THE BEST
BIZARRO FICTION
OF THE DECADE

THE BEST
BIZARRO FICTION
OF THE DECADE

EDITED BY CAMERON PIERCE

Eraserhead Press
Portland, Oregon

ERASERHEAD PRESS
205 NE BRYANT STREET
PORTLAND, OR 97211

WWW.ERASERHEADPRESS.COM

ISBN: 978-1-62105-056-8

Compilation Copyright © 2012 by Eraserhead Press.
Individual works are Copyright © by their respective authors.

Cover art by Alan M. Clark and Kevin Ward
Cover art Copyright © 2012 by Alan M. Clark and Kevin Ward

Printed in the USA.

TABLE OF CONTENTS

I PRAISE THE IDIOT BEAUTY OF THE UNNATURAL WORLD

AN INTRODUCTION BY CAMERON PIERCE

I was a teenager when I discovered bizarro fiction. As an angst-addled punk who played in a death rock band while devouring weird and decadent literature like Sizzler was having a special on surrealist cuisine, bizarro wasn't a revelation; it was a revolution. Lautréamont, Baudelaire, Rimbaud, Lovecraft, Kafka, Breton, Ballard, Burroughs . . . those guys were my heroes, but in the first bizarro books I read, I discovered my life. These were writers who embodied the banality and horror of my upper-middle class California neighborhood. They did it not by examining motifs of alienation in quietly wrought prose, but by stitching those same motifs into Frankenstein-like monsters. The key ingredients? Baby Jesus butt plugs, post-apocalyptic cockroach suits, and pitch-black absurdity.

The stories meant something, but they weren't metaphors. If there was any unifying message between bizarro books, it went something like this: *buckle your seatbelts, because we're in for one hell of a shit storm* (which is basically how the twenty-first century has played out so far). As a young man who had a difficult time understanding that his own behavior was a little left of odd, this was just the right medicine. Aesthetically, bizarro fiction treaded the waters between genre fiction (horror in particular), Adult Swim, and the games and experiments of writers like Andre Breton and William S. Burroughs. In short, it was the quintessential mindfuck.

I had been down rabbit holes before. If you want to see the most beautiful (and ugly) things in life, you've got to take those plunges. But bizarro was different. There was no leaving this Wonderland. That's because I already lived in that space without even knowing it. Now, looking back nearly ten years from when

I read my first bizarro book, I still call this genre home. Bizarro has changed in big ways since then. Evolution has been rapid. I suspect the next decade will be even wilder. Right now, though, let us reflect on the crustaceans we've plucked from our hearts, the slithering (and sniveling) fairy tales of hatred and hope that we tell ourselves to get by, "The Star-Spangled Banner" sung in Klingon by a clown with scoliosis at a four-year-old's birthday party (the parents were frightened, but the kids were happy). Let us explore the *Best Bizarro Fiction of the Decade*.

AT THE FUNERAL

D. HARLAN WILSON

It's been a week already and the funeral isn't over yet. For seven days and nights we've been roaming the hallways of Frinkel's Death Emporium whispering in each other's ears, massaging each other's elbows, politely trampling each other as we ransack the hors d'oeuvre table, which is replenished with a fresh round of fruit punch and cold Swedish meatballs at noon and sundown every day. The Emporium's staff consists of two short, round men in bird costumes. When they're not setting out provisions and cleaning up after us, they wobble around on their big yellow feet and make bird noises.

Seven days and nights of walking around a funeral home is enough to make anybody tired, and yet nobody seems to be tired but me. I start asking people why they don't sit down for a while, maybe take a nap, but everybody just smacks their lips and waves me away.

Annoyed, I decide to look for a bed and take a nap myself. I find one in a secret room. The bed is king-sized and made out of Queen Anne's lace. On the far side of it, my sister Klarissa is sitting there playing with a doll.

In the middle of it, The Deceased is lying there dead.

The upper half of The Deceased's body is hanging out of a black, halfway unzipped body bag. He isn't wearing any clothes and His skin is absolutely colorless. His eyes look like they're on the verge of popping out of His head.

I sit down next to Him and frown at Klarissa. "Did you unzip this body bag?"

She shakes her head.

"You're telling me you didn't unzip this body bag? Is that what you're telling me?"

She nods her head.

"Well, I guess the thing unzipped itself. I guess that's what happened, isn't it?" This time my sister doesn't respond to me. She whispers something into her doll's ear and giggles.

I use my feet to try and stuff The Deceased back into the body bag, but it doesn't work, and when I'm about to lay my hands on Him, my mother walks into the secret room, scolds my sister and I for being there, sits down on the bed and places The Deceased's head in her lap. She strokes His curly brown hair. A few seconds later . . . He coughs.

"Holy moly," I say.

My mother closes her eyes. "No, no. That's just a reflex."

"Reflex? He's been dead over a week."

My mother begins to massage The Deceased's neck. The Deceased coughs again. Then, purring a little, He mumbles, "That feels good."

Before I can say anything my mother shakes her head. "Reflexes. It's all reflexes."

I stare at her.

My mother says, "Listen, I have to go. Aunt Kay's been feeding meatballs to the spiders and I have to try and convince her to feed them to herself instead. You two can stay here, but not for long, okay? Be good." She removes The Deceased's head from her lap, gets off the bed and leaves.

The Deceased flexes His jaw. He coughs again, and again, and again. He keeps on coughing until a rotten apple flies out of His mouth. It sails across the room and shatters an antique lamp. Klarissa and I leap off the bed as The Deceased starts gesticulating like an angry worm. "Get me outta this damn thing," He says.

"I don't think that's such a good idea," I say. Klarissa adds, "We might get in trouble." Then, under her breath: "Is this a reflex, too?"

I purse my lips.

The Deceased gives us a dirty look. "Fine. I'll get out myself. And I'll never forgive you two for being so crummy to me."

Klarissa and I glance at each other. After a brief struggle, The Deceased manages to unzip the body bag the rest of the way. He climbs out of it. He stretches His wiry, naked limbs, rearranges His genitals, and strides out of the secret room without a word. Klarissa and I watch Him go.

Then we leap back onto the bed and fall asleep on either side of the open body bag . . .

Out in the hallways The Deceased approaches the attendants of the funeral one at a time. He taps them on the shoulders and asks if they can spare some clothes and if it's not too much trouble a meatball and a cup of fruit punch. "I'm very cold and undernourished," He says, eyes fixed on his toes. Everybody frowns and pretends they don't understand Him, except for my Aunt Kay, who, in response to His plea, spits a mouthful of tobacco juice on Him and then shoots up into the ceiling on a thread of spidersilk attached to the back of her neck. The Deceased breaks down and cries. My grandfather threatens to have Him hanged. "We'll string you up right here and won't even think twice about it!" he twangs. The Deceased snarls at him. My grandfather signals the Emporium's two bird men and they all chase The Deceased back to the secret room and tell Him not to come out again unless He wants to die.

"I'm already dead," says The Deceased as my grandfather slams the door on His face.

Klarissa and I don't wake up. The Deceased shuffles over to the bed. He stares at us and thinks about what He should do. Should He kill us? Should He maim us? Or should He leave us alone? Since He dislikes us so much, the most sensible thing to do would be to kill us. But He can't make up His mind. He tries to wake us and ask us what He should do. No luck—we're sleeping like dead things. No matter how hard He pokes our shoulders and screams in our ears, we won't open our eyes.

The Deceased sighs. Then, having nothing else to do, He crawls onto the bed and back into the body bag, and zips Himself up as best He can.

ANT COLONY

ALISSA NUTTING

When space on earth became very limited, it was declared all people had to host another organism on or inside of their bodies. Many people chose something noninvasive, such as barnacles or wig-voles. Some women had breast operations that allowed them to accommodate small aquatic life within implants. But because I was already perfectly-breasted (and, admittedly, vain) I sought out a doctor who, for several thousanddollars, drilled holes into my bones to make room for an ant colony.

After being turned down by every surgeon in the book, I finally found my doctor. Actually he's a dentist. I had to lead him on in order to get what I wanted—he only agreed to the procedure because he is in love with me.

"I have all your movies," the doctor told me during our first consultation. "I think you're the most perfect woman in the world."

Since this had never been attempted, I was a study trial. My participation in this experiment had a lot of parallels to modeling, which I used to do before commercial acting. Once a month I went into a laboratory and removed all my clothing. This latter step probably wasn't necessary, but I did it because I was grateful, and also because it was interesting to feel someone looking at my outsides and my insides at the same time. When I laid down onto an imaging machine and certain buttons were pushed, the doctor could see all the ants moving around in my body, using their mandibles to pick up what he said were synthetic calcium deposits. The ants were first implanted within my spine, where their food supply was injected monthly, but then they quickly moved throughout the other various pathways that had been drilled into my limbs and even my skull.

The ants' mandibles were the only part of them that disgusted me; they reminded me of the headgear I'd had to wear with my braces in grades six through eight. I'd refused to wear it to school or even walk around the house when I had it on. Instead I wore it two hours each night before bed, and I spent this time reading fashion magazines in my closet. I wouldn't allow anyone, even my mother, to see me. She used to stand at the door and beg for a kiss goodnight. This was of course before the cancer—she had already been dead for several years by the time the organism hosting movement started. When she began dying I didn't want to watch; I usually grew angry when she'd ask me to come see her in the hospital. The cancer overtook her body until she looked parasitic herself. Near the end, if I felt her lips on my cheek while I was hugging her I'd pull away—I knew it was ridiculous, but I was afraid she was somehow going to suck out my beauty.

"Can you feel them inside you?" As he watched the scan from an outside control room, the doctor would whisper into a microphone that I could hear through a headset earpiece. His voice sounded sweaty. "Does it seem like your blood is crawling? Does it tickle? Are you ticklish?" He'd ask me questions the entire time, but even if I were to answer, there was no way for him to hear my response.

In truth I didn't feel a thing; it was hard to believe they were even there. On my first follow-up visit I made the doctor show me footage of myself in the large ant-imaging machine to prove they were actually inside me. But after awhile I got used to the thought of their presence and even started speaking to them throughout the day. The doctor said this was healthy.

"It's not uncommon to feel a shift of identity," he assured me. "It's okay to talk to your organism, and to feel like it understands you. After all, it's a part of your self. We could talk about this more over dinner?"

But I never actually crossed the line into dating. Then one day I received a frantic call.

"Come in immediately. Where are you right now?"

At the moment, I was in the middle of shooting a commercial for a water company.

"Leave the minute you hang up the phone. What we have to discuss is far more important."

I was very used to people feeling like they were more important than me, but less beautiful. I often felt that every transaction in my life somehow revolved around this premise.

"Refreshing," I said. It was my only line in the commercial, and I'd been practicing all day.

I can tell you this: I did love how invisible the ants were. They were creatures that seemed to consider themselves neither important nor beautiful. Earlier that month, the doctor had given me a videotape of several ants feasting on the corpse of an ant that had died in my femur. This cannibalism was an aberration, he'd pointed out: ants do not normally eat other ants from their own colony. The doctor had worked with an entomologist to specifically breed a contained bone-ant species that would eat the dead, lay the eggs in the dead, and make the dead a part of the living.

Defying these orders, I finished the refreshing water shoot. When I finally arrived at the doctor's he was very upset—he'd cancelled everything and had been waiting in his office, which is covered with wall-to-wall pictures of me, for hours.

"Your left wrist."

I slipped off my glove and held it out to him in a vulnerable way. My wrist was smooth and fragrant and pale and had a nicotine patch on it; the doctor had suggested I quit smoking for the health of the ants. I squeezed my eyes to look beneath my skin for them. "It's like they're not even there," I muttered.

"Grip my fingers," he said, holding two of his own upon my pulse. It was a little difficult to do.

"God," he said. Even though his voice sounded worried, he seemed a little pleased. "Goodness."

He ran out of the room, face flushed. And there I sat alone, or not alone truly.

"We seem to be in crisis," I muttered to them, and put my glove back on.

Since the ants, I have started gloving my arms. I buy the longest gloves I can find. It feels like putting the ants to bed, the way one might place a blanket over the cage of a bird.

"We are all certain this can be resolved." Around the table sat several new doctors I'd never met, or maybe they were dentists. I spotted a magazine that I was in—mascara ad, page seven—lying on an end table in the conference room. Somehow this made me feel safer, more of a majority. There were two of me in the room and only one of everybody else.

My doctor passed me a glossy picture: its subject was a fat, excreting ant. The ant was surrounded by small piles of powder that, when magnified, almost looked like crumbs of bread. I gagged a bit. "Why are you showing me this?"

"This is their queen," he said. The doctor's pupils had dilated to a width universally associated with insanity. "She wants you gone." His fingertip moved from pile to pile on the glossy photo, leaving a print upon each one. "These are piles of your bone. You are being devoured by the ants that live inside you."

"Eaten from within." A dull woman at the very end of the table repeated this in a parrot-like manner. She wore a large dome cap, the obvious fashion of one hosting an organism on her head. Hers appeared tall and slightly conical; I was very interested in what type of creature it might be, but it is considered rude to ask about other people's organisms—they are ultimately too much of a bodily function.

"But we feed the ants so they don't have to eat me. I come here once a month so you can put their food inside."

An authoritarian doctor whispered something to my doctor, who whispered to me. "They're not eating it anymore."

I whispered back to him. "Can we start feeding them something more enticing? A different bone-substitute? Ground bones from animals? Or maybe even the dead?" I knew it was a tasteless suggestion, but I did have money and my life was apparently in danger. The authoritarian doctor scooted back in his rolling-chair and looked at his shoes.

"No," my doctor said, and then he stood. His hands lifted slightly above his head. "This is not about consumption. It is an act of interspecies war!"

In the following weeks, my strength and health deteriorated until I was finally admitted to a very special hospital ward. It was a room my doctor had built onto his existing home just for me.

Around this time, the doctor also started wearing a large sack around his waist—to conceal his organism, I assumed, whatever it might be. It must've grown larger since when I'd first met him. I was grateful my organism wasn't making me wear a sack around my waist, even if it was eating me alive. The sack made a swish noise when he walked; in motion the doctor sounded like a giant broom.

This swishing became more and more of a comfort as I gradually lost my vision. The doctor reminded me that when one door closes another opens, and this was true; I did seem to be gaining a sort of ant-sight. My ears began to turn away from human sounds as well, but soon I could pick up more ant noises. Around the third week I requested that my room's television be taken away. When my eyes were closed I could see various dark caves and swarming ant-limbs, and these images gradually started to feel preferential to anything I might view of the outer world.

"I'm becoming them," I said one night when I heard my doctor swish in. "I'm becoming the ants."

I heard him pull up a chair and sit down next to me. "It is wonderful, isn't it? My swan, my pet?"

He hadn't called me those things before, but I was in no condition to disagree. My arms and legs could no longer move—I could only move through the ants. It was like having hundreds of different hands. I could make them go anywhere and do anything inside my body; I'd even started eating with them. Though I didn't necessarily want to devour my own bone, I had an insatiable hunger, and there was a commanding voice, *Eat, Walk, Lift, Chomp*, it was my own voice but much deeper, not exactly masculine but echoing and confident, like my home was a large cave and I firmly believed in everything I said. I seemed able to express only one word at a time, but this felt more liberating than restrictive—suddenly every word could be a full representation of myself.

I lost all track of time. Eventually I was certain of only two things: the appetite was getting out of control, and my old eyes were completely gone.

"The rest of the world thinks that you've died," the doctor told me. As he swished into the room, there was the sound of yards and yards of material being unwrapped and lifted. His words seemed round with satisfaction. "You cannot see it, but I have just unveiled the portal."

I would've answered him, but I was no longer sure if my voice still made a sound or if words even came out when I felt like I was talking.

"It is right here on my waist; I've been making paths inside of me just as there are paths inside of you. After you first came to see me, I reported to the government that I, too, hold ants inside my body, but I don't. Not yet. It is your ants I'm after. You have now become the ants who have fed on you; your consciousness is united with theirs. And when you all crawl inside of me, we will all be one forever." As his voice continued I could feel the ants rallying, see their legs beginning to kick with heightened motion. "I never actually fed the ants you've become; I simply allowed them to eat you whole. But you will not eat me. I will feed you properly so that you don't. We will share my stomach—I've inserted a tube whereby everything I swallow will also be accessible to your minions, your thousands of minions that are now you entirely and do your bidding. I have always loved you, and when you came to my office, I knew this was my chance to make you mine."

And then I smelled something irresistible and began to crawl towards it, into the new pink-grey cave that must be the doctor. If what he said was true, in a primary way I was somewhat grateful to get inside of him—if I was now just thousands of swarming ants I did not wish to be in the public eye.

Once we had transferred, I was pleased to realize that I could see through the doctor's eyes as well as those of my ants. It is calming, to look through the eyes of another person. It stills your own thoughts almost to a halt.

"Do you love me?"

The doctor likes to ask this; he does so almost every hour. Although I cannot speak, he always smiles afterwards and says that he loves me too.

Throughout the day I have all types of sensations. Some are good, others worry me, but my fears can't grow so big that they reach outside of his body. Nothing can move beyond this body, so in a way I feel like I am the world, and he is the world, the same way that lovers feel. "How strange," I often think, though I try not to let him hear me thinking it, "to have so much in common with an unattractive man."

And then there is the evening, when sunlight pours into the window like nectar. He sits down to the dinner table in front of a large mirror—I think so that I can see him, though maybe he has figured out a way to see me. Then he carefully opens the bag of sugar with a knife. When I hear this sound, each of my ants jump and he smiles, his legs and arms contract whether he likes it or not. And though they are his own, I feel as if I guide his fingertips, that the tiniest of my workers go down into the marrow of his thumb and help to grip the teaspoon.

I love watching him eat. Teaspoon after teaspoon disappears into his mouth; his saliva coats the spoon's surface with stuck granules that change its color from silver to a crusty white. I cannot decide if he did me a favor or if I'm a victim. When I try to think, all I can feel is the sugar fluid, and a rage that comes when I find myself, after our feedings, somewhat hungry.

FIRE DOG

JOE R. LANSDALE

When Jim applied for the dispatcher job, the fire department turned him down, but the Fire Chief offered him something else. "Our fire dog, Rex, is retiring. You might want that job. Pays good and the retirement is great."

"Fire dog?" Jim said.

"That's right."

"Well, I don't know . . ."

"Suit yourself."

Jim considered. "I suppose I could give it a try—"

"Actually, we prefer greater dedication than that. We don't just want someone to give it a try. Being fire dog is an important job."

"Very well," Jim said. "I'll take it."

"Good."

The Chief opened a drawer, pulled out a spotted suit with tail and ears, pushed it across the desk.

"I have to wear this?"

"How the hell you gonna be the fire dog, you don't wear the suit?"

"Of course."

Jim examined the suit. It had a hole for his face, his bottom, and what his mother had called his pee-pee.

"Good grief," Jim said. "I can't go around with my . . . well, you know, my stuff hanging out."

"How many dogs you see wearing pants?"

"Well, Goofy comes to mind."

15

"Those are cartoons. I haven't got time to screw around here. You either want the job, or you don't."

"I want it."

"By the way. You sure Goofy's a dog?"

"Well, he looks like a dog. And he has that dog, Pluto."

"Pluto, by the way, doesn't wear pants."

"You got me there."

"Try on the suit, let's see if it needs tailoring."

The suit fit perfectly, though Jim did feel a bit exposed. Still, he had to admit there was something refreshing about the exposure. He wore the suit into the break room, following the Chief.

Rex, the current fire dog, was sprawled on the couch watching a cop show. His suit looked worn, even a bit smoke stained. He was tired around the eyes. His jowls drooped.

"This is our new fire dog," the Chief said.

Rex turned and looked at Jim, said, "I'm not out the door, already you got a guy in the suit?"

"Rex, no hard feelings. You got what, two, three days? We got to be ready. You know that."

Rex sat up on the couch, adjusted some pillows and leaned into them. "Yeah, I know. But, I've had this job nine years."

"And in dog years that's a lot."

"I don't know why I can't just keep being the fire dog. I think I've done a good job."

"You're our best fire dog yet. Jim here has a lot to live up to."

"I only get to work nine years?" Jim said.

"In dog years you'd be pretty old, and it's a decent retirement."

"Is he gonna take my name too?" Rex said.

"No," the Chief said, "of course not. We'll call him Spot."

"Oh, that's rich," said Rex. "You really worked on that one."

"It's no worse than Rex."

"Hey, Rex is a good name."

"I don't like Spot," Jim said. "Can't I come up with something else?"

"Dogs don't name themselves," the Chief said. "Your name is Spot."

"Spot," Rex said, "don't you think you ought to get started by coming over here and sniffing my butt?"

The first few days at work Spot found riding on the truck to be uncomfortable. He was always given a tool box to sit on so that he could be seen, as this was the fire department's way. They liked the idea of the fire dog in full view, his ears flapping in the wind. It was very promotional for the mascot to be seen.

16

Spot's exposed butt was cold on the tool box, and the wind not only blew his ears around, it moved another part of his anatomy about. That was annoying.

He did, however, enjoy the little motorized tail-wagging device he activated with a touch of a finger. He found that got him a lot of snacks from the firemen. He was especially fond of liver snacks.

After three weeks on the job, Spot found his wife Sheila to be very friendly. After dinner one evening, when he went to the bedroom to remove his dog suit, he discovered Sheila lying on their bed wearing a negligee and a pair of dog ears attached to a hair band.

"Feel frisky, Spot?"

"Jim."

"Whatever. Feel frisky?"

"Well, yeah. Let me shed the suit, take a shower . . ."

"You don't need a shower . . . And baby, leave the suit on, will you?"

They went at it.

"You know how I want it," she said.

"Yeah. Doggie style."

"Good boy."

After sex, Sheila liked to scratch his belly and behind his ears. He used the tail-wagging device to show how much he appreciated it. This wasn't so bad, he thought. He got less when he was a man.

Though his sex life had improved, Spot found himself being put outside a lot, having to relieve himself in a corner of the yard while his wife looked in the other direction, her hand in a plastic bag, ready to use to pick up his deposits.

He only removed his dog suit now when Sheila wasn't around. She liked it on him at all times. At first he was insulted, but the sex was so good, and his life was so good, he relented. He even let her call him Spot all the time.

When she wasn't around, he washed and dried his suit carefully, ironed it. But he never wore anything else. When he rode the bus to work, everyone wanted to pet him. One woman even asked if he liked poodles because she had one.

At work he was well-respected and enjoyed being taken to schools with the Fire Chief. The Chief talked about fire prevention. Spot wagged his tail, sat up, barked, looked cute by turning his head from side to side.

He was even taken to his daughter's class once. He heard her say proudly to a kid sitting next to her, "That's my Daddy. He's the fire dog."

His chest swelled with pride. He made his tail wag enthusiastically.

The job really was the pip. You didn't have fires every day, so Spot lay around all day most days, on the couch sometimes, though some of the firemen would run him off and make him lie on the floor when they came in. But the floor had rugs on it and the television was always on, though he was not allowed to change the channels. Some kind of rule, a union thing. The fire dog can not and will not change channels.

He did hate having to take worm medicine, and the annual required trips to the vet were no picnic either. Especially the thermometer up the ass part.

But, hell, it was a living, and not a bad one. Another plus was after several months of trying, he was able to lick his balls.

At night, when everyone was in their bunks and there were no fires, Spot would read from *Call of the Wild*, *White Fang*, *Dog Digest*, or such, or lie on his back with all four feet in the air, trying to look cute.

He loved it when the firemen came in and caught him that way and ooohheeed and ahhhhhed and scratched his belly or patted his head.

This went on for just short of nine years. Then, one day, while he was lying on the couch, licking his ass—something he had cultivated after three years on the job—the Fire Chief and a guy in a dog suit came in. "This is your replacement, Spot," the Chief said.

"What?"

"Well, it has been nine years."

"You didn't tell me. Has it been? You're sure? Aren't you supposed to warn me? Rex knew his time was up. Remember?"

"Not exactly. But if you say so. Spot, meet Hal."

"Hal? What kind of dog's name is that? Hal?"

But it was no use. By the end of the day he had his personal dog biscuits, pinups from *Dog Digest*, and his worm-away medicine packed. There was also a spray can the firemen used to mist on his poop to keep him from eating it. The can of spray didn't really belong to him, but he took it anyway.

He picked up his old clothes, went into the changing room. He hadn't worn anything but the fire dog suit in years, and it felt odd to try his old clothes on. He could hardly remember ever wearing them. He found they were a bit moth-eaten, and he had gotten a little too plump for them. The shoes fit, but he couldn't tolerate them.

He kept the dog suit on. He caught the bus and went home.

"What? You lost your job?" his wife said.

"I didn't lose anything. They retired me."

"You're not the fire dog?"

"No. Hal is the fire dog."

"I can't believe it. I give you nine great years—"

"We've been married eleven."

"I only count the dog years. Those were the good ones, you know."

"Well, I don't have to quit being a dog. Hell, I am a dog."

"You're not the fire dog. You've lost your position, Spot. Oh, I can't even stand to think about it. Outside. Go on. Git. Outside."

Spot went.

After a while he scratched on the door, but his wife didn't let him in. He went around back and tried there. That didn't work either. He looked in the windows, but couldn't see her.

He lay down in the yard.

That night it rained, and he slept under the car, awakened just in time to keep his wife from backing over him on her way to work.

That afternoon he waited, but his wife did not return at the usual time. Five o'clock was when he came home from the fire house, and she was always waiting, and he had a feeling it was at least five o'clock, and finally the sun went down and he knew it was late.

Still, no wife.

Finally, he saw headlights and a car pulled into the drive. Sheila got out. He ran to meet her. To show he was interested, he humped her leg.

She kicked him loose. He noticed she was holding a leash. Out of the car came Hal.

"Look who I got. A real dog."

Spot was dumbfounded.

"I met him today at the fire house, and well, we hit it off."

"You went by the fire house?"

"Of course."

"What about me?" Spot asked.

"Well, Spot, you are a little old. Sometimes, things change. New blood is necessary."

"Me and Hal, we're going to share the house?"

"I didn't say that."

She took Hal inside. Just before they closed the door, Hal slipped a paw behind Sheila's back and shot Spot the finger.

When they were inside, Spot scratched on the door in a half-hearted way. No soap.

Next morning Sheila hustled him out of the shrubbery by calling his name. She didn't have Hal with her.

Great! She had missed him. He bounded out, his tongue dangling like a wet sock. "Come here, Spot."

He went. That's what dogs did. When the master called, you went to them.

He was still her dog. Yes sirree, Bob. "Come on, boy." She hustled him to the car.

As he climbed inside on the back seat and she shut the door, he saw Hal come out of the house stretching. He looked pretty happy. He walked over to the car and slapped Sheila on the butt.

"See you later, baby."

"You bet, you dog you."

Hal walked down the street to the bus stop. Spot watched him by turning first to the back glass, then rushing over to the side view glass.

Sheila got in the car.

"Where are we going?" Spot asked.

"It's a surprise," she said.

"Can you roll down the window back here a bit?"

"Sure."

Spot stuck his head out as they drove along, his ears flapping, his tongue hanging.

They drove down a side street, turned and tooled up an alley.

Spot thought he recognized the place.

Why, yes, the vet. They had come from another direction and he hadn't spotted it right off, but that's where he was.

He unhooked the little tag that dangled from his collar. Checked the dates of his last shots.

No. Nothing was overdue.

They stopped and Sheila smiled. She opened the back door and took hold of the leash. "Come on, Spot."

Spot climbed out of the car, though carefully. He wasn't as spry as he once was.

Two men were at the back door. One of them was the doctor. The other an assistant.

"Here's Spot," she said.

"He looks pretty good," said the doctor.

"I know. But . . . well, he's old and he has his problems. And I have too many dogs."

She left him there.

The vet checked him over and called the animal shelter. "There's nothing really wrong with him," he told the attendant that came for him. "He's just old, and well, the woman doesn't want to care for him. He'd be great with children."

"You know how it is, Doc," said the attendant. "Dogs all over the place."

Later, at the animal shelter he stood on the cold concrete and smelled the other dogs. He barked at the cats he could smell. Fact was, he found himself barking anytime anyone came into the corridor of pens.

Sometimes men and women and children came and looked at him.

None of them chose him. The device in his tail didn't work right, so he couldn't wag as ferociously as he liked. His ears were pretty droopy, and his jowls hung way too low.

"He looks like his spots are fading," said one woman whose little girl had stuck her fingers through the grating so Spot could lick her hand.

"His breath stinks," she said.

As the days went by, Spot tried to look perky all the time. Hoping for adoption.

But one day, they came for him, wearing white coats and grim faces, brandishing a leash and a muzzle and a hypodermic needle.

CANDY-COATED

CARLTON MELLICK III

Knob Tyler thinks he's the strongest, toughest, most badass motherfucker on Mill Avenue. Unfortunately, Knob has a lollipop for a head. This makes him not quite as badass as he thinks he is.

While he's strutting down the street with his white muscle shirt tossed over his sweat-drenched shoulder, Knob likes to flex his pectorals at the ladies. Whenever he says ladies, he pronounces it laydaaays. But for some reason the laydaaays are never impressed by the size of his pecs. They are too creeped out by his weird lollipop head to notice anything special about his muscles. Knob's lollipop head is the size of a bowling ball and light orange in color. The flavor of the lollipop is Tropical Sensation, which is a mixture of pineapple, mango, and star fruit. His tiny candy eyes, nose, and mouth are clustered together in the center of his large round face. His eyebrows are always curled downward to show how fucking serious he is about shit.

Oftentimes, when the sun is shining hard on Mill Avenue, Knob's lollipop head will begin to sweat, filling the air with tropical sweetness. This smell attracts flies that stick to the side of his face and squirm around his ear holes. Knob tries to wipe them away, but for every fly he frees, three more take its place. This isn't good for picking up the laydaaays.

What also isn't good for picking them up is the gang of bearded truckers that always follow him around, trying to lick his head. It isn't easy to pick up laydaaays when there are bearded truckers licking your head. But you have to understand, truckers really love Tropical Sensation-flavored lollipops. They are addicted to them.

There's something about driving a big rig down the interstate, listening to "Kansas City Lights," and sucking a Tropical Sensation lollipop down to the gooey paper stick that really makes them feel at peace with the universe. Now that Tropical Sensation is a discontinued flavor, these truckers can't do this anymore. The only way they can satisfy their tropical fix is to go down to Mill Avenue, sneak up behind Knob Tyler, and lick the back of his bald candy head.

But even this is becoming a limited resource for their Tropical Sensation needs. There is only so much licking a lollipop can take. Knob has not realized any difference while flexing in front of his mirror each morning. He is too busy watching the size of his muscles increase to notice the size of his head decreasing.

The truckers, on the other hand, have noticed the difference in size as of late. And the thought that his head might shrink away to nothing has sent a wave of panic through the trucker community.

Knob is a connoisseur of fine cheeses. Today, he is at a cheese tasting at the fancy cheesery on Mill Avenue. He holds a tiny chunk of Raclette Poivre on a toothpick, nibbling the edges with his sticky orange lips. The shop is filled with cheese enthusiasts, gathering together for the weekly tasting. Knob struts by goateed men in gray business-casual attire, sizes them up, then moves on. Knob knows that he's the buffest cheese taster in the room. He thinks this will give him an advantage over the competition when picking up the laydaaays. While cruising the cheesery, Knob realizes that most of the women in the room are with other guys. But this doesn't stop him from flirting at a distance. He goes to a turtleneck-sweatered woman speaking to a shrimpy, goateed man. Standing behind the man's shoulder, Knob flexes a single pectoral muscle at the woman as if it is asking her a question.

The woman knows Knob is there but she does not make eye contact, so he raises his pec even higher, then higher. The woman does not acknowledge him. He blames it on the cheesery's absurd no-shirt, no-service policy. He knows she would be much more impressed if he didn't have his shirt on.

Knob gets himself a glass of Nebbiolo and samples a Piave Vecchio. He smiles and bobs his head at the taste.

"This is a good cheese," he says to a woman breastfeeding a baby in a sling. Then he looks down at her bare breast and raises a candy eyebrow. The woman covers the baby's head and steps away.

Knob shrugs and moves on.

After five more failed attempts, Knob decides to focus on the cheeses. He has an extra-aged Mimolette, which he learns goes very well with a Zinfandel or Syrah. He then tries the Emmenthaler, which has hints of flowers, raisins, and wood fires.

"You have to try the Banon," says a voice behind his shoulder.

Knob turns around to see a woman with short blonde hair, square glasses, and a baseball cap. He recognizes her from previous tastings. She's one of the few regulars he hasn't had the chance to hit on yet, because she's always watching old *Flash Gordon* serials on her iPhone and never seems aware of her surroundings. He's checked her out, of course, and thought she was quite the hottie but a little too flat-chested for his taste (only a B-cup).

"It was aged in a chestnut leaf," she says, biting into a piece of cheese on a water cracker.

Knob looks to see if there is anybody standing behind him, just in case she might be talking to somebody else. There isn't. He raises one shoulder and slowly flexes a pectoral muscle.

"Try it," she says, pointing her cheese in his face.

Knob opens his mouth. She drops in the cheese. He chews and swallows.

"It's good," he says, his throat crusty with powdered cracker.

"I see you in here all the time," she says. "Are you really into gourmet cheeses?"

He nods his lollipop head.

"I live for cheese," she says.

"Yeah, me too," he says, his pectoral muscles dancing for her.

They turn back to the cheese table. Knob checks out the girl while she examines the cheeses. Her purple skirt wiggles when she spreads a Brie de Nangis on a slice of crusty bread. He leans in to get a better look at her front, when something wets the back of his head. Knob turns around. There is a beefy, tattooed, potbellied trucker standing behind him holding up a piece of Port-Salut on a toothpick. Knob glares at him.

"What?" says the trucker, licking his lips through a wiry gray beard.

Knob turns back to the girl. Of all the times to have a trucker licking his head, this is the worst.

"I'm Alisa," says the girl, grabbing his hand to shake.

With his free hand, Knob feels the wet spot on his head and pulls away a few curly gray hairs.

"Knobert Tyler," he says, and bows slightly at her.

While leaning down for the bow, Knob feels two more licks on his head. He turns around. There are two more truckers behind him. These two are fatter and hairier than the first. They smile at him, holding glasses of wine and chewing on cheeses.

Knob sizes up the truckers. The truckers size up Knob.

Before they get a chance to confront him, Knob turns to Alisa. He isn't sure if Alisa witnessed the truckers licking him, so he decides to play it off as if nothing happened.

"Try this Stilton," Alisa says, holding a bite of cheese to his face.

Knob opens his mouth. As he bites into the cheese, he feels wide tongues lapping at the back of his head. They squirm against his candy scalp like fat greasy snakes.

While the truckers lick his head, Knob pretends that nothing is wrong. This is his first big chance at scoring in a long time and he doesn't want to mess it up. He chews the cheese and nods at the flavor, as the bearded truckers slobber all over him.

"It tastes like ginger," he says, cringing at the curly hairs that caress the back of his neck.

"Yeah, it has mango and ginger," Alisa says.

Knob doesn't know why Alisa hasn't noticed the truckers yet. He just plays it off cool, hoping that his dancing pectoral muscles have hypnotized her. Many of the other cheese tasters have noticed the licking truckers, however, and are now politely inching away from him. Knob flexes his muscles as tightly as he can, to prove to them that he is not gay no matter how many truckers are licking his head.

"They had a five-year Gouda here last time that was really good," he says, as a warm wetness coils into his right ear hole.

Knob casually breaks away from the worming tongues and switches to the other side of Alisa.

"Yeah, yeah," she says, blinking her blue eyes. "That was terrific. I bought some to take home."

Knob feels another lick, and he turns around. The number of customers in the cheesery has suddenly doubled.

Over half of them are overweight truckers who have sneaked in under Knob's radar like stealthy obese ninjas.

They are spread throughout the shop, mingling with the other cheese enthusiasts. Knob can see them ogling him from across the room, winking at him between sips of chardonnay.

"They always have the most interesting cheeses at this place," Alisa says.

When she turns her back to grab some more wine, a dozen truckers charge the back of Knob's head. They hold him by the shoulders and take turns slurping on him as hard as they can. Knob tenses up like he just hopped into a freezing-cold shower. He retains a manly posture while being gang-licked by the truckers, so that none of the laydaaays watching think he's gay.

The truckers stop licking once Alisa returns to Knob.

She notices that his orange head is soaked and his muscles are tensed.

"What happened to you?" she asks.

Knob slicks his hand across his lollipop head, collecting a mass of orange slime. Alisa examines his head.

"What's this?" she says, wiping her finger across a tender spot on the back of his lollipop.

Knob feels the area her finger wiped. There is a lump.

"It looks like... bone," she says.

Knob can feel it. His lollipop head has been licked down so far that it has finally degraded to the bone.

"It's your skull," she says. "Your skull is showing."

The truckers notice the white lump sticking out of the orange candy like the Tootsie of a half-eaten Tootsie Roll Pop. They bow their heads in shame. Knob fingers his head frantically, wondering what has happened to the rest of it. The other cheese enthusiasts wince at the sight of him.

"We need to get you to the hospital," Alisa says.

She sits him down in a chair. As his head lowers to her level, she gets a whiff of pineapple, mango, and star fruit.

"That smell..." She suddenly forgets about the hospital and becomes lost in the fragrance.

Then she licks his head.

"Is this..." She licks again. "Tropical Sensation?"

Before Knob has a chance to ask her what she's doing, Alisa takes a few more licks and then bites down on his skull, cracking open the bone.

"I'm sorry," she says, wiping orange sauce from her lips. "I've never been able to stop myself from biting."

Everyone in the shop freezes. Yuppies and truckers alike have their eyes locked on Knob and Alisa, their mouths drooped in horror at Knob's cracked-open skull.

Unlike his lollipop head, Knob's brain looks the same as any normal person's brain, only it sweats a deep mahogany fluid that resembles a tawny port.

The taste of this brain fluid mingles with the tropical flavor in Alisa's mouth. Her eyes become distant as she rolls the mahogany liquid across her palate. Then she swallows slowly and smiles.

Knob's pecs cower toward his armpits. He holds back the pain as best as he can so that nobody thinks he's a wimp. But the crowd is no longer paying attention to Knob. Their eyes are glued on Alisa.

"Wow," she says. "It tastes even better on the inside."

Alisa takes another lick of Knob's brain, slower, really trying to get a good taste. She savors the fluid in her mouth, exploring the complexities.

She explains what she is tasting to the crowd: "It's nutty... and sweet. I can taste hints of vanilla... raisins...tobacco... strawberry..."

Then she stabs a piece of cheese with a toothpick and puts it in her mouth. Her eyes roll in euphoric bliss. "And it's just amazing with this Stilton."

Knob gawks at the crazy woman, wondering what is wrong with her, but the rest of the cheese tasters now seem more curious than shocked.

"You have to try it," she says to the cheese tasters.

The manager of the shop nudges his way through the crowd to them. Alisa arches the back of Knob's head toward the manager's nicely manicured goatee. The man dabs his tongue quickly against Knob's brain, catching only a drop of the fluid. Alisa pops a piece of Stilton through his lips and the man bites down. His eyes light up.

"Oh, my..." says the manager. "Yes, yes." He waves his wife over to Knob's head. "It is fantastic!"

After the man's wife gives it a try, she says, "This is divine!"

Knob becomes the hit of the cheesery and a hit with the laydaaays. Everyone wants to take a lick at Knob's brain, especially the truckers. They start a line that winds through the entire shop and stretches out the door.

There is not a woman in the room who doesn't want to lick him. The turtle-neck-sweatered yuppie girl who had ignored him earlier slips her phone number into his pocket when her goateed boyfriend isn't looking. Knob just nods his head and pumps his pectoral muscles to the rhythm of "Kansas City Lights." The truckers raise their wineglasses in approval.

Alisa wraps her arm around Knob's neck and kisses his hard candy cheek.

"Why don't we grab a bottle of wine and go back to my place?" she says.

Knob gives her a wink. Then she cuts through the crowd to the wine section to find something special for them.

"Score," he says to himself, as the truckers and the cheese enthusiasts break off more of his candy-coating to get to the tastier flavor within.

THE TRAVELING DILDO SALESMAN

KEVIN L. DONIHE

CHAPTER ONE

Ralph was a traveling dildo salesman. His selection was vast, and all models were stamped MADE IN HEAVEN.

In truth, he wasn't sure if his name was Ralph, but he thought of himself as Ralph, and, when he happened upon some reflective surface, he saw what he imagined to be a Ralph looking back. It didn't matter if it was really Bill or Bob or Tom or Ted or Sam or Steve. It didn't matter if he didn't have a name at all. All that mattered were the dildos and his ability to sell them.

Ultimately, he wanted to do and be something else, something new that felt old, like a thing he'd been before but somehow stopped being. The only way he could render the unknown known was to continue on the path, be diligent and pick up clues along the way. When the last dildo was sold, the time of wandering and wondering would end; all answers would be revealed.

This process was the one thing of which he was certain.

Ralph trod a flat, featureless road. The morning sun was red on his face, and the eye in the sky looked down at him, unblinkingly. Unlike the sun, it never changed its position, just kept its big blue orb trained on him, day and night. He tried not to look at it very often. It gave him a weird sense of vertigo when he did, like he was about to fall into the eye, even though it was above him.

As he approached the start of yet another neighborhood, his case became heavier, as though ghost hands were loading it with bricks. The weight caused his left side to slump, so Ralph tried dragging it on the pavement.

All around him, the houses were austere, old-looking abodes that seemed to end in needle points, the uppermost stories too high to see. Most were painted white. Spacious yet empty wooden front porches jutted equidistantly from the road, and each yard featured at least one plastic animal sculpture.

Ralph wouldn't try them all. Most he would simply pass, as they weren't the right places. He always knew which were right. He was, in a sense, told. Though the method of transmission was different each time, it was no less apparent.

Suddenly, his neck felt prickly. He turned left and regarded the property across from him. Here, the grass was longer than in the surrounding yards, and it blew back and forth, as if buffeted by gale-force winds. Seconds later, the blades froze into place, all bent towards the house.

He knocked on the selected door. A little girl, licking a lollipop as big as her face, opened it. Ralph wanted to take the lollipop from her, taste something sweet, but restrained himself and said, "Is your mother home?"

She just nodded.

"Wonderful! May I speak with her?"

Again, the girl nodded, and then scampered off.

Too much time seemed to pass. Ralph was beginning to think the girl had simply left when he heard two sets of approaching footsteps. Moments later, a young, harried-looking woman in a flour-coated apron stood before him, the girl by her side.

"Greetings, madam," Ralph said. "I hate to trouble you, but you look like someone who might be interested in my line of products."

"I'm really kind of busy." She looked down. "Kids, you know…"

Ralph didn't, but nodded anyway.

"Though I imagine being a traveling salesman must be hard work, too."

Ralph smiled inwardly. "It is."

She regarded his case. "So, what are you selling?"

"Only the finest dildos. That's my answer, and my guarantee."

Her face went slack. "The finest what?"

"Dildos, madam."

"Don't say that word!" She clutched the girl. "Can't you see a child is present?"

Ralph looked down at the girl, still licking the huge lollipop. He waved, and she waved back.

"I hardly think it's inappropriate," he replied. "After all, my dil—items have a vast array of potential uses, and not just the common one, which you are no doubt considering."

She scowled. "Tell me, how else does one use a d-i-l-d-o?"

"Well, for starters, many mothers buy them for their children to play with, or to fashion into mobiles for infants."

"That's ghastly! You're ghastly!"

"I assure you that's not the case. Kids simply love dildos, especially the colorful floppy ones." He caught his mistake.

"I'm terribly sorry, madam. I'll spell it out next time."

She covered the girl's ears, began humming loudly. "I'm not listening to you!" she shouted between hums.

"Please, if you would just—"

The door slammed in his face. Dejected, Ralph looked down at his feet and saw a bunch of ants crawling in formation across the porch. Their bodies formed a note: AT THE NEXT HOUSE, YOU WILL FIND A CLUE.

Ralph was flummoxed. Why couldn't the sign have been given there first?

Back on the street, a massive billboard caught his attention. IT'S THE GOVERNMENT, it said, the words superimposed over a bunch of happy looking people seated at a breakfast table, eating a bear-shaped cereal called Flang-Os. Ralph made mental note of this revelation and kept walking until he saw something he never remembered seeing, at least not as a traveling dildo salesman.

He ran to the bus stop, plopped himself down on a weathered bench. If a bus was all he needed to escape, then so be it. To hell with selling dildos.

After a few minutes, he drummed fingers on his left leg, shook his right one. A little later, both legs shook, and, after what had to be almost thirty minutes, he chewed on his bottom lip until it bled. Maybe it was an abandoned stop. Maybe there never was a bus.

And then he saw it, first as just a speck on the horizon that could be anything, and then as a big red double-decker. It pulled up, ground to a halt. The door opened, and the oddly familiar driver regarded him.

Ralph grabbed his case, arose.

"Slow down there," said the driver.

"I'm sorry. I'll go slower. I'm just in a—"

"No, no, no. You misunderstand. I'm not telling you to board at a slower and therefore safer pace."

Ralph looked at him askance. "You're not?"

"No, I'm telling you not to board at all."

Hope sank. "What?"

"You heard me."

"But why? Can't I just get on? Please."

The driver seemed perturbed. "Not with that case," he said.

Ralph clutched the handle tighter. "You don't understand; I need it! If I lose it, I'll get in big trouble!"

"Are you sure about that?"

Ralph wasn't sure, at least not exactly. Still, he figured it best to err on the side of caution.

"You know I can't take any riders with cases," the driver continued, "and yet here you are, day after day, asking if you can board."

"I do that?"

"Yes."

He didn't want to let on any further that he didn't recall his last attempts. "Well, uh, I figure if I keep trying, maybe you'll change your mind and let me on."

"That's not going to happen, Ralph."

He was shocked. "How do you know my name?"

The driver smiled. "You've told me a few times."

Somewhere in the back, a passenger asked a muffled question. When the driver finished and turned again towards Ralph, he said, "Try again tomorrow."

"But you'll say the same thing then!"

The driver cocked his neck, raised a brow. "And how do you know that?"

He had a point.

The door closed and the bus shot up into the sky, traveling, it seemed, to the big unblinking eye.

CHAPTER TWO

Twenty minutes after leaving the stop, Ralph found the second sign, the sun shining so brightly upon a house that his view of it was all but obscured. Once the light dimmed, he saw the place and wished he could go elsewhere.

Gravestones jutted from the unkempt yard's left corner, near a rickety, weather-beaten fence and just across from a red-eyed plastic donkey. One stone was cross-shaped, though an arm had broken off. The next had been sculpted to resemble a fat tree stump, a cut branch protruding from center-left. The last one—slate and seemingly the oldest—showcased a bas-relief of a grinning skull framed by garlands. Moss made it seem as though the skull had a mouthful of green teeth.

Unconsciously, Ralph scratched his front tooth with a fingernail. He looked up from the graves. An image in a dark window seemed to be a scowling face, forehead scrunched and lips twisted in some disagreeable way. Still, he couldn't be sure if it was someone behind the glass or an old picture on the wall inside.

Ralph swallowed apprehension. Time to buck up. Time to accost the potential customer within.

He gripped the case and dragged it across the yard, ripping up grass. The red-eyed plastic donkey now faced him instead of the road. Ralph averted his gaze quickly.

He paused at the door. The selling spiel didn't come naturally to him, not even with the easiest or most pliable customers. Saying the words made him feel artificial, like a collection of gears and cogs.

Just then, the dildos started to awaken. He heard their soft, sleepy murmurs, muffled by leather.

"Ssssh," he said. "Relax."

A dildo made a thumping sound. Ralph interpreted this as an act of defiance.

"Be nice today! Don't be assholes!"

Another thump. Then a third one, louder still.

"I said, don't be assholes!"

The dildos ceased flopping, but Ralph still heard them murmur to one another. He couldn't understand their language, but imagined they were saying bad things about him and his abilities as a salesman.

Ralph shook his head, rolled his shoulders a few times and knocked on the door, the noise echoing through the interior, over and over again, then boomeranging back to him and resulting in sounds somehow louder than the original knocks. Eventually, six knocks sounded like six thousand.

A seventh knock wasn't necessary. The door creaked open. Just past the threshold stood an old woman with a face like yellow parchment. Her hair, dyed unnaturally black, stood a foot above her scalp. She wore a stern black dress beneath a shawl that covered her back and shoulders like a web. She didn't seem to have feet, but they had to be somewhere beneath the dress.

No sooner than Ralph introduced himself did smoke start to rise from around her neck, like hundreds of tiny men inside her tall lace collar were smoking cigars. He tried to ignore this and begin his spiel.

"Hello, good lady. My name is Ralph and I'm a traveling dildo salesman." He paused then, waiting to see if the woman might introduce herself or extend a withered hand to be kissed, but she said and did nothing. Thin, bloodless lips remained tightly pursed. She didn't even blink.

Ralph continued. "Now, you might be thinking that such things don't interest you, but I'm here to tell you that dildos are, in fact, one of the most versatile consumer items known to Man. If you'd only—"

He stopped. The amount of smoke pouring from her collar increased. Ralph could barely see her. It was awkward, just standing on the porch, saying nothing, but he didn't think it wise to continue the spiel when the lady wasn't visible.

Before the smoke could clear, the dildos started muttering again. He looked down at the case. "Shut up, you dildos!" he said through clenched teeth. "I'm in the middle of a sale!"

Ralph regained his composure and turned again to the old woman. The smoke had cleared a bit, but she displayed no sign of life other than standing. "Please, forgive the outburst," he said. "Let me just show you, my good lady, what I have to offer."

He opened up the case. His face scrunched in horror. The case brimmed with angry, violent dildos the likes of which he hadn't anticipated. They flopped around like dozens of dying fish, all screaming for water.

He made to close the case. A dildo shot from the opposite end to his fingers. Small yet razor-sharp teeth sank into his thumb.

He dropped the case, and the dildo that bit him scampered off, laughing. He'd never realized a dildo was capable of laughter.

"Excuse me, would you please? This won't take a moment."

The old woman made no response other than continued smoking. Ralph turned from her and saw that the dildo had inched to the cemetery. There, it darted about the graves and coiled around stones. He had to rectify the situation. Not one could be allowed to escape, as a free dildo could never be sold.

Ralph sprinted to the little cemetery. Pausing there, he watched the dildo writhe in overgrown grass and moss, seemingly blissful until it turned to him and hissed.

He tried to pounce on the dildo, but missed and almost cracked his head on a tombstone. No matter. He had to teach the thing a lesson. Reaching out, Ralph seized the sex toy as it curved around the stump-shaped stone. It bared its teeth; bit him again.

"You son of a bitch!" he shouted.

It squirmed in his grasp. Ralph barely maintained his hold. He heard the bray of a donkey, was distracted, and the dildo slipped free, scurried up his shirt and wrapped itself around his neck.

Tighter and tighter it squeezed. Sparks started to fly, and then the world seemed to darken. Ralph couldn't grasp the dildo to free it from around his neck. Falling away, his flopping hand brushed against a stick. He grabbed it.

The dildo shrieked as the stick entered its urethra slit and lodged deep. Uncoiling from his neck, it thrashed on the ground. A blue goopy substance bubbled from the wound Ralph had made.

Gripping what he imagined must be the dildo's throat, he squeezed. "Do you like how that feels?" he shouted. "*Do you?*"

The dildo could not respond. Blue plastic took on a pink tint before becoming a brilliant, swollen red. It went limp in his hand, and Ralph threw its twisted remains against a nearby tree, just for good measure.

Turning back to the house, he noticed that the old, smoking lady had gone, and that the other dildos were inching out of their case, creeping out onto the lawn.

Reclaiming the dead dildo, Ralph ran up to the others and brandished the corpse in front of them. "If any of you assholes move, I'll do the same to you, and I won't hesitate! Do you understand? I'll kill each and every last one of you, no matter how long it takes!"

The dildos stopped flopping on the porch or in the grass, got in line and returned to the case. They seemed cowed and most quieted down, some whimpering like good little sex toys as they took their positions, one atop the other. But a defiant, devilish red dildo didn't get the message. It started flopping the other way.

Ralph pressed the dead dildo against the living one. "No, don't even think about trying that!"

It quieted down, and Ralph threw the dead dildo in with the living ones. Most recoiled in horror, not at all eager to share close quarters with a deceased comrade. Ralph didn't imagine this would pose a problem, at least not for him. He just wouldn't let potential consumers know that the product was deceased. All sales, after all, were final.

He closed the case. Then he knocked on the door a few times, waited, but no one answered.

Ralph hadn't been back on the road for more than a minute when he saw another sign, every cloud in the sky suddenly amassing around a single house. It was hard to remember, but, in the past, it seemed that he had to walk quite a bit, sometimes for miles and miles, before he reached another selected property.

Maybe whatever the other house had to offer had been transferred to this one. Ralph hoped that was the case.

In the yard, a plastic grizzly bear with claws outstretched towered over a birdbath. Its lips: curled in a sneer. A trail of white plastic drool streamed down from a single tooth. The bear had to be at least twelve feet tall. Ralph kept his eye on it as he passed.

A sheet of paper was taped to the front door. The letters were rendered in pencil, words so small he was already on the porch before he could read them. NO FUCKING SALESMEN, PLEASE, they said.

Ralph wanted to respect this homeowner's wishes. He wanted to turn around, go someplace else. Still, he had to try. The sign had been given.

He only had to knock once. In seconds, he heard approaching footsteps, big clomping ones. The door opened with a squeal.

"What do you want?" said the man, a grizzled, but stout, forty-something. His tousled hair made it seem as though he'd just gotten out of bed. Stubble coated his cheeks. He wore an open bathrobe. Beneath it, only briefs.

More disconcerting: a bandage of what appeared to be freshly wrought tiger skin. It covered one eye, most of his forehead and left cheek. Ralph hated the sight of blood, and his mind conjured up images of what might lay below the strange bandage, even as he launched into his spiel.

"Hello, sir! My name is Ralph, and—"

The man didn't let him finish. "Are you a salesman?" he said.

It hadn't sounded like a question. "Ummm, I, uhhhh…"

"Are you or aren't you?"

"I am, sir."

He folded his arms across his chest. "I don't much like salesmen."

"Don't worry," Ralph replied, trying not to stare at the tiger bandage. "I'm not one of those regular guys! I'm a traveling dildo salesman!"

The man seemed neither interested nor impressed. His face reddened and scrunched into a scowl similar to that of the face Ralph had seen in the window.

"But I have all the best models, exclusive ones, and I only come by once. If you miss this opportunity, it's gone forever."

The man's expression didn't waver. A fat forehead vein pulsed, tenting out his bandage. "I'm a guy. What need do I have for dildos? Where am I going to stick them? Up my ass?"

"If you want, yes."

The vein thumped harder. "I don't very much appreciate the kind of people who do that!"

Clearly, this guy would be a hard sell. Perhaps another approach was in order. Ralph thought for a second, began: "The thing about my dildos is that they're not only practical. They're aesthetic, too."

"What the hell are you talking about?" The bandage started to slump. "Those are sex toys, sick and perverted!"

Ralph swallowed hard. His hands quaked, but he had to continue. "They'll look simply lovely atop a mantle, or by a light or candle, should you choose a translucent model." He ducked as blood spurted from the man's forehead. "Can you imagine having such an amazing and versatile item to show your guests?"

"The pulp of your face wrapped around my fists! That's what I can imagine!"

Ralph dropped the case, lifted his hands defensively. "I'm—I'm sorry, but I had no choice! I had to come here! The grass told me so!"

"Are you on drugs?" His face was mere inches from Ralph's. The tiger bandage fell completely, exposing red meat and yellow pus. His left eye: a black raisin in his head. "Are you an addict?"

"No! No drugs! Not an addict!"

The man, now appearing as tall as the room, glared down at him. "Good! Because there's nothing worse than an addict who's also a traveling salesman!"

Blood rained down on Ralph. "Please don't hurt me," he muttered.

"I posted a note!" the man roared in response, and now his nose and ears were bleeding, too. "You can't say I didn't! I have to beat up every salesman that comes to my door, see? It's a compulsion!"

Before Ralph could react, the man landed an uppercut to his jaw. Ralph fell to the porch, and the man started kicking his ribs. The guy's bathrobe flapped back and forth. His penis bobbed up and down in tandem with the balls in his briefs.

Ralph rolled off the porch into the grass. He arose quickly, his mouth and side aching, and saw the man bound towards him.

"Let me finish what I started!" he screamed, every exposed part of his body alternating between shades of scarlet and crimson as it began to swell.

Ralph took off towards the road. "I told you I was sorry!" he shouted, but the man, uninterested in apologizes, continued his pursuit.

His voice sounded clotted, deep and strained. "You are making me very, very mad!"

When Ralph reached the bear, the man jumped out from behind it. Ralph bit back a scream; he couldn't even wonder how he'd gotten there so fast. His body had expanded to four times its normal size. Eyes bulged like angry melons as red fountains gushed from thick, rope-like veins that throbbed audibly.

The man cocked his grossly oversized fist. Instead of a fist, eyes hit Ralph as both popped out of the man's head. "Ah shit," he tried to say, but he had reached critical mass and exploded all over the yard instead.

The initial shock wore off; Ralph felt around. His body was intact and, miraculously, none of the mess had splattered on him or his clothes. It was everywhere else, though, even on some of the other houses.

Then he realized the globs and splatters weren't just random. They spelled out a clue that began by a neighboring tree, stretched from the bear up to the front of the house, went over a fence and ended by a lamppost the next yard over.

DON'T TRUST BILLBOARDS, it said.

Ralph recited these words a hundred times in an attempt to store them in long-term memory. Then he wondered if it really mattered. He remembered nothing specific from past clues, just disembodied references to various individuals, groups, cults and drugs. Perhaps the clues were all being stored in a mental vault of sorts, one that he could access at the correct time, but maybe that was mere wishful thinking.

And how long had it been since he sold a dildo? A year? Ten years? A hundred?

Had he even sold a first one? All he remembered was going to many houses and knocking on many doors, so many that they all blurred together and seemed like the same big door that led into the same big house.

Maybe he just needed another sign, one that would lead him to a new house, a better place where he'd not only find a clue, but sell a dildo, too. To find it, he'd just have to keep walking.

And so Ralph walked for longer than he thought he could without the sun going down.

Maybe he wanted it too much, or wasn't looking hard enough. Fear told him that it was his fault. He was too blind to see what had to be right in front of him. Ralph tried to shake away this thought. It leached into him, instead.

"Come on! Just give me something I can recognize!" Looking up at the eye in the sky, he imagined that it was taunting him silently.

Ralph considered breaking protocol by trying the closest house. Another part of him felt that this might be a bad thing, that he might be punished, somehow and by somebody.

He put the case down. It had become even more of an anathema to him. Stretching his arms and back, he felt something in his pocket press against his leg. He pulled out a cell phone.

Interesting, but he knew no one apart from himself.

Wait. He'd forgotten about Mom. Now, more than anything, he wanted to talk to her. She had been dead for a very long time, but that didn't stop her from being there for him, day after day.

Maybe she would have some answers, too, but Ralph couldn't recall her number. In desperation, he pushed random buttons on the pad. To his surprise, the phone on the other end started ringing. In three rings, it was picked up.

Ralph said "hello" and heard only a lullaby, hummed in his mother's voice. Seconds before, he couldn't remember the sound of it. It seemed so warm and familiar now. Vaguely, Ralph recalled doing stuff with Mom when he was small, things like going to a place full of steel cages and vicious, wild animals. Whenever he thought of her, she had a blank-face.

She finished the lullaby. "How are you doing, dear?"

"About the same ... at least I think so."

Her voice had a caring lilt. "And how exactly is that?"

It seemed now that his mom always had a way of getting the truth out of him. He exhaled and spoke. "I went to a bad house and ... and I just don't want to do this shi—" he stopped himself before he could say a bad word— "anymore. I want to go back home, but to do that, I've got to keep knocking on these doors!"

"I understand. You're frustrated. But trust me, it's not as bad as you think."

He sighed. "I just want you to tell me something about how things used to be. Anything. It doesn't matter. Even the smallest detail will help me feel whole again."

Silence greeted him for too long.

"... Like what school did I attend? What was my favorite color? Where did we live?"

"All those things are confidential, dear."

"Okay, Mom, okay. It's just that ... being dead and all, you must know some of the secrets."

"I do. But you know I can't tell." There was a slight pause. "But I can tell you this..."

His hands tingled. "Please, Mom! Please tell!"

"This happened long ago. I was in the hospital with the flu. Doctors thought I might die, and I felt so terrible I believed them, until The White Man came."

"The White Man?"

"Yes, and he told me that you, who had yet to be born, would grow up to become a very special type of man, a traveling dildo salesman."

"Why have you never told me this?"

"I've told you. You just don't remember."

Ralph looked down at his shoes. "Oh..."

"Don't worry, Son. For now, simply know that you are meant to follow this path. It is your Way. Do you understand?"

"Yes, Mom, I do."

"Good. And never get on that bus. You'd be cheating destiny."

He was taken aback. "How did you know about the bus?"

"Mothers know all. I also know a sign will appear to you soon, and it will make you very, very happy."

Suddenly, the pavement in front of him reared up. Ralph covered his eyes, for a second thinking it might crash down on him like a wave, but it took a detour to the right, shooting through a nearby yard and across the porch where it stopped at the door and landed with a thud.

"Do you see the sign?" Mom asked.

"I do. And yes, I'll do a good job. I'll sell all my dildos, just like you want. But Mom…"

"What, Son?"

He bit his lip. "Can I ask a favor before you go?"

"Of course."

"Will you … will you please call me after I finish with this house, just in case it turns out bad, too?" He hated that he sounded so vulnerable.

"I'll try, but I can't make promises. Getting to the phone more than once a day when you're dead isn't easy."

"I understand, and no need to promise anything. Thanks, Mom."

"You're welcome, Son."

Following the new road, Ralph scanned the chosen property. Physically, the house was the same as all the others, but a fountain towered in the yard. Rusting steel fragments of varying shapes and sizes shot forth at wild angles from a wide, saucer-shaped base. The top ended in a huge nozzle that spurted black, oily water. Ralph wondered if the owner might be an artist, someone who might appreciate his dildos, buy them all, and incorporate them into his or her work.

He stood at the door for a few seconds for composure's sake, but, before he could knock, the door opened slowly, not with a squeal, but a mechanical hum and the sound of uncoiling springs and grinding gears.

Before Ralph stood a robot, or, rather, what looked like a Halloween costume or cheap movie approximation of such. Its body was just a dull tin box with slots and knobs and gauges on it. Some appeared painted on. Its head was similar to a bucket, with a cutout slot for the mouth, two red plastic flares serving as eyes and a black dot for the nose. Legs were thick, woven wire bundles. The wires untangled and split into prongs that served as rudimentary feet; it didn't appear to have functional knees.

"Good day, sir."—Then he wondered if he should call a robot "sir"—"My name is Ralph, and you look like an individual who might be interested in one of my fine dildos."

The robot made bleeping sounds. Ralph took that as a "yes."

He brought his case into view. "Well, then I suggest grabbing one, or even a handful, now, as this is a one-time only opportunity."

The robot bleeped again.

"Why don't we step inside? I could show you some of my finer specimens. Believe me when I say, dildos are one of the world's most versatile inventions."

It started leaking oil onto the carpet.

Ralph felt flustered. Perhaps the best he could do was leave. "Well, good day," he said. "I'm sorry to have bothered you."

As he was about to turn away, a pinprick of light appeared in the center of the robot's chest and lengthened across it in a beam. The beam arched down and became the outline of a door, the demarcated segment opening like a drawbridge as Ralph's case rumbled and light emanated from it in rays. Then locks unfastened, and dildos, dozens and dozens of them, flew from the case and into the robot. When the last dildo was through the breach, the door and case both slammed shut.

For a second, Ralph feared that the robot might take the dildos and leave without paying him. But the door opened again, and a belly-full of pennies slid out from it onto the porch.

He picked up one of the pennies, studied it. The obverse featured a happy-looking walrus head, wearing a monocle. The reverse said only, ONE CENT.

Ralph put this coin in his pocket as a souvenir. The rest, he scooted off the porch. "I give these to the ground," he said. As if on vocal cue, grass blades wrapped around the pennies. The ground swallowed them and, afterwards, expelled air like a burp.

Ralph didn't mind the loss. Money was a means of transaction, and, once that transaction was complete, it became meaningless.

Big-top music started playing in the robot's house. He looked past the robot just as a banner unfurled from the ceiling, stretching from one side of the living room to the other as streamers and confetti fell.

CONGRATULATIONS, RALPH!
—GOD

Knowing something, somewhere, had been watching heartened him. Perhaps certain powers—powers that cared for his best interests—were congratulating him on sticking around and seeing it through to the end.

"Thank you," he said, though to whom exactly he could not say.

The robot spat out a roll of white tape from a slot where a naval would be were it human. When the roll stopped getting longer, Ralph reached down, pulled it off.

Maybe this was his ticket out of the world, but the script was reminiscent of hieroglyphics, and he could decipher none of it. One marking was somewhat evocative, though. It was a heart, and it reminded him of a locket that hung on an old woman's neck. Within that heart image, he realized suddenly, were words too small to read.

He folded the strip, put it in his pocket. "Good day, sir," Ralph said, more out of habit, as he was sure the thing hadn't heard him, then added, sincerely, "And thank you so very, very much."

"Good day to you, too," the thing said in a low, halting electronic register.

On the road, Ralph was met with a feeling like déjà vu. It was, he realized, also a feeling of joy. Before, joy had been just a word, no way to conceptualize it. As he pondered this, he realized that he might just love the robot. It had finally squared his circle.

Ralph glanced up at the sky, looking, perhaps, for a flaming chariot or magic carpet. When would he transcend this place? He hoped it would be soon, but if he had to wait, be patient, then so be it. At that moment, Ralph realized that he still carried his case. How silly of him. He tossed it to the street.

In his pocket, the phone rang. His smile was so wide it felt eternal. He couldn't wait to talk to Mom, tell her the news. "Hello!" he shouted before she even had time to speak.

"My, you sound excited!"

"I am, Mom; I am! You won't believe this, but I sold my dildos to a robot!"

She sighed. "Robots are such nice people."

"They are, Mom. Really and truly."

"I'm so proud of you, Son."

"I'm proud of me, too! It's over and I can go home!"

On the line: awkward silence.

"Mom?" Ralph asked.

"I hate to say this," she said, finally, "but have you looked in your case since the robot bought your dildos?"

"No. Why?"

"I just think you should look, that's all."

Ralph bent down, opened the case. A large pink dildo, threaded with pulsing veins, sat to the left of a smaller translucent blue one and to the right of a realistic-looking yet grossly oversized basic model.

"Oh shi—crap, Mom!" Ralph said. He considered rushing back to the house. There, he would accost the robot, make it buy the last three dildos.

"You are never to return to a house you've already tried," Mom said, her tone a bit sterner. "It's part of the rules."

"Okay. I'm just … a little disappointed."

"Still, Son, this is good," she said. "In fact, it's very, very good. Just think of how much closer you are now…"

"I know. I know. Being close is great, but it's not the same as making it."

"I understand, dear, but you're doing great. I'm so very proud of you. Never forget that and keep plugging away. Do it for your old, dead mother."

"I will. I promise. And thank you, Mom."

Ralph could almost see her smile. "No, thank you. You've said all I wanted to hear."

CHAPTER THREE

Sunrays no longer shined through clouds. Night insects screamed in the distance. In front of and behind Ralph, the lights in all the houses went out simultaneously.

Thinking back, he couldn't recall ever seeing homeowners in their yards after dark. No flickers of light or shadows passing by windows, either. Perhaps everyone left via tunnels or simply ceased to be until morning.

If so, he imagined it'd be okay to sleep in one of the houses, as it seemed a crime for so much space to go unused, night after night.

Then Ralph thought he remembered something about a big, threatening black shadow that warned him never to approach any house after dark. But what if that shadow was just a phantom from some long ago dream? Maybe he'd already entered houses, slept in them numerous times.

A rested salesman, Ralph figured, was preferable to an exhausted one, so he stepped onto the property. In lieu of a plastic animal, a metallic sculpture of a red broken heart sat on a marble base surrounded by a small herb garden. Directly behind the house: a patch of dense woods.

One of the windows was open slightly. From it, Ralph heard a song, its melody warm and happy, its lyrics muffled by walls. Curiosity overpowered him. He walked to the sill, took hold of it and pushed himself up.

Losing his balance, he fell from the window to the floor. His left shoulder stung a bit but the pain was forgotten as he heard the lyrics to the song clearly:

Your trials are near their end.
Relax in memory;
Relax in what soon shall be
And become yourself again…

First his shoulders and then his mind relaxed as he walked through a den populated with comfy looking furniture and charming knickknacks. A set of bronze hands, clasped in prayer, sat atop the TV. Old porcelain dolls lined the mantle above a lit fireplace.

In an adjacent bedroom, colorful jars of perfume were displayed on the dresser. A gray shawl was draped over one bedpost. A rack full of yellowing magazines sat by the nightstand. On the wall above the bed was a family photograph, faded, tattered at the edges and containing three smiling people. The smallest guy looked like the sort of kid Ralph might once have been.

Ralph remembered, suddenly, that this was the room where his grandmother had once slept. Her name was Meg. Or Marge. Or Mabel. Ralph wished he could call her as well, but maybe she'd been dead for so long that her voice was just a whisper.

He entered a short and narrow hall before finding himself in the kitchen. On the refrigerator, held up by an apple-shaped magnet, was a drawing of a stick figure standing beside a stick house in a stick world with a happy sun and no leering blue eye in sight.

FOR GRANNY, said the big, red, crayon-rendered words at the top.

Turning to his right, he saw the entranceway to the dining room and, through it, a massive, ornate wooden table, ostentatious in such an otherwise homespun milieu. China plates and platters and cups held enough food to satiate at least twenty people. Ralph eyed the turkey in the center of the table. His stomach rumbled, and he looked down at his stick-like arms, then felt the ribs beneath his shirt.

Still, he stared at the food for another minute, reveling in the sheer awesomeness of the spread before approaching the table and taking his seat. He touched the turkey leg. It was hot. The stuffing produced warm steam that condensed against his hand. He seized a knife, gold from the looks of it, and dug in, slicing off a chunk of turkey breast. He dropped it on his plate, took a bite and oh did it taste wonderful, like Christmas and Thanksgiving combined.

Quickly, he reached for a spoon buried in a bowl of mashed potatoes, but, upon lifting it, noticed that it was connected by wire to the bottom of the bowl.

Something clicked; a guillotine blade from the ceiling smashed into the table. Ralph looked down. His fork had been halved; the top quarter of his thumb was gone, too.

He stood up. A blade as wide as the room itself descended, splitting the entire kitchen. The left side of the room fell away as the turkey rose from the plate, picked up a carving knife with its wing and flashed it. The severed neck mimicked a mouth and smiled unpleasantly.

A third blade whooshed, this time from the side. Ralph ducked as it sheared away the uppermost quarters of the house. Before he could reorient himself, whirling blades on stalks and nozzles shot up from the floor, busting boards and sending clouds of dust and crawlspace skeletons into the air.

The devices gave chase, playing oddly soothing Muzak from tiny speakers all the while. Ralph's feet wanted to tap against his volition, but he couldn't let these frequencies into his brain. He ignored them as much as he was able and jumped over a fourth blade that threatened his feet.

Outside, he ran in the direction of the woods. The nozzles, hoses and blades shut off their music, made disconcerting chattering sounds. Turning, Ralph saw the open, needle-filled maw of a hose hovering mere inches from his neck.

Running faster, he began to smell pine needles, wild flowers and fragrant roots. He concentrated on these odors and blocked from his mind everything that wasn't associated with them or his pounding feet. Seconds later, darkness gave way to a tangle of browns and greens. The nozzles, hoses and blades attempted to enter alongside, but impacted against tree trunks or were ensnared in vines.

Ralph continued until he could go no farther. Into a bed of pine needles below a dead tree he fell.

It took him a while to regain consciousness, and longer still to stop feeling as though he was about to die. Earlier, he'd breathed so hard that he feared his lungs might burst; he worried that his heart might beat out of his chest or that a blood vessel might explode in his brain. Now, all he felt was a throbbing sensation in his thumb. The bleeding had stopped, but he feared infection. Bandages weren't available on his route, and he'd never seen a doctor's office.

Ralph didn't want to think about this. It didn't make him feel any better. There was, however, one thing that could.

He didn't like killing little animals—or anything, for that matter—but it was unavoidable. Large prey was off the menu. It had to be a creature small enough so that the force of a dildo thrown against its head would either kill it or render it unconscious. Still, a meager dinner was better than no dinner at all.

In a bush, he heard something scamper. He waited a few seconds and saw a rabbit peek out its head, nose twitching.

Ralph felt for his case, opened it. One dildo was awake. He recognized the dildo he'd killed, seized it, and closed the case before the conscious dildo could consider escape. He moved his throwing arm into position, but rustled some leaves. Though Ralph tossed the dildo quickly, the rabbit was gone before it hit the ground.

"Damn!"

He retrieved the dildo, waited for more prey, waited until he imagined he might just as well go to bed. Then the noises came.

He wondered what it could be. The thing sounded decently sized as it trundled through leaves. Maybe it was a skunk. Ralph recalled eating one, and it had agreed neither with his palate nor his stomach.

The thing got closer. It was a groundhog.

"Stay right where you are," he whispered beneath his breath. "Don't move a muscle."

The groundhog turned to Ralph. Had it heard him and understood what he said? Nonsense. Ralph pitched the dildo. It sailed through the air, spinning twice before it hit the fat, furry thing's head and knocked it out cold. A rear leg twitched.

"Gotcha!" Ralph bolted from his position and ran to the animal before it had time to regain its bearings. The blow, he could tell, had only stunned it.

He picked up the dead dildo and put it in his pocket. He wasn't even halfway back to the campsite when the groundhog came to. The thing scratched at his arms and screamed as though human, mouth open wide, nostrils flaring so obscenely that Ralph believed he'd see the animal's brain were the lighting better.

He couldn't take the sight, much less the sound. He pinned the groundhog against a nearby tree and slammed the dildo hard against its head.

It still twitched, so Ralph struck the thing, again and again.

"Just die already!" he screamed.

Minutes later, the groundhog's head lolled around the side of Ralph's hand. He watched it for a few minutes more, half-expecting it to twitch or scream. When it did neither, he set out to build a small fire and then go about the unpleasant task of running the groundhog through with a stick.

Groundhog flesh crackled and popped in the fire. When the meat was done,

Ralph removed it from the flames, wiped off a blanket of black, melted fur and brought the crispy groundhog to his lips. He took a bite and had memories of cold, sweet things on sticks that tasted nothing at all like this. Though he hoped it would be a long time before he ate groundhog again, he finished all the meat but the face and tail.

With a belly full of vile, hairy food, Ralph laid down to sleep. For warmth, he layered pine needles atop his chest before coiling into a fetal ball. It took a few minutes, but he drifted off as the fire died down and blackened pieces of wood turned into crackling red and white embers and then became nothing at all.

Ralph awoke with a start. A nearby rustling had disturbed his sleep. He turned the way of the sound and beheld the white, glowing bodies of those he called the Orb Passers. He'd forgotten about them and the name he'd given them. Now, it seemed that he saw them every night, and they always did the same inscrutable thing, carrying illuminated silver orbs like sacred objects, passing them back and forth, holding them aloft briefly, letting the light from the moon kiss them, or maybe giving the eye in the sky a better look.

Who were they? What did they want? Were they living clues? Angels? Devils? Messengers?

He had to approach them.

Ralph sat up, dusted himself off and started walking. The twigs under his feet made very loud noises, louder than they had any right to sound. He cursed them, but the Orb Passers didn't seem to care or notice. They continued passing and lifting, lifting and passing.

Closer still, he saw that the things were naked, but didn't have genitalia.

He crept up to them, addressed one. "Could you help me? I want to know why I'm here and what's happening."

The thing just glowed. It had no face.

"If you can say or do anything, I'd be much obliged."

More lifting. More passing…

Ralph bit his bottom lip. "Can't you do anything else?"

The being reached out a bright finger, pointed to his pants pocket.

Ralph was confused until he remembered what he'd stored there. He reached in, wincing as fabric scraped across his wound. Now with his other hand, he dug deep and brought forth the paper strip that the robot had given him. "Do you mean this?" he asked.

The glowing thing nodded and took the strip from Ralph. A black hole opened in the center of its head. It put the strip into the hole.

Ralph wanted to shriek, perhaps even punch the Orb Passer. It had destroyed a vital piece of the puzzle. But his anger quieted when the thing presented its orb for Ralph's inspection. Inside the crystal, he saw the image of the strip, close up on the heart, and now the tiny words inside it were legible:

THE FIRST HOUSE OF THE DAY WILL BE YOUR LAST, IF YOU ARE A GOOD SALESMAN.

Ralph staggered back to his campsite, body tingling. It took almost an hour before sleep claimed him. His thoughts raced, but in a good way, as he imagined all the things that might soon be.

CHAPTER FOUR

Ralph awoke to a perfect spring morning. He took to his feet moments later, as it seemed wrong to waste time lying around on a day that held so much promise.

But what if you mess it up?

That thought tried to dissipate the good feelings taking root inside him, so he shook it away. He would make the best damn sale in the history of salesmanship, and be rewarded for it.

Ralph freshened up by a stream of bright, almost navy blue water, a color more soothing than the bright red of the streaks that crisscrossed his mangled thumb. Blood infection, he thought, but tried to worry no more about it. It was something a doctor could treat once he sold his last dildo and left this place for good.

He returned to his case, opened it, looked inside, but no dildo fought him or tried to escape, the two survivors content to just undulate quietly. Maybe these were the better-behaved ones. Or maybe they were less rambunctious now there was no more safety in numbers.

Ralph closed the case and picked it up to begin his day. It felt almost weightless in his grasp, not like a burden at all.

Ralph stepped out onto the road and came face-to-face with another billboard. It featured the same artwork of the happy, breakfast cereal eating family, but, this time, the text read: IT ISN'T THE GOVERNMENT.

His memory of the day before was already degrading, but he was almost certain that the previous sign had implicated the government. Then he remembered the clue by the exploded man's house, though he wasn't sure if it had told him to trust or not to trust billboards.

No matter. He had better, more important things to consider.

The bus was already at the stop when he passed it. He gave it a second glance, but only because he couldn't recall ever seeing a bus on his route. He'd be receiving a better way out than via public transit soon enough.

Before him, the houses were all in the form of squat, almost featureless rectangles. There was no way of telling which would be the special one, the deciding factor, but it was along the line, somewhere, and, if necessary, Ralph would walk all day to find it.

He passed just ten houses, and there it was: the shadow of a tree cast upon the house elongated, losing its branches and leaves, becoming a line, which then became deep black, like paint instead of shadow. The base of the line bifurcated into an arrow that pointed down at the door. Within seconds, the arrow was gone, the innocuous tree shadow once again cast upon the house, but that brief sign was all he needed.

On the lawn: a plastic statue of a fat, rosy-cheeked cherub. When Ralph first noticed it, it wore a neutral expression. Upon a second glance, it smiled at him. Plastic eyes twinkled. Ralph couldn't help but smile back.

The smile faded as he glanced down at his case. It was streaked with red and yellow discharge from his thumb. Ralph sat the case down, scrubbed it in the grass. He considered looking at his thumb again, but didn't want that image fresh on his mind as he tried to make the sale.

He stepped onto the porch, knocked at the door. When it opened, a young, neat-looking man dressed in beige slacks and a white button-up shirt stood at the threshold. His face was soft and pleasant, reminiscent, somewhat, of the cherub.

Ralph launched into his spiel. "Hello, my name is Ralph, and I'm a traveling dildo salesman."

"Hello, sir," the man said. "My name is Steve, and I'm your potential customer."

Ralph was taken aback. He'd found someone who was polite, well-spoken. "Well, nice to meet you, Steve," he said. "Might I interest you in one of my fine dildos?"

"I could take a look..."

Of course you could, Ralph thought. He opened the case, afraid that the dildos might be in a rambunctious mood—Murphy's Law—but the two living ones were as quiet and orderly as before.

Steve craned his head to see inside. In Ralph's estimation, he looked impressed.

"I simply love the color and texture of that one," Ralph said. "Don't you?"

"My, it is pretty!" Steve pointed at the red one just beside it. "But I think I like this one even better."

Ralph smiled. There was no way he wouldn't make this sale. "I'd say they both have positive attributes," he said.

Steve studied the third dildo; his face scrunched. "Isn't that one dead?"

Ralph bit his bottom lip. "No, it's not."

"Oh, okay. Guess it's just a quiet one."

"Yes, and personally, I've found that quiet dildos are the best dildos."

"These are all nice, yes." He paused, looked at Ralph. "But tell me, are they expensive?"

"Just a penny each."

"Really? I thought you'd ask for more."

"I just need to sell these. I don't care about making a profit. I'd give them away if I could, but that's against the rules."

Steve scratched his chin. "Okay, the price is good; the product is good. Everything looks good."

"So, you are interested! Wonderful!" He flashed a smile that he sensed would seal the deal.

The man reached out—*This is it!* Ralph's mind screamed—but he only took two dildos and gave Ralph two pennies.

"You forgot one, sir," Ralph said.

Steve looked confused. "No, I didn't."

"But you did." He tilted the case, pointed. "See, here it is."

"I simply cannot take that last one."

Something flipped in his stomach. "What?"

"I'm terribly sorry."

Ralph fought rising horror, but Steve had been an easy customer before, and he hadn't closed the door, was still standing at the threshold smiling, being pleasant, but, most importantly, available. Getting Steve to take the last dildo had to be the true and final test of his salesman's mettle.

He composed himself, threw the two pennies to the ground, said, "Really, these are a set, and you wouldn't want to break up a set, would you? Individual pieces might become lonely."

"It's just not possible. No offense."

Control over the situation seemed lost. Was the ship already sunk? What if … what if he wasn't supposed to lie? If that was the test, then he'd already failed. Ralph wanted to bite his nails. Run his hands through his hair. Fling his body off the porch and flail in the grass.

Compose yourself, damn it!

He cleared his already clear throat before making himself speak coherently. "You must take it, sir. This is my last house, and, really, I can't have remaining inventory."

The man just shook his head.

Ralph clenched his fists. "If you don't take it, so help me, I'll—" He made himself stop, realizing he was losing his professional cool, becoming disrespectful. "I'm sorry," he said. "Must be the heat." Suddenly, snowflakes fell from overhead.

"No problem," Steve replied, but didn't utter a word about purchasing another dildo.

"Come on, just take the thing."

"But that would be one too many dildos, and you know what they say about that."

Ralph had no idea. All he knew was that his emotional floodgates were about to burst. "Why can't you just buy the dildo, you son of a bitch!" he shouted. "Do you want me to do this shit forever?" He lifted his thumb, now swollen, pulsing and green. "Do you want this to kill me?"

Steve lifted his hands, a placating gesture. "No sir, and I don't want to do this forever, either." He glanced at the remaining dildo. "Still, I told you it was very nice, and I haven't changed my opinion."

Ralph seized the dildo, brandished it in his customer's face. "Then take the fucking thing!"

"But I can't, no matter how much I may desire it. God always buys the last dildo from salesmen."

Ralph thought back to the banner. "God?"

Steve nodded.

"And you said: salesmen?"

"Oh yes, I've seen plenty of traveling dildo salesman. They're all over these parts."

He never imagined there might be others, and wasn't sure whether to believe this news or not.

"I just ignored them in the past," Steve continued, "or was mean to them. Sometimes very, very mean." His eyes lost focus. "One I even chopped up and stored in the basement until the smell got to me."

Ralph took two steps back. "You did?"

"And I made love to the parts like you wouldn't believe! But I'm a different man now. I understand what it's like to have to do the same thing, day in and day out, with scant hope of ever stopping." He seemed suddenly wistful. "I had a life too, you know. We all did, and, my lord, I see it so clearly now."

Watching this man, Ralph almost wanted to cry. "I'm sorry for getting mad at you earlier."

"Oh, that's okay. I'm sorry it took me so long to finally help out a traveling dildo salesman, but I've got to go." He paused briefly. "Good luck."

With that, Steve's body shimmered like a Christmas tree. He waved as the sparkles intensified, smiled and then disappeared.

Turning, Ralph noticed a fork in the ordinarily straight road. He couldn't wait to take this path, see where it led. Then he remembered someone named Mom, and realized that he should call her, tell her of this wonderful news.

He reached into his pocket. Found the phone. He dialed numbers at random, heard the other end start ringing, and waited for Mom's sweet, sweet voice to fill his ear.

Instead, all he heard were distant murmurs, like several people speaking to one another far from the receiver.

"Hello," he said.

It sounded as though the people were walking towards the phone. One voice sounded gruff, masculine.

"I—I would like to speak to Mom, please," Ralph continued.

Suddenly, an angry man shouted into the receiver. "Hang up the phone!"

Ralph did so quickly. His nerves jangled, but he made himself relax and not think too much about it. Maybe he'd gotten the wrong number. Perhaps he could tell Mom about the events of the day himself, in person, once it was through.

On the new road, the only thing Ralph noticed was more billboards, hundreds if not thousands of them, lining both sides and blocking all other sensory input.

ALIENS ARE DOING IT, said one.

He wondered if this related to his predicament, or was a mere sexual declaration.

Another: YOU ARE REALLY DEAD.

And on the next billboard, just a few yards up: YOU CAN NEVER DIE.

This was followed by a litany of positive statements rendered negative by subsequent ones. So many groups implicated, then vindicated: bankers, masons, illuminati, televangelists, working mothers, electricians, dental hygienists and, more prosaically, the bus driver, Ralph's customers and even himself.

He decided to pay no further attention, as he now recalled the exploded man's clue quite clearly. These were just falsehoods and distractions he had to pass before the truth was revealed.

He soldiered on. The road curved. Beyond, billboards vanished and a vista opened, revealing a hill, the base of which stretched for miles. The change in topography stunned Ralph, and he walked to it like a supplicant towards an idol.

Pavement soon changed into an overgrown footpath that snaked up the hill. It felt weird, but very welcome, traveling upwards after so much time spent on flat and monotonous ground.

Near the summit, he noticed a sign posted in front of a thorn bush. A SLIGHT LEFT FOR UNDERSTANDING, it said. Ralph turned in the direction indicated, entering a path that traveled between parallel lines of oaks, each tree equidistant from the others. Overhead, branches tangled in an organic canopy.

He walked this path until he noticed space where a tree was missing. In its place was another sign: GO HERE.

Ralph found himself in a clearing. Looking up, he beheld a towering dildo-shaped building looming a field's length ahead. Its chimney—jutting from the penis tip—was actually a smokestack, belching out puffs of steam.

He ran to the building, stopping when he saw another sign, this one posted at the door.

THIS IS THE PLACE; KNOCK FOR ANSWERS.

When he did, the door did not swing open, but slid away so quickly that it seemed to disappear. Before him stood the robot, then the old, smoking woman, then the exploded man and a hundred and then a thousand different other faces, all he'd seen before, though most he had forgotten.

Finally, his eyes settled on a beautiful tow-haired woman. She wore a simple white dress that sparkled. A disk of wan light surrounded her head.

"Are you God?" Ralph asked her.

"Yes, I am."

"I thought you might be scary." He looked down at his feet as he spoke, humbled in her presence.

"Please, look me in the eyes." She touched his cheek, her hands warm. "There's no need for fear."

Ralph glanced up reluctantly. Her irises were electric blue islands in white seas, and, as he looked into them, nervousness fled.

"So," she said. "You are finally here."

He forced himself to look past God's eyes, and behind her, saw a huge metal room, filled with machines on which thousands of old women in hairnets toiled.

"Yes," he said, "but where am I?"

"This is Heaven, the factory in which all your dildos were made."

"Really?" Ralph craned his neck to see farther. He noticed a group of old women gathered on a bench by the adjacent wall, painting a line of floppy sex toys. To the right, additional old ladies sat in chairs, hands behind their backs as younger-seeming people in black clothes and helmets stood over them, shoving dildos into their mouths and moving them back and forth, testing for proper circumference, perhaps. To the left, others stuffed finished products into suitcases identical to the one Ralph carried.

She placed a hand on his shoulder. "If you want, we can tour the factory later, but we should be outside now. The eye in the sky must bear witness to this event."

God stepped across the threshold and Ralph followed. She sat down in a lotus position on the grass. He took this as his cue to take a seat as well, though he couldn't manage the lotus.

"Tell me, Ralph," she said, "what is it you want to know most?"

"So, my name is Ralph."

"Yes, but do tell…"

"I want to know the answer."

She nodded. "After coming so far, you deserve it. Many dildo salesmen never sell even a single dildo. You sold yours in your first two weeks, though years passed before you sold another." A smile. "Despite the odds, you remained steadfast, diligently picking up and piecing together clues. Now, it's time to reward your efforts."

His nerves felt positively alive, his spine, electric. "Oh thank you!" he effused. "Thank you so much!"

"No need to thank me. Thank yourself for what is to be." She looked down at his mangled thumb. "But first, let me take care of that. Please, extend your hand."

Ralph did, and God touched the stump where his nail had once been. Warmth branched through his fingers and down his arm as, like a mushroom, the missing tip grew. "My god," he said, surveying the digit, looking for seams but seeing none.

"Now, I must prepare…" God closed her eyes, tilted her head towards the sky, linked her forearms and lifted them so that her unfolded hands were bunched near her sternum. It looked as though she might be holding an orb Ralph could not see.

She maintained this position, and total silence, for what seemed to be a very, very long time. Ralph wished she'd hurry up, but said nothing, imagining it wasn't wise to rush God.

Finally, she arose. "I am ready, so stand, Ralph. Present unto me the final dildo in your case."

"And then I can be free?"

God said nothing, just smiled, so Ralph handed her the dildo. The passing felt like a sacrament.

She outstretched her other hand, opened it. "And here's your penny."

Ralph looked at his ticket out. He saw the usual walrus-face-wearing-a-monocle, but there was now a single word below it, rendered in bas-relief: CONGRATS. He took the coin from her, flipped it over. NOW BEGIN AGAIN said the reverse.

Suddenly, the case by his feet started shaking, and then was enveloped in white light. When the light faded, Ralph beheld at least a hundred violent, angry dildos, flopping on the ground, gnashing their teeth.

"Now go on," said God, "continue your endless journey."

Ralph held up his hands. "No, wait … this … this is supposed to be the end! This is supposed to be—"

"There is no end, Ralph. Not here, but that's okay. It's the quest that's noble, not the outcome."

He shook his head back and forth. "I can't do this anymore!" A dildo crept up to his foot, and he stomped it. "I just can't!"

"Don't worry. Tomorrow, you won't remember a thing."

"But I know now, and that's the problem!"

"There's no problem."

He felt on the verge of crying, screaming and breaking things. "Come on, God! Isn't there something you can do?"

"We could tour the factory," she said.

"I don't want to tour the fucking factory!"

God drummed her fingers on her hips. "Okay, Ralph, I'll lay it on the line. Freedom just doesn't work for you. You'll always swirl back to the center, and that's exactly where you're going when we're done here."

"I don't understand."

She laughed. "You sound like someone who hasn't had this conversation with me a hundred times before, but that's to be expected."

Ralph could only look at her.

"You may be mad now, you may even want to kill me, but you'll come back with that same awe-struck expression you wore earlier, overjoyed to see me and wanting what you think you desire, but ultimately getting what you need."

He lashed out. "I'll never come back to you! And this isn't what I need!"

Her tone was palliative again. "Without dildos and the unfurling road to nowhere, you have no direction, no purpose. You're not strong enough to assign meaning to life in any other way."

"No, this isn't—"

"You're concerned and agitated, but don't be. Many have the same problem, and, when the time is right, they'll return to the center, too. It's the way it must be, now and forevermore."

"Maybe they'll return, but I refuse!"

"But you've returned every time before." She twirled an index finger in the air. "Swirl, swirl, swirl..."

Ralph smacked her hand down. "Not this time! Now is different!"

God laughed. "Now is never different. If it was, do you think this factory would be here, churning out all the dildos for all the traveling dildo salesman of the world? Business is booming."

Ralph tried to get a word in edge-wise, but God wouldn't let him.

"You remember that woman on the phone? It wasn't your mother. It was a voice actor." She grinned. "Your mother works for us now, in the advanced product testing department with all the other old, dead mothers who have traveling dildo salesmen for sons."

"No, that's not true! There's not a shred of truth in you!"

"The only truth lies in your case, so pick it up."

"I will not!"

God reached out, caressed his face. Her hands felt cold now. "You know this is a mistake," she said, "but you have time to correct it. Just do as I say. We can pretend that this never happened."

Ralph repeated his declaration.

God shook her head. "I don't always give traveling dildo salesmen this chance, believe me." A small flipbook appeared in her hand. "I've got pictures. Want to see?"

Ralph didn't, but she opened the flipbook, showed him a few of its pages.

"This is a mere sampling. I've got a bigger book in my office."

His stomach twisted; he wanted to gag. His legs tried to fold and carry him to the ground, after which they would surely arise from it and carry him back to his case and to his life as a traveling dildo salesman, *ad infinitum*.

No, he wouldn't allow it. Maybe terrible things had happened to those poor guys, but that didn't mean they had to happen to him ... and so what if they did?

"My mind hasn't changed," he said. "You can do nothing to me. I'm not someone in your book. I am Ralph." Suddenly, it seemed that there was more to his name than simply that.

Then it dawned on him. "Ralph Stevens," he added, and couldn't help but grin.

God's ears bled at the sound of that name. "Pick up your case!" she shrieked. "Someone must take it, and you're the only one here that can!"

"No, I'm not the only one!" He dumped the dildos from the case. "I'll give these to the ground!"

The ground took the dildos not into its mouth—that was a place for pennies—but into its womb. Exiting the resting state, dildos germinated, entangling beneath the surface, becoming a network of helices as the earth spewed a mound of pennies from its bowels.

Ralph smiled. "The transaction is complete."

The world felt the new growth, started shrieking. God threw herself atop the copper mound, shrieking the loudest of all the shrieking things. She looked up at him, her mouth filled with ivory tusks. "You can't do this!" she screamed. Her words were muffled and slurred.

"I already did!" He pointed at the pennies. "They are mine, and there's nothing you can do!"

The bottom half of God's body became that of a walrus. Ralph almost laughed at the sight. Seconds later, her top half followed suit. She even had the monocle, though it was hard to think of God as female now.

The God-thing barked and belched as its flesh started to flake, then crack and peel. It tried to clutch at Ralph's pant leg with a flipper. That flipper fell off, followed by tusks, the other flipper and even more vital parts. Something white and foamy shot from God's mouth before the remains of its brown, flabby body went rigid and rolled to the left of the penny mound.

Ignoring God, Ralph took handfuls of pennies and dumped them into both coat pockets, then into his pants.

Up ahead, he heard a sudden commotion. A mob clamored up the hill, approaching him from the west.

Ralph recognized some of the people, though he did not see his last customer. The man who had beaten him prior to exploding headed the line. To his left was the once-motionless smoking woman, now running as fast as the newly reconstituted man. Behind them, in an unbroken and seemingly eternal line, fanning out from left to right, were potential customers from days and months and years past. Some carried impromptu torches, fashioned from sticks or broken furniture legs wrapped in kerosene-dipped cloth. Others carried pitchforks.

From the opposite direction, orb passers sprinted from the woods. They shook their fists and hurtled their balls at him. One impacted against a tree, leaving a hole big enough for Ralph to see through.

The closest thrower hurtled a second orb. There was no avoiding it. Ralph stopped, took a deep breath, knowing that, if he died, at the very least, he wouldn't die as a traveling dildo salesman, but the thing passed through him, leaving only an electrical sensation in its wake.

The first pitchfork-wielder reached him. Like the orb, his weapon had no effect.

"Die already!" screamed the man who had exploded. His body swelled as he tried to stab again.

The old smoking woman said nothing, but attempted without success to brain him with her torch.

The robot bleeped, and then caught fire. But it wasn't just the robot that had malfunctioned. Everything started to burn as dildos completed the germination cycle.

He turned away from it all then, away from the rows of houses, the endless streets, the orb passers, killing machines and the factory and its god. As he walked, the world peeled slightly at its edges. The bright tip of something different shined through. Ralph could barely see whatever it was, but, somehow, it seemed like stuff from memory.

In his pocket, the phone started ringing. It was his faux-mother. Fuck her. She was probably on fire, too.

EPILOGUE

Ralph took the path back down the hill, surrounded by burning trees and sky, but didn't get far before he noticed that the footpath ahead of him had changed into a road. About twenty yards farther, Ralph saw a bus stop.

He only had to wait a minute for the bus to arrive. Its door opened and the same driver—it was always the same driver—regarded him, seemingly not fazed by the conflagration going on all around him. "Hello, Ralph," he said.

Ralph nodded, but did not move. He'd been rebuffed so many times before, and, worse yet, flames had broken out on the street between him and the bus.

"Why are you just staring at me? Get on."

"I can't. Too much fire."

"Just walk through it."

Figuring he had little to lose, Ralph did. He was impervious to the flames. Still, he paused just before reaching the bus. Crossing its threshold seemed more challenging than a walk through fire. "I can get on now? Really and truly?"

"Really and truly."

"It's ... as easy as that?"

The man smiled. "Sure is, but hurry. I've got other salesmen to pick up down the line."

"But I don't have a ticket."

"That's alright." The driver pointed to his case, lying in the middle of the road; Ralph didn't remember dropping it. "Leaving that behind is better than a ticket."

Ralph put his left foot on the step, then his right foot. Past the steps, he looked around at his fellow passengers. The bus was packed. He noticed that no one carried cases or luggage of any kind, and all were dressed in suits identical to Ralph's.

Finally, he found a seat. The passenger across from him, a scrawny-looking middle-aged fellow, turned his way. "Hello, there," he said as the bus took flight.

"Hey," replied Ralph. "You're a salesman, too?"

He grinned. "Was."

"Oh, sorry." Ralph tried to smooth over his faux pas with pleasantry. "So, how long were you selling?"

"87.3 years."

The man didn't look a day over forty. "Are you serious?"

"As a heart attack."

"But how do you know? And how were you able to keep track of time?"

"I didn't know, and I couldn't keep track."

"Then I don't understand."

The man shrugged. "It just came to me a few minutes ago, and, if you wait, I bet the same will happen to you."

It was all coming back to him now. "You're right," Ralph said.

"So, how many years has it been?"

"11.6."

A toothless old man in front of them turned, said, "Hell, you're both youngins! I've been doin' this for 121 years!"

A look of amazement spread across the other man's face. Ralph was amazed, too. He almost wished he could bow, but couldn't, as he was sitting down. Instead, he stared out his window, watching people burn from on high until they flamed out. Then larger things crumbled: trees, the factory and the ground beneath it, falling away and becoming nothing, or maybe something else entirely.

When he was too far up to see anymore, Ralph turned back to the front of the bus. The eye in the sky was so big that it filled the driver's window.

"You were watching it burn, weren't you?" the man across from him said.

"Yeah," replied Ralph, still staring at the eye. "But couldn't you see it, too?"

"No, buddy. That was your stop. But I watched it burn at mine and loved every minute of it."

He turned to him then. "Wait… You saw God and the factory and got the coin, right?"

The man nodded.

"But if it burned for you, then it couldn't have burned for me."

He shrugged. "I guess we all have our own versions of this place."

"I wish every version would burn," Ralph said. "And I almost wish I could stay to help burn them."

"Nah, that's too much responsibility for one man. We can't help other salesmen, you know. We can only help ourselves."

With that, the man picked up a magazine wedged between the seats in front of him, and Ralph sat back to enjoy the rest of the ride, the eye so prevalent now that only the big blue iris and pupil were visible. When he glanced back out his own window, Ralph saw a billboard, hanging in the middle of nothing in the sky. YOU ARE NOW RE-ENTERING, it said.

It seemed as though the sign was incomplete. You are now re-entering what? But then he thought about it, and decided it really did make sense.

Turning around, Ralph saw what was on the back of the sign through the bus's rear windows:

YOU HAVE RE-ENTERED.

The bus traveled into the pupil of the eye, and the eye blinked.

WE WITNESSED THE ADVENT OF A NEW APOCALYPSE DURING AN EPISODE OF *FRIENDS*

BLAKE BUTLER

1.

The complications of the coming death of Earth or some part of it became apparent as 59.6% of all television-owning American households were watching *Friends*. Families sat huddled around their flat-screen LCDs with take-out containers and microwave-safe plates, eating in silence under the blaze of weird color as Ross and Rachel and Chandler and Joey and Monica and Phoebe moved about the screen. The viewers viewed without blink or comment as the handsome actors delivered their lines with a timed precision and jocular wit many at home had tried to replicate in their own lives—employing small approximations of the ease and subtle exit strategies demonstrated by these now all-too-familiar characters in their amusing manifestations of minor duress—and yet most had yet to find such triumph. Despite buying the products by the same designers as provided in the actors' wardrobes, having their hair quaffed by professionals into some approximation of what they'd seen on screen, most of the viewers' days went on the same as they always had, one after another. Many sat alone in their cars on the way home from work thinking of who they'd been and what they might be, sick for the simple arbitrary direction of a popular television sitcom. Still they smiled wryly to themselves at the jokes not funny enough to laugh aloud at despite the bright intonation of the canned studio response, intended to make their brain more rapidly produce serotonin and other similar chemicals that would leave them with a feeling of productiveness and goodwill. At night they'd sleep that much more soundly. They would hold the tickle in their heads.

On this particular evening at home, some certain viewers would get down on their hands and knees and kiss the screen, while outside in the streets, beyond the glowing windows of so many homes, the sky overhead sat wide and ready, a white so bright it appeared reflective.

2.

This evening's episode, like most others, begins with several quirky concurrent plotlines, each meant to build in gentle tension that would be resolved by the half-hour's end:

(1) Phoebe introduces a new song she's recently written about ass itch, worded without any direct reference to the shameful cavity itself. Despite the remotely unpleasant subject matter, the song is cute and clever and oddly catchy in a way that many viewers will have trouble dislodging from their minds which, were the airwaves not about to be reduced to static by some inexplicable sonic interference, causing the demise of all worldwide broadcast stations, the show's producers and the song's nameless writer could have made a fortune in royalties and iTunes downloads.

(2) A problem between Joey and the noisy neighbors on the other side of his bedroom wall quickly spins into a war of retaliation, seeing who can bother the other the most. Though at first he is confident and joyous, brandishing the loud trombone he played in high school, Joey quickly finds himself at a disadvantage when he realizes his neighbors are college students who stay up all night and own quite a collection of Swedish black metal that leaves him sleepless and wrecked and desperate, all quite to the amusement of the other characters and the crowd at home.

(3) In her frustration after being treated rudely by a convenience store clerk while buying tampons, Monica throws a banana against the wall of her apartment. The banana inadvertently knocks over an antique lamp Ross had

salvaged from a local garage sale, which he'd planned to sell on eBay in hopes of raising extra money for a nose job operation. Via flashback we learn that for years he's been obsessed with the shape of his nose, for which he blames his inability to maintain a healthy relationship with Rachel. Though he declines to allow his sister to pay him for the loss, he excuses himself politely and goes to sit in the closet in his bedroom and buries his face in an itchy sweater and bangs his head against the wall.

It's not until the second scene after the first commercial break, though, that Rachel's baby begins coughing.

The croup is nominal at first—perhaps the baby has swallowed a gnat or has tummy trouble. Rachel props the small child on her shoulder and pats her back with authentic-seeming motherly care and poise. She continues to deliver her lines uninterrupted, though the next time we see the baby, her cough has redoubled. She hacks with her whole newborn body, making such noise that there are several lengthy moments where the actors have no choice but to stop and wait to deliver their lines or else repeat them loud enough to be heard. The baby's face is small and weird, not at all the gorgeous little girl we'd grown accustomed to, made to seem like something that could have come from Jennifer Aniston's stunning loins. This child looks malformed or sick or sad. The actors look at one other uneasily. Something is wrong. This is not correct. Shouldn't the director or even the baby's actual mother have stopped the taping of the program and fixed the child, or at least replaced her? Shouldn't somebody do something?

Often during the scenes not including the baby, she can be heard hacking from off-screen. The actors appear flustered. Lines are fumbled, muttered, dubbed. No one seems quite sure what to do.

The next time we see Rachel she carries the baby low in her arms. She seems repulsed or confused or frightened, no longer fully ensconced by the immersive demands of her acting duties. It seems almost as if she's been caught inside the program—as if she has no choice but to go on.

After a long blank stare of no clear distinction, with weird light coming in through the back window, we cut to a commercial for all-beef franks.

3.

From here on, the plotline begins to veer slightly—

During a performance of her ass itch song at Central Perk, Phoebe is interrupted by booing and catcalls. The audience doesn't like the song. They are angry, tired, overhauled. They are sick of being fed garbage, they shout. The scene culminates in a rather violent coffee-flinging riot in which Phoebe's acoustic guitar is ripped from her hands and smashed on the coffee counter and she runs bleeding from the venue.

Simultaneously, after the third day of the neighbor noise, which has now turned into a nonstop onslaught of Cradle of Filth's *Midian*, Joey looks sickly and moth-eaten. His hair is falling out of his head. His muscle sheen is slumping. He has bright sacks under his eyes and refuses to laugh or smile. He mumbles his lines in a half-assed monotone.

Though Ross reconstructs the antique lamp and lists it with a high and quickly met reserve price well more than four times what he'd paid, he begins to get threatening messages from anonymous users that at first seem playful and even funny, yet soon begin to take on a more violent and disturbing edge. One message uses words banned from public broadcast and includes an explicit description of what the author would like to do to Ross's mother's vulva, and yet there is no editing or censored bleeping as he reads the extended lines. The regretful language is therefore broadcast into the ears of the viewing young. The station will be fined several hundred thousand dollars.

At some point, Ross looks directly into the camera as if searching for someone behind the lens. His cracking eye whites reflect a kind of tremor sheen.

The other Friends also find themselves subjected to unfortunate events. Monica suddenly develops a rash over her chin and neck that makes her sort of stutter and, despite the laugh track, looks more disgusting than funny; Rachel begins to find her normal speaking voice subverted to lower and lower tones. Suddenly she sounds much older and like a heavy smoker; Chandler witnesses a car accident in which two are killed. He finds his new pink polo shirt covered in an old lady's blood as he tries to salvage her from the burning wreckage, only to see she is already dead, as are the Chihuahua and young granddaughter in the backseat.

The normally sunny and peaceful skies programmed to overlook the televised makeshift setting—except in the event that the story called for snow or heavy rain as a punctuation mark to some joke or amusing turn—now take on the color of a rotten eggplant, scratched and bubbled, the light through the windows of the soundstage dwellings now going limp and dim, as if someone had set a cake lid over the encased fake skylight; as if there's something unknown overhead.

The Friends all return, then, to the girls' apartment to find each other ruined or wrecked or awful. The baby is now brutally whooping and her skin has begun to flush. Her face and arms are now a subtle off-color, her eyes strained and agonized and squealing. She seems covered in fuzz. Rachel has laid her on the sofa and stands several feet away, wringing her hands, her hair a mess. No one can think of what to do to help. At this point the cast and the audience have become aware that something is very wrong with this episode—that whatever kind-hearted plight or windfall the team of well-paid writers had concocted has somehow been subverted and wrongly altered and they are breaching territory unrehearsed. There is broken dialogue. There is sweating. The actors stand looking into the soundstage wings and into the cameras, as if expecting those on the sidelines to come in and interrupt and fix this obvious run-over error, though no one does and the broadcast continues, and when the requisite amount of exposition leading up to the next commercial break has passed, the cameras continue rolling and the scene goes on unbroken.

4.

Rachel begins to gag. Ross pats her back, yet he's still too distracted by his own turmoil to really put in too much effort. The baby squirms and sputters. Rachel throws up blood. Monica throws up crackers she put in her purse at Central Perk and snuck into the bathroom to eat in guiltless private. Chandler throws up booze. There is throw up everywhere. The other Friends hesitate. They hold each other's hands. Something is beating at the walls. The wallpaper is coming off in long strips. Whole sections of wall crumble, revealing the bare soundstage concrete. The canned laughter is going haywire. The actors seem to have forgotten about the baby now lying facedown on the bright blue loveseat. Joey is standing off from the others, talking to himself, his neck visibly pulsing. Rachel begins writhing on the floor. Her body levitates from the carpet. Her cleavage gleams in the flickering studio lights. Her makeup runs in sweat. Her nipples are hard. Chandler can't resist reaching out and tweaking them through her fashionable sweater. Monica throws up again, though this time it is mostly clear. She moves to sit down on the floor and cradles her head. All the glass in the apartment shatters. The ceiling cracks and puckers, allowing some appendage from a piece of a futon or desk or crib. There is screaming above and below and outside in the street. Phoebe, already sobbing, finds a nit burrowed in her hair. She finds another. She finds another. She begins to roll on the floor, clawing at her face and crowing something that sounds like gibberish but could be an impassioned call for help. Ross tries to shout for everyone to just calm down a second but his voice is overrun by the laugh track and the plod of horrendous thunder. It is clear through the apartment's shattered windows that the sky has turned another color. Although it is not raining yet, and won't again for months, something gathers there above. Something embedded overhead and brooding.

In the viewers' homes, father or mothers or children go to the windows to compare their sky to the one on *Friends*. They find the same strange, puckered vortex, the crudded bruise made on their horizon. They go, then, to check the locks. They sit again together in front of the TV, slightly closer together or further apart, depending on the constitution of their family's internal crisis system.

Critters begin filtering through a crack in the ceiling. Soon, nits and gnats and moths and salamanders and many-legged things no one can name are crawling all over the apartment. The walls are cracking, spraying shattered paint flecks that make abrasions on the Friends' skin. The sink is overflowing. The water is gathering in the floor. There's a smell like something burned forever. The baby's body is already becoming mush. Several others are unconscious. Ross ducks and covers. The carpet begins to smoke. All the cameras have been abandoned. Only Joey is left standing.

He is in the center of the room. His hair is wet with something dripping from the ceiling. His skin is taut and pasty. His eyes are bright. He twitches.

Joey moves toward the camera.

With his small mouth, Joey speaks.

5.

"Are you watching? Have you been here? Is this the room that you remember? Where we laughed and gassed and flirted? Where we've been for all these years? Shit. Motherfucker. Your children are already getting old. Your skin as thick as clay mud. Let's go. Let's have a chicken sandwich. Eat while you can, is what I'm saying. Chew the rubble. Suck the fat. Is that your Timmy on the floor beside you? His small eyes wide and full of curse? He's going to die. Your little Timmy. He's going to perish from something dumb. The Book says all first babies busted. Like sexy Jenny's here. [*Joey turns to pick up the suffocated infant from the sofa and wield it before the camera by its feet.*] You will watch your young boy die. Feed him antiseptic, vitamins, and chicken soup. Kiss him on the face. By month's end he will be zero. [*He throws the baby on the floor.*] His ghoul will clog your pretty home. Evenings of screech, of squawk, and rattle. Prepare yourselves. Turn the TV loud. Hide the windows. Clench the gun. Every home will fill thick with the souls of those it once covered over. The walls will move in smaller. The ceilings will come down. You've had all these years to pay attention. You've had time for spinach salads and Sunday football and summer beer. You've prayed for air conditioning. You've fixed your eyes to the small screen. Bastard. Bitch shit dicksucker. God is tired. Think of all the doors you've never opened. Of the photographs you've allowed to filch your image. Think of nothing. Think of shit. I can see you from here, you know. I've sniffed you. I am the Alpha and Omega. I am the Fonz. I've been inside your bed. Think of drought, then think of water. Years absorbing. Endless rain. The phonebooks fattened, roof beams buckled. Your brother underground grown rot with wet. And after the rain, the infestation. The moth eggs in your ear holes. The growth of hair. You won't see that. You won't listen. There is something in your eyes."

6.

The screen went blank then. The hall lights sputtered and went out. In the distance outside the windows billboards sat like large blockades against further dark. The families sat around the cold screen with the light's short remainder buzzing in their skull. They sat on the cushions full of bugs and old sweat and did not move or blink or gurgle. They did not speak or look at one another, though in the dark they felt for one another's hand. Even the youngest child's skin felt cracked now. Even the air seemed sopping wet. They went on sitting, looking straight ahead with veins bulging in their arms, while outside the sky shrunk and the night fried and the bugs hummed and the stars pinched for traction to hold in place.

CARDIOLOGY

RYAN BOUDINOT

Years ago there was a town not far from here where nobody had their own heart. They shared one gigantic heart located in a former water purification plant near the center of town. When enlivened by physical activity, the heart beat more rapidly, sending its blood to the neighborhoods, rattling silverware on restaurant tables, shaking portraits off walls, tickling bare feet on cobblestones with its vibrations.

The townspeople were connected to the heart by a vast system of valves and pipes distributed throughout the town. The streets boasted five or six blood hydrants for every one fire hydrant. Every home came equipped with as many blood outlets as electrical outlets. Nobody could travel very far beyond the reach of these outlets and hydrants, as they were tethered to them by sturdy surgical tubing that came in a variety of fashion colors. These tubes snaked through alleys and parks, under doors, up ladders, and down stairwells. One never left the house without at least 20 feet of tubing and a portable placenta which they kept in purses, also in fashion colors. Children walking to school became adept at quickly refilling their placentas from one hydrant to the next. Some kids even developed elaborate games around the tube transferal process, choosing sides, cruelly leaving "captured" children tethered to hydrants with little hope of rescue. There was an etiquette to removing the tubes from one's chest and replacing them with a new pair. To travel without a pair of clamps with which to momentarily cease the flow of blood while switching to new tubes was considered a faux pas. To drip blood on a table cloth or a friend's shoes was also bad form, but tolerated. Everyone carried a travel-size packet of absorbent wipes and was an expert at removing blood stains from carpet.

The blood moved slower at the edges of town, where the senior citizens lived. One widower named Ike lived in a one bedroom place with a garden full of untended perennials that his wife had planted before she died five years previous. Every Sunday, Ike's grandson Magnus visited to make him dinner and watch a video together. While they ate, Ike would tell Magnus stories about when he worked in the vast, subterranean plant where they maintained the heart. Ike had belonged to the department that monitored the left ventricle.

"We stuffed our ears with cotton down there cause of the thudding, but my hearing still went to hell," Ike said, "Night shifts were the worst. We'd get a sudden increase of flow on account of everyone making love. I was there during the murmurs of '03, the Great Aneurysm of '08. The very life of this community was in our hands. I just thank God we never had to use the paddles to get that ticker started again."

One Sunday night after a dinner of macaroni and cheese, salad, and bread, with coffee ice cream for dessert, Magnus set up the video, "Beverly Hills Cop," and sat beside his grandfather on the sofa. The tubes snaked out from between the buttons of their shirts, one tube delivering blood to their bodies, the other one sending it into the wall and back to the center of town. The slow flow always made Magnus feel sleepy at his grandfather's house, and it took some effort to stay awake during the video. During the part of the film where Eddie Murphy stuffs bananas into the tail pipe of a car, Magnus suddenly heard a loud hissing. Ike's vein tube had come loose from his chest and was squirting bright red blood all over the lampshade and a paint-by-numbers portrait of Jesus that hung on the wall. It wasn't the first time Ike's tubes had come loose, and Magnus knew what to do. He quickly clamped the tubes, opened his grandfather's stained shirt, and located the two hair-ringed orifices in his chest. After reinserting the tubes and making sure they were secure, Magnus wiped down the mess with bleach on a rag.

Frustrated that his movie had been interrupted by his grandfather's incontinence, Magnus threw down his rag and said, "I hate this place! Why can't we live somewhere like Beverly Hills? Why can't we have palm trees and funny police officers? I want to be able to walk down the street without worrying about whether the next blood hydrant is already being used. Why can't I walk freely wherever I want? How come I have to live in this stupid town with everyone sucking blood from the same stupid heart?"

PART TWO

Ike didn't say anything for a moment and immediately Magnus feared that he had offended his grandfather. After all, the man had devoted himself to the heart for sixty years, had scraped fat from inside its chambers, had watched friends die in horrible diastolic accidents. As long as Magnus had been alive he had associated Ike so closely with the giant cardiac muscle that maligning the heart was akin to maligning his own family.

As Ike's circulation picked back up, he sighed and made his mouth into an expression that in better light might have been a smile. "Of course, if you want to get out of this town, you'll have to create your own heart."

Magnus laughed. The suggestion was absurd. But quickly he saw that his grandfather was not joking; in fact he had adopted an expression of the utmost gravity.

"There is a man who can help you," Ike said, "His name is Gatton. You can find him in the tumor farm deep beneath the plant. Tell him that you come to claim my payment for what happened during the blood poisoning of '99. He'll know what you're talking about. He can supply you with a hand-made heart and you will be able to get out of town."

"But they'll know I don't belong there as soon as I get to the plant. How will I even make it to the tumor farm?"

"You'll wear my old uniform, and have my key card. It should still work. They never deactivated it when I left."

The rest of the movie passed unmemorably through Magnus' eyes. He tried to imagine the tumor farm, where the polyp trees grew, where they sent the convicts to work. He'd heard horrible things about the place, workers inadvertently fused to tumors, unable to escape, eventually becoming one with the cancerous cells, packs of rats who feasted on the growths and cysts, developing mutations that gave them five sets of legs, horns, wings.

Nonetheless, Magnus took the cake box that contained his grandfather's uniform and badge home with him and spent the next few weeks avoiding making a decision about whether he was going to pursue acquiring his own heart. One afternoon on his way home from school Magnus became entangled in the tubes of a girl named Carly, with whom he shared a fifth period AP Calculus class. They had never spoken to each other in school, but here on an elm-lined lane, trapped in a knot of surgical tubing, they had no way to avoid each other. As they slowly moved their bodies in such a way as to disentangle the tubes without disconnecting them, they started talking about their plans for the following year.

"After graduation I think I'm going to spend a week fishing, then look for a job," Magnus said, "What about you?"

"I hate this place," Carly said, "I want to go to a big college thousands of miles away from here."

"But you'll have to be connected to your placenta the whole time, and get regular blood transfusions, and those aren't reliable for more than a few days at a time," Magnus said.

"That's what they tell us anyway," Carly said, "I don't care. If I die out there it'll be better than staying in this place where people think you're crazy for liking plaid pants."

"I might know another way," Magnus said, then revealed to Carly everything his grandfather had told him about the tumor farm and portable hearts.

"Magnus, you have to go! This could be your chance out of this place."

"I'm afraid to go down there," Magnus said sheepishly.

PART THREE

Carly's cell phone rang. It was one of those new phones with the camera attached, and over Carly's shoulder Magnus could see the scrunched up face of Carly's mother, inquiring as to when she planned to come home for dinner.

Carly and Magnus parted ways, with Magnus continuing toward the center of town. With every tube transfer he felt the flow grow stronger, as though he were wandering upstream into the tumultuous rapids of a river. Every fourth house or so was replaced by a coffee shop or book store, then the houses began inching closer together, blocks interrupted by restaurants, then apartment buildings, and finally no place to live at all, just businesses with lit-up signs and wares on display. Men and women conducted conversations on hands-free phones, speaking into buds dangling from their ears, weaving from hydrant to hydrant, intersections turning into cats cradles of tubing that miraculously resolved with every light change.

Magnus rarely made it this far into town, and he couldn't tell if it was his own excitement or his proximity to the gigantic, energy-giving organ that made him feel as though he was being hit in the chest with a fire hose. He stopped and leaned against the front of a bagel shop. When the owner told him to get lost, he turned into an alley, hurrying past a couple junkies shooting up directly into their vein tubes. Luckily, the detoxification department would scrub the drugs from the blood when it returned to the plant.

Magnus changed into his grandfather's uniform behind a dumpster. It was clearly too big for him. How would anyone be fooled? He'd be found out, tossed into jail, left to die of lethal disattachment on death row. Then he imagined the swaying palms of Beverly Hills, the witty people in turtlenecks, and it was enough to propel him forward, onto the sidewalk, toward the decrepit former cathedral that served as the plant's main point of entrance.

The cathedral's exterior was all sooty stone and busted stained glass windows. One of its spires had crumbled long after the god worshipped here had been forgotten. Workers in uniforms like Ike's hurried in and out of the opening where the doors used to be, trailing tubes, great red ropes of speeding blood. Magnus fell into a mass of workers on their way to their shifts. Inside the cathedral, the workers branched off toward various banks of escalators marked with different departments: Aorta, Left ventricle, Right ventricle, Pulmonary Vessels, Mitrial Valve. There didn't appear to be any sign for the tumor farm, so Magnus headed toward the elevator leading to the Left Ventricle, where his grandfather had worked.

"Hey, hold it a minute there, son."

PART FOUR

A security officer of some sort grabbed Magnus by the shoulder. He had a big, blond mustache and wore the heart-shaped insignia of the plant on his chest, with all the chambers highlighted in green to indicate he had full access. "You're obviously new here. You can't go in with these wimpy surgical tubes, they can't stand the pressure. You'll need to go to the Bypass office and get some new ones. And whoever issued you this uniform, they must have been in a real retro mood. Let them know you're going to need new duds."

"Where is the Bypass office?" Magnus said.

"Man, you are green. Up there." The officer pointed to a point high above the floor, a kind of balcony just out of reach of the pipe organ. Magnus took the appropriately labeled elevator and exited into an office overlooking the throng of workers below. Administrative types wearing shirts and ties hurried about, making photocopies, faxing spreadsheets. A woman at a broad, ebony desk motioned for Magnus to have a seat, telling him she'd be with him after she completed an email. A minute or two later she turned and said, "So. First day. We're glad you're here, Magnus. We've been looking forward to your arrival since your grandfather retired. You'll find that around here he's a real legend. You'll need new tubes, a new uniform, a real ID card."

Magnus plugged into a nearby outlet that sent blood coursing so powerfully into his body that he felt he could climb a mountain, and filled out some paperwork.

That day Magnus was put to work in the outskirts of the vast underground operation, monitoring flow to and from the poorer neighborhoods. Someday, his shift supervisor, Jim, told him, he could work his way up from these dank, subterranean passages to work on an actual valve, maybe even the Purkinje fibers. His grandfather had started out at the bottom of the totem pole, repairing capilaries. Through hard work he had become one of the most respected valvemen this operation had ever had the honor of employing.

For the first weeks of his employment, Magnus walked for miles under the city, pressing his stethoscope against the pipes through which oxygenated blood flowed, noting changes in pressure in his palm computer, and calling in the repair crew whenever he detected a leak. Magnus learned to locate leaks by following rats and other misshapen vermin who could smell the blood before any human. One morning Magnus followed a gaggle of rats down several flights of stairs and came upon an entrance to the tumor farm. The space was as big as a stadium, the floor, walls, and ceiling high overhead covered in strange fleshy forms that almost resembled trees. The floor was rubbery down here, and occasionally viscous fluids squirted up from underfoot like clams spitting on a beach. While the handbook had assured Magnus that nothing in the tumor farm was contagious, the place still put him ill at ease. He swept his mag light across the trembling mounds of flesh, each grotesque growth fueled by the same blood that beat quickly in his own body.

"You lost, kid?" said a man perched on a tumor in the vague shape of a couch. He wore the insignia of his department on his dirty jumpsuit next to his name, Kyle, and a cap drawn low over his eyes. He picked his fingernails with a knife. Magnus hurriedly introduced himself and explained he had come here following rats, but this didn't provoke any change in the bored expression fixed on Kyle's face.

"I'm looking for someone named Gatton, who worked with my grandfather Ike. My grandfather said Gatton could help me."

Kyle nodded and motioned for Magnus to follow him. They wound their way through a forest of abnormal growths. "We keep this tumor farm for a reason, case you hadn't figured out by now," Kyle said, "For years we been trying to develop individual hearts for folks to carry around in they own chests, not bein' dependent on the big thumper up there in the cave. Down here's where the cardiac scientists cultivate materials and toss their failed experiments. When the breakthrough comes we'll be turning this place into a giant factory of hearts, with the people coming in one end empty-chested and leaving the other with independent tickers allowing them to not have to hook up to the blood hydrants every goddamn day. Then we can destroy that big muscle that keeps us all enslaved to the ebb and flow."

They found a slippery staircase and made their way down deep enough for Magnus to have to pop his ears. Finally the stairs opened into an echoing chamber more vast than the tumor farm, and reeking of blood. As Magnus's eyes adjusted he came to understand that he was standing on the bank of an underground river of blood, too wide to see across to the other shore.

"They'll come soon enough," Kyle said, taking off his hat, wiping his brow. As if lying in wait, the sounds of a vessel came across the flowing plasma, ringing with percussion and horns. From the dark emerged a craft about forty feet long. At first Magnus thought the people crowded on its deck were men in armored suits, but slowly they revealed themselves to be birds the size of humans, standing upright, some of them wearing jeweled clothes or helmets, squawking hideously with their long beaks.

"I wasn't supposed to see this place yet," Magnus said, though the words seemed as foreign in his mouth as the creatures manifest before him. He couldn't help feeling that some sealed repository of knowledge had been opened within his mind, some place that had existed prior to his birth, now revealed on the path his curiosity had so dangerously compelled him to follow. The bird beings in their craft raised a great squawking din of horns and drums upon seeing him standing petrified on the shore, a sound panicked and angry, and this was enough to frighten Magnus back up the stairs to the tumor farm, into the labyrinth of vessel-lined halls, and out an exit into the night of a town he no longer understood.

PART FIVE

Magnus tried to cleanse himself of the disturbing scene he had witnessed by throwing himself into his routines. That night was movie night with his grandfather. He chose a video at the video store and walked across the park in the middle of town with it tucked under his arm, a bag of burritos from his favorite taqueria in the other. He decided the only way to relieve his fear of the bird creatures on the river of blood was to convince himself that they had been a hallucination. By the time he reached his grandfather's house he decided that he must have been working too hard these past few weeks and suffered a fatigue-related mental lapse. This idea comforted him, more so than the possibility that there existed beneath his feet an underground blood river navigated by alien forms.

If he had peeked in the windows when he arrived at his grandfather's house, Magnus would have certainly noticed something awfully wrong about the place. But instead he instinctively grabbed the doorknob and entered without knocking as was his habit. Instead of being met with Ike's friendly hello, a wall of blood swept Magnus off the porch, depositing him in the gnarled rose bushes in the front lawn. He'd heard of this problem before but never seen it. A leak that slowly fills an entire house. Waves of the red stuff rolled out to the street. Inside he found the entire place awash in blood, covering every surface, saturating every permeable material. He rushed to his grandfather's bedroom, where he found the drowned body still in bed, unrecognizable, covered in all this mess. Crying, he carried the body from the house.

After the ambulance arrived, leisurely, with its sirens off, Magnus sat in the blood-soaked front lawn watching nightcrawlers emerge from the tunnels hidden beneath the grass. Some police officers may have spoken to him, he couldn't be sure. As the light faded and the seizure crew exited the house, Magnus felt a hand on his shoulder and looked up to see Carly in her plaid pants, holding a suitcase.

"It's time to leave this place," Carly said.

"I think there's only one way to leave this place," Magnus said, "And it's underground. At least until they start manufacturing individual hearts."

Carly opened her suitcase, moved aside some shirts and showed him the two mechanical hearts inside. They were made of bright yellow plastic, like waterproof electronic equipment.

THE SCREAMING OF THE FISH

VINCENT SAKOWSKI

I once had a friend who had a fishbowl for a brain. So needless to say, he had a rather large head. But he carried it well—powerful neck muscles built up over the years—and he carried it with pride.

He changed the water regularly; he liked to keep it fresh. But he also lost a lot of it, since he was an avid jogger. Despite his strength and poise, sometimes that water bounced right out of there. He never worried about it though, or complained about the loss. The water kept him cool inside and out. There wasn't anything he could do about the evaporation, but he always carried a full water bottle just to be safe.

The two goldfish in the bowl didn't seem to be too crazy about him jogging every day—with all of the rocks from the bottom getting stirred up, swishing around and scraping their sides. Way too many scars over the years, but what could they say?

My friend kept them well-fed, and they certainly got their exercise. And even though they were stuck in a small home, they got to see a lot of the sights. Especially since my friend liked to jog a new route every day if he could. He enjoyed new scenes himself.

Folks thought he was a pretty strange sight, and since he passed some new people each day, word about him traveled fast. So, he was often sought after, and although there was little he could do about video cameras and photographers, he never granted an interview. Nor did he pay any attention to the occasional rude person who would call such lame remarks as:

"I see you have a little water on the brain today, buddy."

And: "You mind if I go fishing with you sometime?"

And: "Do you want me to feed your fish while you're away?"

It didn't matter who was doing the shouting, and it didn't matter what they were shouting out. Or if his two fish could speak and they could tell him all about the unpleasantness of bouncing around in the bowl swimming for their lives and how his knee joints were getting rubbed raw and how he was developing shin splints and if he wasn't careful how—

None of this would matter because he wasn't much of a listener. In fact, he couldn't hear anything at all—no ears. He only felt the pressure of their voices. . . the pressure of the sounds

. . . and the pressure said enough. And he was quite happy not to know any more than that.

Until the day he died.

My friend died while jogging, of course. He tripped over somebody's Chihuahua, which happened to get off its leash. So even though the dog was barking, and the owner was trying to call it back and shouting at my friend at the same time—and even I was foolishly trying to warn him—my friend didn't hear a word, he only felt the sudden agonizing pressure from all around. It caught him totally unaware, confusing him. So he tripped over the Chihuahua, and he fell, and man did those fish fly!

Just as the fishbowl shattered on the sidewalk, the Chihuahua scurried over to the flying fishes and it snapped one right out of the air. The dog quickly chewed that goldfish, likely hoping to get to the other one before it got too dirty on the sidewalk; not that the dog still wouldn't eat it anyway. The second goldfish lay there flopping around in its own small way, gasping, gills contracting, watching its schoolmate being gobbled up. What else could it do?

Without wasting another moment, I scrambled over to the second goldfish. I popped it in my mouth, hoping that the moisture would keep it alive until I could squeeze it into my friend's water bottle, or into a glass of water or a fountain, or—but it was still flopping around in my mouth—so much so that I accidentally (or perhaps instinctively?) swallowed it.

As the goldfish digested, I got a real taste of my friend's memories . . . his life . . . particularly before he met me. And although I'm not sure if I understand him any better, I'm just really glad that he kept his fishbowl so clean.

ATWATER

CODY GOODFELLOW

Life was not so unkind to Howell as it seemed to the world at large—it offered few surprises, and predictable rewards. Where there were explicit directions, Howell found he could go anywhere, do anything, but whenever and wherever he got lost, he found Atwater.

The first time it happened, he believed, at first, that it was as real as everything else in his life up to that point had been. On his way to a business appointment in Burbank: he'd given himself plenty of time to get there, leaving the office in Mid-Wilshire an hour ahead of the departure time on the Triple A itinerary he'd printed out the night before. After living in LA for over a year, he still did this for any place he had never driven, and kept a binder and three map books.

Traffic shut him down within sight of his office. Parked on the 101, swimming in sweat, and he suddenly, absolutely, needed to pee. He couldn't just give up and get off; it had to get better soon, but it got worse, so clusterfucked by Hollywood Boulevard that he couldn't even get through the glacial drift of traffic to the exit. Watching as the time of his appointment came and went, and he wasn't even in the Valley, yet he was committed. The southbound traffic was almost as bad. Howell left a message to reschedule with the client in Burbank. The secretary treated him like some idiot who'd tried to ride a horse into town.

Wondering which of the empty coffee cups at his feet he'd like to try going in, wondering why the sensible Volvo people had never tackled this crying need of the long-haul motorist, Howell crawled through the pass and into the Valley.

With a dramatic flare that must be truly impressive from a swiftly moving car, the 101 burst out into Griffith Park, and a blazing Catherine Wheel avalanche of sulfurous afternoon sunlight speared his brain. Cascades of shaggy green hills and shadowed black canyons of wilderness under glass lurched up to the shoulder and Howell was looking somewhere else when horns sounded behind him, and the road ahead was a vacant plain.

Howell whooped with joy and stomped on the gas. The Triple A directions had wilted into pasty slime from the heat and smog and sweat from his hands, pages stuck together. The damned thing was supposed to be foolproof, distances totaled out to the hundredth of a mile, but 42.62 crept by on his trip odometer, and no Burbank Avenue. No off-ramp at all, and then he saw from the baffling menu of interstate and city highway junctions in the southbound lanes, that he was on the wrong freeway, and headed east to Pasadena.

No one let him out of the left lane until he'd passed under the Golden State Freeway. With a defiant berserker roar, he kamikazed the next off-ramp and slammed on the brakes, power-sliding up a hairpin chute between blank brick walls. He skidded to a stop just short of the sign.

ATWATER, it said. No population or elevation, no explanation, no Kiwanis or Lion's Club chapters. Just ATWATER.

He idled at the intersection for a good long time. No other cars came. There were no other cars. Anywhere.

In the middle of LA. No cars. No pedestrians, either. Howell waited for something, for a director to scream, "Cut!" and a crew to spill out from behind these painted murals of a ghost town to resurrect the scene he'd ruined.

On the three corners opposite the off-ramp, a 7-11, an AM/PM, and another 7-11, all abandoned, windows shattered, roofs askew and foundations cracked. All angles subtly off, and apartment buildings down the street had collapsed, crushing their ground floors or spilling their contents out into the street. All the entrances were swathed in CAUTION tape, and Condemned notices were pasted on all remaining doors. "By order of FEMA—"

The last real earthquake in Los Angeles was in 1993. Howell looked into this before taking the job and moving here. A decade later, and they never tried to rebuild? Unless it was a movie set… or something else happened here—

Imagination did nothing good for Howell. He let it go and set the Volvo rolling down the main drag.

Atwater wasn't large; he could see the same brick wall cutting across the street only a few blocks from the off-ramp. The whole area was walled off from the rest of the city, a pitcher plant with only one mouth, into which he'd stumbled. The sounds of the city outside were almost completely muzzled. He heard only the hushed hum of distant traffic and something like electronic wind chimes, or a Don't Walk alarm for blind pedestrians, but here, nothing moved. Fine then, he'd turn around.

A man threw himself across the hood of his car. Threw himself, those were the right words, because Howell certainly didn't hit him—

"Please," the man bleated, beating on the windshield, "please help—"

The man came around to the passenger side, and Howell hadn't locked it. He wore a navy blue suit and tie, shabby and shiny, the kind of thing an exceptionally cheap prison might parole its least promising inmates in, but he didn't look like a bum, and Howell supposed he wanted to help, so he let the man fumble it open and fall into the passenger seat. "You don't know how long I've been waiting," the man said, "for someone to come…"

"Where the hell are we? Where's everybody?"

"No onramp," the man wheezed, hauling the door shut and turning to look at Howell. "We have to go back up the off-ramp, but nobody comes in here, ever… For God's sake, let's go!"

Something buzzed past Howell's ear. He whipped his head around so fast something tore in the back of his neck, but he let out a sharp yelp and shouted, "Did you see it? You let a—let it in—" He couldn't bring himself to say the word.

Howell looked at the man's face, at gaping pores all over his face and neck, tessellated hexagons like tiny, waxy mouths. Black, buzzing bullets oozed out of them. His head was a honeycomb.

"It's not as bad as it looks," the man offered, his humming hand shooting out to bar Howell in his seat. "Please just drive."

Howell shrieked. He was allergic to bee stings. He was allergic to the *word* Bees. He yanked open the door and threw himself out, but the fucking seatbelt trapped him, hanging upside down in the street. His hand slapped at the button, or was it a latch…

Bees swarmed and formed a beard on the man's face. "You're making them mad," the man said, his eyes wet, nose streaming snot and furious bees drowning in it. Tiny feather-touches of agitated air played over Howell's face, the microscopic violence of thousands of wings. A homicidal halo roared around his head.

The seatbelt snapped free and Howell rolled out of the Volvo, hit the street running on all fours, out of the intersection and into the nearest shelter, the underground garage of a three story townhouse.

He slid on his belly down the steep driveway and crawled under the gate, jammed open on a toppled Vespa scooter. The dark was his only cover, here. He had no real hope of finding help, only of hiding until the lunatic either stole his car or abandoned it, but he was not getting back in there. He'd walk out onto the freeway and hail a Highway Patrolman, he'd get out, he'd go home and never come back...

Almost nauseous now with relief, Howell unzipped and pissed in the dark.

A sound, and then another, behind him. His bladder slammed shut; his balls crawled up and wrapped around his femoral artery, legs tingled and fell into a coma. Small sounds, but distinctive, and if not threatening, then in this alien place they portended a myriad of things, all awful.

It was the sound of a metal tool striking a metal tray, and the sound of a miniature saw biting into something hard, and the cloying reek of burning bone. Howell turned and sought something to hide behind as he saw how far from alone he was.

A moth-battered ceiling fixture lit up a shining steel table in the center of the empty garage. Two gaunt figures in black smocks and leather aprons hovered over it. They wore cages over their heads like old-time insane asylum alienists, or else their heads *were* cages, for they seemed to imprison nothing but shadows.

Between them on the table lay a nude female body, painfully white, viciously thin, a naked sprawl of cruel angles and lunar planes, decoratively inked with dotted lines that encompassed her whole form. Freshly sutured cuts ran down the arms and legs, and perhaps the worst of it was that Howell saw nowhere a drop of blood.

Deftly, one of the alienists sawed down the bridge of the dead woman's nose, while the other peeled the parted skin away from the skull. Howell didn't know how long he watched; their procedures were so methodical, he got sucked into infinite minutiae, only to take a sudden, stabbing breath when suddenly, with a magician's flare, the peeler laid bare the skull and held it up.

The skull was black glass, toxic onyx ice, squealing and smoking as it met the hot, stale air. The alienist dropped it into an oil drum, changed into a fresh pair of heavy rubber gloves and opened the gilded doors of a medieval reliquary on a sideboard.

The cutting alienist continued his master ventral incision at the jaw, laying bare the fuligin struts of the rib cage, which spewed ribbons of oily black vapor across the table.

Its colleague selected an ancient yellow skull from the reliquary and deftly slipped it into the hollow pouch of the face, arranging the features just so, then stitching the lips of the incision together with colorless spiderweb thread as fast as a sweatshop matron.

Cowering behind a Camaro half-propped up on cinder-blocks in the far corner of the garage, Howell started to creep backwards to the gate. He'd face down the honeycombed man, or just run out onto the freeway, and get out of here—

When the woman on the table spoke.

"I felt that," she whimpered, and Howell was gored by the wonder in her voice, as much as by the fact that the speaker was a filleted cadaver, with two headless surgeons elbow-deep inside her. He trembled, but it was thousands of misfired reflexes warring with each other as he tried to frame a reaction.

An alienist set a crumbling, fossilized rib cage into the empty thorax and sewed it up as the other prepared to join his incision with the cleft of her groin.

Howell rushed at the cutter, screaming, "Get off her!" with his fists pounding its broad back and he almost fell into it when the towering form collapsed on itself with no more resistance than an airborne shopping bag.

He blundered into the edge of the table and knocked the wind out of his lungs as the alienist with the needle calmly reached for something on the tray that looked like a nail gun.

On the table, the woman looked at him. Her eyes, impossibly vast black pupils, ringed by violet irises like bone-deep bruises, drank him in and stole something he needed to breathe. "Take me," she said, "take me away—"

Howell's hand found the knife and lashed out across the table at the other alienist. The blade slashed through unresisting fabric, the black form deflated and melted into the oil-stained shadows.

Howell dropped the knife and looked for something to cover her with, trying to say, "I'll get you—get you out—"

"What's your name, here?" she asked.

He took off his jacket and draped it over her, arms out, awkwardly trying to size her up to lift. "Um, Howell, Roger, um, Howell. Listen, are you okay to move? I saw them…"

She sat up on the table and leaned into him. The exquisitely fine stitching down the center of her face creaked when she smiled and put the knife to his throat. Her other hand hustled his crotch. "I'm cured."

He looked away, but she forced him to look with her knife. "Get hard," she commanded, and tore herself open.

Her breasts, almost imperceptible swells but for her angry, erect nipples, like bites from some enormous spider that lived in her bed, like accusing snail-eyes.

His stomach rolled and everything was hot, rushing water, drowning him. He wished he could melt and flow away through her fingers, but where he wanted it least, he swiftly became solid under the harsh ministrations of her bony hand.

Using the knife and his cock as levers, she got him up onto the table, peeled away his slacks and boxers. "Let me see you," she husked in his ear, "show me what you really are."

He couldn't melt or run away, so he just took it. Froze solid as she lowered herself onto him, cold, tight and dry, spat on the head of it and impaled herself.

Inside, she felt like anything but flesh, ground-glass needles and gnashing teeth and mortuary marble, doors within doors opening in a cold black cathedral. He thought of the operation he'd interrupted, the looted fossils of a saint swapped out for her toxic necrotic skeleton, and in the open reliquary he saw a pale yellow pelvis, untransplanted—

Spastic reflex wrapped his arms around her, protruding ribs like notches for his fingers. Her concave torso shook as if she was full of panicked birds, and she hissed, to him or to herself, "Take your medicine."

Shuddering, she rose up and dropped herself hard against him, and spider webs of black ice shot through his hips and into his guts. In his head, he reviewed sums, columns of expenditure figures for the projected relocation scheme his company had sent him up here to investigate. Culling them fiercely in the quiet corners of his mind, he noted two adding errors and committed them to memory, as soon as he got back to his laptop, he'd correct them—

The knife never left his throat. It sawed back and forth as she smashed herself against him, eyes rolled back, breath choppy gusts of frigid mist that grew colder with every stroke, despite the unbearable friction.

"Take it, take it," she growled in his ear, and in rushing waves of cold and heat, he knew he'd lost what he'd put into her, it was hers now, and she was fucking him to death with it. He could only hold on.

Her rhythm sped, stiffened, such a ferocious blur of motion that he could not open his eyes, and she screamed, "He's coming, faster, he's coming—"

The sensation spreading through him now pulled him further away from the world, fired his gut-sense that the agony of pleasure he felt was really her coming inside him, taking him over. He hid from it, crying inside, *please God, just let it be over*—

She clung to him and froze, screaming like a rabbit in a trap. His skin was slathered in cold motor oil, and then she was gone.

He did not look around or try to cover himself, huddled on the icy steel table in a puddle of oil and urine, shocked mute by the sudden, sepulchral stillness.

The ground shook.

Dust and grit sprinkled his cold, raw skin. He rolled off the table and hitched his piss-soaked pants up over his bloodied hips.

He was alone in the dark. It was so quiet, he could hear the Volvo, still idling out on the street, and those faint, phantom chimes. But something else was coming, an itch in the soles of his feet, a tremor that shivered through his bowels, and he remembered what she'd said, just before she vanished.

He's coming—

A steady, subsonic rumble spread up through the floor, a silent sound of pure terrestrial protest. A whole patch of ceiling gave way, dumping plaster and shattered concrete and spark-spitting washing machines into the garage.

Howell crawled under the gate and scrambled up the driveway on all fours, uttering a weird, panicked hooting sound with each hard-fought breath. He could still hear his car, so close, he could hear the seat belt alert beeping endlessly, and the dull burble of a public radio talk show on the stereo, but he could also hear voices on the street, and those chimes, growing louder, reverberating off the encircling walls of Atwater. And buzzing—

Howell hit the sidewalk and had to remind himself to keep moving to the Volvo. He saw no one inside it, but the honeycomb man stood in the middle of the street, and he wasn't alone.

Another man, short, with a head like a claw-hammer, and snarls of piano wire running from his arms and legs and torso to a jumbled mound of marionettes in the street behind him, like the sole survivor of some sort of street-mime's massacre. A little girl stood beside them, sucking her thumb and holding a length of an impossibly long albino python, which wrapped around her so many times, showing neither head nor tail, that she might have been made of snakes.

She pointed at Howell as he ran for his car. The honeycomb man shouted, "Wait! Take us with you!"

He said something else, but though Howell saw his mouth working, he could hear nothing but the sound of jets, a squadron of them, flying up out of the secret, hollow heart of the earth.

Behind Howell, the townhouse lurched forward with an orchestral moan and settled down into the underground garage. The apartment block behind it bulged and broke open, rooms bursting like bubbles full of abandoned human lives and flaming, flying debris, a wall of dust and smoke and something coming through it, something that made the freaks on the street race for his car.

Howell got in and slammed the door, locked it and threw the Volvo in gear. He threw the wheel to the right, jumping the curb and flattening a street sign. The honeycomb man spilled across the hood in a roiling cloud of bees. Howell screamed and stomped on the gas, batting the air vents shut.

The puppeteer waved at him, hurling screaming marionettes into the grill of the car. Their wooden claws gouged out his headlights and chrome and ripped off his antenna as he passed, looking for the narrow niche in the wall that he'd come in through, but it was gone, the intersection with the three convenience stores was now a T-junction facing a blank brick wall.

The insanity, the injustice of it all, finally broke him. He kept going forward, but he saw nothing.

And then the ground shifted, and the car was going uphill, but he only went faster up the tilting fragment of the street. The wall fell away as the ground rose, as something unspeakably heavy gained on him, making a sinkhole of Atwater from which he could not hope to escape.

Howell saw the freeway. The cars were hurtling by and he was headed into their midst in the wrong direction, but he did not care. He saw only fire and black smoke in his rearview mirror. He wrenched the wheel around as the Volvo sailed off the ragged edge of the broken road and over the wall, and he saw a flash of white in the mirror.

He looked back and saw her face, a snowflake in the collapsing furnace, and then he was over the wall, and the car's axle nearly snapped as the car hit the onramp with the wheels at a right angle, sailed down the dry ice-plant embankment and swerved, amid a chorus of horns, into the flow of traffic.

Howell got off at the next exit and cleaned himself up in a gas station restroom. He did not look at himself in the mirror. Then he went to his appointment in Burbank.

It was some weeks before Howell could admit to himself that he wasn't going to report the incident. To tell it would make it real, declare that he believed in it, but no one would believe him. How much easier to just go on, to leave it behind, when it fit nothing else in his life but his dreams, which he never remembered, anyway. For over a year, a bad dream was all it was, and all it would ever be.

Until he got lost again.

Driving up to Sacramento, an interview for a senior accounting position with the state comptroller's office, and he would have flown, if not for the terror of handing over his life to some unseen mumbler with a bar tab in eight states. If he had been meticulous in his planning before, he was now obsessive. He bought maps and plotted his route and itinerary, and he researched Atwater, and made damned sure that nothing brought him any closer to it as he passed the junction he'd stumbled into last time.

He'd been stunned to discover it was a real place, an odd, isolated knothole in the haphazard sprawl of the San Fernando Valley, encircled by freeways and largely undeveloped since the early Seventies, but an unremarkable, ordinary place that had suffered only a few broken windows in the last earthquake. What might have driven a more curious man mad only salved the fear he hadn't dared confront since it happened, because it confirmed that it was all a bad dream. He drove through the Valley, and passed Atwater unmolested.

He had the itinerary folded in his lap and the GPS unit in his new Volvo told him he was in the San Joaquin Valley on the northbound 5, entering Chow-chilla, but the GPS unit had no way of knowing about the truck wreck, bodies strewn across both lanes and up the scrub-brush shoulders, naked children everywhere, and all he could do was clutch the map to his breast and tell himself, you're not lost, not lost, don't look—

But they were only pigs, scattered by the impact with a truck loaded with tanks of flammable gas that came off the Chowchilla onramp too fast. A pair of highway patrol cars was parked sideways on the highway, the troopers hanging their heads at the waste of good bacon.

Detour signs and sawhorses with rusty orange blinking lights diverted the traffic up through Chowchilla onto the two-lane eastbound 140. Howell followed the signs through the tiny town and turned north on the 99 at the promise of eventually reaching Sacramento thereby. Remarkably, almost no other cars joined him on the detour, preferring to sit in gridlock while the dead pigs were mopped up, and he should have sneered at their stupidity, but instead, he couldn't stop wondering what they knew.

He was on the 99, he was sure of it, when it started to rain. Suddenly, he was driving through a car wash, and the GPS unit in the dash, in fact everything in the dash, blinked and went black.

He hit the windshield wipers, but they didn't work. He braked soberly to a stop, angling to the right shoulder and hitting his hazard lights, though no sign that they worked, either. He was about to call Onstar and have them send a tow truck, and he had his map out on his lap, when he saw two men in workman's coveralls step into the tiny arena of his headlights, arm in arm and grappling, legs crazily digging for traction in the slick mud.

Howell had his phone in his hand when the two men smashed their heads together and staggered back into the dark. He was pushing the number he had programmed to speed-dial the friendly Onstar operator somewhere in Bombay or New Delhi, who would use satellite imagery and impeccable, pleasingly accented English to guide him back to the highway, even though he was definitely not lost—

His eyes roved over the map, up the aortic 5 to the blue branching 140 to the 99, and up the 99 past Merced, and a tiny town just off the highway, though no roads to or from it showed on the map. The town was called ATWATER.

He looked out the window at the two men, but despaired of asking them for directions.

Each fighter had his hands around the other's throat, and throttled his foe for all he was worth. Faces purple and streaming in the rain, they had wrung each other half to death when one suddenly kicked the other in the gut. The injured man folded, and his attacker pressed the advantage with ruthless abandon, smashing his head again and again into the pavement.

Howell sat there watching, even after the dashboard lights came back on, and the windshield wipers gave him a clearer view.

The victor lifted the vanquished up by his head, looking deeply, longingly, into the eyes of the man he'd beaten. Then his arms tensed and he squeezed the skull, crushing it as his mouth opened wider, jaw unhinged, skin stretching, to engulf the top of the broken head between his lips.

Howell's hands fumbled for the gearshift, switched on the hi-beams. Oblivious to the light, the victor opened his mouth still wider, hoisting his twitching enemy off his feet and forcing the body, inch by inch, into his own.

Howell reversed and floored it, headed back the way he'd come. But the road was different. Corn crowded in on both sides. He saw peaked Victorian rooftops behind the waving stalks, but knew he'd find no help there. His brain crawled out of his skull and flew above the racing Volvo. If he hadn't been so meticulous in his bathroom stops this trip, he would have voided his bladder as he screamed through the town of Atwater.

Not a single board of a building looked familiar, but he knew that somehow, it was the same town.

He passed an intersection that wasn't there before, a big black sign swinging above an old wire-hung traffic light said, PENTACOST ROAD.

He passed a man dressed in his mother's skin, that still screamed and nagged in his ear; a naked old woman who sweated fabulous tumors of molten gold, and goggled at him through crystalline growths like malignant diamonds, shining out of her eyeholes; an armless, legless nude woman in an eyeless rubber mask and a ball-gag stuffed in her mouth, racing alongside the car, borne aloft by black segmented tentacles growing from her gaping, snapping vagina.

The crumbling Victorian mansions crept closer to the road until they strangled it. In its death-throes, the road thrashed from left to right until a sprawling, misplaced mansion blocked it entirely. Howell aimed for the narrow alley between the colossal house and its neighbor, but the car wedged itself into the space and refused to budge in either direction. Howell climbed over the seats and out the back.

The storm battered the land with an ever-growing ferocity, but still he heard the somnolent music of those molten chimes, coming from everywhere and nowhere—and growing steadily louder. He looked frantically all around, waving a flashlight in the rain-slashed dark, but he still ran full into the honeycombed man before he saw him.

Howell fell on the pavement, but rolled and aimed the flashlight at the man. His problem with the bees had gotten worse. They were bigger, the size of hummingbirds circling his head, dancing secrets to each other on his shoulders, the hexagonal combs like shotgun holes in his face and neck and down beneath his shirt.

"Hurry," the honeycombed man said, and the bees echoed, "she's waiting for you."

Howell backed away from the man, from his car, from his own body. There had to be a way out of this, a way to escape, to wake up—

He turned and took a long stride to run away, but there was the man who'd beaten—and eaten—his doppelganger. "Get me out of here," the man said, and fingers squirmed out of his wide, froglike mouth, clawed at his lips. The fighter bent over, wracked by spasms and surges of movement under his muddy coveralls. He screamed, and Howell saw something thrashing in the seat of his pants, tearing away the fabric, a tail—no, a leg...

Howell backed away again, but he heard angry bees circling behind him. The fighter threw himself at Howell's feet, screaming so loud, so wide, Howell could see the man inside him screaming, too.

"Come on," the honeycombed man took his arm and dragged him to the porch of the mansion in the road. Cobalt blue lanterns saturated the darkness in the parlor, vertebral shadows of legions of ferns, and among them, a bed, and on it, a woman's body.

But no, it wasn't her, and had he hoped it would be? This one was enormous, a monstrous puffball belly with drained, flaccid limbs trailing away from it like the knotted fingers of empty surgical gloves. Sizzling wings at his back drove him closer.

"Mr. Howell," she said, and he started, because underneath all that, it was her. "I know all about you, Howell. I even know your real name. What do you know?"

"I—" he looked around, at anything but her, and he heard creaking, crackling sounds, the ferns growing up through the floor so fast they glowed, feeding on the fever-heat, the light, pouring out of her. "I don't know anything."

"You got away, but you only think you keep getting lost... you keep coming back."

"I got away because I don't belong here. This is all some kind of—"

"A mistake?" Her breath hitched hurtfully inside her, like laughter, or something inside trying to escape. "You escaped because you have no imagination. You don't dream."

"I had a dream... about you, before. You—This... this is a dream..."

"This is a dream," she agreed. The ground rumbled. Pictures and knick-knacks shook off the walls. A window looking out on the street shattered, the wind and rain pried away the storm shutters. Her massive belly shivered and stirred. "But it's more real than where you think you came from."

Her hand shot out and caught his. He pulled away so hard he staggered into the wall. His shoulder went right through the moldy plaster. "You… did something to me. Why did you do… that?"

Her face brightened. "You remember! I didn't want to give you the wrong idea, but there was no time. There's no time, now, either." Her hand caressed the turgid globe of her abdomen.

"I don't understand what's going on, here, but what are you?" He swallowed and choked as he realized he was most afraid that she was not real. "All of you? What happened to you?"

"*You* did." She convulsed, pain drawing her into a ball around her pulsating womb.

He pointed and stammered, "No, that's not mine."

"You sound like you've done this before." She shrieked and made ribbons of the sheets. Her heels dug into the mattress, kicking divots of flea-infested stuffing across the rumbling room.

Howell knew he should take her hand, but was terrified of coming any closer. Her belly contorted as if it caged a wild animal, then two animals battling, as each of them began to transform to catch the other at a disadvantage. Her skin stretched out into wild formations, stalks like roots and the eyes of overripe potatoes looking for anchorage or food to fuel its runaway metamorphosis— looking for him.

Howell backed into and right through the wall. He tripped over crumbling plaster and spilled into the atrium, narrowly dodging the heavy front door swinging in the whipping wind. The rain was no longer rain. Hot ash and bits of still-flaming trash swept by his face.

The hordes of Atwater, a hundred or more of them, crowded into the cul-de-sac before the mansion. On the horizon, a blood-red sun rose and swiftly grew, for it was not rising into the sky, but rolling up the road. The horde met this sight with bestial screams and wails of despair, but they remained rooted, distracting themselves with desperate last-minute orgies, battles and suicide attempts. Though they seemed incapable of coming, killing or dying, still they chased these forbidden states in the burning rain even as the red sun drew closer.

The chimes grew louder, a steamroller trampling a forest of tubular bells. Inside, the pregnant woman called out to him, but he was fixed to the spot.

As the sun swelled, it came clear to Howell. A towering, brazen idol, taller than the highest weathervane on any of the mansions it shouldered aside as it rolled down the street on gigantic iron-shod wheels.

A huge, saturnine head and torso, with great hands outstretched to lift its worshippers to its grinding mechanical jaws. The whole idol glowed dull red with the heat of the furnace raging inside it. All that it touched crumpled in white flames, but the hordes of freaks crowded closer, herded by cage-headed alienists armed with baling hooks and pikes.

The horde tortured itself, each tearing at the deformities of his or her neighbor as the heat between them came alive with white light and fire. Packed closer and closer together as the advancing idol trapped them in the cul-de-sac, they approached an ecstasy of panic, yet they meekly stepped or knelt, singly and in knots of writhing bodies, onto the spreading bronze palms of the glowing idol.

Howell knew this was the thing from which he had averted his eyes, the last time he got lost in Atwater. When she said, "He's coming," she meant this. Now, it was too late to escape. The horde danced on his trapped car. He could go through the mansion, dive out a window on the other side and run all the way home, if he had to, but he got no further than the parlor, where the woman's ordeal was, for better or worse, nearly over.

The woman who raped him told him the thing inside her was his. He could come no closer than the hole he'd made in the wall, but he could not run away from it. Her legs jerked and wrenched impossibly akimbo, laying bare her outraged genitalia, and a glimpse of something fighting its way out of her.

No one had ever asked for what she took from him. No one had ever wanted anything from him but his facility as a calculator, and so the violence with which she had taken his seed had left him curiously stronger than he'd been, before. He'd never realized how much he feared human contact, and he saw in her slitted eyes, now, how much like him she was, how loathsome the act had been for her, but how desperately necessary.

That the act had produced some offspring, here in this place that was insanity itself, was the only sane thing Howell could find to cling to.

He went to her and took her hand. He tried to soothe her with words and touch, but she seemed beyond noticing. "If you're going to be the mother of my child," he said, "I think you could at least tell me your name."

Her eyes rolled but focused on him, and in the midst of her panting seizure, she found breath to laugh at him. "Your *child?* Oh, Howell, you idiot—"

A wash of scalding heat raised blisters on his face, and the mansion's outer wall melted away like a tortilla under a blowtorch. Outside, all he could see was a single red eye, glowering cruel and absolute with the fires of a collapsing sun behind it, a brain that blasted all it touched to atoms. It looked full on them, now, as, all at once, the woman gave birth.

Her hand clasped his and the mountain of her belly tore open like a waterballoon smashing into a wall.

Ferns curled and turned to silver tornadoes of ash. Swamps of sweat vaporized out of the sheets. The woman's hand went slack and deflated in his grip, crumbled like a sheaf of autumn leaves. Howell's own clothes smoldered and gave off puffs of steam and smoke, but he noticed none of it.

The thing that squatted in the ruined chrysalis of the woman at first looked like nothing more than her insides come to life: bones, muscles, guts and all, stirred and resculpted into a crude effigy of a newborn child, but it redefined itself as he watched. Swaddled in blood and shreds of uterine lining, the thing uncoiled and opened its eyes. Swollen sacs of tissue burst and unfurled into membranous wings, and Howell understood.

"Thank you," she said, her voice piping and unsteady in its new vessel, "for helping me escape. I'm sorry you won't."

The iridescent wings snapped and beat the stagnant air, shaking off slime and lifting the newborn body out of its cocoon in one swift motion. Howell ducked, then made a half-hearted attempt to catch her, but she eluded him and dove out the window, into the eye of the idol.

And then the whole house was flying sideways, and Howell had no choice but to go with it. The chiming, roaring explosion went on forever, the room rolling end over end and dancing wheels of fire all around him. And when it all stopped, he was too broken to move, but somehow, he was outside.

The brazen idol clawed at the sky, at a fleeting dart of light that was well away from its glowing grip, and the idol seemed to rust and come unhinged inside, all its parts simply disconnected from the others and the furnace, unleashed, spilled out waves of fire upon the hordes.

Howell ran and ran and still the sound of the fire rolling, gaining, eating up the land, grew in his ears, but he kept running, in his mind calculating his speed and caloric consumption and estimated time of arrival if he just ran and ran home, if he ran to Mexico, if he just ran around the world and came back to this exact point—

Somewhere, long before he got home, he dropped in his tracks and fainted, mind and body completely spent.

And he woke up in a ditch beside the 99 just outside the town of Chowchilla, a sheriff's deputy in an orange poncho poking him in the ribs with a flashlight.

"Thought you was one of them pigs," said the deputy.

He held his life together pretty well, after that, all told, and most of the time, he didn't remember his dreams.

He worked from home, toting up accounts for several small, borderline il-legal companies. He did not, could not, go outside. The fear that he would get lost again, that he might lose track of the route down the street to the corner store, kept him inside. In every corner of every place he did not know as intimately as his own body, a doorway to Atwater waited.

And yet he kept working, eating and sleeping, because, though he did not admit it even to himself while he was awake, he hoped for something.

He lurched on through life like this for months before the dreams started to push through into work, into the blank spaces on the screen and the black pauses between commercials on TV. Her face, her luminous blue wings lifting her out of the fire and into the sky. He still lived, he began to see, only because he hoped she would come back.

He began to seek out some sign, some message to affirm that she was not just a dream, but nothing came forth to save him. He looked for other Atwaters and found one, in Minnesota—"a small, friendly community which welcomes people with open arms…" said the website of the town "named for Dr. E. D. Atwater, of the land department of the St. Paul and Pacific Railroad"—but nothing to distinguish it or marry it to the others, except its name. He did searches, found hundreds of people, streets and companies named Atwater, but nothing that resonated… until he found a listing in a San Diego phone book, and did a search on the computer.

Atwater Transpersonal Institute. The website gave a breezy outline of treatments, but Howell didn't read them. He looked only at the picture on the home page, of a row of couches with people lying on them, sleeping peacefully with spider webs of electrodes pasted to their skulls. He studied the woman on the nearest couch, the planed bones of her face, the black wings of hair flared out on the pastel pillow, and he got his car keys.

At the end of a quiet residential street, on the peak of a hill overlooking Presidio Park with its Spanish colonial fortress, the Atwater Institute looked like the first outpost of yet another colonization. A low, faux-adobe building honeycombed with courtyards huddled around a conical tower of tile and glass. It hid itself from the street behind white brick walls and eucalyptus trees, but the gates readily swung open when Howell pressed the button at the unmanned security checkpoint. He drove up the cobblestone path to the front doors, where a nurse waited. He wanted to turn around and go back home, but he forced himself to get out and walk up to her. "I think I know a woman who is being treated here. I'd like to see her, please."

The nurse only stared, backed away and went inside, leaving the door hanging open. He followed, pausing helplessly as a valet slipped into his car and whisked it off to an underground garage.

Inside, the atrium was dimly lit by a soothing cobalt light. Banks of ferns in hanging pots softened the outlines of the room, and a soft, almost inaudible music played somewhere, an atonal carillon stirred by alien wind.

Howell wanted out, needed in. She's here, somewhere, it's all here, it wasn't in your mind, *oh God, it was all real*—

"I'll just get Dr. Atwater," the nurse said, and fled the room. Howell looked at abstract pictures on the walls, at a watercolor of a man with a beehive for a head, at another of a puppeteer being strangled by marionettes with their own wires, which sprouted out of his flesh.

"Art therapy," said a voice over his shoulder. "It's not pleasant to look at, but it makes them healthier."

"What else do they do?" Howell turned and looked at the Doctor's feet. He could not look at his face, but he heard the man's reaction.

"I—my God, what're you doing out here?" asked Dr. Atwater.

"You treat people with sleep therapy here, right?"

"That's correct. Maybe you—"

"I have been having bad dreams for a long time, Doctor. About this place."

"I can't say I'm surprised. Maybe if I could show you…" Dr. Atwater beckoned him through a door into an even darker corridor. Howell followed, looking around him. The music was louder back here, liquid chimes that made him feel sleepy.

"Binaural tones guide the treatment," Atwater said. "Shamanic cultures use them in rituals, in drumming and trance-inducing states to guide the shaman into the realm of the spirit. It's subtler than medication, and it doesn't blunt the subconscious input from the limbic system. It lets lucid dreams become the patient's reality."

"For how long?"

"In my papers, I recommended regimens of three-day sessions over several months, but the modalities promised so much more for extreme cases, if we could only push deeper, longer. But you know all this."

Howell stopped avoiding the Doctor's eyes. Against the tanning bed bronze skin, they were cold, faded gray. "Where is the woman? The one in the picture?"

Atwater opened a door, waved Howell closer. A body lay on the couch that filled the tiny cell. Howell leapt at it, but froze. It wasn't her.

The honeycombed man twitched and shivered on the couch. He wore mittens and restraints, but still his face was red and chafed, all facial hair plucked out from compulsive grooming.

"One of our most challenging cases. He suffers from a massive OCD complex, but in his therapy, he externalizes his disorder, manifesting it in terms he can metaphorically abolish. He's been dreaming for a month on, a week off for two years, and he's getting better."

Blinking, seeing the bees like ravens on the patient's face, Howell muttered, "No, he's not." Then, rounding on the Doctor, he demanded, "Where is she?"

Atwater's eyes flatly regarded him, but he saw the lambent red glow kindling in them. His mouth made a bold pretense of smiling openness, but his brow was forked with wrathful wrinkles, and his rusty red beard formed a mask of flames. "I'm afraid I don't understand. Who are you looking for?"

"You know, don't you lie!" Howell flinched at his own voice, but he took hold of the Doctor's arms and pushed him back against the wall. "You were there! You tried to eat her up like all the others, but she got away from you!"

Atwater's eyes flashed, his jaw dropped. "So, you found a back door into the group… Well, that's a mystery solved, at any rate."

As if done with Howell, he made to turn away and go about his business, but Howell slammed him into the wall. "Where is she?"

Atwater sighed. "Gone. Transferred to a private institution. Her parents might not sue. They're very wealthy, powerful people, and they were very upset when their neurotic, drug-addicted daughter came to us to be cured and emerged a full-blown autistic."

"Your dream therapy wrecked her brain."

"No, my friend, *you* did. She got it from you." Atwater opened another door onto darkness. "Here, I'll show you."

Howell stepped inside. A body lay on the couch, but there were many machines, a congregation of automated mourners beeping and wailing their grief and providing the only light, trees with dripping IV solutions and the atonal music of binaural chimes.

Atwater spoke into his ear in a low whisper. "He was our first extreme case. Semi-vegetative autistic from birth, ward of the state. We secured power of attorney before the first bricks of the Institute were laid. He was going to be my greatest triumph."

Howell approached the couch, feeling like he did in the mansion, as if he were about to ignite and combust from the heat pouring out of the body on the couch.

"At first, he responded swimmingly, but the deeper we tried to drive into his subconscious, the more he retreated… until one day, about three years ago, he just stopped waking up. I concluded that the psychic disintegration—for that's what it looked like, to me—was a result of his distorted self-concept, his lack of imagination. But I underestimated just how powerful his imagination really was, didn't I?"

Howell tried to remember where he went to school, who his parents were, anything more than three years old, and wondered why none of it had ever mattered before. Because he was a hermetically sealed, self-contained world unto himself, and nothing outside him had ever been anything but numbers, until she forced him to touch her, and escaped.

"At the time, we never reckoned on the possibility that our patients were manifesting in a shared environment, let alone that one could escape it. When Ms. Heaton began to exhibit your symptoms, we thought it was a ploy. Ms. Heaton was very cunning, manipulative, and had attempted suicide more times than her family bothered to keep track of. We never dreamed she could contact the other patients, let alone that she might find you. But *you* found *her*."

Howell leaned closer to the sleeper, eyes roving over the only truly familiar face he'd ever known. The geography of it, seen from any angle for the first time, totally engrossed him, so that he didn't notice when Atwater locked the door and took out a syringe.

"His name is Jeremy Ogilvie, but we use code names for our patients, to protect their privacy. The nurses coined his—he used to scream at the top of his lungs whenever he was touched, so they called him the Howler."

Atwater's shadow loomed across the white desert of sheet, but Howell only leaned closer to the sleeping face.

"For so long, I've thought of you, Mr. Howell, as my only failure. It would appear that you are the only one I ever really cured."

Howell reached up and touched the mouth of the sleeping face, and smiled when its eyes opened.

THE DARKNESS

AMELIA GRAY

"I think I'd call us strange bedfellows," the armadillo said.

The penguin barely heard her. He was, at that moment, attempting to hold a straw between his flippers.

The armadillo centered her shell on the barstool. She was drinking a Miller High Life.

"Strange bedfellows indeed," she said.

The penguin gave up on holding the straw and stood on his stool to reach the lip of the glass. He could barely wet his tongue with a little gin. "What's that?" he asked.

"You are a penguin, and I am an armadillo," the armadillo said. "My name is Betsy."

"That's a beautiful name," murmured the penguin, who was more interested in the condensation on his glass. "I fought the darkness."

"You did not."

The penguin swiveled his head to look at Betsy. He had very beady eyes.

"What's your name?" she said.

"Ray," said the penguin.

"That's a nice name."

"I fought the *fucking* darkness."

"Neat," Betsy said. She let her long tongue dip into the bottle, lapping the surface of her beer. "What was that like?"

"Well Betsy," Ray said, "it was evil incarnate."

"Oh."

"Imagine the worst evil ever done to you in your life."

Betsy thought of the time she was locked in a shed.

"Got it," she said.

Ray pecked at his highball glass in anger. "Well," he said, "imagine that, except fifteen times worse. That's what the darkness was like."

"That sounds terrible," Betsy said. She was trying to be noncommittal about the whole darkness thing in the hopes that Ray would drop it. Before coming to the bar, she had used vegetable oil to shine her shell to a high sheen. In her peripheral vision, she could see the lights above the bar playing off her shoulders.

"What do you think of my shell?" she asked.

Ray leaned back a little to appraise the situation. "It's nice," he said.

"I like your coat."

"This old thing," Ray said, patting his feathers. "It'll smell like the bar for weeks. You can't get this smell out."

"That's the good thing about a shell," Betsy said.

They sat in silence. Betsy wondered if she had perhaps said too much about her shell. Ray wondered where the bartender got off serving a penguin a drink in a highball glass. He would have rather taken his gin out of an ashtray.

Betsy tapped her claw against the beer bottle. "Have you ever protected an egg?" she asked.

Ray realized that he was at the state of intoxication where anything Betsy could possibly say was going to piss him off. *Keep your cool, buddy*, he said to himself. *She's just trying to make conversation.*

"Usually that's a job for the lady penguins," Ray said. "I am a male penguin and therefore, no, I have never protected an egg."

"Right," Betsy said. "Well, I saw a documentary once, and a male penguin was protecting an egg. I figured maybe you'd have some experience."

"Sorry, I don't have any experience. I guess that makes me less of a penguin."

"I wasn't saying that."

"I suppose you think I'm some kind of *lesser* penguin, just because I fought the *fucking darkness* and tasted my own *blood*, because I haven't protected a stupid fucking *egg*."

Betsy felt tears welling up. *Don't cry*, she said to herself. *It would be really stupid to cry at this moment.*

"I honor your fight," she said. "I did not mean to disrespect you."

Ray sank back. "It's no disrespect," he said. "I'm just a penguin in a bar, drinking my gin out of a fucking highball glass for some reason."

"I was wondering why they did that," the armadillo said.

"Doesn't make any goddamn sense," said the penguin.

LI'L MISS ULTRASOUND

ROBERT DEVEREAUX

June 30, 2004

Mummy dearest,

It's great to hear from you, though I'm magnitudinously distraught that you can't be here for the contest. Still, I'm not complaining. It's extremely better that you show up for the birth—three weeks after my little munchkin's copped her crown!—and help out afterwards. The contest is a hoot and I want to do you proud, I *will* do you proud, but that can be done from a distance too, don't you think? What with the national coverage and the mega-sponsorship, you'll get to VCR me and the kid many times over. And of course I'll save all the local clippings for you like you asked.

It made my throat hurt, the baby even kicked, when you mentioned Willie in your last letter. It's tough to lose such a wonderful man. Still, he died calmly. I read that gruesome thing a few years ago, that *How We Die* book? It gave me the chills, Mom, how some people thrash and moan, how they don't make a pretty picture at all, many of them. Willie was one of the quiet ones though, thank the Lord. Nary a bark nor whimper out of him, he just drifted off like a thief in the night. Which was funny, because he was so, I don't know, *noisy* isn't the right word, I guess *expressive* maybe, his entire life.

Oh, before I close, I gotta tell you about Kip. Kip's my ultrasound man. I'm in love, I think. Kind face on him. Nice compact little bod. Cute butt too, the kind of buns you can wrap your hands halfway around, no flabby sags to spoil your view or the feel of the thing. Anyway, Kip's been on the periphery of the contest for a few years and likes tinkering with the machinery. He's confided in me. Says he can—and will!—go beyond the superimposition of costumes that's been all the rage in recent years to some other stuff I haven't seen yet and he won't spell out. He worked some for those Light and Magic folks in California, and he claims he's somehow brought all that stuff into the ultrasound arena. Kip's sworn me to secrecy. He tells me we'll win easy. But I'm my momma's daughter. I don't put any stock in eggs that haven't been hatched, and Kip isn't fanatical about it, so it's okay. Also, Mother, he kissed me. Yep! As sweet and tasty as all get-out. I'll reveal more, next missive. Meantime, you can just keep guessing about what we're up to, since you refuse to grace us with your presence at the contest.

Just teasing, Mummy dear. Me and my fetal muffin will make you so proud, your chest will puff out like a Looney Tunes hen! Your staying put—for legit reasons, like you said—is a-okay with me, though I *do* wish you were here to hug, and chat up, and share the joy.

Love, love, love, mumsy mine,

Wendy

Kip brightened when Wendy came in from the waiting room, radiant with smiles.

Today was the magic day. The next few sessions would acquaint Wendy with his enhancements to the ultrasound process. He wanted her confident, composed, and fully informed onstage.

"Wendy, hello. Come in." They traded hugs and he hung her jacket on a clothes rack.

"You can kiss me, you know," she teased.

He shook his head. "It doesn't feel right in the office. Well, okay, a little one. Mmmm. Wendy, hon, you're a keeper! Now hoist yourself up and let's put these pillows behind your back. That's the way. Comfy? Can you see the monitor?"

"Yes." Eagerly, she bunched her maternity dress up over her belly. Beautiful blue and red streaks, blood lightning, englobed it. A perfect seven-months' pooch. Her flowered briefs were as strained and displaced as a fat man's belt.

"Okay, now," said Kip. "Get ready for a surprise. This'll be cold." He smeared thick gel on her belly and moved the hand-held transducer to bring up baby's image. "There's our little darling."

"Mmmmm, I like that *our!*"

"She's a beauty *without* any enhancement, isn't she? Now we add the dress." Reaching over, he flipped a switch on his enhancer. Costumes had come in three years before, thanks to the doctor Kip had studied under. They were now expected fare. "Here's the one I showed you last time," he said, pink taffeta with hints of chiffon at the bodice. There slept baby in her party dress, her tiny fists up to her chest.

"It's beautiful," enthused Wendy. "You can almost hear it rustle." What a joy Wendy was, thought Kip. A compact little woman who no doubt would slim down quickly after giving birth.

"Okay. Here goes. Get a load of this." He toggled the first switch. Overlaying the soft fabric, there now sparkled sequins, sharp gleams of red, silver, gold. They winked at random, cutting and captivating—spliced in, by digital magic, from a captured glisten of gems.

"Oh, Kip. It's breathtaking."

It was indeed. Kip laughed at himself for being so proud. But adding sparkle was child's play, and he fully expected other ultrasounders to have come up with it this year. It wouldn't win the contest. It would merely keep them in the running. He told Wendy so.

"Ah but this," he said, "this will put us over the top." He flipped the second switch, keeping his eyes not on the monitor but on his lover, knowing that the proof of his invention would be found in the wideness of her eyes.

Eudora glared at the monitor.

She had won the Li'l Miss Ultrasound contest two years running—the purses her first two brats brought in had done plenty to offset the bother of raising them—and she was determined to make it three.

Then she could retire in triumph.

She had Moe Bannerman, the best ultrasound man money could buy. He gestured to the monitor's image. "She's a beaut. Do you have a name yet?"

"Can the chatter, Moe. I'll worry about that after she wins. Listen, I'm dying for a smoke. Let's cut to the chase."

Moe's face fell.

Big friggin' deal, she thought. Let him cry to his fat wife, then dry his tears on the megabucks Eudora was paying him.

"Here she is, ready for a night on the town." He flipped a switch and her kid was swaddled in a svelte evening gown, a black number with matching accessories (gloves and a clutchpurse) floating beside her in the amniotic sac.

Eudora was impressed. "Clear image."

"Sharpest yet. I pride myself on that. It's the latest in digital radiography, straight from Switzerland. We use intensity isocontours to—"

"It looks good. That's what counts. We win this round. Good. Now what about the swimsuit?"

"Ah. A nice touch. Take a look." Again his hands worked their magic. "See here. A red bikini with white polka dots."

"The sunglasses look ordinary, Moe. Give her better frames, a little glitz, something that catches the eye."

"I'll have some choices for you next time."

She shot a fingertip at him. "To hell with choices. You get the right ones first time, or I'll go to someone else." She'd heard rumor of a new ultrasound man on the horizon, Kip Johnson. He deserved a visit, just to check out the terrain. Handsome fuck, scuttlebutt said.

"Yes, ma'am. But take a look at this. It'll win us this round too. We show them the bikini, a nice tight fit that accentuates your baby girl's charms. I've even lent a hint of hardness to her nipples, which will most likely net you a contract with one of the baby-formula companies. But watch. We flip a switch and . . ."

Eudora had her eyes on the screen, her nicotine need making more vivid the image she saw. It was as if the kid had been suddenly splashed with a bucket of water. No twitch of course. It was all image. But the swimsuit's fabric lost its opacity. See-through. Gleams of moisture on her midriff. Her nipple nubs grew even harder, and her pudendal slit was clearly outlined and highlighted. Moe, you're a genius, she thought.

"Cute," she said. "What else you got?"

Thus she strung the poor dolt along, though his work delighted her. Dissatisfaction, she found, tended to spur people to their best. It wouldn't do to have Moe resting on his laurels. People got trounced by surprise that way. Eudora was determined not to be one of them.

When they were done, she left in a hurry, had a quick smoke, and hit the road. The Judge was due for a visit. There were other judges, of course, all of whom she did her best to cultivate. But somehow Benjamin—perversely he preferred the ugly cognomen "Benj"—was The Judge, a man born to the role.

Weaving through traffic, she imagined the slither of his hand across her belly.

Benj walks into the house without knocking.

In the kitchen he finds her dull hubby, feeding last year's winner (Gully or

Tully) from a bottle. The beauty queen from two years prior toddles snot-nosed after him, wailing, no longer the tantalizing piece of tissue she had once been. Her name escapes him.

But names aren't important. What's important are *in utero* images and the feelings they arouse in him.

"Hello, Chet," says Benj.

Stupid Chet lights up like a bulb about to burn out. "Oh, hi, Benj. Eudora's in the bedroom. Have at her!"

Benj winks. "I will."

He winds his way through the house, noting how many knick-knacks prize money and commercial endorsements can buy. Over-the-hill, post-fetal baby drool is all *he* sees on the tube once the little darlings are born. It never makes him want to buy a thing.

"Why, Benjamin. Hello." She says it in that fake provocative voice, liking him for his power alone of course. As long as he can feel her belly, he doesn't care.

"Touch it?" he asks in a boyish voice. "Touch it now?" He thickens below.

"Of course you can," says Eudora, easing the bedroom door shut and leaning against it, her hands on the knob as if her wrists are tied.

Stupid Chet thinks Benj and Eudora do the man-woman thing. Chet wants money from the winnings, so he's okay with it as long as they use rubbers. But they don't *really* do the man-woman thing. Nope. They just tell Chet they do. Benj rubs her belly and feels the object of his lust kick and squirm in there, touching herself, no doubt, with those tiny curled hands, thrashing around breathless in the womb, divinely distracted.

Breathless.

Baby's first breath taints absolutely.

"Touch yourself, Benjamin."

He does. He wears a rubber, rolled on before he left the car. Later, he'll give it to Eudora so she can smear it with her scent and drop it in the bathroom wastebasket. Chet's a rummager, a sniffer. It's safer to provide him evidence of normalcy.

To Benj, normal folks are abnormal. But it takes all kinds to make a world.

His mouth fills with saliva. Usually, he remembers to swallow. Sometimes, a teensy bit drools out.

The baby kicks. Benj's heart leaps up like a frisky lamb. Eudora pretends to get off on this, but Benj knows better. He ignores her, focusing on his arousal, and is consumed with bliss.

July 12, 2004

Mummy dearest,

I'm so excited! Kip is too! The contest cometh tomorrow, so you'll see this letter *after* you've watched me and the munchkin on TV, but what the hey.

I could do without the media hoopla of course, though I suppose it comes with the territory. The contest assigns you these big bruisers, kind of like linebackers. I don't think you had them in your day. They deflect press hounds for you, so you don't go all exhausted from the barrage or get put on the spot by some persistent sensationalist out to sell dirt.

Then there are the protesters.

Ugh! I agree with you, mumsy. They're out of their blessed noggins. Both sorts of protesters. There are the ones who want the contest opened up to second trimester fetuses. The extremists even scream for first trimester. What, I ask you, would be the point of *that*?

Then there are the ones who want to ban pre-birth beauty contests entirely. Life-haters I call them. Hey, I'm as deep as the next gal. But I was never harmed by having a beauty queen for a mother nor by winning the Baby Miss contest when I was three months old. All that helped me, I'm sure—my self-esteem, my comfort with putting my wares on display, which a gal has just got to do to please her fella. I don't mind if Kip likes me for *all* of me, and I sincerely and honestly believe he does. But that includes the packaging. The sashay too, though mine's got *waddle* written all over it these days. Hey, I can work off the belly flab as soon as my baby's born. I know I can. I'll slim down and tighten up you-know-where even if it's under the knife with sutures taking up the slack. That's a woman's duty, as my momma taught me so well!

My point is that I'm *all* of me, the brainy stuff and the sexy stuff too. It's all completely me, it's my soul, and right proud of it am I. Well, listen to me gas on and on, like a regular old innerlectual. What hath thou raised? Or more properlike, whom?

Wish us luck, mumsikins!

Your loving and devoted daughter,

Wendy

Kip was alone in his office, making final tweaks to his software. Wendy had been by, an hour before, for one last run-through prior to their appearance onstage.

Five more minutes and he would lock up.

His ultrasound workstation, with its twenty-four-inch, ultra-high-resolution, sixteen-million-color monitor, had become standard for MRI and angiography. Moe Bannerman, last year's winning ultrasound man, had copped the prize, thanks to this model. But Kip was sure, given the current plateau in technology, that whatever Moe had up his sleeve this year would involve something other than the size and clarity of the image.

Butterflies flitted in Kip's gut. Somehow, no matter how old you got, exposure to the public limelight jazzed you up.

The outer office door groaned. Maisie coming back for forgotten car keys, thought Kip.

A pregnant woman appeared at the door. Eyes like nail points. Hair as long and shiny as a raven's wing. Where had he seen her? Ah. Moe's client, mother of the last two contest winners.

Wendy's competition.

"Hello there," she said, her voice as full-bellied as she was. "Have you got a minute?" She waddled in without waiting for an answer. "I'm Eudora Kelly."

He opened his mouth to introduce himself.

"You're Kip, if I'm not mistaken. My man will be going up against you tomorrow."

"True. Look, according to the rules, you and I shouldn't be talking."

She approached him. "Rules are made to keep sneaky people in line. We're both above board. At least, I am." Her voice was edged with tease, a quality that turned Kip off, despite the woman's stunning looks. "Besides, even if I were to tell Moe what you and I talked about or what we did—which I won't—it's too late for him to counter it onstage, don't you think?"

"Ms. Kelly, maybe you'd better—"

She touched his arm, her eyes intent on the contours of his shirtsleeve. "I'll tell you what surprises *he's* planning to pull tomorrow. How would that be?"

"No, I don't want to know that." He did, of course, but such knowledge was off limits. She knew that as well as he.

"They say you've got new technologies you're drawing on. A background in the movies. Maybe next year, you and I could pair up."

Kip reviewed his helpers, looking for a blabbermouth.

No one came to mind.

"In fact," she sidled closer, her taut belly pressing against his side, "maybe *right now* we could pair up." Her hand touched his chest and drifted lower.

"All right, that's enough. There's the door. Use it." His firmness surprised him. It was rare to encounter audacity, rarer still therefore to predict how one would respond to it. He took her shoulders and turned her about, giving her a light shove.

She wheeled on him. "You think you're God, you spin some dials and flick a few switches. Well, me and Moe're gonna wipe the floor with your ass tomorrow. Count on it!"

Then she was gone.

The back of Kip's neck was hot and tense. "Jesus," he said, half expecting her to charge in for another try.

Giving the workstation a pat, he prepared to leave, making sure that the locks were in place, the alarms set.

"Fool jackass," Eudora said. "The man must be sexed the wrong way around."

"Some people," observed The Judge, his eyes on her beach ball belly, "have a warped sense of right and wrong. They take that Sunday school stuff for gospel, as I once did long ago."

"Not me, Benjamin. I knew it for the crock it was the moment it burbled out of old Mrs. Pilsner's twisted little mouth. Ummm, that feels divine." It didn't, but what the hell.

Benjamin would be pivotal tomorrow. No sense letting the truth spoil her chances.

The Judge's moist hand moved upon her, shaky with what was happening elsewhere. Soon he would yank out his tool, a condom the color of rancid custard rolled over it like a liverwurst sheath. "Yeah, I wised up when I saw how the wicked prospered," he said. "How do you *do* it, Eudora? This is the third sexy babe in a row. Your yummy little siren is calling to me."

"She wants it, Benjamin," said Eudora.

Perv city, she thought. It would be a relief to jettison this creep as soon as the crown was hers. Three wins. She would retire in glory and wealth. At the first sign he wanted to visit, she would drop him cold. No bridges left to burn after her triumph. Let the poor bastard drool on someone else's belly.

Benjamin groped about between the parted teeth of his zipper. Eudora said, "That Kip person's going to spring something."

"Who's he?" asked The Judge, pulling out his plum.

"You know. The ultrasound guy that Wendy bubblehead is using. Scuttlebutt says he's doing something fancy."

"Ungh," said Benjamin.

Eudora pictured Kip's office receptionist, her hand shaking as she took

Eudora's money. She was disgustingly vague and unhelpful, Maisie of the frazzled hair and the troubled conscience. All she gave off were echoes of unease: he has this machine, I don't know what it does, but it's good because he says it is and because they both look so sure of themselves after her visits. Worthless!

"My baby girl's getting off, hon."

"Me too," he gasped.

"You're a sweet man," she said. "Show us your stuff. Give it to us, Benjamin, right where we live. That's it. That's my sweet Benjamin Bunny."

Benj really gets into it. Eudora's bellyskin is so smooth and tight, and as hot as a brick oven. He smells baby oil in his memory.

Eudora has no cause for worry, he thinks. Moe Bannerman's a stellar technician. What Moe's able to do to tease naked babes into vivid life onscreen is nothing short of miraculous.

Benj conjures up the looker inside Eudora's womb by recalling what hangs on his bedroom wall, those stunning images from *Life* last year—better than the real thing though a boner's a boner no matter how you slice it.

He dips into Tupperwared coconut oil, smearing it slick and liberal upon her belly, as he does upon his condomed boytoy. Oil plays havoc with latex, he knows, but Benj isn't about to get near impregnation or STDs.

Benj bets Moe Bannerman will carry his experiments in vividness forward in the coming years. Headphones will caress Benj's head as he judges, the soft gurgle of fetal float-and-twist tantalizing his ears, vague murmurs coaxed by a digital audio sampler into a whispered *fuck-me* or *oh-yeah-baby*.

Or perhaps virtual reality will come of age. He'll put on goggles and gloves, or an over-the-head mask that gooses his senses into believing he's tasting her, the salty tang of preemie quim upon his tongue, the touch of his fingertips all over her white-corn-kernel body.

Benj shuts his eyes.

Eudora starts to speak but Benj says, "Hush," and she does. This time the rhythms are elusive but *there*, within reach if his mind twists the right way. The beauty queen to be is touching him, indeed she is, those strong little fingers wrapped about his pinkie. Her eyelids are closed, the all-knowing face of the not-yet-born, lighting upon uncorrupted thoughts, unaware of and unbothered by the sensual filtering imposed by society on the living.

Her touch is as light as a hush of croissant crust. This, he thinks, is love: the wing-brush of a butterfly upon an eyelash; a sound so faint it throws hearing into doubt; a vision so fleetingly imprinted on the retina, it might be the stray flash of a neuron.

With such slight movements, love coaxes him along the path, capturing, keeping, and cultivating—like a seasoned temptress—the focus of his fascination, so that the path swiftly devolves into a grade, hurrying him downhill and abruptly thrusting him into a chute of pleasure. He whips and rumbles joyously along its oily sides once more, *once more, ONCE MORE!*

July 13, 2004

Mummy mine,

I'm writing from the convention center, just having come offstage from Round One, where our little dolly garnered her first *first!* I had a hunch I'd want to disgorge all these glorious pent-up emotions into my momma's ear. So I brought along my lilac stationery and that purple pen with the ice-blue feather you love so much. Here I sit in the dressing room with the nine other contestants who survived Round One. Ooh, the daggers that are zipping across the room from Eudora Kelly, whose kids won the last two years. Methinks she suspects we've got her skunked!

Baby's jazzed, doing more than her usual poking and prodding. Kip just gave me a peck (would it had been a bushel!!!) and left to check out his equipment for Round Two. If I were a teensy bit naughtier, I'd mention how much *fun* it is to check out Kip's equipment, ha ha ha. But you raised a daughter with that rarest of qualities, modesty. Besides which, it would be unseemly to get too much into that, Willie being so recently deceased and all. But life goes on. Oh boy howdy, does it ever!

I passed through those idiotic protesters with a minimum of upset, thanks to my linebacker types. Joe, he's the beefiest, flirts outrageously, but both of us know it's all in fun. Still, he's a sweetie and you should see the scowl that drops down over his face whenever some "news twerp" (that's what Joe calls them) sticks his neck out where it don't belong, begging Joe to lop it off.

There were twenty of us to start with. 'Taint so crowded here no more! The audience sounds like an ocean, and the orchestra—you heard me, strings and all, scads of them, like Mantovani—set all things bobbing on a sea of joy. Kip gave me a big kiss right here where I sit—no, you slyboots, on my lips!!! Before I knew it, I was standing onstage amidst twenty bobbing bellies, all of us watching our handsome aged wreck of a TV host, that Guy Givens you like so much, his bowtie jiggling up and down as he spoke, and his hand mike held just so. The judges were in view, including the drooly one—you know, the one whose hanky is always all soppy by the end.

First off, oh joy, we got to step up and do those cutesy interviews. Who the heck can remember what I gassed on about? I guess they build suspense at least in the hall. At home, all I remember is that you and me and Dad used that dumb chit-chat as an excuse to grab a sandwich or a soda.

Then Round One was upon us, and we were number 16, not a great number but not all that bad neither. I lifted my dress for Kip—not the *first* time I've done that, I assure you!!!—to bare my belly and of course to show off my dazzling red-sequined panties. For good luck, I sewed, among the new sequins, an even dozen from my Baby Miss swimsuit. The crowd loved my dumpling's first outfit, a ball gown that might have waltzed in from the court of Queen Victoria. It reminded me of a wedding cake, what with all the flounces and frills and those little silver sugar bee-bees you and I love so much. Baby showed it off beautifully, don't you think?

Then Kip played his first card. With a casual gesture, he brought life to her face. Of course, her face *has* life, but it's a pretty placid sort of life at this stage, what with every need being satisfied as soon as it happens. So there's nothing to cry about and no air to cry with if she *could* cry.

Then it blossomed on her face: a flush and blush of tasteful makeup spreading over her cheeks and chin and forehead, a smear of carmine on her lips, turquoise blue eyeshadow and an elongation of her lashes. Huge monitors in the hall gave everyone as clear a picture as the folks at home on their TVs. I could taste the rush of amazement rippling through the hall at each effect.

Then, her darling eyes opened! Just for a second before Kip erased the image. Of course they didn't *really* open, any more than my baby really wore a ball gown. But they weren't just some painted porcelain doll's eyes. Kip's years in Hollywood paid off, because you would have sworn there was angelic intelligence in the deep gaze Kip gave her face—

Oops, we just got the five-minute call, mumsy, so I'll cut off here and pick back up at the next break. Wish us luck! Gotta go!!!

Kip followed close behind a stagehand, who wheeled the ultrasound equipment to the tape marks, locked down the rollers, and plugged the cord into an outlet on the stage floor. Wendy had already settled into the stylish recliner.

"Hello, darling," said Kip, taking her hand. Wendy returned his kiss. "How are you two?"

"Fine." Her voice wavered, but Kip judged it near enough to the truth.

The stage manager, clipboard at the ready, breezed by. "Two minutes," he said. Hints of garlic.

Beyond the curtain's muffle, the emcee pumped things up. A drum roll and a cymbal crash rushed the orchestra into an arpeggio swirling up to suggest magic and pixie dust. Kip squeezed Wendy's hand.

When the curtain rose, Guy Givens strode over. "And here's our first round winner, Miss Wendy Sales. Round she certainly is. And ready for another round, I hope. Wendy, how does it feel to be the winner of our evening wear competition?"

"Well, Guy," said Wendy, as he poked the mike at her mouth, "it feels great, but I don't bet on any horse until the race is over's what my momma taught me. All these great gals I've met? Their babies too? They're *all* winners as far as I'm concerned."

"Ladies and gentleman, let's give the little lady's generosity a big hand." The emcee's mike jammed up into his armpit so he could show the audience how to clap with gusto. Then it jumped back into his grip. "Wendy, with that attitude, you'll be a great mom indeed."

"I sincerely hope so."

Ignoring her answer: "And now . . . let's see your adorable little girl *in her bobbysoxer outfit!*" The tuxedoed man backed out of the spotlight, his free hand raised in a flourish.

Deftly fingering a series of switches, Kip hid his amusement at the emcee's tinsel voice, as the orchestra played hush-hush music and Wendy's child came into view.

A tiny pair of saddle shoes graced the baby's feet. Her poodle skirt (its usually trim stitched poodle gravid with a bellyful of pups) gave a slight sway. She wore a collared blouse of kelly green. A matching ribbon set off her tresses, which Kip had thickened and sheened by means of Gaussian and Shadow filters combined with histogram equalization.

When the crowd's applause began to fall off, Kip put highlights back into baby's face, an effect which brought the clapping to new heights.

As if in answer, Kip turned to two dials and began to manipulate them. The baby's eyes widened. She gave a coy turn of the head. Then her eyelids lowered and Kip wiped the image away.

The effect looked easy, but the work that had gone into making it happen was staggering. To judge by the shouts and cheers that washed over the stage, the crowd sensed that. Wendy glowed.

"*Judges?*" screamed Guy Givens into his mike.

One by one, down the row of five, 10s shot into the air. A 9 from a squint-eyed woman who never gave 10s drew the briefest of boos.

Wendy mouthed "I love you" at Kip, and he mouthed it back, as the music swirled up and the curtain mercifully shut out an ear-splitting din of delight.

Eudora watched from the wings as the TV jerkoff with the capped teeth and the crow's feet chatted up her only competition one last time.

The swimsuit round.

Moe's water-splash effect had gained Eudora an exceptional score, but from the look on the ultrasound man's face out there, that insufferable Kip Johnson, she was afraid he was poised to take the Wendy bitch and her unborn brat over the top.

Dump Moe.

Yep, Moe was a goner. Yesterday's meat. Spawn the loser inside her, let her snivel through life, whining for the tit withheld. A dilation and extraction might better suit. Tone up. Four months from now, let Chet poke her a few times. Stick one last bun in the oven.

Then, adrip with apologies, she would pay Kip another visit, playing to his goody-two-shoes side if that got him off. Hell, she'd even befriend his lover. If Wendy had a two-bagger in mind, Eudora would persuade her—strictly as a friend with her best interests at heart—to retire undefeated.

Onstage, that damned tantalizing womb image sprang to life again, this time dressed for the beach. Her swimsuit was a stylish fire-engine-red one-piece that drew the eye to her bosom, as it slashed across the thighs and arrowed into her crotch. Nice, but no great shakes.

Then the kid's face animated again. Eudora knew that this face would bring in millions. For months, it would be splashed across front pages and magazine covers. Then it would sell products like nobody's business.

Would it ever!

Instead of repeating its coy twist of the head, the intrauterine babe fluttered her eyelashes at the audience and winked. Then she puckered her lips and relaxed them. No hand came up to blow that kiss, but Eudora suspected that Kip would make that happen next year.

Her kid would be the one to blow a kiss. *Her* kid would idly brush her fingers past breast and thigh, while tossing flirtatious looks at Benjamin and viewers at home.

Eudora scanned the judges through a deafening wall of elation. There sat the oily little pervert, more radiant than she had ever seen him. Another year would pass, a year of wound-licking capped by her triumph, and Kip's, right here on this stage. *Then* she'd dump the drooler. One more year of slobber, she assured herself, would be bearable.

Eye on the prize, she thought. Keep your eye on the prize.

Benj is in heaven. His drenched handkerchief lies wadded in his right pants pocket. Fortunately, his left contained a forgotten extra, stuck together only slightly with the crust of past noseblows. It dampens and softens now with his voluminous drool.

The curtain sweeps open. Midstage stand the three victors, awaiting their reward.

Wendy's infant has quite eclipsed Eudora's in his mind. The third-place fetus? It scarcely raises a blip. Its mother comes forward to accept a small faux-sapphire tiara, a modest bouquet of mums, and a token check for a piddling sum. An anorexic blonde hurries her off.

Eudora's up next.

Replay pix of her bambina flash across a huge monitor overhead. Beneath her smile, she's steaming. He's in the doghouse for his votes; he knows that. But there's always next year. She needs him. She'll get over it.

A silver crown, an armful of daffodils, a substantial cash settlement, and off Eudora waddles into oblivion, her loserkid's image erased from the monitor.

Then his glands ooze anew as the house erupts. Like a bazillion cap guns, hands clap as Wendy's pride and joy lights up the screen with that killer smile, that wink, oh god those lips.

"AND HERE'S OUR QUEEN INDEED!" screams Guy Givens, welcoming Wendy into his arms. Gaggles of bimbos stagger beneath armloads of roses. The main bimbo's burden is lighter, a gold crown bepillowed. Wendy puts a hand to her mouth. Her eyes well.

Then it happens.

Something shifts in the winner's face. She whispers to Givens, who relays whatever she has said to the crown-bearing blonde. Unsure what to do, the blonde beckons offstage, mouthing something, then walks away. Wendy leans against the emcee, who says "Hold on now" into his mike. A puddle forms on the stage where she is standing. "Is there a . . . do we have a . . . of course we do, yes, here he comes, folks."

Benj feels light-headed.

The rest drifts by like a river ripe with sewage. Spontaneous TV, the young doctor, the ultrasound man, a wheeled-in recliner, people with basins of water, with instruments, backup medical personnel. Smells assault him. Sights. Guy

Givens gives a hushed blow-by-blow. And then, a wailing *thing* lifts out of the ruins of its mother, its head like a smashed fist covered in blood, wailing, wailing, endlessly wailing. Blanket wrap. The emcee raises his voice in triumph, lowering the tiny gold crown onto the bloody bawler's brow.

It's a travesty. Benj is glad to be sitting down. He rests his head on his palms and cries, mourning the passing of the enwombed beauty who winked and nodded in his direction not five minutes before.

Is there no justice in the world, he wonders. Must all things beautiful end in squalor and filth?

He craves his condo. How blissful it will be to be alone there, standing beneath the punishing blast of a hot shower, then cocooning himself under blankets and nestling into the oblivion of sleep.

July 14, 2004

Mumsicle mine, now GRAN-mumsicle!

Well I guess that'll teach me to finish my letters when I can. I'll just add a little more to the one I never got 'round to wrapping up, and send you the whole kitten-kaboodle [sic, in case you think I don't know!], along with the newsclips I promised.

I'm sitting here in a hospital bed surrounded by flowers. Baby girl No-Name-Yet is dozing beside me, her rosebud lips moving in the air and making me leak like crazy. I do so love mommyhood!

But I never expected to give birth in public. They were all so nice to me at the contest, even that Eudora woman, who seems to have had a change of heart. That creepy drooly judge came up to wish me his best, but Kip rough-armed him away and said something to him before kicking him offstage. I'll have to ask Kip what that was all about.

Oh and Kip proposed! I knew he would, but it's always a thrill when the moment arrives, isn't it? I cried and cried with joy and Kip got all teary too. He'll make a great father, and I'm betting we spawn a few more winners before we're through. We'll give you plenty of warning as to when the wedding will be.

He's deflected the media nuts so far, until my strength is back. They're all so antsy to get at me. But meanwhile Kip's the hero of the hour. There's even talk of a movie of the week, with guess-who doing the special effects of course. But Kip tells me these movie deals usually aren't worth the hot air they're written on, so he and I shrug it off and simply bask bask bask!

I'll sign off now and get some rest, but I wanted to close by thanking you for being such a super mom and role model for me, growing up. You showed me I could really make something of myself in this world if I just persisted and worked my buns off for what I wanted.

I have.

It's paid off.

And I have you to thank for it. I love you, Mom. You're the greatest. Come down as soon as you can and say hello and kootchie-koo-my-little-snookums to the newest addition to the family. You'll adore her. You'll adore Kip too. But hey, hands off, girl, he's mine all mine!!!

Your devoted daughter,

Wendy

CRAZY SHITTING PLANET

MYKLE HANSEN

THE FAT PEOPLE

The fat people are hundreds of feet tall, clad in the finest exoskeletal fashions, giant zeppelins of money and power and fat. They block out the sun with their immensity, staring down at us from the heavens with their pale, simple, hungry faces, their compound eyes as big as soccer balls, their bulbous bellies vast as astrodomes. Usually they eat us, though occasionally they toy with us, strafing us with food or clean water or scraps of the past. Either way, they own us. The fat people own everything: the air, the water, the sky; words, speech, thought; the past, the future. All of these things belong to the fat people now, while we little creatures on the ground are left to scavenge in their shit for crumbs and scurry to evade the punishment of their mighty crushing feet.

Call me Cheeseburger. I have no family; my mother died from the general sickness long ago, the same disease of everything that gives me this cough, cough, cough. My father was eaten by a fat person, almost a year ago. A particularly obese, giggling pale sky-bag that swooped down on us one day as Father and Son foraged for edible plastic in one of the many massive piles of shit and debris which rain down from the bloody orange sky. I had just discovered, half buried in stinking fat-person feces, a beautiful antique laptop computer from the late Stuff Era. Praising our luck, we had begun to dine together on the tiny morsels of keyboard, when the sky went dark. Silent and deadly, the fat woman smiled down at us, the bulbous folds of her face pinched into a tent-like mask of hungry anticipation. There was nowhere to hide.

To save my life, Father shoved me into the feces, rendering me grody and unpalatable. As I scraped the stinking brown paste from my eyes I watched an immense pink hand, encrusted with stunningly huge jeweled baubles and two massive Rolex replicas, plunge down and scoop up my father, who struggled not a twitch. He only cried out "Eat or be eaten, kiddo!" as he slowly ascended out of earshot, towards the hideous bloated jowls of the levitating obesity. It studied him for a moment, sniffing him with its massive, surgically enhanced nose, and then with incredible vicious speed it gobbled him up.

Inside the fat person, I knew, lasers and grinders and robotic viscera flayed Father alive, stripping him skin to bone, boiling him down to nutrition and energy, and injecting his jellied existence directly down the gullet of the rich bastard at its core. Satisfied, the fat person emitted a jet of flaming methane from its rectal thrusters and shot back up into the sky, to the place where the fat people float forever.

And then I was alone in the world. Except for my friend Aimless.

My friend Aimless found a telescope, and now makes a study of the fat people. Gazing through his telescope at the floating city of fat, he says, is a quiet way to pass the time. They have built Fat Heaven up there, he tells me. In their titanic city of pearl and silver, held aloft by the constant effort of nuclear reactors, the fat people dance and sing, hold beauty contests, stage immense operas, copulate on clouds, stuff giant bales of money adoringly in one another's asses, and endlessly elaborate upon their total consumption of everything. They fling their refuse down to earth, where we tiny things that remain crawl out of our holes and race to feed upon it, while low-flying fat people make cruel sport of us.

I hate them. But Aimless watches them and only laughs.

The fat people are strong, they are smart, they have every good thing that ever was, all of it. All the earth's bounty is tightly concentrated in their gargantuan fists. They do not share. They don't have to. The great struggle is over and the fat people have won. I used to dream of a day when they would eat the last rock of the earth and find themselves, at last, hungry and unfed. But Aimless has watched them soar away into space, perhaps searching for other planets, other universes to eat and shit upon and throw away. The fat people want to eat the sun, and when they've run out of sun I'm sure their hunger will lead them on to other stars. They'll never have enough.

GERTIE THE WHALE

Aimless says he's in love with a whale. He says the whale comes to him in his dreams, singing to him when he's sleeping. He says the whale has beautiful eyes. He says the whale's name is Gertie, and he wants to find her something for her birthday. Aimless tells me all this as we pick through a layer of potato chip bags, used diapers and syringes with our digging sticks. I'm looking for something we can eat, smoke, or feed to Mrs. Teeth. Aimless is looking for a present for his whale.

A thing about Aimless: he loves animals. And loving something that is dead and gone can be hard. I try not to think about my family; sometimes in my dreams I see my Father's face rising into the sky, and I'm overcome with anger, I shake with rage, I weep. But Aimless is always excited to tell me about rats he almost saw, or insects he found traces of, or bones he dug up which might not have died too long ago. He's ever hopeful.

There are no more animals, I try to explain. We ate them all. The fat people ate all the tasty ones and the starving people ate the rest a long, long time ago. Every now and then someone might discover a dead animal in the general piles of trash and shit that we dig through, but those animals are ages dead, mummified by trash. And if we do ever find such a dead, rotten, disgusting animal, we have to feed it to Mrs. Teeth.

There are no more animals, but there are lots of drugs. Drugs are one of the things the fat people happily shit on us. Six months ago it rained feces and marijuana for two days. Everyone in our colony smoked and smoked and smoked it, adults and children both, until our brains ran out our ears. Then, while we lay passed out in a happy blue haze of shit-stinking bliss, the fat people came down and ate dozens of us. That's how stupid we are.

Aimless lives in a rusting automobile, I think it was once a Dodge Caravan, that is lodged in the side of a cliff of scrap metal just above the reeking, reeling tide of the shit-dark ocean, overlooking a beach of slime. Nobody ever comes here because the smell is so terrible. This is where Aimless lives alone, and hoards his treasure, and smokes the leftover marijuana and dried feces.

Aimless is very rich. All of us dig through the rotten trash to survive—what else is there to do?—but Aimless is luckier than the rest. Aimless finds incredible things, constantly. He has magic powers. He has The Knack. And while most people throw back what they can't eat or smoke or burn for fuel, Aimless is a collector.

Aimless collects animals. He has hundreds of metal fish, several rubber snakes, a stuffed bird with no head, and numerous porcelain cats, or parts of porcelain cats, or broken shards of porcelain which he says remind him of cats.

All of these decorate his tight, frozen, stinking metal home, or are hoarded in the catacombs of scrap underneath.

Aimless collects photographs. Pictures from the times before the fat overlords owned absolutely everything, the times when stupid people like us still had clothing and lived indoors and ate food. Most photographs from the Stuff Era are curiously inedible, but I would still gladly burn them for heat. Aimless, however, would rather sleep in the cold than sacrifice these scraps of paper.

Aimless collects nautical supplies. He has an anchor, and some rope. He has glass floats and old, rotten nets, useful for catching the fish that used to live in the sea, but no longer. He has an eye patch—I'm not sure what makes this a nautical supply, but he insists it's crucial. He has a rusty compass and a pile of mildewed nautical charts. He once caught me chewing on one of them— mildew is considered a delicacy in our colony—and smashed me in the nose with the anchor.

"Without those charts," he said, "how can I find Gertie?"

Aimless collects so many things ... anything bright and shiny, anything ancient and hand-worn, anything that might be at home in his dreams. Anything and everything useless and inedible, he caches and catalogues in the holes he's dug beneath his van in the side of his cliff, all of his lovely collections waiting to be someday dragged down into the shit-dark sea by a tidal wave of crap.

Aimless is insane. But he's also rich, and he has a lot of drugs. I'm happy that he calls me his friend. Sometimes he vanishes for months at a time, but when he's around, we dig in the trash together. I watch the sky with his telescope, ready to dive for cover if the fat people notice us, while Aimless waves a crooked stick back and forth over the shit-greased piles of debris, his eyes closed, listening, wandering in short steps, sniffing the fetid air ... and then suddenly he dives, attacking the earth with his digging stick, scraping and scuttling at the plastic bags and debris with silent assurance until he conjures forth some beautiful or meaningful or edible fragment from the Age of Stuff.

This time, it's a small plastic model of some kind of boat. He holds it triumphantly up to the sky, smiling with pride. A toy. A yellow submarine.

I ask him the ultimate question of my people: are you going to eat that? But I know better. What he has found is clearly a nautical supply. So we keep digging, searching for the perfect gift for an imaginary whale.

ARE YOU GOING TO EAT THAT?

Rubber is chewy. I can chew on a piece of rubber for days before it loses its flavor and finally begins to crumble. One of my favorite things to chew is an old shoe, especially if it carries the flavor of an antique human foot.

Plastic is crunchy. There are many kinds of plastic; some kinds I can eat, others make me vomit. But they all provide texture. Because I am always coughing, I must eat very slowly. It's easy to choke on plastic.

Shit tastes terrible. But it's all over everything. The turds of the flying fat people are the only steady component of our diets. We scrape, we rub, we tap and polish everything we pull out of the shit-soaked ground, but still, we eat an awful lot of shit.

Every now and then, the fat people throw us a bone. It amuses them to do so. The day I was born, it rained shit-covered cheeseburgers. They shot down from the sky in hot greasy fusillades, smacking people in the heads and backs, exploding on the ground. I'm told it was the most beautiful day in our history, a day without hunger, a day my father loved to remember. That's why he named me Cheeseburger.

Or else he planned to eat me.

THE WEATHER

Today it rained shit and exercise videos. These were shit-coated cardboard boxes painted, on the front, with a picture of an incredibly clean, well-fed woman, a woman with all her teeth and perfect skin, clad in angelic blue and grey clothing, standing in a warm, sun-filled room, smiling, smiling, smiling. And on the back of each box, her solemn promise: you will lose the weight you want to lose. And keep it off.

Inside each box was a black plastic tray, and centered on each tray was a shiny, reflective disc. I find these discs in the trash piles all the time. They are difficult to eat. But the cardboard box itself wasn't bad. The ink tastes terrible, but the boxes were flat with a smooth surface; you could scrape just about all the shit off of them.

One month ago, it rained shit and George Foreman Grills. Giant useless iron apparatuses from the era of propane gas in canisters. One of these grills fell on my cousin Beef and killed him. Then Mrs. Teeth ate his body. Many of the other grills exploded into bits of jagged metal when they hit the ground, scattering razor-edged shards that still cut my feet when I step on them. My aunt Crazins stepped on one, and her foot became infected. Her leg turned fat and yellow, and she was unable to run. So Mrs. Teeth ate her too.

One thing about the weather: if you don't like it, stick around and it'll get worse. Sometimes it rains Sony PlayStation Twos and shit. Sometimes it rains flat plasma televisions and shit. I remember the horrible day when it rained NordicTrack Fitness Systems and shit. Many people died.

MRS. TEETH

The woman in our colony called Mrs. Teeth is much bigger than the rest of us, and older. She's not fat or huge like the people in the sky, but compared to my own gaunt stick-frame of a body she is like a great pillar of angry meat with huge, loose, hairy breasts and long, snatching fingers. She is very very clean and white, because she refuses to eat shit.

Mrs. Teeth doesn't suffer from the general sickness. She doesn't cough, she isn't racked with chills or pox on her skin. She is tall and wide and healthy. She has all her teeth, and she likes to bare them. "Grrrrrr!" she says. Her eyes are close together and her voice is loud and frightening.

Because Mrs. Teeth doesn't have the sickness, there isn't much she can eat. The fungus in my belly, I've learned, can break down almost anything and convert it into fuel for The Host. That's me—I am The Host. The fungus in my belly is slowly eating me, very slowly it is eating us all, but it also helps us to survive on this landscape of trash and shit. The point of my survival is lost on me, but feeding the hunger is a habit I can't break. The fungus in my belly is like a starving child, always crying. I like to think that it loves me, my hungry sickness. I try to be a good host.

Mrs. Teeth is a poor host. Her fungus left her.

Mrs. Teeth is family. She's my mother's sister's husband's mother's sister. Since my father's sister's husband was also her half-brother, Mrs. Teeth is also my aunt. We are all family in this colony. That's why my lower lip curls around toward my left ear, and also why my cousin Beef had no arms to deflect the George Foreman Grill that crushed him. We are defective recycled products.

But we're family, so we look after each other. Whenever one of us finds something in the trash that Mrs. Teeth could eat, they set it aside for her, even though we too are starving. We do this for her out of love.

We also do it so she won't eat us. Mrs. Teeth is so strong, so fast, so hungry. When one of our colony dies, or is about to die, or shows signs of possibly nearing death, Mrs. Teeth smiles, and begins to drool.

Mrs. Teeth is a very pious woman. She worships the fat people in the sky, the gods of Fat Heaven. She believes our fat owners are the source of all goodness, wisdom and justice—not that we have any of that down here. But you must never argue with Mrs. Teeth, because she bites, and her teeth are full of diseases that stick in your flesh and make you sick. Then, when you grow ill, Mrs. Teeth follows you around waiting for you to fall.

Mrs. Teeth becomes very angry if anyone ever complains about the precious gifts the fat people have shat upon us. "Rejoice!" she cries whenever it comes dumping down. "Hallelujah!" she screams, and dances, and points at the sky. "Praise them!" And if you are near her when this happens, then you had better bow down and pray, because, as I said before, she bites.

Mrs. Teeth is very insane, very dangerous. I try very hard to stay away from her. But I would rather be eaten by Mrs. Teeth than give anything, even thanks, to those evil fat pigs in the sky.

AIMLESS'S GUITAR

Last night it was too cold to sleep, so I went to find Aimless and his drugs. I found him on the edge of the cliff, sitting cross-legged on a dry patch of elevated sky-turd ... and do you know what I found him doing?

I found him playing a guitar!

He found it in the trash, he said. An entire guitar! I have never even found a box the size of a guitar, and if I had found such a box it would have been crushed and full of feces.

Aimless's guitar is clean, uncrushed, it has three intact strings and spaces for three more. Maybe Aimless will find those too, the lucky bastard.

Oh, how my stomach churned, gazing at that beautiful, beautiful guitar. I have never even found a stick as thick as the neck of that guitar, in all my years of trash. Oh, how I dreamed of seizing it from him and lighting it afire, just to bring a moment's warmth to my cold, naked life. How I longed to bite off a corner of that guitar—just a tiny corner—and feel the splintery wood dissolving in my stomach.

Aimless strummed the guitar tunelessly, gazing out into the freezing, shit-dark sea. He ignored my astonishment over his sudden production of this astounding relic, and my anger at the useless way he toyed with it—as if he and I and all of us in the colony were not tumbling down a long slope of hunger and desperation. As if trees still existed, and guitars grew on them. Madman!

In my mind's eye, I killed Aimless right there, and I ate him. Aimless is even smaller and scrawnier than me, and oblivious to danger. I could kill him with my bare hands. In my mind I built a fire of his guitar, and roasted his flesh over it, and ate him. And I was warm and full and happy and alone, in my mind's eye.

But I couldn't really do that to my only friend.

Aimless ignored me. He just strummed the guitar, and sang a song to his girlfriend:

Gertie, baby sweetie,
Meet me by the shore,
Where nobody is wailin'
On the whales no more.

Open up your ocean,
Lead me to your deep,
Lay me in the cradle
Where the baby whales sleep.

We will swim into the sun,
We will dive into the sky,
We will float along the river
And we're never gonna die.

I will hold you in my arms,
I will love you 'till I'm sore,
Oh Gertie, baby sweetie,
If you meet me by the shore.

"How are you going to hold a whale in your arms?" I had to ask.

Then Aimless stopped playing his guitar. He gazed at me, annoyed.

"Are you saying Gertie is fat?" he asked.

"Well, she's a whale, isn't she?"

He made no reply, except to return to strumming his guitar. It was clear he wasn't going to eat that.

Eventually he said: "Yes, she's a whale. But she's special!"

Later we smoked some drugs and Aimless fell asleep on the cold cliffside. I was hungry, shuddering, confused and angry. And there lay Aimless's guitar next to him, begging me to take it.

Love makes no sense to me. You can't eat it, you can't smoke it, you can't burn it for fuel. I feel the dull warmth of my family ties, but family ties are provisional. Family is a courtesy that everyone extends because everyone so desperately needs the favor returned. When it's time to feed Mrs. Teeth, family love weighs as much in one hand as one edible plastic door handle weighs in the other. Love is flimsy and disposable. It may be worth something, but not much.

I could never, ever fall in love with an imaginary whale.

But neither could I eat my friend's guitar.

EXTREMELY BAD NEWS

I am doomed!

I always wondered how long I had to live, and now I know. I am definitely going to die, I can see it all coming now.

This morning I heard the news from my cousin Earwax, as we worked the trash pile together. He laughed when he told me, and poked me in my cough-wracked chest with his trash stick:

Mrs. Teeth has fallen in love with me!

Me!

Earwax laughed and laughed, until he folded over in a fit of wheezing. And then I spied Mrs. Teeth, far off over the bluff of trash. Just her huge head poked above the horizon, watching us, peering at me with her close-together eyes, and I knew this was no joke. Even at that distance I could see the passion burning in her like infection.

Why me? How did her mind settle on me? She ate her previous husband less than a month ago. How can she need another one so soon?

It's only a matter of time now. I am doomed, doomed, doomed! I need to hide. I need to escape.

Ever since this morning she has been following me! She keeps her distance, for now, but I know she'll be coming closer.

Probably she is carrying a present for me, probably some disgusting bouquet of my relatives' bones. When she catches me she will blush, and then bashfully hand me these bony flowers, the fingers and toes of my cousins and uncles.

She will ask me if I like this, and if I tell the truth she will kill me.

She will ask me to hold her hand, and if I refuse, she will eat me.

That horrible madwoman will clutch my head with her huge grasping fingers and pull it towards her own, and ask me to kiss her on her diseased, toothy mouth! If I refuse, she'll bite out my tongue! That is what love means to Mrs. Teeth!

And on top of all that, other bad news: a storm is brewing in Fat Heaven. That's what Aimless told me when I went to visit him. He has been studying them through his telescope, and he says they're angry. Some fat person has offended some other fat person, and they are all up there taking sides, getting ready to fight. Aimless says it has something to do with a spoiled romance.

This has happened before. The last time the fat people pummeled each other in the sky above us, they oozed blood and shit and vomit and useless consumer products for days and days. My cousin Snackables was swept up in the putrid gore and washed away to drown in the shit-dark sea, it fell so thick and slippery. Even our trash was contaminated with their bile and their blood. We had to dig for weeks to reach some relatively clean garbage. All because two floating fat men had to prove their relative worth to some floating fat woman in the sky.

Love! If the word Love had a head, I would stab it in the eye with my stick.

It's so bad, this news, I can't even think. I can only sit on the cliff next to Aimless, clutch my head, and listen to him babble while he plays his guitar.

Aimless says that there's nothing to worry about. Aimless says everything will be fine, because Aimless is building a submarine. As soon as this submarine is ready, he says, the two of us can sail away into the shit-dark sea, thence to meet up with his whale girlfriend. "I think she has a sister," he tells me, winking, while he strums the notes.

Aimless is insane, but I appreciate his willingness to help. I sit there beside him on the cliff, and listen to him sing his song to his whale, and for a moment I forget to worry. Foolish me.

Did you know that people in love are drawn to music? Yes, music attracts lovers like shit once attracted flies, before we ate all the flies.

Music now attracts Mrs. Teeth. Here she comes, shambling across the trash-mound toward us, shoving through the twisted scrap. I could run, but she would catch me. I could hide, but she would tear Aimless's home apart looking for me, scatter his collections, sink his submarine. So I sink deep inside myself, perched there on the cliff, hiding inside my own skin, waiting for the horror.

I never knew love could feel like this.

Mrs. Teeth tramples up behind us. "Such beautiful music!" she barks, clapping her hands in glee. Before either of us can react, she has grabbed Aimless's guitar out of his hands and is shaking it upside-down, trying to dump the music out of the hole so she can eat it. Aimless grabs at the guitar and she slaps him to the ground with one meaty hand. She shakes it and shakes it, a dumb confused look on her face, but no edible musicians fall out of the guitar. Then, she holds it out to me.

"It's a present," she says. "I like you. Take it!"

I take it, and hand it back to Aimless.

"Now we're friends!" she giggles. "Do you like that?"

I know it's important to lie when answering this question, but I just don't think I can do it. Honesty is my handicap. Honesty and my harelip. I want to say nothing, but I know Mrs. Teeth will reach down my throat with her ravaging hands and pull the truth up out of my belly if I don't speak it.

"It's a nice guitar," I offer.

She reaches between my legs and grabs my genitals in one cold, clutching hand!

"Wanna be my boyfriend?" she asks, grinning. With her other hand she raises a hairy breast toward my face. A drop of saliva runs from the corner of her stinking mouth.

"Be my boyfriend and fuck me? Wanna?" she asks, leering.

I really don't want to answer this question! But she leans over me, pushing her idiot lips at mine, squeezing me painfully. I go cross-eyed just looking into the beady eyes in her pinched-together face.

Just then, two things happen for which I will always be grateful.

First, there is a loud cracking clunk! Mrs. Teeth releases me and staggers to the side. Aimless has bopped her on her ugly head with his beautiful guitar! He strikes her again, and I hear the sound of wood preparing to crack. She screams with rage, and fixes Aimless's tiny frame in her murderous eyes, grinding her disgusting teeth.

And then the other thing: an explosion in Heaven.

FLAMING FAT PEOPLE FALL FROM THE SKY

There's a bright white flash, and for a moment my vision is full of blinking pink pain and squirming lines. I rub the heels of my hands against my face as pink lightning slowly subsides to sky-orange throbbing. Eventually I can see points in the orange plane: high up over the shit-dark sea, there are tumbling, burning obese bodies, growing larger, falling down out of the sky, trailing black smoke.

Mrs. Teeth sees them too, and the sight throws her into religious ecstasy. She hurls herself to the ground and moans, screaming "Forgive them! Masters, forgive them!" She tears at her hair, bashes her face against the scrap-strewn ground, and starts to weep.

The fat people loom larger in the sky now. At least a dozen of them are falling down on us.

Aimless shouts "Submarine!" and scurries over the edge of the cliff, climbing down to his battered Caravan with the battered guitar over his shoulder. Given the choice of following Aimless or remaining with Mrs. Teeth, I decide in a heartbeat. But once in the van, I can see we are well and truly trapped.

Aimless rolls up the windows, adjusts some dead knobs on the dashboard, buckles himself into the driver's seat, and looks out over the sea. The fat people are about to splash down. The first one strikes far out to sea, and with a massive crash it explodes, tossing blubber into the sky.

Aimless asks me if I want to smoke some drugs. Never have I wanted this more.

Through the smoky haze of the Caravan's atmosphere, I see a tidal wave of crap rising up on the horizon, and other flaming fat people shooting over to land behind us, striking the land with booming impacts. The scrap metal cliffside rattles and shifts. Either we will be dropped into the sea and drowned, or flattened by a tidal wave, or else the trash will fall on us and suffocate us.

I'm grinning with relief as I buckle my seat-belt. All of these deaths are so much nicer than being eaten by Mrs. Teeth.

Aimless is grinning with excitement. He's going to meet his girlfriend in the shit-dark sea.

The wave strikes the cliff, and we're flipped over as we plunge down, down, down into the ocean of excrement. The roar of explosions, crashing metal, distant screams, and the loud moaning of Mrs. Teeth are all suffocated in a cold wet plop. All is stinking blackness, while we wait to hit the bottom. Aimless peers through the glass into the sea of crap, looking for fish.

Time passes. Feces seep in slowly through cracks in the floor. The vehicle bobs and sways. We smoke more drugs. There's nothing else to do.

I tell Aimless that I'm really enjoying dying like this. This is almost beautiful.

Aimless asks me if I still think his girlfriend is fat.

I wonder when the ocean is going to crush us.

After a while, I hear the slapping of waves against the roof of the van. We are floating. But we can't see through the windows because they're slathered with feces. And the bottom of the van is filling up, slowly but surely, with the ocean's diarrhea. Aimless unbuckles himself, opens the hatch in the roof and climbs out. I follow.

Our submarine is floating on the ocean, far from home. Shit surrounds us on all sides, and the smell is twice as revolting as it is on land. But the sun is shining in the orange sky, and not far away we see a shape on the surface of the water.

It is the bobbing, charred body of a fallen fat person, still smoldering. A woman, perhaps.

Very slowly it bobs closer, facedown in the slime, while gently sloshing waves of shit lap higher against the side of the van. The roof of the vehicle is slick and treacherous, so we stand perfectly still, even as the van begins to tip, ever so slowly.

The massive black corpse is our only salvation. I don't know how to swim, but as I slide into the shit-black sea I thrash my weak, gangly limbs and wave my trash stick in an effort to push myself towards the fat person's body. I manage to keep my head mostly above the waves, and soon I am climbing the hot fragments of the fat person's burned-up pearl necklace, clambering up onto its deflated back. I collapse, heaving and choking, but safe. But where is Aimless?

Aimless is still standing atop his capsizing submarine, gazing out over the waves, ignoring the fact that he's about to drown, strumming his guitar. Oblivious to danger, that's Aimless.

"GERTIE!" he sings over the waves. "GERTIE BABY SWEETIE!"

If any imaginary whales can hear him shouting, they're keeping mum about it.

After much screaming, I finally convince him to throw me a line: a knotted-together collection of short lengths of twenty kinds of rope. His rope collection.

Using it, I haul his van alongside the bloated body, and he hops aboard, guitar in one hand, telescope in the other, just as the vehicle rolls upside-down and bubbles under. Aimless stares down in dismay as the sucking whirlpool steals his submarine, home to his nautical-supplies collection, his collection of vintage soda cans, his dead insect collection, his rubber snake collection, his charts, his dreams and his drugs. All his riches, his life's work, slithering down into the shit-dark sea.

"Don't worry," I tell him. "Gertie's going to love it."

With my trash stick I scrape a hole in the back of the fat person, through its expensive dress, its expensive blouse, its expensive blubbery skin. Beneath that is an expensive metal shell which blunts my stick. My father told me the fat people were floating castles full of food and money. But even in death they won't share it with us.

I'm hungry. The fat person's skin itself is delicious, especially the parts that have been char-broiled in the sky. The flame-roasted Prada dress is tougher than most clothing I've eaten, but not bad.

We sit on the floating fat woman's back—our own private island, warm, soft, round, upholstered in wool and food. We watch the urine sun sink down into the toilet Earth. Our bellies are full, and we're free.

That night the sky is clear and I can see the sky full of perfect stars. The stars are the only things I know that don't have shit all over them. They're beautiful. I would give anything to prevent the fat people from soiling them, but I'm not hopeful.

Aimless sings to his girlfriend for a while, and then we both lie down to sleep.

MARTHA HILTON-TRUMP THE TWELFTH

In the middle of the night, a booming, blubbery, gurgling panic of a voice starts screaming beneath us:

"Lice ... maggots! Get them off me!"

It appears that the floating fat person is not quite dead.

"Parasites! Daddy!"

For a moment I see my latest death: drowning in shit, while the fat person pisses on me. But it remains motionless.

"Daddy! I'm stuck! Help me right now! They're eating me!"

Not a twitch from the giant fat fingers. Not a nod from the huge floating head. I stab into the ground with my trash stick.

"Ow! Stop it!"

Stab, stab, stab.

"OW! Daddy! Mommy!"

And still, it doesn't move.

Stab! Stab, stab, stab! The giant fat bastard is crying now! The ones who ate so many of us, the ones who ate my father, who shat on my family! Stab, stab! It cries out in pain and yet it's still powerless! The ones who humped each other screaming in the sky for hours, while we buried our heads in the shit to block out the sound ... the ones who fucked up the world ...

Stab! Stab! Stab!

Then Aimless puts a hand on my stabbing stick. He looks pained, worried.

The anger drains out of me in an instant. We listen to the pathetic, booming sobs of fat pain and fat fear. So human.

"I'm sorry," I say.

"Yeah, right!" it sneers. "Parasite! Maggot! Let me go! My daddy is going to eat you! Waaaaaaah!"

Eventually it stops crying. It tell us its name: Martha Hilton-Trump the Twelfth. It tells us it's one of the richest women in Heaven, it's college-educated, and its father, Danforth Hilton-Trump the Eleventh, is an extremely powerful and important fat person who is going to eat us. We take turns watching the sky with Aimless's telescope, but no fat people are approaching to eat us at this time.

I tell Martha my name is Cheeseburger, and she laughs. So I stab, just a little bit. This upsets Aimless, but I hate when people laugh at my name.

Aimless asks Martha Hilton-Trump if she sees any whales down in the ocean.

And Martha Hilton-Trump the Twelfth laughs some more.

Night turns back to day. The sky is still empty of fat people. Aimless and I fix breakfast, to the loud protestation of Martha Hilton-Trump.

"AAAAAAA!" she gurgles. "Daddy! They're eating me!"

"We're eating a tiny, small piece of your clothing," I say. "Shut up."

"Ow! It's mine! And you're eating it!"

"Why not? You're dead anyway."

She is silent for a while, as thick waves of shit lap against her body, as her greasy shit-soaked hair floats out around her face-down head like a blonde carpet, as we eat her dress and welcome the day.

Then the weeping begins. No more threats, no more complaints, just loud, hacking, heaving sobs that swell into loud bawling, retreat back to sobbing, swell and retreat.

We sit and listen to this all day. We scream at her to shut up! We stamp on her flesh, pound her, stab her, pull her hair, but the wailing carries on. I wrap long strips of her shitty fried clothing around my head to block out the sound, but the sound is too loud.

Such pain! Such anguish! Such terrified misery! Never did I cry as loud or as long as this, not when the fat people ate my father, not when Mrs. Teeth ate my mother, never. Oh, how the sobs of this enormous fat woman claw at the armor of my soul!

The fat people are sadder than we are; they have so much more to lose.

Eventually, to block out the noise, Aimless starts to strum his guitar as loud as he can. Finding a tune, he sings a lullaby for Martha Hilton-Trump the Twelfth:

Sleep pretty baby,
darling, sleep,
Rock on the tide
of the warm dark deep.

Your Daddy will come,
in the morning you'll ride.
Sleep pretty darling
and rock on the tide

Sleep pretty baby,
rock on the tide
Your Mommy is waiting
at home in the sky

At home in the sky,
your Mommy will keep.
So rock on the tide,
and sleep, baby, sleep.

He sings this over and over, strumming the guitar, and Martha Hilton-Trump the Twelfth seems to hear it. The sobbing boils away slowly as night falls, receding into deep wracking coughs, and then silence. But Aimless keeps on playing his guitar for hours, as the sun goes to sleep in its bed of shit, and even the stars lower their orange screen and come out to listen.

The next morning, the dead fat person called Martha Hilton-Trump has changed her dead fat-person tune. Now she wants to know Aimless's name, and where Aimless's from, and what it was like for Aimless growing up in a stinking pile of shit instead of a fluffy floating cloud of food and money. And he tells her some stories about his youth, and she says "Oh, you poor dear!" and "I never even imagined!" And she tells us some stories from her youth, all of which are revoltingly luxurious, even the supposedly bad parts.

Martha Hilton-Trump says she likes Aimless's singing. She asks for more. And for a whole day, she doesn't once threaten us with being chewed up and swallowed by her rich daddy.

I think Martha Hilton-Trump the Twelfth is in love with Aimless.

But she has nothing to say to me.

THE BLOODY HATCHET

All this time, we have been taking turns watching the skies with the telescope, waiting for the arrival of Martha Hilton-Trump's father, or any other fat people. When we see them, we know we're dead. But so far we don't see them.

However, that afternoon, we see something else: a shape on the horizon.

A ship!

Father told me about ships. I've even seen ships. Aimless had half of a book about ships somewhere in his submarine. They are like big floating boxes with sticks coming out of them, and on the sticks are bags of wind. And this is one of them, a sailing ship, sailing to meet us. Atop the tallest spire it flies two flags: one red, one black.

Aimless gives Martha Hilton-Trump the news, and Martha starts to cringe and whinge and weep all over again.

"It's the Bloody Hatchet! The terror of the shit-dark seas! Daddy!"

It grows slowly on the horizon, at the rate toadstools used to grow before we ate all the toadstools. It takes most of an hour to reach us. Fat person Martha Hilton-Trump is inconsolable the whole time. The Bloody Hatchet is a scavenger ship, she tells us, a zombie ghost ship that picks apart the dead and rapes the living. The ship's insane crew never stops laughing. "They'll flay me and fillet me!" says Martha.

"Why doesn't your fat daddy just eat them for you?" I ask. And Martha starts bawling.

She begs Aimless to protect her. As if Aimless could do anything with his little guitar against a ship full of laughing zombies.

Slowly, slowly, the Bloody Hatchet looms closer. It's a beautiful ship, fast and tall. Through the telescope I can make out shapes of people on the bow, staring back at us through their own telescopes. Two of them wave. I wave back. They seem friendly.

"They'll boil my bones! They'll steam my spleen!" Martha is howling in fear now, as Aimless frantically strums on the guitar, trying to calm her down.

The ship glides toward us. The people on the deck are still waving their greeting. I can hear their laughter. I can see their faces now.

And on the very bow of the ship, arms outstretched to embrace us, I see a member of my family! My aunt!

Mrs. Teeth!

"Hallelujah!" she cries.

THE PEOPLE'S COMMITTEE FOR RAPING AND PILLAGING

The Bloody Hatchet pulls up alongside Martha Hilton-Trump; its pirates swing down from the deck on ropes, happy, laughing, eager to meet us. They are all so nice! And so well-fed! They are muscular and tan and strong, you can tell they eat well. And they wear clothing: ragged red sweaters and tattered black trousers, all of it warm and beautiful. They're so healthy, so alive. They shake our hands, pat our backs, and offer us water.

Water! I've heard of it, but never seen it. It's the cleanest thing I've ever tasted.

Mrs. Teeth smiles from the deck, waving down at me, drooling.

The largest of the pirates boards us. He is a huge tree of a man, wearing a heavy black coat and a black beret with one gold-embroidered red star. He introduces himself as People's Captain Slasher-Jones, the chairman of The

People's Committee for Raping and Pillaging. He bows a long, elegant bow, and asks us how long we've been stranded, if we're sick, if we're thirsty, and if we'd like to come on board to drink grog and dance a jig in celebration of our rescue.

Mrs. Teeth is hopping up and down with mad glee, waving at me, blowing kisses. Aimless sees her too, but says nothing.

While People's Captain Slasher-Jones congratulates us on our impressive catch, and tells us how thrilled he would be to take us aboard and introduce us to the members of the Steering Subcommittee and the Jig Subcommittee and the Grog Subcommittee, a team of men from the Pillaging Subcommittee are already stripping Martha Hilton-Trump of valuables. Using long pole-hooks, they expertly snag the pearl necklace, sever it from her neck and hoist it on deck. Then they lasso an arm, hauling it up from the fecal depths, and strip it of a ladies' Rolex, some gold rings and a few other giant baubles of gold and silver. The pirates gather around the pile of booty on the deck, whooping with joy.

Through this all, Martha Hilton-Trump remains silent, playing dead. Through it all, Mrs. Teeth leers at me from the deck, drooling with excitement.

The People's Captain is waiting for our answer. He says if we join the pirate crew, we will sail together, battling the fat people and living on the sea. He says I can be the People's Watchman, riding on the top of the mast with my telescope, and Aimless can be the People's Singer-Songwriter, composing some desperately needed new jigs, subject to the approval of the Jig Subcommittee.

Aimless asks the captain: what will happen to our fat person?

Captain Slasher-Jones is sympathetic to Aimless's concerns. He places his beret over his heart and solemnly swears that absolutely nothing will happen to Martha Hilton-Trump without a plebiscite of the People's Pillaging, Raping, Devouring and Jettisoning Subcommittees.

All around us, the pirates are yelling: join us! Please, join us!

I stand at the edge of Martha Hilton-Trump's expansive ass and gaze deep down into the shit-dark sea. I've always known I'd end up down there. The only question has been when.

I look to Aimless. Aimless stares into the hole of his guitar, thinking.

But what choice do we have?

When we announce our decision, the pirate host shouts a unanimous "Hurrah!"

Then, Martha Hilton-Trump the Twelfth commences to weep.

STATUS REPORT FROM THE PEOPLE'S LOOKOUT
SUBCOMMITTEE

For three days I have sat on the top of this pole. I will probably die here.

For three days Aimless and I have been pirates. As soon as I climbed on deck, Mrs. Teeth chased me around the ship, while all the pirates laughed. So I scurried up this pole with my telescope and my poking stick. Captain Slasher-Jones says my job is to keep the lookout. I am the Special Investigator of the People's Lookout Subcommittee.

With one eye I gaze out across the shit-dark sea with the telescope, confirming the ocean's constant, stinking emptiness, and the sky's curious lack of marauding fat people. With my other eye I watch Mrs. Teeth, who leers up at me from the bottom of the pole, making kissy-faces.

Mrs. Teeth can't reach me here—she's too thick and clumsy to climb this pole. If she tries, I will poke her eyes out with my stick.

But she waits for me. Sometimes she wraps herself around the mast and humps it, and it shakes, and I must hold on with all my might.

The other pirates pay her no heed, except for Captain Slasher-Jones. Three times a day, the Captain emerges from his cabin, marches to the base of this mast, and shouts up to me: "WHAT HO, LOOKOUT OF THE PEOPLE?"

Three times a day, I shout down to him, as instructed: "NOTHING HO, PEOPLE'S CAPTAIN." And he laughs, and Mrs. Teeth laughs, and he gazes longingly into her eyes. Then he struts around the deck, inspecting the work of the other pirates, shouting, laughing, acting tough and important. It's plain to see he's trying to impress her.

Yesterday I saw Mrs. Teeth vanish into the Captain's cabin for a short while, and I heard horrible screams and clatter. I was terrified; I thought she was eating him. I could have slid down and run away at that moment, if I had anywhere to run to. But she returned soon enough, giggling, dressed in rags, her hair matted on her sweaty face, and then continued her leering as if she'd never left. A few minutes later, Captain Slasher-Jones crept out of the cabin and wandered in a different direction entirely, to peals of laughter from the other pirates.

They find everything funny, these pirates. Everybody is always laughing on this ship, except for me and Aimless ... and Martha Hilton-Trump the Twelfth, if you count fat people.

Martha Hilton-Trump trails the boat by a long rope tied to her hair, but her loud, desperate moaning and burbling still reaches us. It comes and goes throughout the day, deafening at times. I can tell the crew is growing irritated with her. Her misery interferes with their laughter. The only coherent word she ever speaks is "Daddy!"

Aimless sits at the stern, watching Martha Hilton-Trump as she bobs on the reeking waves, strumming his guitar for her. His song is sad and plaintive, but a few pirates from the Jig Subcommittee gamely attempt to dance to it, trying their best to ignore the sobs of the giant floating fat person, even when the weeping drowns out Aimless's little wooden guitar.

The pirates have given us clothing, and water, and committee assignments, and for all that I am grateful, especially for the water. But hospitality is only worth so much at the top of a cold pole.

And their customs are strange. When I shat from up here, down onto the deck and all over Mrs. Teeth, there was much laughter. But later the Captain scolded me.

"We be a civilized people," he said. "And this be the People's Ship. Keep it tight!" As if every single plank of the deck, every single particle of this ship and of the earth, did not have shit all over it already.

I was not punished, except that now I must shit in a bucket on a rope, which I am then required to empty over the edge of the ship. I must hold the bucket under myself with one hand while I shit, while I hold onto the pole with the other hand, while Mrs. Teeth stares directly up into my asshole.

Thankfully, I haven't had to do this often. We've had no food for three days.

At night, after Martha Hilton-Trump sobs herself unconscious, facedown in the shit-dark sea, and after Mrs. Teeth curls up around my mast and falls asleep drooling, and after the pirates have sung each other lullabies and laughed themselves to sleep ... then, Aimless tiptoes to the mast and quietly puts drugs in my shit-bucket, and I haul them up and smoke them, and we talk.

Aimless says I mustn't get the wrong idea. He's still in love with Gertie the Whale. Martha Hilton-Trump he only pities. She lost everything there is to lose, he says. She is young, he says, and foolish.

And rich, I add. And tasty.

Aimless has made special petitions to the Raping and Devouring Subcommittees, asking them to postpone their raping and devouring. He told them they can ransom her for infinite treasure when her Daddy finally comes. The pirates are intrigued by this idea, but also very hungry.

"If Martha's daddy were coming," I said, "we'd all be dead by now."

It's a perfect mystery: why did the fat people explode? Why did they fall to earth? One day they were up there, the next day they were gone. Are they dead? Or will they rise again? Aimless has asked Martha Hilton-Trump what happened, but the question only makes her cry.

Even if Mrs. Teeth eats me in my sleep, even if the pirates toss me in the sea for shitting on their deck, there is one thing on this ship that was worth coming for, and that is this excellent view of the overhanging stars. Since the fat people exploded, the sky has been clear of orange smoke at night. The winking, glittering stars overhead are my blanket. Aimless agrees: the stars are cleaner and more beautiful than anything on earth. I wish I could keep the fat people away from them.

A DREAM WITH MY MOTHER'S VOICE IN IT

It seems I am going mad, just like Aimless.

At night I tie ropes around my arms and legs so I can sleep without falling into the jaws of Mrs. Teeth. For three nights I've fallen asleep this way, a sack of bones hung to dry under the precious stars, and each night I've had the same dream. I dreamed I heard the voice of my mother, a woman I've never met.

In this dream, I am watching the sky with my telescope, when each of the stars in the sky explodes, one by one, with a huge flash and a loud bang. Then the sky itself bursts into flame. Fire and smoke and feces and burning guitars rain down on the shit-dark sea. The pirates hide under deck, but I am still dangling from the mast. The wind whips me as the ocean churns. Huge waves of shit juggle the Bloody Hatchet. Shit crashes over me, shit pounds the deck. I am whipped back and forth as the creaking ship spins and dips and shudders, tumbling under breaking waves of shit. My pole becomes slick with crap; I lose my grip and I'm tossed into the ocean. I thrash around, grasping at the smoldering guitars that float on the surface. I grab several of them and try to lash their strings together to build a raft. But then a huge wave pounces on me, shoving me down, down, down into the sickening turd. I can't see, I'm choking. The hideous reeking muck squeezes into my eyes, my ears, my nose. I open my mouth and it pours down my throat, as I sink deeper and deeper ... but then I fall through the bottom of it, and open my eyes.

Under the ocean of shit there is another, larger ocean—an ocean of transparent clean water! Water that washes the shit out of my eyes, my skin, my fingernails, my hair, my red pirate shirt and my black pirate pants. I inhale, drinking in this water, and it rushes through my body, destroying all the filth in me, filling me with life. And, drinking it, I can fly!

I zoom in crazy circles, surrounded on all sides by life—a world of animals floating all around me: horses, snakes, giraffes, leopards, dinosaurs, jackalopes. All the animals we killed are still alive here, swimming in circles. And flowers, and trees, and cars, and toadstools too, all twirling through space, drifting gently in the pure, delicious water that surrounds us. A black and white cat rubs against my feet and swims away. Two goldfish chase past me, swimming upside-down. They're so beautiful I can't even eat them.

The water itself glows, bathing everything in a pure shimmering moonlight. And down below me, a brighter light beckons, shining up like an upside-down moon on the ocean floor.

I swim deeper, faster, toward the glowing thing that hangs there in the bottom of the sea. It is like a huge glowing fat person, but in the shape of a fish. Its skin seems to be made out of the full moon itself, all blue-gray and glowing, and covered with tiny craters. It wears no clothing, no jewelry, not even any arms or legs. It only has fins, a tail and a huge, smiling face with beautiful blue-green eyes.

The glowing fat fish sings to me in my mother's voice.

It tells me its name is Gertie.

NUNS HO!

On the morning of the fourth day, we sighted the Ship of Nuns.

As on the first three mornings I awoke upside-down, tangled in a dangling strangulation of ropes that cut into my limbs and left my fingers and toes numb. As on the first three mornings, the first thing I saw when I opened my eyes was Mrs. Teeth, patient as gravity, batting her eyes and licking her lips.

After righting myself and rubbing the pain out of my arms, I took up my telescope to check the condition of the emptiness. But I was startled to see something quite near on the horizon: a ship, with tattered sails!

Through the telescope I saw women on the deck of the ship, kneeling around the mast, clothed in long black dresses and long black hats, all gazing up wistfully at the place where their sails had been. And up there, lashed to the mast of that ship, was a desperate-looking naked man. With his limp arms outstretched on the rigging, he appeared at least half-dead.

When I heard the women shouting "Hallelujah!" at him, I could not help but sympathize.

Captain Slasher-Jones stormed onto the deck. "LOOKOUT OF THE PEOPLE!" he cried. "WHAT HO?"

"NUNS, CAPTAIN!" I cried. "NUNS HO!"

I pointed out the ship. Every pirate rushed to the railing to see, and to cheer, and to laugh. They hoisted the sails and caught a wind, and we made for our rendezvous with the Ship of Nuns.

MY POSITION ON THE EATING OF NUNS

I would have preferred not to eat them. In a world of choice, a world of options, I would have opted out of the nun-eating. Although they were delicious, and I was hungry.

But I would have preferred not to. When the strong, friendly pirates pulled alongside the nun-ship, waving and smiling and greeting them so politely, I expected ... I don't know. Something other than what I saw, from above.

I have never seen so many women raped in one day.

I'm so tired of this life.

My father's mother used to tell him incredible stories of the past when he was small, and when I was small my father would tell these same stories to me. Stories about the Easy Times, the Age of Stuff, when every person got to decide what to do with their own life. In the times before shit, before poverty, even the littlest people were incredibly rich and wealthy and happy and stupid. When Grandma was young, Father told me, life was an endless banquet of options, a feast of fascinating choices with exotic names: Right, Wrong, Democrat, Republican, War, Peace, Regular, Unleaded.

All day long, every single day of her life, the waiters of the world brought steaming trays of fine, delicious, enticing lifestyle options to my grandmother's table, each fresh and ripe with unfolding possibility. All my grandmother had to do was pick the ones she wanted. That was her life! Can you even imagine it?

As the People's Committee for Raping and Pillaging seethed over the helpless nuns, making meat of them, stripping them of clothing and then of flesh, drowning their screams with mad laughter and darkening the decks with their blood, I found, finally, that I could no longer watch.

And when I looked away, I caught the eye of the other man, the man on the mast of the other ship. He was still just barely alive, though the whole height of his mast was painted red with his blood. Blood seeped in rivulets from wounds in his hands and feet. Looking closer, I saw the nails in his flesh.

I asked the man how he ended up in such a fix, but he never told me. He only begged for mercy.

"Please, sir," he croaked in a weak, bloody whisper, "please spare my sisters. Eat me instead! I'm delicious and tasty, I promise! I'll give you my body gladly, but please have mercy on the women. They are innocent and good! I'm crispy and tender and full of magic! I'll feed you all, with just my body. Please, let them go! You'll live forever if you eat me instead!"

I told him he was asking the wrong guy.

A moment later, the People's Captain cut him down and fed him to Mrs. Teeth.

Here's the thing: I am completely different from everybody else in the world, in a way that completely does not matter. In Grandma's time, in a world of choice, a world of either-or, I could be the People's Captain. I know it. I could live, grow and flourish in a world like that. I could hew to a righteous path. Or I could even hew to a terrible, hideous path, in a world where I get my choice of paths for hewing. If I could have chosen nun-eating, then I would have gone forth and boldly eaten nuns until I died. I have a strong mind. My ancestors' decision-making power still flows in my blood. I could do everything I chose to do, if I could choose.

But all the choices worth choosing drowned in the shit-dark sea a long, long time ago.

Live or Die?

Kill or Be Killed?

Starve or Eat Nuns?

These are the only items on my menu.

Aimless ate no nuns. He refused their meat, though I know he's more hungry than I am. Even at sunset, when the members of the Jig Subcommittee slow-roasted a nun-foot on a spit, just for Aimless, and offered it to him on a jeweled plate, he refused and turned away. I watched him clamber over the stern, lowering himself carefully onto the head of Martha Hilton-Trump. The jilted pirates ate the foot without him, and did not try to follow.

Martha Hilton-Trump saw nothing of what happened to the Nun Ship—her eyes are still pressed against the shit-dark sea —but did she overhear? I wonder what Aimless will tell her.

He's stopped strumming his guitar. In the moonlight I can see him crouched cross-legged on Martha Hilton-Trump's floating head, whispering something to her, I don't know what.

Tonight I hate the stars. Tonight the stars are ugly stupid specks, flaws in the darkness. They can't help me and they never could. Tonight I'm hanging upside-down in my bed of ropes, watching Mrs. Teeth suck the marrow from another man's bones while the giant floating fat woman wails and the mad pirates laugh and the never-ending world of filthy shit reeks in all directions. Tonight I stare out over the shit-dark sea watching the nun-ship burn. I eat my piece of nun, and wait for Gertie the Whale to take me down.

MORNING OF THE SHITTIEST DAY

This morning it rained shit, laptop computers, Leatherman Super-Tools, and blood. A laptop struck me in the hand, I think it broke a bone in my wrist. One Leatherman Super-Tool smashed a porthole in the People's Captain's Cabin. Captain Slasher-Jones came storming out, demanding a report.

"SHIT HO, PEOPLE'S CAPTAIN!" I cried. "SHIT AND LAPTOPS!" All the men took cover, while I hung in the mast, weathering the storm. For better or worse, I'm still alive.

The fat people are back. I can see them through my telescope high, high up in the orange sky, zooming angrily to and fro, swarming the way startled wasps once swarmed, before we ate all the wasps. The fat people are back, and they're angry.

I shouted the news to the whole crew this morning, including Aimless, but Aimless is busy. From my vantage point I can see that he has opened some kind of hatch in the back of Martha Hilton-Trump's giant skull, and climbed inside her head. What he's doing in there I don't know, but he'd better not let Daddy catch him.

Nobody missed the fat people, but they have returned anyway.

After the squall, Mrs. Teeth found a Leatherman Super-Tool on deck, licked it clean of shit and blood, and now, whenever the Captain isn't watching, she uses its tiny saw-blade to saw away at my mast. The tiny, persistent scratching sound reverberates up through the pole and scrapes at my ears. Scrape, scrape, scrape. Saw, saw, saw. It will take her a long while to saw through all that wood, but Mrs. Teeth is persistent.

While she saws daintily away at my mast, she bats her pinched-together eyes at me, and asks when I'm going to come down and marry her. And then fuck her.

Honesty is my handicap. I tell her: never in a hundred years will I do either of those things.

Saw, saw, saw. Scrape, scrape, scrape.

My broken wrist has swelled up like a tiny fat person. I can't use my right hand. With my left hand I am tightening the ropes around myself, lashing myself to the mast as tightly as I can.

The pirates aren't laughing anymore. They're sharpening their pole-hooks and their harpoons, preparing for battle. The People's Captain barks orders from the bow, while the men hoist heavy iron cannons up onto the main deck. The shit-stained sails are spread tight under heavy wind. The mast groans and flexes as we rush across the slick water.

Scrape, scrape, scrape.

THE MOTION OF THE PEOPLE'S CAPTAIN

The wind is howling now. The snapping of the sails hurts my ears. Boiling black clouds are filling up the orange sky, and the shit-dark sea is lumpy and churning.

The People's Captain stalks the deck with a sword and a bottle of vodka, delivering an inspirational message to the People's Committee for Raping and Pillaging.

"Comrades," he says, "look at the sky! See how it quivers and sags! See how Heaven itself quakes at our approach!

"Comrades, the sea! How it trembles! How it roars! See how the Bloody Hatchet strikes fear into the waves themselves!

"Comrades, look around you, at our terror ship, at the cruel blades and the heavy cannon and the long, nasty harpoons. Look at the nun-meat piled high on the stern, at the blood boiling in pots by the cannon, at the stacks of nun-heads ready to be dipped in the boiling blood, loaded in the cannons and fired! Do we not strike a fearsome figure? Are we not pirates to the bone?

"Comrades! Today is the day I've promised you! Today we take the fight to the fat skies! Today we will storm the pearly gates! Today we will shit in the eyes of God, and feast upon the flesh of the infinite! We will plunder the vaults of Heaven! We will pillage the Garden of Eden! We will fart in the face of power, and piss in the mouth of destiny!

"Some may die. Nay, many may die. Nay, nay, all shall die, I promise it. Nay, even that is false. Know this, Scalawags of the People: we are all dead already! Every one of us is dead, for ours is a ghost ship, a ship that fishes drowned souls up out of the shit-dark sea, and grants them one last chance for glory!

"Today, the Bloody Hatchet sails home to oblivion! Oblivion and glory!"

"Comrades! I make a motion that we strike, that we fight, that we die! In the name of the People! For the glory of the People! For justice! For freedom! And for the love of bloody vengeance! Who among ye might second this motion?"

A hearty cheer rang out from the crew.

"Who among ye might place this motion on the agenda?"

Another cheer rang out.

"Who among ye might move this motion to the top of the agenda, given its priority?"

Another cheer.

"Who among ye might discuss this motion?"

Then began much shouting and confusion, as the People's Committee carried the Captain's motion through their arcane decision-making process. The motion was affirmed, recorded, amended, reaffirmed and re-recorded. Debate was extended, although there was no opposition. Fiscal impact and environmental impact were both assessed. Fingers were wiggled. It was very boring. And through it all, Mrs. Teeth scraped away at my pole from below. Scrape, scrape, scrape.

Then I noticed Aimless. He was standing waist-deep in the hatch in Martha Hilton-Trump's floating charred head, waving at me.

And I saw that the fat, toasted carcass of Martha Hilton-Trump rode very high in the water, much higher than before. And I thought I heard a rumbling, a mechanical hum, in the tone of her voice.

What is Aimless doing in there?

The ire of the fat people is rising. The clouds are blistering brown-black smoke dragons, pregnant with thunderbolts. Hot diarrhea starts to drizzle down on us. The pirates have finished their plebiscite, two hours after they begun, with much laughter and much shouting.

It is finally resolved: the pirates will fight the fat sky-bastards to the death.

Mrs. Teeth is making good progress, I think. As the rough sea tosses our boat, my pole flexes farther than ever, and I sometimes hear tiny splintering crackles in the wood.

Scrape, scrape, scrape.

Martha Hilton-Trump is making ominous noises: whirring, sucking, pinging, gurgling, ticking. Aimless is in there somewhere, busying himself with something insane. Occasionally he scurries out of Martha's head, runs down her back, peers at something in the water below her huge charred buttocks, then scurries back inside. But not before waving at me.

THE FINAL SHITSTORM

Now it begins. Shit-encrusted lambskin steering wheel covers flutter down from the sky and plop on the deck. Then come shit-covered iPhones. The men slash at the sky with their swords, deflecting the hail, laughing. They've seen worse.

Then, the My Little Ponies come tumbling down, covered in feces. They bounce and skitter across the deckboards. One smacks directly on my skull, kicking me with its little plastic hooves. I feel what might be a tiny trickle of blood behind my ear, or perhaps just diarrhea

Boardgames covered in shit. Air Jordans covered in shit. It keeps coming, but the men just laugh. Really it's not so bad. We've all seen worse.

I wonder, have the fat people grown weak? Have they not yet recovered all their power?

But then come the children's bicycles. Crashing down hard and shitty, exploding into whirling pink plastic and steel skeletons when they strike. One pirate is crushed by a direct hit. Another man's throat is impaled on a seat-post decorated with plastic horses. Shrapnel flies everywhere. The captain is felled by a ricocheting Spider-Man chain guard to the face, but he regains his footing. "Fight, scalawags!" he cries as blood streams from his eye, but the smarter pirates dive below deck and cower, while the pink and black metal hail smashes apart the railings and chops at the deck. Only myself, the Captain, and Mrs. Teeth remain topside. Oblivious to the danger, Mrs. Teeth is still sawing frantically with her little metal knife. I see the blood-blisters in her hand, and the madness in her eyes.

Then a sideways-gliding pink mini-bike shoots down from on high, coming straight at me, its handlebar streamers screaming! It strikes the mast hard, just below my foot. With a rough crunch of yielding wood, the mast tips sideways a dozen degrees, settling into a wounded stoop.

The People's Captain stands on the bow, surveying the carnage with his remaining eye, as death bombs down from the sky on little girls' pink bicycles. He sees the mast teetering, and then he spots, for the first time, what Mrs. Teeth is doing and has been doing all this time with her rotten little knife.

In a glance, he sees why she has spurned him. He understands the object of her obsession, and why she is so often by the mast and so rarely at his side. He sees what love has wrought.

With a great leap Captain Slasher-Jones crosses the deck and draws his scabbard. With a wrenching scream of misery, he decapitates the woman he loves. Mrs. Teeth's hideous head tumbles through the broken railing and plops into the shit-dark sea, her animal eyes leering at me all the while.

But her headless body clings to the crooked mast, and keeps on scraping away with its little metal saw.

Scrape, scrape, scrape.

Then the storm pauses. Up in the sky, directly above us, a bright orange light boils away a hole in the clouds, as a roaring, swirling wind yanks at the broken sails. The hole in the clouds opens wider, and through the telescope I see clearly the immense Prada shoes on the fat feet of, the vast Dolce & Gabbana sport-coat around the lunar girth of, the enormous Tommy Hilfiger necktie around the angry, flabby neck of, the titanic Gucci sunglasses on the scowling evil face of … the biggest, fattest, ugliest, meanest fat person I have ever seen in the whole of my filthy useless life. My life that is about to end.

I look to Martha Hilton-Trump, whose daddy is finally coming.

But now, with Aimless waving from the hatch in her head, Martha Hilton-Trump's body is slowly rising, fattening, re-inflating with gas, and now I see that mad Aimless has actually repaired something in her, because she rises above the waves, dripping with shit, and slowly hovers closer.

The Captain stares in shock at the oncoming family drama. Martha Hilton-Trump's charred body floats up beside me, and from the top of her head Aimless tosses to me the frayed end of his rope collection. I tug weakly on the line with my one good hand.

"Aimless!" I yell through the roaring wind. "What are you doing? You're going to get killed!"

"We're going traveling!" he yells. "Come with us! There's lots of room!"

"What about Gertie?" I ask. "Aren't you in love with a whale?"

For a little while, there's nothing but the whirling of the wind and the roar of fat engines.

"Gertie's a wonderful lady," he says. "But me and Martha have a really special thing going. I mean ... there's a kitchen in here!"

The mast teeters and creaks. Down below the Captain stares up in shock and horror, as the headless lady scrapes, scrapes, scrapes.

Love! You can't burn it, you can't eat it, you can't depend on it, or argue with it, or explain it. You can't even kill it! It just grabs you by the neck and marches you into the shit-dark sea.

I wouldn't take ten buckets of Love for one handful of my own shit.

"We gotta make time," shouts Aimless. "Just tie the rope around you and I'll haul you up. There's a sofa in here. And a mini-bar!"

"Go eat your fucking mini-bar!" I say. "*I'm* in love with Gertie! And *I'm* going to meet her!"

Admitting that miserable truth, I let go of Aimless's rope-collection. It twirls down to the deck below.

The horrible fat father looms over us like a toxic cloud, staring down, clenching and unclenching its fat fingers, its sunglassed face grimacing in horror. Its fat anguished voice thunderclaps in my ears:

MARTHA!

Aimless shrugs. Then he ducks back inside the head of his new girlfriend, and they rocket past Daddy into the sky.

But Captain Slasher-Jones will not be denied. He seizes the other end of Aimless's rope collection and expertly lashes it around the stout brass anchor cleat on the bow. When the slack runs out, the ship jerks violently and my broken mast tips sideways, dangling me over the edge of the ship.

Gazing down into the shit-dark sea, I search for my beloved.

With a mighty roar of Martha Hilton-Trump's engines, the Bloody Hatchet is dragged, creaking and swaying, up out of the ocean and into the sky! The pirates peer out from below deck in confusion, while the People's Captain laughs and laughs. The knots of Aimless's threadbare rope shudder as the they tighten, the fibers crackle and twist under the strain. The wind screams.

Now we rise up past the face of the fat father, its huge head twice as large as the ship. It removes its sunglasses. Where its eyes should be are two bloody, grinding metal mouths. Its third mouth gapes open, screaming with the horror of a father's love:

MARTHA!

Its seizes the ship in a stubby squeezing hand. Captain Slasher lassoes the huge fat fingers clawing at his deck. The loud ticking of three gigantic Rolex watches echoes from its wrist.

"Now, my comrades! Now!" screams the People's Captain, and the mad pirates of the Committee for Raping and Pillaging pour out from below deck and swarm over the monstrous hand, stabbing and slashing at it. They climb up its fat wrist, into the fat sleeve of its fat sport-coat, slashing and stabbing and setting fire to the fabric. Captain Slasher winds more thick ropes around the fat father's fingers and lashes them to the cleat. Two other pirates drive red-hot harpoons under its fingernails.

The powerful machinery of Martha Hilton-Trump's ascension roars still louder, straining still harder, and we rise still higher into the sky. The ratty, knotted tow-rope twitches and shudders. The fat father writhes and screams, helpless. It's so fat and round that its left arm can't reach its right to rescue it. The laughing horde of pirates surges forward up its arm, toward its fat neck and head. It flails blindly, swatting our boat against its great belly again and again, trying to flatten the crawling attackers. The hull fractures, the deckboards snap, the bow bends in upon itself, and my mast snaps cleanly free from the hull and tumbles to the broken deck, snagged in various ropes and turnbuckles. Through it all, Captain Slasher-Jones clings to the brass cleat, laughing and laughing as we rise higher and higher.

I look out over the wide horizon, shit-dark and pestilent in all directions, without a scrap of land, a scrap of anything clean or safe to cling to anywhere

Martha Hilton-Trump and her father tug against each other with all their power. From far on high, Aimless shouts my name.

CHEESEBURGER! CUT THE LINE!

Me? But I'm still strapped to this pole, unable to move, my broken hand throbbing as the mast spins around the deck, as the Bloody Hatchet whips through the sky, as the fat father howls in pain and panic, as the pirates crawl all over the fat father's face and through its hair, laughing, stabbing.

And now, the headless body of Mrs. Teeth is staggering blindly toward me, humping its way along the length of the mast, stabbing the air with its sharp little saw. Even headless she won't leave me alone!

Love!

I call to the Captain: "Cut the line!"

The one-eyed Captain sneers at me with wounded laughter. "Drown in shit, ye treacherous pond-scum!"

"Please, Captain! Cut the line! We're rising too high!"

The Captain shows me the middle finger on his free hand. "Rise high on this, ye filthy pigeon! Ye deck-crapping troglodyte!"

I recognize the sadness in his mad laughter. "What have ye got?" he cries, staring at me dumbfounded. "What speck of manhood? What did she find in ye so desirable, ye drifting dingleberry? I'm the People's Captain! And I loved her so!"

Then he releases the giant brass cleat, draws his bloody sword, and climbs toward me across the heaving deck with murder in his one good eye.

Love!

I AM ABOUT TO DIE

It seems certain that I am about to die in one of the following awful ways:

I may be raped and sawn apart by a headless madwoman.

I may be crushed to diarrhea between the rolling mast and the flying ship, or impaled on broken, twisted planks.

The People's Captain may slice me in two, in his jealousy.

The fat father may eat me, as my father was eaten before me.

I may asphyxiate in space, if we rise much higher.

I may fall down into the shit-dark sea and drown.

Or, most likely: all of these, in quick succession.

I've always expected to die, and I never held any hope that my death would be pleasant. Lately I have even longed to die, fantasized of escaping this cruel, tiring, pointless life.

But I would like to have a choice, just one choice, before I die. I would like to do one thing for any reason at all besides this awful habit of prolonging my life and this piercing hunger in my guts.

Nobody gets what they want, or what they deserve. Nobody gets anything anymore, except the fat people. For the rest of us this world is a hell of shit and pain; only the mad are suited to it.

But I demand to make a choice! I demand that one thing about this world be changed by my brief suffering. I can't die until I've left my mark! I don't care if it's selfish, but I just want to change the world in some tiny, lasting way. Any change at all would be an improvement.

The fat father writhes, and the ship heaves, and the mast skitters and rolls, and suddenly the Captain and Mrs. Teeth's body and the mast and I are piled up on the bow, on top of the big brass cleat. My arms are caught—the pain in my hand is agony! But from where I lie I can just about stretch out and lay the back of my neck across the rock-hard knot that holds Martha Hilton-Trump's tow line.

Captain Slasher-Jones is first to recover his balance and his blade.

"Kill me, Captain!" I scream! "Cut my miserable throat!"

Mrs. Teeth stumbles to her feet, gore oozing from the stump of her neck, waving her dirty saw.

"Take me, Mrs. Teeth!" I yell! "Saw off my head! And fuck me!"

I arch my head back, pressing my neck harder against the bitter end of Aimless's rope-collection. If just one of them will slice my head off, they might cut the knot as well, and set Aimless and his stupid girlfriend free.

But then, the headless body of Mrs. Teeth, instead of raping me, finds the Captain with its blind fingers. It molests him savagely, grasping at his genitals and slashing at his face.

And then Captain Slasher-Jones, instead of slicing my head off, cuts the line.

A whip-snap whistles away into the sky, and we are falling.

The fat father roars in pain. Pirates are cutting his face, cracking open his skull, crawling down his throat, and we are falling.

The Captain and Mrs. Teeth copulate on the deck of the ship while they slice one another apart, and we are falling.

The ship shatters, the mast cracks apart and I tumble away into space, falling.

The burnt-black body of Martha Hilton-Trump the Twelfth rockets away into the starry sky.

And I am falling, falling, falling, down into the shit-dark sea to drown.

I'm so happy! I'm so ready to die!

Gertie! Baby! Sweetie! I'm coming!

GREETINGS FROM THE BOTTOM OF THE SEA!

Gertie the Whale changed my life! I really mean that. I used to be bitter and depressed, but now I've found my reason to keep living! I know it sounds corny, but you know everything they say about true love? Well, it's true.

We live together at the bottom of the sea, down here in this wonderful bubble of life. Sure, it's kind of dark and damp, but we think it's the best place in the world. It's so beautiful and alive; it's full of great scenery and really excellent food. The water is delicious, clean and healthy, and it turns out that the fungus in my belly is able to breathe it. Imagine my surprise!

Now I'm in better shape than I've ever been. I've put on weight, my skin has cleared up, and I've gotten to be a pretty good swimmer. I hardly even cough anymore. All thanks to Gertie.

I know what you're thinking: sure, she's kind of fat. But she's special!

Sometimes we float for hours, singing and gazing into each other's eyes.

Every now and then, Aimless and Martha come down to visit us. But rarely; it's tricky sneaking past their in-laws. It's always great to see them though, even if Martha is kind of annoying sometimes.

The two of them used to travel around the solar system a lot, but now they've more or less settled down on a nice crater on the far side of the moon.

Aimless keeps busy. He's been fixing up Martha; he's organized and displayed his space-junk collection in her abdomen, and remodeled the kitchen and the wet-bar. He still plays a wicked guitar, too, and he's learning the drums.

Martha plays the Sousaphone, but she's not very good.

Aimless and Gertie never talk about that romance they used to have. But they're still very fond of one another. It's funny how things work out.

Life is good, great, grand; Gertie and I are really happy … except, if the truth be told, I really do miss my dear friend Aimless sometimes. I wish he could visit more often. I've tried to talk the two of them into moving down here, but Martha says she'd find it depressing, and I'm sure she's right.

It seems like forever ago, when Aimless and I used to dig for nautical supplies together in the mountains of trash on the crazy shitting planet's surface. I often ponder moving back up there with Gertie; she could meet my family, and maybe we could build an aquarium. But now's not the right time. The world, sad to say, is still fatally fucked and shat upon by mighty floating assholes. Except down here.

But sooner or later those fat people will choke on their own shit. We will wait them out.

That's my philosophy: things are so shitty, they can only get better!

CATERPILLAR GIRL

ATHENA VILLAVERDE

ONE

Something was wrong with Cat Filigree. Ever since her seventeenth birthday, her skin felt tight, like someone had dipped her in glue. It slowly hardened and peeled off. Her feet seemed too big for her body. Her vision was intermittently blurry and her sense of smell went haywire. Constantly feverish, she was burning up and freezing cold simultaneously. Her body itched. Her skin blistered and peeled off in layers. She was undergoing chrysalis.

Her mother, who had butterfly wings like stained glass windows, told Cat that soon it would pass. Soon, all the loose skin on her back would form into her own beautiful set of wings and she would discover what type of butterfly she would be. But for now, she was still Cat, the caterpillar girl. High school student. Outcast.

Cat's high school was filled with the typical assortment of insect kids. There were the praying mantises who met after school in the courtyard every day. A tough Christian youth group, dedicated hardcore to praying and saving the country. They loved getting into sparring matches to show off for the ladybug girls how tough and pious they were.

The ladybug girls were the rich preppy girls that liked only the trendiest clothes and popular music. They all had the same style of perfectly coifed hair, light red skin with just the faintest smattering of freckles. They always kept their nails perfectly manicured and their antennas bent at the cutest and most stylish angles.

Then there was Larry, the stoner slug. Every day, he sat like a Buddha under the Bodhi tree in one of the few patches of shade in the desert schoolyard sorting through his *Magic: The Gathering* cards and eating Cheetos through his dreadlocks. Sometimes Cat ate lunch with him.

Other days, Cat ate lunch with Paulette, the moth girl. Paulette had naturally white hair and her waifish body and big eyes made her look just like the cartoons she drew. Everyone knew that Paulette would grow up to be a famous cartoonist. She had an ongoing strip in the school newspaper about a colony of bees in outer space. She and Cat liked to talk about comic books.

But Cat's favorite person, her best friend, was Lilith, the spider girl. All the boys were in love with Lilith—the preps, the jocks, the nerds and even the gay boys.

Lilith had long, slender black-and-white striped legs, a perfect ass, a tiny waist and high round breasts. No matter what she wore, she'd look amazing, but she always had the coolest styles. She altered all of her clothes herself, accenting them with punk rock embroidery and safety pins or cinching the seams on the sides of her shirts so they were more form-fitting.

She was the only spider girl at their school. There was a stigma against female spiders because after they had sex they would usually eat their mates. Lilith definitely had been known to do that.

When boys disappeared, people didn't talk about it much but all the girls hated her for it. They thought she was a dirty whore. Bad news.

Even though the boys knew that Lilith was dangerous, they still managed to get involved with her. Some of them probably even liked her because she was dangerous. Lilith called herself a nymphomaniac. She couldn't help it, she said, she just liked sex.

Lilith especially liked sex with butterfly boys, with their slender bodies and large colorful wings. They were usually musicians and artists. They would sneak her backstage at punk shows and buy her beer even though she didn't have a fake ID. Sometimes she would let them paint her portrait naked or sing songs they composed for her. But it never lasted long. Lilith's appetites always assured it.

Cat spent most of her time reading comics and keeping to herself. Sometimes boys would act interested in Cat in order to get closer to Lilith. But Cat had never been physically attracted to any of them.

She had lots of male friends, but she didn't think of them sexually. They really always seemed interested in other girls anyway and only liked her because she could carry on conversations about video games, horror movies and comic books. She'd never dated anyone and thought that maybe she just wasn't meant to be with anyone that way.

TWO

Cat didn't know at first that she was in love Lilith, it just happened over time. She found herself always wanting to be around the spider girl. It got to the point where it was actually painful to be apart from her.

Cat felt that Lilith understood her. They could talk for hours and never run out of things to say. Usually, when Cat met someone new, the person would entertain her for a while but quickly became boring. Cat found it was more interesting to read about comic book characters. But Lilith was endlessly fascinating.

Cat tried to let Lilith know that she was attracted to her. She started dressing like Lilith and listening to the same music she liked. She dyed her hair green, so she would look less plain, and wore black and white striped stockings to cover up her pasty white caterpillar legs so that they would look like Lilith's naturally candy-striped legs.

Cat's mother didn't approve of her new look. She told her that she didn't want Cat hanging out with Lilith anymore. Her mom said that Lilith had a bad reputation and you had to watch who you hung out with or you risked damaging your own. But Cat didn't care what her mom thought. She continued to hang out with Lilith and then lied to her mother about where she was going.

However much she tried, Cat could never look like Lilith. Lilith had the body of a ballet dancer. She was muscular and limber with strong thighs and toned arms. She liked to go dancing and mountain climbing, neither of which Cat had ever been coordinated enough to do.

Cat was awkward and had two left feet. She could never maintain good posture, and she was always knocking things over and accidently spilling her drinks. Cat figured that Lilith would never be interested in her.

THREE

One day at school, the ladybugs were teasing Cat. They spit on her and called her trash. They were always picking on her thrift store outfits even though Cat prided herself on the creativity of the fashions she designed herself.

"What are you reading, geek?" they asked Cat.

The ladybug with the most freckles, Marsha, grabbed the comic book out of Cat's hands.

"Give that back," Cat said.

"You're reading comic books? What stupid baby trash. Are you a stupid baby?"

Lilith, who happened to be passing through the hall, looked over at Cat, as if noticing her for the first time. She saw what was going on, stepped over, and said to the ladybugs, "Leave her alone."

"Ooo, the whore likes you, little caterpillar girl," Marsha said to Cat.

Lilith grabbed Marsha's hand and yanked the comic book away from her and calmly handed it back to Cat.

"Ew, don't touch me you disgusting witch. Who knows what those hands have been doing." Marsha shook the hand that Lilith had touched as if it had something disgusting on it.

After that, Lilith told Cat she thought the ladybugs were stuck up bitches. All they cared about were appearances. They judged everyone on their looks, and anyone who didn't fit in was an outcast.

Cat showed her the comic book she was reading; it was *The Invisibles* by Grant Morrison.

"*The Invisibles* is my favorite comic!" said Lilith.

"Who's your favorite character?" asked Cat.

"Lord Fanny, the Brazilian transsexual shaman, of course. Who's yours?"

"Ragged Robin, the psychic time traveling witch," said Cat.

"We're going to be great friends," Lilith said. "Like the girls in that movie, *Heavenly Creatures*, who bond over both of them being deformed in some way."

Lilith looked down at Cat's peeling skin.

Cat suddenly became embarrassed. She wasn't sure what Lilith meant by it. Lilith didn't seem deformed to Cat in any way at all.

FOUR

Cat ditched P.E. class to smoke a cigarette behind the gymnasium. She liked to sneak away by herself. She was always worried about getting caught, but that just added to the excitement of doing it.

As she inhaled the smoke, she felt defiant and indulgent. She heard strange noises coming from underneath the bleachers on the soccer field and walked a little closer to see what was going on.

It was Lilith. She quickened her walk, heading toward her. Cat opened her mouth to call out when she realized that Lilith wasn't alone. She was underneath the bleachers with a blue butterfly boy.

Cat had seen him around school before but she didn't remember his name. He had a black pompadour hairstyle and wore a Sisters of Mercy t-shirt with black jeans and checkerboard creepers. His wings, which looked almost too large for his body, were pierced six times on each side. A black leather D-ring dog collar circled his thin neck.

Lilith wrapped her hands around his shoulders and jumped up onto him, her strong thighs gripping his torso. He stumbled back a little, before regaining his balance as Lilith crushed her berry-colored lips against his black lipstick mouth.

She thrust her hips against his while he gripped her ass. Then she forced him down to the ground, his blue wings spreading wide beneath them like a blanket.

She fumbled with the zipper to his jeans before yanking his pants down around his ankles.

Lifting her skirt, her legs intertwined with his as she straddled him. Her long black hair veiled his face like a spider web. She gripped the back of his throat and tugged on the clasp of the dog collar, tightening it.

His indigo eyelids fluttered, his long eyelashes tickling her cheek. She kissed him on his lipstick-smeared mouth and he let out a deep moan and slid his hands up her firm belly to stroke her breasts underneath her shirt.

Cat had never seen two people have sex before. It made her feel weird, but while watching the two of them she found herself wondering what it would feel like to kiss Lilith.

She inhaled smoke slowly from her cigarette and let it roll around on her tongue imagining it as a kiss.

The boy closed his eyes. Lilith pushed her stomach harder against him and extended a long pointed appendage from her abdomen. Without the boy being aware, she gently pierced him in the chest. A thick red liquid pumped through the sharp tip and under the boy's skin.

Cat stood there motionless. The ash on the end of her cigarette grew longer and then dropped off and landed on the top of her boot. She couldn't tear her eyes away from Lilith. It was the most intimate thing she'd ever witnessed. She wasn't grossed out or afraid, even though Lilith's body was covered in blood. Lilith wore a smile unlike any Cat had ever seen her make before. There was an ecstatic look in her eyes, her skin glistened.

The blue boy's chest heaved as he struggled to breathe. His chest pulsed from navel to neck. His massive wings withered.

His body started to shrivel, drying up as all of the liquids were sucked out of him. His life drained away, into Lilith's abdomen. His eyes bulged out of his head. A thin line of dust outlined where his wings had been, a small husk like an empty chrysalis where his body was, his clothes in a heap.

Later that afternoon in Biology class, Lilith walked in and took her usual seat next to Cat. Lilith was neatly dressed, her hair was pulled back and she looked completely back to normal except Cat noticed a glittering blue piece of butterfly wing stuck to the bottom of her chin.

It hung there for a few seconds before Lilith scratched her chin and it stuck to her finger. She discretely wiped her finger on the edge of the lab table and, when she noticed Cat watching her, she gave her a conspiratorial wink.

Cat felt embarrassed, as if maybe that wink meant that Lilith knew Cat had just seen her have sex behind the bleachers.

FIVE

Cat wanted to tell Lilith about her secret crush but was too shy to actually articulate how she felt. She was also terrified that if Lilith knew that Cat was attracted to her, she would stop being her friend. So Cat started a game. She passed Lilith a note in class that said, "We do not see things as they are, we see things as we are."

Lilith smiled at the note and said, "Anaïs Nin?"

Cat nodded her head.

"I like it," said Lilith.

"I've left you another note in the library."

"Where?" Lilith asked.

"That's for you to discover," said Cat hoping that Lilith would be able to figure it out. Cat thought the idea of Lilith reading erotica was romantic. She had always liked playing games like this. There was only one book in the library written by Anaïs Nin: *The Collected Works of Erotica*.

Lilith checked out the book and inside it found a note that said "Henry Miller had an affair with Anaïs Nin."

Lilith had never heard of Henry Miller so she looked him up and discovered he had several books in the library. She searched through each one and in a book titled *Tropic of Cancer* she found a note in Cat's handwriting that said "Tag! You're it."

Lilith took the cue and left a note of her own inside *Tropic of Cancer* for Cat to find. When the note was answered in return by a new note appearing in the Anaïs Nin book, the game had been established and the two girls exchanged quotes and messages in between classes this way on a daily basis from that point forward. Cat left Lilith notes inside *Tropic of Cancer* and Lilith left hers inside Anaïs Nin's book of erotica.

They always joked about how funny it would be if someone actually checked out one of those books and found their notes hidden inside.

SIX

"It's not that I don't feel bad about it," Lilith said when Cat asked her if she ever felt bad about eating the boys she had sex with, "It's just, I can't help it. It makes me feel so alive—I just lose myself in the moment, you know?"

Cat nodded her head, even though she didn't know. All she knew was that this made *her* feel alive, being with Lilith this way, weaving her long black hair into tiny braids, painting their toenails matching colors, staring up at the stars while lying in the grass next to Lilith. These were the things that made her feel alive.

SEVEN

Cat wanted to do something special for Lilith. Lilith's favorite band, Chainsaw Millipede, was coming to town. Lilith had been talking for weeks about how much she wanted to see the show but said there was no way she could afford it. Cat skipped buying lunches and babysat for her neighbor's bratty crickets so she could scrounge up enough money to buy tickets for the two of them to go to the show.

The night before the show, Cat was hanging out with Lilith in her backyard. They had made snapdragon cocktails with homemade sour orange liqueur from Lilith's mother's liquor cabinet. The air was warm and smelled like mesquite. They sat on the swings in Lilith's old swing set looking up at the stars.

"When's Chainsaw Millipede coming to town again?" Cat asked.

"Tomorrow night," Lilith said. "Why did you have to remind me? I am so bummed out that I can't go."

"What if you could go?"

"What do you mean? Do you know someone who could get us in?" Lilith's face lit up.

Cat held up the two tickets and Lilith screamed.

"Oh my god! How did you get these? These tickets cost like a fortune."

"I have my ways," Cat said, trying to sound cool.

"Ahh! Are you for real? This is so amazing. I have always wanted to see Chainsaw Millipede live and they hardly ever tour the U.S."

Cat was beaming. She and Lilith went out together all the time to the mall and the coffee shop. But this would be different. It would be the first time that Cat had ever been to a show. Before this, Lilith had always gone to clubs with butterfly boys.

The next night, Cat made up an elaborate excuse for her mom about why she needed to borrow the car and she picked Lilith up like they were going on a date.

Lilith opened the door to her house dressed in a black leather corset that made her already tiny waist look even tinier. She had her hair up in a messy bun and wore a black knee-length pencil skirt that hugged her hips, accessorized with black stiletto ballet slippers which pointed daintily at the ends on her black and white striped legs. Cat thought she looked like a sexy secretary.

Lilith eyed Cat's outfit—a tutu skirt, striped stockings and a baggy Bauhaus t-shirt—and said, "You're not going to the show looking like *that,* are you?"

Cat looked down at herself, suddenly self-conscious.

Lilith said, "Come in, I'll get you fixed up," and took her inside.

Cat had been in Lilith's bedroom many times. One time she had even spent the night and they stayed awake until morning watching Japanese anime and reading Francesca Lia Block books aloud to each other. But this time, when Lilith took Cat into her room, she felt different.

"Stand still," Lilith said, brushing out Cat's green hair with an oversized comb.

Lilith styled Cat's hair with gel and hairspray so that it stood up on her head like a hornet's nest. Then she stuck out two little black butterfly barrettes on either side of her temples. She drew spider webs around Cat's eyes with black mascara and painted her mouth with the same berry lipstick as her own.

The lipstick felt sensual, like a kiss, as Lilith slowly applied it to her top lip and then her bottom.

When Lilith was done with Cat's hair and makeup she opened a secret compartment at the bottom of her dresser, revealing a stash of clothes Cat had never seen before.

"This is my collection of corsets," Lilith said, as she pulled them out and arranged them on the bed. "I don't bring them out on just any occasion because they are very expensive and mean a lot to me, but tonight feels like a special night. And I just know that one of these is going to look great on you."

There were different shapes and colors. There were under-the-bust styles and over-the-bust styles, waist trimmers, and fancy brocaded corsets lined with silk and trimmed with lace.

Lilith picked up an oily black leather corset with steel boning and a silver zipper on the front.

"I think this is the one," she said to Cat, holding it out to her.

Cat took the corset from her. It was smooth and almost felt warm to the touch. It smelled like velvety mocha and peaty campfire. She wrapped it around her torso over her t-shirt and fumbled with the zipper, unable to connect it in the front.

"I don't think this will fit me," she said.

"Oh darling, don't worry. It *will* fit you. These things are designed to hold you in," Lilith said, waving her hand in the air, dismissing Cat's fears.

Lilith reached around behind Cat and started to loosen the laces on the back of the corset, adjusting it so that the bottom of the fabric rested against her hipbone. Lilith told her the corset was custom-made to fit her shape by a famous corsetiere in Paris who used only finest earwig leather and narwhale boning.

Cat tugged on the sides of the leather until she could finally connect the zipper in the front. But as soon as she started zipping it, the cotton fabric of her t-shirt got caught in the teeth of the zipper.

Lilith and Cat both struggled to free the excess fabric from the jammed zipper. Cat couldn't believe that she was fucking up this special corset and worried that she had broken the zipper.

Lilith just laughed it off and said, "I think this might work better without your t-shirt."

Cat was shy about her blotchy peeling skin. The reason she liked to ditch P.E. so often was really because she didn't want anyone to see her naked. She didn't want to take her shirt off. She thought Lilith would think she looked like a freak.

"I won't even look," Lilith said, reassuring her.

"But my skin is disgusting and peeling," Cat said, looking at Lilith's smooth delicately striped skin.

"Who cares about a little flakey skin?" said Lilith. "In the lighting at the club no one will even notice. Plus, you have a really cute figure and you should flaunt it."

Lilith handed Cat a hairspray bottle.

"What's this for?" Cat asked.

"Liquid encouragement," Lilith said.

"Huh?"

"It's liquor, silly. I stole it out of my mom's liquor cabinet and hid it in my hairspray bottle.

"Oh..." Cat said, bringing the spray bottle cautiously up to her mouth.

Cat spritzed a little of the liquid into her mouth. It tasted like air freshener. She winced and then coughed.

Lilith laughed at Cat.

"It works better if you just take the top off and drink from it."

After a couple of swigs off the hairspray bottle and some more compliments from Lilith, Cat turned around so that her back was facing Lilith and pulled off her t-shirt.

As Cat was unclasping her bra, she felt Lilith approach her from behind and reach around her, wrapping the corset around Cat's body. Cat could feel Lilith's warm breath on her neck as she slid the leather against her torso, almost embracing her but not actually touching her.

Then Lilith told Cat to hold her breath and lean forward as she clasped the zipper and slowly zipped the front of the corset. Cat's nipple hardened underneath the leather when Lilith's fingers just barely grazed her breast as she pulled the zipper up to the top. Lilith didn't seem to notice but Cat felt her skin prickle and it sent a chill up her spine.

"Brace yourself against the doorframe while I tighten the laces," Lilith told her.

Cat felt like they were playing dress up and she was the doll.

Once she was laced up, Cat looked at herself in the mirror. Her waist was cinched in the center, her stomach flat as a board, and her breasts looked firmer and more voluptuous. She thought that if she were taller and her legs a little thinner she actually would look a little like Lilith. The corset felt like a second skin. She imagined she was wearing Lilith's skin and it made her feel powerful, sexy. Cat didn't care anymore that her own skin was loose and peeling because she had this new skin holding her together, embracing her, protecting her.

EIGHT

At the show, Cat and Lilith made their way to the front of the stage. The club was packed with people and there was barely any room to move. But Lilith had an effortless way of making people get out of her way. It was in the way she carried herself; her posture and natural grace.

Cat liked the way the corset restricted her movements. She felt more elegant and self-possessed. It was as if by proxy some of the spider girl's grace had rubbed off on her. She felt more confident and less shy. But she had to take shallow breaths because the corset was laced so tight, which in addition to the alcohol made her lightheaded.

The lead singer of Chainsaw Millipede was a dragonfly boy wearing metal-studded leather jeans, no shirt, and steel-toed combat boots. He was a few years older than Lilith and Cat, about the same age as the guys that Lilith usually went out with.

He head-banged his black liberty spikes along with his bass guitar rhythm. Upon his tattered purple-tipped dragonfly wings were sewn a patchwork of punk band logos, political statements, sigils and movie references. He had a neon pink patch on his right wing that said "kill yourself" and an Abbie Hoffman quote about revolution on the other wing.

His eyes were dark and sensitive. The way he held a focused yet ambivalent gaze made it appear like he was staring straight into the eyes of every single person in the room simultaneously. His hands and arms were veined and knotted; the muscles on his chest were tight with energy and it looked like he was carving sound out of the air with his chainsaw guitar and throwing light into the audience as he bounced to the music and sang into the microphone.

Cat loved the way the music made her feel and even more than the music she loved watching Lilith dance.

The music moved through Lilith's long body as she wove patterns on the floor with her hands and feet. She craned her neck and stared up at the singer, her eyes caressing his hairless chest.

"I think patch-wing boys are the hottest," Lilith whisper-screamed into Cat's ear.

Cat nodded and Lilith stared back up at the singer. Lilith bounced around like she was catching his sound with her arms and swallowing it with her ears.

When Chainsaw Millipede played their most popular song, the crowd went wild. People were screaming out the lyrics along with them and skanking in the circle pit.

Cat had never been in a circle pit. But before she knew it, she found herself caught up in the one that spontaneously formed in front of the stage. People slammed her from every direction. They elbowed her in the chest and smashed her toes until they were bleeding in her boots.

She couldn't control her direction and spent most of her energy just trying not to get knocked down. A few times she lost her balance and thought she was going to fall over, but the people on the edge of the pit buoyed her up before she hit the ground.

Lilith slam-danced in the center of the pit, turning in circles as if she were controlling the crowd around her. She spun on one leg and then the other like a spider in the center of a web. Then she locked eyes with Cat and pointed one finger at her beckoning her to come into the center of the circle with her. Lilith wore a huge grin on her face and even though Cat was scared of the pit, Lilith's smile encouraged her to jump through, get knocked down and around until she reached the center.

In the middle of the swirling group of dancers, Cat found the calm at the center of the storm. The spider girl grabbed onto her and held her tightly. Their shiny leather corsets rubbed together, making their torsos stick and Cat felt for a moment like she was a part of Lilith, moving as she moved, effortlessly.

Cat's body tingled. She could feel heat rising in her face and thought her skin was going to flare up again. Her heart pounded like the bass in the speakers.

Lilith's face looked like an H.R. Giger painting in the greenish glow of the club. Dancing in the center of the circle as the crowd bounced in frantic chaos around them, the caterpillar girl never felt more alive. Cat knew in that moment that she wanted to be with Lilith forever. She never wanted to be apart from her. She felt safe and powerful when she was with Lilith.

As the song ended, they spun around, facing each other. Their hips pressed gently against one another. They locked eyes. Cat wanted to kiss Lilith. Confidence rose within her and she felt capable of anything.

She leaned in toward Lilith's face, eyes lowering toward the spider girl's ripe blackberry lips. Tilting her head, she puckered her mouth.

But just as she was about to connect, Lilith turned her head and Cat's kiss landed awkwardly on Lilith's cheek. Lilith was looking over her shoulder at a red-winged butterfly boy who put his hand on her back.

"Kas, how are you!" Lilith said, turning around and hugging the butterfly boy.

Cat didn't know what to do. Did Lilith think it was weird that she had kissed her? Did she even notice?

Cat stood there for a few seconds waiting to see if Lilith would acknowledge her, or say anything, or even look at her. But Lilith was turned the other way, flirting with Kas. She touched him on the shoulder, staring into his eyes and laughing at the inaudible phrases he shouted over the noise of the crowd.

Then the band started their next song and the crowd began slamming again.

Before she could say anything to Lilith, Cat got knocked to the ground by an ant boy's knee and a beefy cockroach dude stepped on her fingers, crushing them under his thick-soled boot, causing crippling pain to shoot up Cat's arm. She screamed out, but the guy didn't even notice her and no one else paid any attention to her either.

Lilith had completely forgotten about her and was dancing with the butterfly boy. His red wings fluttered in a swirling motion around him. His hands caressed the curve of Lilith's hips.

Cat scrambled to her feet and stuck her crushed fingers into her mouth to soothe herself and then forced her way through the crowd all the way out to the lobby where the bathrooms were located.

A long line queued in front of the women's room, and Cat couldn't handle the thought of waiting in it. She noticed a couple of impatient girls walking shamelessly into the men's room, where there was no line. Cat thought about following them but was too shy.

She wanted to escape, to be somewhere she could be alone. The night was ruined. She couldn't believe that she had embarrassed herself like that.

After getting all the way through the line to the bathroom, the show was almost over and Cat couldn't stand the idea of going back into the room to watch Lilith dance with the butterfly boy. She felt stupid for daring to think she could kiss Lilith. She wanted to rewind time and erase the awkward moment between them. Instead, she went outside and waited through the rest of the show in her mom's car.

Lilith came out of the club clutching Kas's shoulder and giggling. Cat was leaning against her car, smoking a cigarette. Lilith walked straight over to Cat and gave her a hug. Cat was relieved to see her and to feel her in her arms. As she hugged her she thought maybe things weren't going to be any different between them after all, maybe Lilith thought it was completely normal for Cat to kiss her on the cheek while they were dancing. But then she heard Lilith whisper in her ear.

"Thanks for waiting, but I won't be needing a ride home. Kas is going to take me for a ride on his motorcycle."

Cat felt rejected. She had spent all her money on these tickets, her toes were bleeding, and she had just spent the last hour waiting at the car for Lilith, who was now running off with this guy she just met.

"Are you sure?" asked Cat.

"Don't worry about me," Lilith answered and winked at her.

Kas grabbed Lilith by the waist and pulled her away toward his motorcycle. Cat felt like her heart had been stomped on.

NINE

Over the weekend, Cat spent most of her time obsessing about what had happened. She was worried that the next time she saw Lilith, things were going to be weird and she didn't want anything to mess up their friendship. But she also couldn't control the feelings she had every time she was around Lilith.

She still had Lilith's corset.

She closed her eyes and rubbed her hands along the smooth leather, imagining it was Lilith's skin. She caressed the leather with one hand and reached down between her legs with her other, rubbing the knuckle of her thumb against her clit through her wet panties.

Imagining the shape of Lilith's body, she ran her fingertips along the boning of the leather corset. Her flesh turned hot and cold and the skin on her back shifted and changed shape.

She looked in the mirror at her naked body and saw her back was covered in red welts where her skin had stretched. Wings started to form. The loose skin on her back became thicker and molded into two bulges just beneath her skin that were tender and hurt when she poked them.

TEN

Lilith came to school wearing a dress made from red butterfly wings. It looked like couture fashion that should be on a runway in Paris. A lot of people complimented her on it, telling her the wings looked so realistic. The girls all gossiped about how they thought that she'd probably made her skirt out of real butterfly wings. Most of them didn't really believe it was true, but the anti-arachnid kids thought it was disgusting. They called it inhumane and told her she should be ashamed of herself.

Cat could tell that Lilith didn't care what anyone thought. It was obvious the spider girl knew she looked hot in the outfit she'd created and there wasn't anything anyone could say about it that would change her mind. Cat loved that about her.

"I wanted to apologize for the awkwardness on Friday night," Cat said when she saw her in Biology class. "I just wanted you to know that I..."

"No, no don't even worry about it," Lilith said. "I should have made it clear earlier in the night that if I met anyone I probably wouldn't need a ride home."

Cat could tell that Lilith didn't know what she meant. Cat wasn't talking about the ride situation—she was worried about the kiss.

"Kas was incredible by the way," said Lilith. "He tasted like raspberries ... Oh and his bike was awesome. He drove me out to this bonfire party in the middle of the desert where there were dozens of hot butterfly boys. We danced and drank tequila and talked all night long." She licked her lips. "It was one of the best nights of my life."

Cat decided to change the topic.

"What did you get for the answer to number seven on the math homework?" Cat asked.

"Math homework? Oh shit! I completely forgot about it. You don't mind if I copy yours, do you?"

Cat sighed and handed over her completed homework.

ELEVEN

Cat wore Lilith's corset to school every day underneath her clothes. She looked at herself in the mirror as she was getting ready and knew that no one would be able to tell. She liked having this secret. Her posture was straighter because she found that it was impossible to slouch in a corset and she noticed that boys kept staring at her breasts.

Lilith sat up on a tree branch in their usual lunch spot. Her stuff was scattered across the ground under the tree and Cat noticed a scrap of green butterfly wing stuck to the inside of Lilith's purse like a used tissue. She was talking to Paulette who was eating a sausage sandwich. When Cat came over, Paulette offered her half of her sandwich, even though she should have known that Cat didn't eat stuff like that.

"I don't eat sausage, remember?"

"Oh that's right, you're a vegan," said Paulette.

"Not a vegan, I just don't eat cooked food."

Cat only ate raw fruits and vegetables because she thought it was gross to eat anything that wasn't alive.

"You look like you've lost weight," Lilith said to Cat. "That diet must be working for you."

Cat felt her face turn red. She shrugged.

Lilith jumped down off the tree and came over to Cat.

"No seriously," Lilith said, "you look great. What's your secret?"

Cat looked down at her feet. "Nothing."

"And your waist has gotten so tiny," Lilith said, reaching out and squeezing the side of Cat's stomach.

Lilith's eyes widened when she felt the corset. Then a big smile broke out on her face.

Cat was mortified. She knew that Lilith felt the stiffness of her corset through her t-shirt. She was afraid that Lilith was going to laugh at her and tell everyone that she was wearing a corset.

But instead, Lilith patted her stomach and whispered in her ear, "I sometimes like to wear that one, so I'm going to need that back from you."

Cat was embarrassed. She knew that she was going to have to give the corset back to Lilith. She hadn't intended on keeping it so long, but she'd not mentioned it because subconsciously she didn't want to give it back to her.

"Yes, of course," said Cat.

Lilith smiled at her and said, "You have been looking good lately. Your skin really looks like it's clearing up."

Cat couldn't decide if that was a compliment or not. She worried that Lilith thought she was a freak and was just trying not to embarrass her out of politeness.

TWELVE

Cat woke up the next day with her head between her legs. Muscles tight. Sore back. Cramps in her abdomen like knife blades stabbing her from inside. Charlie horses seized the muscles in both her legs. She couldn't see. A foggy haze blocked her vision.

She reached her hands to her face and the lumps on her back cracked open oozing oily liquid. The skin on her neck loosened as she stretched forward. Her spine cracked like a xylophone, the haze cleared from her eyes and wings unfolded from around her body.

She stretched out her new muscles. They were strong and full of energy. She circled her neck and lengthened her spine. Wiggling her antennae, she reached back with her fingertips and touched the wings. Oily residue from the metamorphosis coated her nails as she scratched the bits of dead skin off the slick surface of each side.

Like a blooming flower, she widened her wings, stretching them out as far as they would go. Tall and shimmering, they doubled her size. Turquoise blue and translucent as the Mediterranean Sea. Delicate veins laced each wing in thin black spiral patterns and small yellow dots the shape of miniature skulls decorated her shoulders.

She looked down at her new shape and admired her upward-turned breasts, her shapely hips, her long lean limbs. She stood in front of the full-length mirror on her bedroom wall and spun around, bending over to inspect herself from every angle.

She felt beautiful. Her heart was on fire. This was what she had been waiting for. No more peeling skin, no more strange lumps and thick doughy legs. She was finally a butterfly.

THIRTEEN

Freddy Centipede was throwing a party that night and everyone at school was invited. He was one of the richest and most popular boys at school. His parents had a giant mansion on the side of a cliff overlooking the valley. Cat normally didn't like Freddie's parties but Lilith had been trying to convince her to go for weeks. When she imagined the look on Lilith's face watching her arrive for the first time in butterfly form, Cat decided to go.

She spent all day getting ready, doing her hair in different styles, deciding what to wear. After discarding about two dozen outfits she decided to go with a black minidress that Lilith had picked out for her that she had never worn because she thought it was too revealing. Her new wings protruded from the back of the strapless dress like blue dragon flowers. She added red plaid thigh-high stockings with vintage button garters. Then strapped herself into 32-buckle platform boots that came up to her knees. She affixed a pair of vintage goggles to her head in front of her antennas to complete the look.

Everyone was at the party. All the popular kids, unpopular kids, geeks, freaks and jocks. People kept staring at Cat. She could tell they were shocked by her appearance. It always fascinated people to discover what type of butterflies the caterpillars became.

This time, Cat didn't mind that they were looking at her. She had always been the weird outcast geek that no one really paid any attention to. Now, everyone gawked at her like she was some kind of celebrity. She felt ready to show everyone, especially Lilith, what she always knew she was like on the inside. But where was Lilith?

Cat searched for the spider girl but it didn't seem like she was at the party yet. So she wandered around enjoying the way her body moved. She felt taller, more graceful. She heard people whispering her name under their breath, but could tell by their smiles that they were only admiring her.

A swimming pool took up a big portion of the backyard with a fire pit on one end of it. Large flower-shaped sculptures lined the patio that looked out onto the lights of the city below.

Cat imagined what it would be like to fly over the city with her new pair of wings. But the most she was able to do was hover.

She found some of her friends in the kitchen drinking cans of PBR and passing a bong.

"Oh my god," Paulette squealed when she saw Cat. "You've turned! Let me see, let me see." Paulette jumped in circles around Cat. She tugged on the end of one of Cat's wings pulling it out from her body so she could inspect the pattern.

Cat stretched her wings out so that Paulette could get a better look at her. A crowd circled around Cat.

"You look absolutely beautiful," Paulette said. The moth girl reached out a finger and touched the yellow skull-freckles on Cat's shoulder. Her touch made the skin on her wings vibrate and ripple. "And I *love* your outfit."

"You look hot," said Larry, exhaling a cloud of smoke under his heavily lidded dome-shaped slug eyes.

"Thanks you guys," said Cat, feeling really good about herself for the first time in a long time.

One of the popular jock beetles from her algebra class waved from across the room. And the butterfly boy from A.P. English said, "Hey Cat," even though he hadn't spoken to her all year outside of the one time he asked to borrow her flash drive. Cat wondered if Lilith thought he was attractive.

Then she saw Lilith walk through the front door. Cat almost didn't recognize her. Lilith's hair was pulled back into an elaborate up-do like a samurai warrior princess. Her face was painted white with black symbols drawn on her eyelids.

A purple-winged butterfly boy ran over to Lilith and circled his arm around her corseted waist. The corset had a red hourglass emblem painted on the front of it like the abdomen of a black widow.

Cat couldn't wait to see Lilith's reaction to her butterfly wings. She waited for Lilith to look across the room and notice her, but instead, Lilith followed the butterfly boy in the other direction.

Cat went after them but was blocked by the crowd and lost sight of where they went. Freddy's mansion was huge.

"Have you seen Lilith?" Cat asked everyone she passed. They were all either too drunk to understand her or would say, "Yes, she was just here," and then look around blankly.

She searched behind closed doors and behind one of them she accidentally found two cicada boys having sex. The high-pitched sound of their voices was deafening and it looked like one of them was shedding his skin. Cat closed the door quickly and decided to only check the common areas.

Finally, she gave up and returned to the kitchen, where Paulette and Larry were still passing a bong, and Lilith walked in behind her.

"I've been looking all over for you!" Cat said to Lilith.

"I didn't know you were coming," Lilith said.

Cat stood in front of Lilith, expecting her to make some type of comment about her butterfly wings but she didn't. Instead she just went on like normal, talking about some guy.

After pretending to listen for a few minutes, Cat said, "Great outfit."

"Yours too," Lilith replied.

"I like your shoes," Cat said, looking down at Lilith's Fluevog heels.

"Thanks," said Lilith.

Cat waited for something more. But instead of commenting on her metamorphosis, Lilith said, "Where's the booze?" and bent down to open an ice chest by the refrigerator.

Lilith grabbed a can of PBR and walked outside. Cat followed her. The swimming pool had a glass edge alongside the cliff and looked like it was a part of the horizon. Some mosquito boys were skimming the surface of the water with hockey sticks, whacking a beach ball. Two spotlights at the bottom of the pool illuminated the water, making the mosquitos' wings shimmer.

Ladybug girls in bikinis lay out on the lounge chairs even though it was nighttime. A group of boys stood off to the side, watching the girls. The ladybugs pretended to ignore the boys.

Marsha's hair spiraled up in a beehive do that looked like something out of a 1950's Hollywood film. She wore oversized white sunglasses and a bikini that highlighted her petite ladybug curves.

As Cat walked by, the ogling boys turned their eyes on her. It felt weird to have people noticing her. Lilith was usually the one everyone was looking at.

Lilith seemed preoccupied with other things. She scanned the patio, watching the partiers. Cat started to wonder what might be wrong with her. She thought Lilith would have said more about her wings. Maybe Lilith didn't like the way that she turned out.

"I was thinking about getting my wings pierced," Cat said, trying to draw Lilith's attention to them.

"I've always thought about getting something pierced," said Lilith wistfully.

"What would you get?"

"I don't know, I was thinking maybe my lip or my eyebrows. But it might be fun to get my nipples pierced."

Cat pictured in her mind what Lilith's nipples would look like pierced. It turned her on.

"Yeah, that would be hot," she said, biting her lower lip.

Lilith smiled and put her hands on her hips.

Cat studied her mouth and her eyebrows. She imagined sucking on Lilith's pierced lips and pulling on her eyebrows. She felt herself start to blush.

"Who was that guy you were with earlier?" Cat asked.

"Oh, Tyler?"

"That was Tyler?" Cat asked. "Caterpillar Tyler?"

"He just turned. Doesn't he look incredible? His wings are like rose petals."

Cat's stomach sank. Lilith must only be attracted to butterfly boys. She'd not even mentioned Cat's wings. Cat stretched out her wings and leaned forward pretending to adjust the buckle on her boot, hoping to capture Lilith's attention.

Lilith crushed her beer can and said, "I'm gonna get another drink, do you want one?"

Cat looked up at her.

"No," she said, coldly.

Lilith shrugged and walked back toward the kitchen. Cat watched her through the window. She laughed and drank and flirted with the butterfly boys. One of them came over to her and she grabbed the loose flesh on his elbow, yanking him toward her and pressing her mouth to his throat. Cat couldn't watch anymore. She wanted nothing more than to be with Lilith. She had waited all of this time in the hope that once she became a butterfly Lilith would want her, but now she could see she was wrong.

FOURTEEN

When Lilith came back out she found Cat on a bench by the swimming pool, away from the rest of the party. Cat had tears in her eyes. She wiped them away as Lilith approached.

"What's going on with you tonight?" Lilith asked. "Why have you been avoiding me?"

"Me avoiding *you*?" Cat said. "You are the one that's been avoiding *me*."

Cat tried to act normal like nothing was bothering her, but her eyes welled up again when she looked at Lilith.

"Shh, it's okay." Lilith came over to her and put her arm around Cat's shoulders. "Tell me what's wrong."

Lilith's embrace was painful for Cat. The feeling of the spider girl's arm around her made Cat imagine what she could never have.

"I can't," said Cat.

"Does it have to do with your transformation?" Lilith asked.

Cat looked at her. It was the first time that Lilith had even acknowledged her transformation.

"It has everything to do with that," Cat whispered.

"What do you mean?"

"I thought you would notice me," Cat said. "I thought once I became a butterfly you would think I was beautiful."

Lilith looked deeply into her eyes. "I have always thought you were beautiful, Cat. Once you changed, I just saw more of who I already knew you were."

Cat started to tear up again, but this time it was from happiness.

"Remember the corset that I lent you?" Lilith asked.

"Yes," Cat said sheepishly.

"After I found out that you were wearing it under your clothes, I kept imagining you that way. I liked that you enjoyed wearing it. I thought it was totally sexy."

"Oh my god, I was so embarrassed about that!" Cat said.

"And you look great tonight," Lilith said. "I'm so happy to see you finally feeling good about yourself. Why do you care what I think anyway? You know you look hot. I've seen the way people are looking at you."

Cat felt different knowing that Lilith thought she was hot.

"I thought that things would be different." Cat paused and looked down at her hands. She lowered her voice and in barely a whisper she said, "I thought things would be different between *us*."

Lilith didn't respond. Cat started to sweat. She knew that if she didn't tell Lilith how she felt about her she would burst.

"It's hard for me to talk about it because we are such good friends," Cat said. "And the last thing that I would want to do is mess up our friendship. In fact, I have been terrified to tell you this because I am afraid of what you will think of me. I don't want to lose you as a friend."

Cat didn't want to look at Lilith's face. She was afraid of seeing her expression. She was afraid of being rejected.

"Lilith, I'm in love with you."

Lilith was silent for what seemed like a long time. Cat felt all the air go out of her chest. Then Lilith touched Cat's chin with her palm and turned her face toward her, forcing Cat to look her in the eyes.

"I love you, too," Lilith said in a sweet voice like the one she would use to speak to a child or a puppy-fly.

Cat felt her heart sink. She had to make it clear to Lilith what she meant.

"I don't just mean that I love you, I mean that I am attracted to you."

Lilith's expression didn't change.

"Please don't hate me," Cat said.

"I don't hate you." Lilith took her arm off of Cat's shoulder and took her by the hands. "I'm attracted to you, too."

"Wait, what?" Cat said. "Are you just saying that?"

Lilith smiled. "I've always been into you. Even before we met, I used to check you out every time that we ran into each other at lunch."

Cat couldn't believe what she was hearing.

"You used to check me out?" Cat said, arching her eyebrows in surprise.

Lilith laughed. "Yeah, is that so hard to believe?"

"But I thought you were just interested in boys."

"I am interested in boys. But with them, it's just sex. With you it's different. It goes deeper than that. You are my best friend. And you are the cutest chick I know. Just look at you." Lilith stroked her finger along Cat's wing.

Cat shivered.

"I love these skull-freckles," said Lilith.

"Why didn't you ever let on that you were interested in me?" Cat asked.

"You know why ... It's awkward. I thought that you would be afraid that I would eat you."

Lilith's eyes consumed Cat. She was sucked into them like two vortexes and for the first time she saw what she'd been longing to see. Lilith was telling her the truth. She was attracted to Cat. Her stomach knotted up. Her breath caught in her throat.

Lilith leaned in toward Cat and put her hand on her cheek. She brushed a lock of hair out of her eyes and pulled Cat's face toward hers.

The kiss was a magical crazy starlight popcorn-filled explosion. Cat's tongue was sucked into the spider girl's mouth, sharp fangs caressed its curve. Every muscle in her body relaxed. She felt like she was floating. She couldn't believe it had finally happened. She closed her eyes.

A cricket boy stumbled into them, splashing beer on the toes of Lilith's shoes.

"Hey, watch it," Lilith said to him.

"Whoa, were you two just making out?" the boy said, stumbling sideways.

"It's none of your business," Lilith said, turning her body to face him.

"Hey, it's cool. I'm totally into it. If you want, I'd be happy to join in."

"Fuck off, asshole," said Lilith

"Lesbian bitch," the cricket boy said, and stumbled drunkenly around the pool.

"Can we go someplace more private?" Cat said, suddenly aware of where she was and who might be watching.

"Jerk," Lilith said, turning back to Cat.

"I noticed the back gate was unlocked," Cat said, pointing behind them to fence at the end of the patio covered in darkness.

FIFTEEN

The two girls sneaked into the desert behind the fence at the cliff's edge, holding hands and helping each other over the rocks. They brought a blanket and two bottles of strawberry wine cooler. Laughter, music, and all the sounds of the party still raged in the background.

Lilith spread the blanket on a soft sandy spot between two mesquite trees. She and Cat took off their shoes and stretched out on their stomachs. A tingle of expectation buzzed between them. Cat knew where she wanted things to go, but she didn't know if it would actually happen.

Cat fluttered her wings and rose a few feet into the air. Lilith flipped over onto her back and looked up at Cat. The butterfly girl dangled her plaid toes above Lilith and they both started to laugh. Lilith hugged Cat around the legs and pulled her down to the ground again.

"Don't fly away from me," said Lilith.

Cat melted into Lilith's arms. The spider girl held her close and kissed her neck. Snuggling her head against Cat's chest, she closed her eyes.

Cat kissed the black symbols drawn on Lilith's eyelids, marking them with lipstick rings like a bull's-eye. She caressed Lilith's muscular arms, feeling shy about touching her body anywhere else.

Lilith stroked Cat's green hair, winding her fingers through it, tugging slightly. She licked the skulls on Cat's shoulder and ran her sharp teeth along the edge of her ear.

"You taste like Halloween candy," she whispered, her hot breath raising the hair on Cat's arms.

Cat flickered with anticipation. She felt wetness spread between her thighs. Without speaking, Lilith slowly unzipped her corset in front of Cat. The spider girl's dark nipples hardened in the cool night air. They looked like they were stained with blood. She removed Cat's dress, unbuttoned her garters and peeled her stockings off one at a time, kissing Cat's legs, and tickling the back of her knees. After shedding the rest of their clothes, they lay naked together under the stars.

Lilith took Cat's hand and brought it to her breast, tracing her nipples with Cat's fingers. Cat climbed on top of the spider girl, straddling her, and pressed down on her shoulders with the palms of her hands. She spread her wings, creating a canopy above them. Lilith stared up with eyes like burning stars. Even though Cat had Lilith pinned to the blanket, the butterfly girl felt that the spider could eat her at any moment.

She waited for Lilith to respond, to throw her off or pull her close but the spider girl just lay there staring up at her.

"What's wrong?" Cat asked, feeling self-conscious.

"Nothing," said Lilith, nuzzling her head against Cat's arm.

"Why aren't you getting into it?" Cat asked.

"I am into it," Lilith said, stroking her forehead.

"But not like with the boys."

"Boys are different." Lilith smiled and took a sip of her wine cooler. "What do you want me to do?"

"I want you to *want* me."

"I *do* want you," said Lilith. "I want you so much. But I have to hold myself back. I don't want to get carried away and go too far."

"I'm not worried about that," Cat said. "I want you to make love to me with all of your passion."

Lilith gazed deep into Cat's eyes and stroked her hair. The butterfly girl's eyes were pleading.

Lilith reached up and kissed her deeply. Her mouth tasted like strawberries and alcohol. In the middle of the kiss, she grabbed Cat's hair and flipped over on top of her. She paused and took another sip of her wine cooler. She didn't swallow it. She brought her lips to Cat's and let the liquid slide from her tongue down the butterfly girl's throat.

Lilith slowly lowered herself down the length of Cat's body, kissing her neck and shoulders. She reached her nipples and took another sip of her wine cooler. She placed her lips over Cat's nipple and sucked. The liquid swirled around Cat's areola. Cold. Stimulating.

The strawberry liquid slid between Cat's breasts and pooled in her belly button. Lilith lapped the liquid from Cat's center, slurping it up through her conical-shaped tongue. Then she lowered her head between Cat's legs.

"I want to taste you," said Lilith, licking her lips.

Thighs wet with butterfly nectar, strawberry wine cooler, and spit. Lilith drew spirals across Cat's clitoris with her tongue, sending waves of heat through her body.

Cat stretched her arms out above her head and elongated her spine. Spreading her legs wider, she invited Lilith's tongue between the folds of her vulva. She ground her hips against Lilith's face, pushing her deeper with her hands.

Lilith came up for air and smiled at her hungrily, baring her fangs and licking her chin. The look in her eyes was suddenly wild, ferocious.

When Cat saw that hungry look in Lilith's eyes, the muscles inside her pelvis tightened. Her skin tingled. It was the same look Lilith had the time she ate the butterfly boy under the bleachers.

"Why are you looking at me like that?" Cat asked, the spider girl's face between her quivering thighs.

Lilith stared deeply into Cat. Her eyes were on fire. Cat could see the lust burning behind them.

"Are you going to eat me?" Cat asked in a shaky tone.

Lilith realized what she was doing and shook her head, trying to shake the hunger away.

"I'm sorry," said the spider girl. "I didn't mean to get carried away."

"It's okay," Cat said.

"I would never do that with you."

Cat broke eye contact. Suddenly, she felt rejected. Her eyes began to water. Then she said, "Why not?"

Lilith giggled. "What do you mean *why not?*"

"I thought you loved me," Cat said.

"I *do* love you," Lilith said.

"Then why won't you eat me?"

Lilith stared back at her in disbelief.

"What are you talking about, Cat? You're my best friend."

"You ate all of those butterfly boys. I want you to love me like you loved them." Cat wiped tears from her cheeks. "I want you to eat me."

"No way," Lilith said.

"But you have to!"

"You mean too much to me."

Then something snapped inside of Cat's butterfly brain. She lunged forward.

"Eat me," Cat screamed, forcing herself against Lilith, probing at her belly searching for the extra appendage that would inject the poison. "I *need* you to do it."

Lilith's appendage started to emerge. She couldn't help herself from getting turned on. She had never been with anyone so insistent.

"Don't," Lilith whispered.

"Put it inside me," Cat said, pulling on the stinger.

Cat slid her clitoris up against Lilith's stinger. She felt a drop of poison slip out the tip and numb the skin around her vulva.

Then Cat reached down and guided the stinger inside her vagina. It felt hard and sharp.

"Okay, just for a minute," Lilith gasped as the stinger slipped inside. "Then I'll pull out."

She thrust herself against the butterfly girl.

Lilith and Cat fucked under the stars. They screamed like cicadas and slammed their bodies against one another.

As Lilith was about to pull out, Cat locked her legs around Lilith's thighs. She held her inside.

"Do it," Cat said as she pictured being stabbed in the abdomen. Cat wanted to orgasm but she stopped herself, holding out for the actual moment. She opened her eyes and looked at Lilith.

"Let me out," Lilith screamed.

"Suck me dry," Cat said.

"No," Lilith struggled to free herself, but Cat's thighs had grown strong and held firm. She pushed Cat, trying to get away but it just made Cat more excited. Lilith started to cry.

"I don't want to kill you," Lilith sobbed. "I love you too much."

She could no longer contain herself and exploded in poisonous orgasm. Cat felt Lilith's essence spread through her. Every muscle in her body convulsed. Her breath quickened. Her wings felt stiff.

With fading strength, she pushed Lilith's body back down to her crotch and shoved herself against the spider girl's mouth. Lilith, lost in her own orgasm, could no longer resist.

Cat looked down as Lilith lapped the red fluid oozing out of her vagina. She couldn't tell if it was her blood, the poison, or her insides melting away. She smiled as she looked into Lilith's eyes.

Tears streamed down the spider girl's face as she hungrily sunk her fangs into Cat's stiffening flesh.

"It's okay," Cat whispered, brushing the tears from Lilith's cheeks. "It's what I've always wanted."

Cat's orgasm came in waves, surging forth from her pelvis. She arched her back. Her skin pulsed as Lilith sucked the fluid from between her legs. She felt the moisture being drawn out of her and her skin starting to wither.

Lilith sobbed and gripped her friend's hands. She could no longer pull herself away, her tears mixing with the red goo oozing forth between her lips, until the butterfly girl crumbled to dust and drifted away.

COPS & BODYBUILDERS

D. HARLAN WILSON

A bodybuilder in a purple spandex G-string snuck into my home and started to pose. His tan seemed to have been painted onto his skin, and his muscles seemed to twitch and flex of their own volition. His grin was as white as the image of God.

I reached underneath the couch cushion I was sitting on. Pulled out a crowbar. "I'll teach you to invade a man's privacy," I exclaimed, and made like I was going to swing at him. He didn't flinch. He went on posing, turning his broad back to me and tightening up his gluteus maximus.

Impressed, I couldn't help making a comment. "Nice glutes," I said. The bodybuilder thanked me, straightened out one of his arms and exhibited a sublime tricep muscle. I made a frog face. "That's pretty nice, too. But could you leave please? My wife will be home soon and if she sees us here together she might get suspicious. Anyway you're breaking the law. You can't just sneak into somebody's house, start posing, and expect everything to be all right. Please go."

The bodybuilder shook his head. "I'm sorry but I can't do that. Once I start posing, there's no stopping me." He placed a foot out in front of him and mockingly jiggled his profound thigh muscles back and forth. "I may take five now and then to shoot up an anabolic cocktail and fix myself a protein shake, but otherwise, you're stuck with me. You're stuck with me for a long, long time."

I called the bodybuilder an asshole. Then I called 911. "You're going to jail for what you've done." The bodybuilder shrugged. The shrug was as much a pose as it was a gesture of indifference.

In light of the severity of the crime I reported on the phone, the police didn't bother knocking on my door when they arrived. They simply crashed through my door like a stampede of psychotic oxen. There were three of them, each equipped with a bushy handlebar mustache, each wearing two articles of clothing: a ten-gallon police hat and a purple spandex G-string. Their tans seemed to have been painted onto their skin, and their muscles seemed to twitch and flex of their own volition. Their grins were as white as the image of God.

"What seems to be the problem here, sir?" asked the cop in charge, and struck a pose. It was an impressive Front Double Bicep pose. Following his lead, the rest of the cops also struck it.

I said, "This bodybuilder is an intruder. Take him away."

"We weren't talking to you," replied the cop in charge. He and his colleagues synchronously shifted into an equally impressive Side Chest pose. "We were talking to the bodybuilder."

Confused, I glanced at the bodybuilder. He nodded at me. "This man is inhospitable," he said. "Take him away."

The cops made belittling, sniggering comments about my less than rock hard body as they frisked me, cuffed me, and led me out to the squad car . . .

A MILLION VERSIONS OF RIGHT

MATTHEW REVERT

It was certainly no surprise that what I had once referred to lovingly as 'the gentle little rub' had eventually become frenetic masturbation, resulting in my first orgasm. Under the bed that one lunch time hiding from my clockwork father. I was excited and disgusted, my pockets chock full of scabs. My hands were adorned in filthy fingernails, all chewed and torn. I lay there under the bed, cribbed among uncomfortable refuse. The sound of approaching footsteps combined with the sight of a looming shadow panged excited nerves throughout me. I jerked quickly, my breathing heavy and then there was an experience of overwhelming build. A distinct sense that this feeling couldn't elevate any higher overcame me. When that point of no return had been reached it was nothing but intense pain. My toes curled, my lips were bitten into leaking sores, sweat lathered me. That was the first time I ever ejaculated a moustachioed tiler.

The moustachioed tiler climbed down my erect shaft and immediately got to work. Retrieving all the tools he needed from a seemingly infinite back pocket, he began to lay miniscule tiles upon my stomach. It wasn't long before my entire lower torso had been well and truly tiled. The tiler extracted a thermos and a sandwich from his pocket, sat down and had a break. With his gruff exertions, sweaty brow and dirty white overalls, the tiler was a sight to behold. He chewed upon his tiny sandwich, spitting out chunks he didn't like.

When my clockwork father finally vacated the house I remember squirming my way out from beneath the bed. The tiler appeared angry at the inconvenience these movements caused.

"Sorry," I whispered, as if atonement was necessary.

He momentarily stopped eating his sandwich and stared hard, right into my eyes. A very awkward silence ensued. I had the distinct impression that I shouldn't move at all, lest I further irritate this strange little man. I watched as he retrieved a cigarette from his upper front pocket and started exhaling the filthy smoke into the room. There was little I could do.

So there I lay, pants around my knees. A good half of my body entombed in miniature tiles. If there was one thing to be said it was that this tiler had a remarkable work ethic. If only he would stop tiling for a while and get off my body. Burning with hunger, I remember desperately wanting to get up. Stomach acid was knocking against my insides like waves to a shore. Each stomach grumble forced barely spoken profanity from the tiler. I figured it best to stay where I was. My penis was pathetically exposed and flaccid, my urethra still recovering from the enormous stretch of the moustachioed ejaculation.

Hours passed and my clockwork father was due home any minute. My entire body was tiled except for my face and genitals. I assumed this was an attempt by the tiler to maximise the shame and embarrassment I would feel when my father found me in such a peculiar position.

The sound of the car rumbling up the driveway struck me with fear. The tiler cruelly laughed to himself despite the fact the situation was anything but amusing. No, it wasn't a laugh as much as a verbalised rictus.

My father's footsteps clopped up the front steps. He unlocked the door and entered the house. He gently closed the door behind and began making his way ever closer toward his son's sheer embarrassment and shame.

I lay prone, tiled to the hilt. That tiny bastard was eating a sandwich that never seemed to end. The crumbs had achieved an alarming accumulation in his moustache. I could clearly make them out despite their microscopic nature.

The words of my father upon entering my bedroom still ring in my ears to this day. In a screeching tenor he exerted the words, "Now fuck me if you ain't covered all up in tiny tiles!"

My father moved closer, eyeing the moustachioed tiler as he ate his sandwich. "One thing you should know, son, is that when faced with a situation such as yours, when you ejaculate something untoward, you should respond in a manner that is at least equally as untoward as the ejaculate."

In fascination I stared at my father. Without the slightest hesitation he picked up the tiler in a pinch of his fingers. The tiler dangled ever so awkwardly in my father's grip but remained as apathetic as ever. Once my father nabbed the little sandwich right from the tiler's tight little grasp the apathy turned into a miniaturised rage. My father just laughed in a self-assured way as he inserted the tiler into his anus.

"I'm just going to keep him there," he said to me with a pleasant wink.

He turned around and walked toward the lounge room. Moments later I heard the sound of the television coming to life.

Still lying flat, covered in tiles, I pondered what my father had said. He was undoubtedly right, as the tiler certainly wasn't a problem anymore. It was as if my father had demonstrated the positive nature of fighting fire with fire. Birthed from the cock but destroyed up the arse. It was an understandable conclusion to his little life. That it was demonstrated with such ease still dazzled me and filled me with an admiration for my father that I'd never previously experienced. My father was somehow a little less clockwork.

I remember the mild sensation of pain as I peeled the tiny tiles from my ravaged body. Each tile cluster stung my skin as if tearing off a bandaid. With the deed finally complete, I stood straight up and examined my naked body in the mirror. I was covered head to toe, excluding face and genitals, in a red, itchy rash. *Tile rash*, I thought to myself, *what a peculiar development.*

I lay in bed, covered in itch and deep contemplation. Looking back on it now, I feel as if I was robbed of my first orgasmic experience. Where I should have been reflecting on the strange physical sensations that shot through my body, all I could see was the gruff face of the apathetic tiler as he munched on his bloody sandwich. This would eventually affect my sexual life deeply. Suffice to say, during moments of sexual intimacy the tilers face continues to invade my fragile thoughts. It has ruined many a promising night. To this day I call it 'the flaccidity of the tiler's curse.'

My first ejaculatory experience may have been my first visit from the moustachioed tiler but it certainly didn't prove to be the last. As you may imagine, the outcome of my first act of self-love filled me with trepidation. The situation I found myself in was unfortunate. As a pubescent teen I was in a near constant state of intense arousal which was perpetually at odds with my fear of masturbation. I would go to bed at night and pray to a higher power I didn't quite believe in, to ward off the potentiality of a wet dream. I may have been able to reject the masturbatory temptation in the waking hours but I had little control over myself when in a state of sleep. Wags at school would boast of the sticky mess they awoke to on a constant basis. I would have loved to wake in a sticky mess; my concern however, was that I would awake covered head to toe in tiles and tiny breadcrumbs, unable to move.

The pretty young things in my class would invade my dream state regularly and it was only a matter of time before this translated into an unconscious eruption in my lower regions. This eventuality did indeed occur. It had been nearly three agitated years since my first and only orgasm.

That night, in my dreams, the girls pranced about in their short little dresses, winding me up like a toy, willing me to snap like a faulty twig.

The next morning I awoke, and like I did every morning, patted my sleepy chest, feeling for tiles. I breathed a sigh of relief, for my chest was still naked as the day I was born. I threw back the blankets, ready to start the day. But, the sticky, wet sensation in my pants became apparent. I couldn't quite believe it. By all accounts, it appeared I had successfully orgasmed without the appearance of a tiler. It aroused me instantly and masturbatory thoughts entered my head immediately. But wary of the time, I had to shelve them.

The next day at school was full of braggadocio on my part. Sure, I had bragged about my wet dream prowess before but this was the first time I had actually experienced a wet dream to back it up. I boasted loudly and proudly to all and sundry. Quizzical stares assailed me from the chums and wags as my enthusiasm was in direct contrast to my previous, untrue boasts. I'm still not sure whether two and two was ever successfully put together but that is by the by.

I was determined to masturbate myself into a gooey stupor upon my arrival home. My erection had been a barely tamed beast all day. I felt it could sense the possibilities. Tentatively, yet excitedly, I threw myself on the bed and went to work. I clung to myself ever so tightly as I jerked and pulled the last three years of repression away. The moment of climax was a terrifying yet brilliant one. There was that split second where I feared the worst but the worst simply didn't come. Instead I erupted all over myself in pure ecstasy. The tiler, for whatever reason, had been vanquished from my loins.

This was my ticket to pubescent paradise. My life became a dizzy blur of climax and seminal fluid. No tiler, no problems. It wasn't until my first real sexual encounter some years later that the tiler reappeared and caused all manner of problems for me and my ill-fated sexual partner.

I met her in crying class. She was struggling with the basic methodology involved in crying ribbons. I approached her with pure intentions, failing at the time to notice her exquisite beauty. She sat pathetically with a second generation beginners ribbon hanging lifeless from her right eye. I asked her if she needed help. She accepted. Her acceptance revealed a shame in her voice. I found the display of shame endearing. I gently tugged on the ribbon, being careful not to irritate her eyeball. The ribbon slipped out, her eyes blinked frantically as if shaking out the cobwebs, 'Ribbon Jitters' they were called according to the literature. We got to talking. There was a mutual affection and it wasn't long before we were what the other wags called an 'item.'

Sexual intercourse was the inevitable conclusion of our trajectory. Our affection had grown rather deep and the 'love' word had been used on more than one occasion. As it happened, the intercourse was a result of passionate spontaneity. My clockwork father was out for the night at a 'dreary old function.' We were alone in my room discussing matters of interest. The conversation arrived at the topic of nipple wheeze. We lost ourselves in passion. I was blissfully inside her before I could fully comprehend my actions. Our awkward movements had a resonance of innocence that was purity embodied. As is common during one's first sexual encounter, it was all over relatively quickly. The moment of climax was problematic. For the first time in years I felt the familiar discomfort as my urethra stretched beyond reasonable limits. My deposit was a treacherous one. It quickly became apparent that I had just ejaculated another moustachioed tiler, only this time into my sweetheart.

I had pulled out too late. It was post-coital devastation of a most unusual kind. I could detect the look of concerned confusion in my sweetheart's eyes. I owned up almost immediately. I explained in detail about the tiler and the high probability that he was now residing somewhere in her vaginal tunnel. Her tears flowed endlessly. Between sobs I was implored to get it out at any cost. My efforts to calm her down via Rastafarian impersonation were an instant failure. I asked her to wait while I sought out a torch to shine directly up her region. Although I was gone mere seconds I'm sure it felt like hours to my poor little sweetheart as she sobbed wretchedly. Coils of smoke were floating from between her legs, filling the room with the scent of tobacco. I requested my sweetheart remain deathly still as it appeared the tiler inside her was smoking a cigarette. She fanned at the smoke as it attacked her pretty face. I asked her to part her vaginal walls, which she did in a surprisingly ladylike way. I shone my torch deep within her, searching out the moist crevasses. I could just make out what appeared to be a little hand, waving about a cigarette like some form of diva. I informed my sweetheart that I could see him and she again implored me to hurry. With a long-handled spoon I scraped about inside her, trying to ensnare the tiler. He was definitely privy to my intrusion as he dodged about, attempting to find sanctuary within the limited space available. Above me, my sweetheart squealed in a discomfort that I'm sure she viewed as pain. The real pain unfortunately was soon to come. As if the tiler was aware of the love I felt for my sweetheart he began to stab at her insides. I felt every little stab and slash. Her squeals of agony were intensified. I felt helpless as I desperately reached for the horrid little man. I did eventually manage to get his kicking body out but I tore my sweetheart up rather badly in the process.

With the bastard tiler in my tight grip I surveyed the scene. Bits of my poor little sweetheart seemed everywhere around the room. Needless to say, my carpet was sodden. My stony gaze returned to the squirming little tiler in my hand, the source of so much misery in my life. My first sexual experience had concluded with the death of my first true love. I felt worthless. My mind began to occupy itself with thoughts of the tiler and what I should do with him. I was at quite a loss until I remembered the previous actions of my father. That day, lying on the floor, covered in tiles, my father had indeed come to the rescue. His actions were so sure. He did what he did with barely a thought and it had worked. *One thing you should know son, is that when faced with a situation such as yours, when you ejaculate something untoward, you should respond in a manner that is at least equally as untoward as the ejaculate.* These were the strange words my father had said. With conviction I slid the moustachioed tiler into my tight anus.

The tiler's presence was by no means muted. I could feel every movement as he writhed about my inner workings. A profound sense of discomfort over-whelmed my being as I contemplated the purpose of my actions. On top of the discomfort was the feeling that my bowel tract was at that very moment being tiled. Just how long the tiler was to remain inside me I didn't know. The first few minutes had been extremely unpleasant and I shuddered at the possibility that the fate which had befallen me was a permanent one. How was I to go about my basic toiletries or even walk appropriately given the constant clench required to keep the wretched tiler inside? Clearly I needed to consult my father in the matter, which is precisely what I did.

I awkwardly walked toward my father in a style that could best be described as an elongated crab. He was in his sitting chair watching his stories. I wasn't aware of my father's televisual tastes but the show seemed especially unusual. There was a man on the screen, among the shrubbery, and the hat he wore was clearly incorrect. In a mild panic I averted my gaze. My father looked up at me, examining my blood spangled body. Rather than the shocked or horri-fied reaction I had anticipated, he simply nodded knowingly with a degree of genuine warmth that momentarily elevated me from the emotional doldrums I had been lost within. Explaining the situation in detail, with several well-timed points of the finger toward my backside, the gist was understood completely. He informed me that although *he* had chosen to dispose of the tiler via his anus, it wasn't a path that I needed to take. He looked me square in the eye and repeated something that will resonate within me for the rest of my life:

"There are a million versions of right."

Those were his exact words. They circulated throughout my mind as I tried to grasp their import.

I spent a great many weeks with the tiler inside me as I couldn't find any alternative solutions to my woe. My precarious bowel movements were infused with miniature tiles and cigarette butts. I spent some time mourning for my sweetheart on the odd occasions where my mind wasn't obsessed with the beast inside me. I had completely stopped attending classes and accepting guests into my home. These were dark days as I retreated more and more within myself, almost shunning the reality of the world around me. My father's words were still but an unbreakable cipher in my mind. Any efforts made to convince my father to expand upon his statement were met with a solemn shake of the head and in-explicable gesticulation. Descending deeper into a private hell I beat upon walls with bare fists and slapped my weeping rump, trying to knock the tiler about. He remained very much alive inside me, assumedly remaining so via a back pocket full of never-ending sandwiches and God knows what other edibles.

When an unfortunate situation removes all vigour from life there comes a time when you must seek a conclusion. It appeared as though having the tiler inside me simply wasn't working out as I'd planned. My bowels were pregnant with a life that irritated me to a completely unreasonable degree. After many sleepless nights, I finally arrived at the decision it was time for the tiler to go. I simply couldn't tolerate his presence anymore. He had ruined all that was worthwhile about my life and if *it* didn't end soon I feared my life would.

The bowel movement was dramatic in the worst possible way. Based on the sensation of my anal stretch and eventual tear, I was sure the tiler had grown in size. Sprays of gassy blood painted the toilet bowl murky red. Tiny tiles shattered upon impact with the porcelain. Stools of the most improbable shapes, colours and consistencies rocketed from my tiny hell hole. Then there was the smell! The fetid, miasmic stench engulfed the toilet room. I felt as if caught in a death tempest. Eventually, with much pain and applied pressure, the object of my woe slowly began to slide out of me. Bloody flatulence and splatterings of faecal inhumanities accompanied its exit from my worn and torn body. When I thought the pain could get no more severe I finally felt the tiler exit me completely and drop into the toilet stew with a mighty splash. I sat upon the toilet for upwards of an hour as I tried to assimilate the intense pain and fatigue I was feeling. When I had sufficiently recovered, it dawned on me that I could hear no sound whatsoever coming from the toilet bowl. I expected to hear the angry tiler splashing around, fighting for breath and swearing emphatically in my general direction. I tuned in closely to the minutiae of sound within the room. I concentrated so deeply that I heard the blood rushing through my veins but still, no thrashing, splashing tiler. *Could it be true? Was the tiler dead?* I was almost too scared to look. I had to psych myself into it. I slowly stood up with my pants still around my ankles and stared hard into the revolting bowl. Nestled within the grisly muck, exactly where I would have expected to find the tiler, I found something else; something that filled me with immense concern. If my eyes weren't deceiving me, instead of the tiler's body, all I could see was a rather large black stapler!

My mind was in cartwheels of wretched confusion. I immediately picked up the stapler, completely unaware I was subjecting my hand to pure filth. I held the stapler up, studying it. Toilet juice ran down my arm. I was far too preoccupied with the reality of the stapler to be overly concerned. Before I knew it I had entered into tiny mental spasms. I ran from the toilet room, stapler in hand, arms flailing, pants still at my ankles. A wall, which I swear should not have been there, eventually cut short my little episode by knocking me out cold.

I awoke to my father standing over me, staring down, face full of concern. I was covered in blood, tiles, faecal matter and cigarette butts. The stapler was still firmly in my grip. Once again my father had found me in an unfortunate situation with my genitals exposed. Through a daze of concussion I relayed the events which had just occurred. He nodded, as if completely unsurprised by my experience. He helped me up into a chair, looked hard at me and simply said, "Have you tried the stapler yet?"

I watched him walk away, taking position back in front of the television. I sat for a while, once again contemplating my father's words. Everything appeared so simple to him. Perhaps the truth really was that simple. Perhaps I had let this whole situation work me up into a ball of neurosis for nothing.

I showered thoroughly, scouring every speck of my body several times over until I felt sufficiently clean. The stapler had been soaking in a cleaning solution that I'd purchased from a discount balm factory. By the time I was dried off and changed, it too was sufficiently clean. I took it with me into my bedroom and sat it on the desk. I ruminated for a while before I worked up the gumption to test its functionality. I squared a short stack of loose paper and readied the stapler for work. The result was an utter failure. There were roughly ten sheets in the paper stack and the staple barely penetrated the first couple. I kept subtracting sheets, seeking the threshold. As it turned out, the threshold was only three and even this appeared a struggle for the bowel stapler. This was the tiler all over again, I could sense it. He had seen fit to make my life unpleasant from the first moment I ejaculated him all those years ago. I didn't know whether he had turned himself into the stapler or whether it was a naturally occurring phenomenon but it fit his modus operandi to a tee. I cursed his wretched name. I picked up the wretched stapler and motioned to hurl it against a wall. I stopped. I couldn't bring myself to do it. I placed it back on the desk, glared at it, cursed the tiler once more and finally sought refuge in my bed. I fell asleep almost instantly with a conviction to never have an orgasm again.

The older you get the more difficult it seems to repress your sexual urges. At least this was my experience. I had blossomed into a rather attractive young man. I was understandably attracted to women and they me. I avoided relationships and situations that would provoke unwanted urges. The unpredictability of an urge-inducing situation was a constant problem. For instance, I might glance across and see a lady tying her shoe and nearly explode in my pants there and then. Life was a frustrating struggle and of course I eventually garnered a reputation for being either stuck up or of homosexual proclivity. To tell them the truth was not an option. Shortly after my 25th year, another wet dream struck.

I woke up completely draped in tiles save for my face and genitals. There was another moustachioed little monster, sitting on my chin, blowing foul smoke into my face. I passed out.

When I awoke the second time there was another tiler. They were fighting each other. Throwing tiles and kicking at shins. I watched the strange spectacle for some time, completely enthralled. Unusual feelings began to well within me. Staring at these little men, these little men whom I was responsible for creating, I felt somewhat like a god. Even if their purpose in life was to cause me discomfort and frustration, I was still their creator. Not even *they* could deny me that. I freed my right arm from its tile encrustation and began to masturbate ferociously. The ejaculation birthed forth yet another tiler from my weary penis. This tiler instantly joined the first two in their brawl. I kept masturbating, again and again. Each new ejaculation introduced new tilers into the fight. They were all identical with their moustaches and little white overalls. Hours passed, days passed, I lost all track of time. When my body finally gave in, there must have been close to a hundred tilers. The ongoing fight was full of violence. There were bloody corpses strewn throughout my room. Those still alive wouldn't give up. They were each determined to be the only one.

Once again I awoke to the sight of my father standing over me. As my vision cleared it became apparent he was holding my testicles in his hand. They were no longer attached to my body. I slowly scanned the bedroom. There were no more tilers. What I plainly saw was a large black garbage bag. Through a small hole in one side a miniature, lifeless arm poked free. My anal stapler was still on the desk. It hadn't been disposed of. As I stared once more at my severed testicles in my father's hand, I pondered. My father had stopped being clockwork long ago. This further proved it. He carefully inserted my testicles into his anus and walked away, calling back, "This is just another version of right."

HELLION

ALISSA NUTTING

I never had breasts until I went to Hell. When I died at the age of thirty-nine I was barely an A-cup. I often used to purchase bras from the preteen section. The bra I died in had tiny unicorns patterned across one nipple and tiny rainbows patterned across the other.

At first I thought it was a be-careful-what-you-wish-for type deal. All my life I had wanted a bigger chest, and now I was going to be saddled with one and learn all the ways that it's inconvenient—back pain, unwanted attention, etc. But as I walked around I began to notice that all the females had them. I was looking down my shirt when another woman patted me on the back. "They're for defense," she winked. I didn't understand until later that day when a fellow Hellion began hitting on me, a real know-it-all. The kind of person who always has a toothpick in his mouth. When I first got to Hell, I was shocked they'd let people have sharp objects like toothpicks; I expected the rules of prison. But that is lesson #1. Hell is not the same as prison.

As I grew angry with the guy, my breasts began to make a percolating sound. It felt like they were being forcibly tickled. My nipples hardened into nozzles and a bubbling green liquid that smelled like motor oil shot out of them. It sprayed all over the man's face and his skin began to smoke and blister. I watched him run over to the lava pond and look at his reflection. "I'm a mutant for eternity!" he screamed.

A giant man named Ben walked up and put his hand on my shoulder. Ben is intimidating at first: he is covered from head-to-toe with eye implants. "Sorry about that," he muttered. A bat poked its head out of Ben's beard. The bat was wearing an eye patch. Some people in Hell are nice. They just happened to have done a very reprehensible thing at one point. I killed my husband once, for instance. But I felt bad enough about it to also kill myself.

Hell isn't that awful, but it does smell. People often ask, "What died in here?"

The answer is complicated. It could be a lot of things. Our currency is little coins made of hair and liver that we have to spend before they rot. We get a weekly allowance, enough to keep most people entertained, but if we want more money we can mop the floors, etc. It's common for people to start a collection as a hobby. For example, Ben collects eyes and surgically embeds them all over his body. His best eye is in his belly button. He wears little high-rise t-shirts so that his belly-eye can see and be seen at all times.

I expected a lot of axe murderers to be running around, licking bloody knives and looking sinister. But Hell really isn't that violent. Something about the heat. Everyone is lazy and sluggish except the Caribbean pirates—they were already used to high temperatures. But now they can't ravage women because of the bosom-acid, so they try to catch their flies with honey and are really quite chivalrous. If someone accidentally drops her purse into a lava river, they'll use their peg legs to fetch it out. Wild serial killers are totally the minority down here. Hell is mainly full of people with tempers, or people like Thor.

"I still feel bad about Thor." I heard the devil mumble this one night at the bar and inquired around. Apparently every few millennia Hell gets a case like Thor's. He lived during the 1600s and was a brain-eater in both his real and after-lives. Normally Hell's heat encourages people to slow down, but in Thor's case it seemed to give him momentum. It became quite problematic, Thor running around brain-eating, so the devil turned Thor into a large rhesus monkey whose brain had already been eaten out.

But the change was too dramatic. It was like a father yelling at an irritating kid who then becomes completely quiet and joyless, so much so that the father feels remorseful. Prior to the change Thor was known for his relentless war chants, but after the metamorphosis he forgot all their words. He did nothing but silently pick insects from his fur, and the devil felt this silence as guilt. To make amends he gave Thor a sort-of brain, something similar to the motor from an electric pencil sharpener. Now everyone in Hell treats Thor with kid gloves.

Hell also has an incredible number of nurses, so many that it's ridiculous. I don't know why, but the bar is always full of them, guzzling fake beer and talking about how they wish they could go back to earth for just a second and pull someone's catheter out really fast. There is only one small bar in Hell but everyone manages to hang out inside. The beer is nonalcoholic.

I was complaining about this the first time I actually got to talk to the devil one-on-one.

"You'd get dehydrated," he mumbled. "Alcohol is a great idea if everyone wants a headache."

The devil's voice sounds like that of a leprechaun who's been smoking for centuries. He wants to quit, or so he says. He began telling me how he once put on a trench coat and went into an earthly gas station to buy nicotine gum.

"I never had any luck with it," I commiserated. I think that's when he took a shine to me.

Newcomers experience a placebo effect in the bar during their first couple visits, and I was no exception. As the night progressed, I started to feel intoxicated and my conversation with the devil took a turn for the worse.

"And what's up with the ceiling?" I added. "It's like the inside of the biggest dead animal in the universe." The walls are all bones and stretchy tendon.

The devil put out his cigar and stood up. "It's worked for a long time," he argued. "Why change it now?" But from his expression I could tell he was hurt.

A few days later there was a knock on my door, and it was none other than the devil.

"You were right," he nodded, "what you said the other night."

"I was drunk," I offered. His eyebrows rose. "Though not technically."

"No, some things could be updated." We began to gaze at one another. His eyes turned a fiery red that didn't exactly scare me but was hypnotizing in an assertive way.

I thought for a moment. "You could build a roller coaster?" I described my favorite ride ever, the Demon Drop, which plummeted straight down and made my stomach feel insane every time I rode it.

He thought for a while and agreed it would be a good thing to try. "Thor could operate it," he suggested.

We had a raffle contest to decide what the ride would be called. The winner was Betty, a former Wisconsin housewife, who chose the name of SKULLKRUSH.

As the ride was being built, the nurses wanted to know if they could set up a triage hospital next to SKULLKRUSH. "No one will get hurt," I said. I put a supportive arm around Thor. The devil and I had outfitted him with a SKULLKRUSH uniform and nametag in preparation, just to get him into the role. As I looked to Thor for reassurance, he grabbed the devil's lit cigar and crammed it up his nose.

"Just in case," they insisted.

The hospital turned out to be very beneficial—Thor has his good days and his bad days. They're actually the same day. He likes to ignite and smoke his own tail, and have seizures. Sometimes Thor will appear to be safely stopping the ride, but then at the last moment he'll defecate into his paw instead and throw it at the riders just before they're pulverized. Of course no one can die, but there is no shortage of mangling, reconstruction, and extreme transformation. The whole concept that energy can never be destroyed really works out in Hell. Physics, etc. Examples of this abound.

There is Varmint Man, who lost a rib in a poker game. The hole it left was annoying, because Hell varmints waste no time packing up inside of cavities. I accepted an invitation from Varmint Man to try his yoga class, which wasn't the best because of the twelve baby raccoons romping around in his chest hole. They were cute, but were demon raccoons, so they had green buckteeth and puss flowing freely from their eyes.

After a wonderful date riding SKULLKRUSH with the devil (it was nice to feel the crazy stomach feeling while holding his giant claw), I spoke to him about Varmint Man and he was more than happy to help. He suggested we take Varmint Man dumpster diving to find something to seal up the chest hole. The dumpsters in Hell have unbelievable finds. I always thought I was hot stuff on earth, wading through the old éclair piles behind Dough Knots. I had no idea. We ended up outfitting Varmint Man with an elaborate series of copper piping: resistant to rodent teeth. I also found an intestine that had been stuffed with rat poison and fashioned into a noose. I decided to hang the whole thing from my chandelier. "You're becoming more comfortable with entrails," the devil commented. I liked the way he took notice of my growth.

SKULLKRUSH turned out to be a very lucrative venture. The best part was how the devil and I had succeeded in it together. I'd always wanted to be someone's right-hand go-to girl, and there I was.

We were keeping the bags of profit from SKULLCRUSH in my house, but soon it started rotting. "Our money is beginning to smell," I told him. He stared at me for a while, weighing whether or not to say what was on his mind. Finally he sighed and took my hand and said to get all the money together. His hands in mine give me that great feeling of dating someone my father would completely not approve of.

We walked the bags down a long tunnel that was like an everlasting gobstopper of horrible smells: first dead cats then dead dogs then dead cows then dead whales until I couldn't even take it. "This stinks," I managed. The walls were boiling with blood.

"We're almost there." He picked me up and put me inside a pouch in his stomach that I didn't even know he had. Actually I'm positive he just tore his flesh open and let me hang out inside so I wouldn't have to walk anymore.

The inside of the pouch was wet and oozy and took me back to when I was little. Each time my family had to go on a long car ride, my grandma first sat me down on the toilet and poured warm water between my legs to make me pee. It's something I was trained to do from the earliest age onward, and suddenly I found myself sitting in a warm blood-organ puddle. "Whatever you do," I thought, "don't pee inside the devil." I think he felt it before I did, but suddenly we both got really quiet and it was the most awkward moment of my life. Or it would've been, if I weren't already dead.

I defensively took my boobs into my hands before confessing, just in case he was sore about the whole thing. "Sorry." After it was still quiet for a moment I added, "I didn't mean to." For a second I thought I was going to faint from embarrassment but then he started laughing and so did I; I started laughing so hard that I cried. My tears were acidy and smelled like motor oil. I think my new boob ducts are connected to my tear ducts.

Finally we arrived at the end of the tunnel, where the dead smell seemed to disappear. I wriggled out of his pouch then he reached down and did a squeegee-like wringing motion; all sorts of things splashed onto the ground and then the flap was instantly gone. It's cute how he doesn't make a big deal out of his ability to do such amazing things. Although he tells me I do amazing things that I don't think are amazing at all, like have hair on my head.

"Do you feel the air?" I asked, but he was already smiling. This was his coup de grâce.

We'd arrived at a cave where cold air was literally blasting. Feeling cold after being hot for so long hurt somewhat; it made me realize that it probably was painful to breathe for the first time when I was born. I kept breathing the cold air and soon it started to feel pleasant, like stretching a muscle that's sore.

He flipped on a light switch. In front of us there were hundreds and thousands of rows of frozen liver and hair. After stacking the bags of money in the back, he nervously put one of his arm hooves against the other and locked their grooves together. "I've never shown anyone this place before." He paused. "You can imagine how popular it would be."

"I won't tell anyone. I promise." I stretched out on a liver strip near the lip of the cave so only the top half of my body was in the freezer. I wanted to bask in the difference.

"I know you won't tell," he said. "If I think about things in the future hard enough, I can see what will happen, and you don't tell anyone."

This pleased me. To be honest, I've never been able to keep a secret.

We stayed there breathing cold air for quite awhile. It reminded me of the first time I smoked a cigarette. How strange it was to just breathe and feel better.

"I should be getting back," he said finally. "If I'm gone for too long, it's not good."

I nodded. Usually in Hell it's so hot that my skin is bright pink. But when I looked down I saw a very pale chest, and for the first time ever, the purple-green veins running through my acid boobs.

"You can stay if you want," he offered. "I can come get you later."

"No," I said, "I'm ready." It wasn't true. I figured he'd know that I was lying to be polite. Hopefully, this would let him know how much I liked him.

He grew wings and giant claws to hold me so the journey back would be faster.

"I love this," I said. "We should fly more often." He seemed unsure. I pressed the issue until he admitted that he doesn't like to grow wings and talons. He thinks they make his head look disproportionate. I had been pinching my nose because of the smell, but I let it go before speaking. I didn't want to sound like some annoying mother-in-law from New Jersey.

"I think you look really terrific," I whispered, and his claw tightened just a little.

Later that week he and I had such a good afternoon that we decided to go ahead and make a night of it. I tried to bake him some scones, but we got to talking and I forgot the oven and they burned. I'm horrible at baking and cooking. It was a point of contention between my husband and me before I killed him.

"Let's go back to my place," he said.

In my old life (we're encouraged to do that, to call it an "old life" rather than "life," as though it was left behind rather than taken), I did not do many exciting things. I never went on a real vacation, for instance. And I only remember swimming once when I was young. I certainly did not have sex with the devil.

"Sex with the devil," I said flirtatiously. I thought he'd like that but instead he completely clammed up.

Maybe because his house is not an evil dungeon. I expected, as many women might, a type of Transylvanian sex-lair. This is not to say I wanted to be tortured, but pain is different and more relative in Hell, less "ouch" and more "I guess I don't have anywhere else to be."

But his bedroom was plain and ancient. There was the usual smell of rot, which in Hell is not a visceral, unbearably fresh smell. Instead it's like something died a while ago on its own and had never been found or cleaned up. It made me think of my husband. I imagined how much I'd freak out if the devil dragged my husband's corpse out from behind the bed, or worse, if my husband was actually in Hell at that very moment, still bearing all the death-stains I'd given him, and he'd been following me and was going to jump out at us in the middle of our intimate evening and ruin everything.

"I'm glad he's not here, but why didn't my husband go to Hell?" I asked. "I just always thought it would be the other way around, that he'd be in Hell and I'd be somewhere else."

We walked into a small cave that had a single torch and a bed, and the devil lay down and then gazed at me. I took the cue and curled up next to him.

It's amazing how perspectives can change. I was always on my husband to cut his fingernails, but the devil has the longest ones I've ever seen and they don't bother me. They're thick and very yellow—their color is very unimposing, like blood that has sat for several centuries whose weight has left only a quiet stain. They remind me a little of paper in a really old book.

"Your husband was mean, but he wasn't evil." The devil's breath on my neck was hot and brothy. He kissed me, and it was like being kissed by a pot of soup.

"Are you saying I'm evil?" I was curious, not upset. Hell also has a Prozac effect—regarding nearly everything, I both care and don't care at the same time. When you know you have an eternity to get over things, you tend to just go ahead and get over them.

"You did an evil thing," he said in a fatherly and chiding way that I liked beyond words. "Everyone's capable of doing evil things."

When I took off my shirt his eyes grew panicked. For a moment I thought it was my weapon-breasts. "Will they shoot you?" I asked. "Or do they only do that when I'm angry?"

He got up and pulled a curtain across the opening of the cave, then moved towards the torch. "Devil," I whispered, "what are you doing?"

"Don't you want the lights out?" The way he said it, it wasn't really a question.

"I want to see you," I whined. In a way, this was the biggest part of the excitement. The devil is millions of folds that I know somehow unfold. He is the largest insect in the universe, and a dragon and a goat and a man and a beard and skin that has been burnt clean.

"I can't," he said. "Right now, I can't."

I thought Hell would be all give or all take. But there's just not enough room to plunder. We're all here; we all have to go to the same small bar.

Most importantly, we have to learn that we are wrong sometimes. That there was at least one time, in our old lives, when we were very wrong.

I nodded and he blew out the torch. I couldn't see him but I could feel him swelling, becoming fifty shadows almost as big as the room. My hand had been on his chest when the torch blew out, and now I felt his skin begin to slide up under my palm like he was a magic plant growing and growing; soon my hand was on his hip.

I began to explore his bones with my hand; I felt far more bones than legs or wings. I tried to count with my fingers their hundreds of knobs and ends. He lay back down, though he hardly fit upon the bed, and coaxed me up onto him. His warm breath was coming from every direction at once.

"This part is a little normal," he said. But it wasn't true.

Afterwards he fell asleep quickly. I felt him shrinking back, his entire body receding and folding, everything tucking neatly into place. I listened to the deep years of his lungs and decided to have a cigarette. We are smokers, he and I.

It's true, the lighter was cheating. "Respect his wishes," I told myself, "haven't you learned anything?" But I was too excited to learn.

When I clicked the lighter, years seemed to pass. I could see through all the parts of him. His skin now looked like a clear bat's. In his wings, cells were beating far faster than I could see; behind his lids his pink eyes were spinning. His long tongue flickered in his mouth and his stomach was full of small limbs. He was a machine, a riddle. Looking at him, I felt that I was growing smarter every second. I was able to watch him like children watch fish.

Then he woke up and caught me peeking.

"I've been in love before," I told him, meaning the other time was not one bit like this. I felt my ribs and my stomach begin to grow and unfold like his skin.

He shot me a smile. Don't go getting swept away, it said, a grounding look to tell me that Hell is different from my old life, but not as different as all that. Not so different that I couldn't get hurt, or hurt him. He let me look on just a moment more, then the flame was blown out by a wind that came from nowhere.

MR. PLUSH, DETECTIVE

GARRETT COOK

Until a month ago, my name was Hatbox. Then, I woke up as a teddy bear in a trench coat and fedora. I wasn't just a teddy bear, I was worse; I was a teddy bear and a lowdown dirty private dick, the kind of gumshoe you hire when you want somebody found and don't care if somebody else has gotta get lost. From a hearty six-one, I went down to three feet high, all because I needed money and Plush needed to be somebody else. When you got money, you can be anybody, which was lucky for the no-good, cuddly brown bastard that double-crossed me. Next time a teddy bear offers to pay off your gambling debts in exchange for your body, you'd better think twice. I sure as hell should have.

Had I thought twice and not ended up as Jimmy Plush, I wouldn't have been sneaking into the warehouse where Lillian Benzedrine was being held. If I hadn't ended up as Jimmy Plush I wouldn't be padding around, palms frozen onto the oversized-trigger of a custom fingerless forty-five.

This was my eighth trip to warehouses like this in a month. Kidnappers are sloppy in this town. One look at the perpetrators said why. One of the two was a big guy, his face was clenched tight, his jaw square and he had a forehead you could serve a round of drinks for the house off. The other one, who looked like a ferret standin' on its hind legs, wore a long tie decorated with hearts. I knew them well by now, Halperin's men—Johnny Hideous and Skinny Valentine. Not much for brains or creativity, but I will admit that in the past they had been known to press their size advantage with some degree of effectiveness. In short, men who I'm embarrassed to say have literally knocked the stuffing out of me.

But, lucky for me, I've gotten used to this body (as much as a guy can get used to being a teddy bear the size of a toddler) and being tiny and made out of plush and stuffing makes you quiet. Quiet enough to sneak up behind a huge bruiser and shoot out the back of his knee at point-blank range with a modified teddy bear .45. Mean enough to do it, too. If this warehouse had neighbors, Hideous definitely would've woken them up.

"Jimmy Plush, I'll teach ya! I'll teach ya to sneak up behind me!"

He was right. His falling to the floor writhing and screaming definitely taught me that I should sneak up on him. His partner reached for his gun, but I was quicker on the draw and shot him in the hand. Last time I'd encountered these two a week back, I was the one getting shot in the arm, while Hideous reached into me and started pulling cotton out. This was definitely a change for the better. Tangle with a couple of thugs nine times you start to figure things out.

Angry and bleeding, but not down for the count, Skinny charged me and, though he wasn't the stronger of the two, I was still a teddy bear. I realized now would be the time to make use of some of the Chinese fighting arts that my chauffeur Chang was training me in, fighting arts used by the real Jimmy Plush to put thugs like these in their places. The Angry Hamster Kick was perfected by vicious Shaolin dwarves for just these occasions. Sure enough, one good quick Hamster Kick used Valentine's momentum and size to cave his ribs in on themselves.

Since the two thugs would be more eager to get to a hospital than finish me off, I untied Mrs. Benzedrine and brought her out to the limo for delivery to her husband, who had tried to open a competing Chinese restaurant across the street from Vic Halperin's gaudy Chinese pleasure palace, J.L Wong's. Vic Halperin had never liked competition and David Benzedrine's mother was actually Chinese. As well as hating competition, Halperin hated the Chinese since his greatest desire in life was to be one of them. I pitied Benzedrine, since inheriting this body left me on Halperin's bad side from day one, and like him there was nothing I could do about what body I inhabited. Unlike him, I owned a gun and was training in the Chinese fighting arts. For a race of wisecracking chauffeurs and crooked restaurateurs, those Chinese sure know their fighting arts.

I proudly brought Mrs. Benzedrine to the door and rang the bell. Nothing. Knocked. Nothing. Something stank. I worked the knob and it turned out the door was open.

"I'll go in first, Mrs. Benzedrine. I think something's going on."

My chauffeur rolled down his window, perfect to the beat. It was uncanny how he did that all the time.

"Should Chang accompany most honored Mr. Plush inside?"

"Stay out here and wait."

"As you wish. But Chang is not sure…"

"Wait outside and be ready if I don't come out."

"Yes, Mr. Plush." Chang mumbled what must have been something rude in Chinese. I'll have to learn to speak slanty someday and take him by surprise. Someday.

Chang was right. Chang has an awful habit of being right. I opened the door, walked into the sitting room, and a walrus shot me in the chest. It was probably just a furry dressed as a walrus, but I still didn't expect to be shot in the chest by anything resembling a walrus. A squid, also definitely a furry, walked into the sitting room with a hand drill. Luckily, I black out from pain easily and am something of a fainter. Otherwise, I would have felt something nobody should ever feel.

When my eyes opened, I was disappointed but not surprised that the first thing I saw was the long, arrogant, wrinkly face of Vic Halperin, "the Pale Peril" as he's often called. The squinty eyes, the long, skinny fake moustache, the awful goatee, the cheap fez on his head. Halperin was no easier to look at than he was to talk to. He ran his press-on nails over what I now understood to be a gaping hole in my stomach, proudly exploring its contours. I'm grateful that teddy bears don't bleed or vomit, because otherwise I'd be doing plenty of both things. He backed off, so I could look at the two Furries who knocked me out cold. And appreciate that Chang and the Benzedrines were all tied up beside me.

Chang's head was hanging.

"Chang apologizes to Honored Mr. Plush. There is no counter for squid-style martial arts."

"That's all right, Chang," I said, mortified that all my stuffing was hanging out, "the cotton comes out of your next check."

Halperin cleared his throat and as expected, began a lengthy reprimand in his deep voice that was as far from being Chinese as he was, maybe more because it didn't have a cheap kimono and a fez to hide behind.

"Jimmy Plush, we meet again, detective, but this time, the advantage is of course my own. I'm sure that you were finally able to put Skinny Valentine and Johnny Hideous in the hospital, but as you can see, I have taken on a higher class of thug, men who can't be outwitted by a two-bit stuffed bear who likes to stick his nose in the wrong honey pots."

It took a lot of willpower not to laugh. I restrained myself not out of any kind of fear of Halperin, but out of the knowledge that laughing would make more of my stuffing start to fall out.

"How do you know it was me?"

"Mr. Plush, you have a very familiar face."

"Common too. You ever been to F.A.O. Schwartz?"

Halperin liked to banter, but was always quick to get steamed. I wanted him to be off balance and give me some kind of advantage. It didn't work.

"That's very funny, Mr. Plush, but the fact is, something must be done about you."

"Give him to me," the walrus furry cooed. "He's so beautiful, so soft. I could have so much fun with him…"

The squid crossed his arms.

"I don't think he's so special." There was a hint of jealousy in his voice, but I didn't want to think about it.

"We could both have him, and it would be a delight."

"I suppose we could. He *is* beautiful."

"His fur has a lovely texture…"

Now I was starting to get afraid. Halperin was the kind of scum that would hand me over to his gunsels to have god-knows-what done to me. He also appreciated these guys more than he did Hideous and Valentine, even though they'd only been in his service a little bit. I hoped I could either get out of here before they did or lose enough stuffing to die so I wouldn't have to experience their plush flippers and tentacles on me.

"You see, Mr. Plush, what happens when you interfere with me? I'm sure you don't want Tusky and Bernstein to have their way with you, do you?"

"I must confess I would not." I tried to say it with my tough façade intact. I'm pretty sure I didn't pull it off quite right.

"So stay out of my way, or you'll be left to serve as a kind of toy which you were not intended to be."

"All right. I'll lay off your operation."

Halperin applauded softly.

"Excellent, Mr. Plush. Tusky, Bernstein, untie Plush and my countryman."

The walrus and squid complied.

"I hope to see you later," the walrus whispered in my ear. I hoped I never would.

I eased into my modified limo, feeling like I'd been hit by a truck full of lightning being driven by my girl and the man she was making time with.

"Chang," I said to my chauffeur, "that was demoralizing."

"I cannot apologize enough, most honored Mr. Plush."

"Funny you say that, Chang. *That* was just enough. Next time we go against Halperin, I hope there won't be any squids involved," I choked a little, "or walruses. God, I hope there aren't any walruses."

"The squid and walrus' success means there will be more of them. Maybe the time has come that for once you keep your word and leave Halperin alone."

I didn't like hearing that, especially coming from a Chinaman who was working for me. Chang had a tendency to say the wrong thing, particularly when it was the right thing. One of the few joys in my life of teddy bear detective inadequacy was messing with Halperin, especially since I had just gotten an innocent man and his wife killed for opening a Chinese restaurant on the wrong side of town. On the other hand, next time we squared off, I'd have to face Halperin's Furries. I didn't like losing and I didn't like admitting that I couldn't win. Chang had done something impressive: found a spot where I was even more vulnerable.

"It's your fault I got in this mess, Chang. Don't tell me whose cage I can rattle and whose I can't! This little bear's got teeth, Chang and don't you forget it."

The argument ended abruptly when we both noticed the same thing: there were more furry girls on the streets. Usually they were rare and hard to pick up, but now there were squirrel girls and skunk girls and kitty cat girls and even killer whale girls peddling their wares everywhere. First Halperin employs Furries, now every pimp in the city must be doing it. Something didn't add up.

"You remember there being so many Furries in this town, Chang?"

"I can honestly say, Mr. Plush, that I do not. I have never seen two prostitutes dressed as turtles arguing over which lamppost to lean against in my life."

"Smells like Halperin."

Chang shot down my theory immediately.

"Mr. Halperin has been running the flesh trade in this city for years. Why would he just now put more furry girls on the streets, most honored Mr. Plush?"

"You've got a point Chang. Let's go to Jean's. There's nobody else I know who can patch me up and tell me about Furries in this town."

"A most wise suggestion, most honored Mr. Plush."

We drove to Jean's. She answered the door in her evening clothes, somehow having figured I'd come by. Her evening clothes happen to be a tight, head-to-toe fox suit. Somehow she pulls it off. I never bought into that Indian shamanic totem stuff, but that suit makes me wonder from time to time.

Being a teddy bear kind of blunts the impact of a near-fatal wounding. Most guys show up with their guts hanging out, their girlfriend faints. Me? It's always the same:

"What have you done this time? Let me get my sewing box…"

"Your compassion moves me to tears."

"Your sarcasm bores me to tears. Come in and sit down on the bed."

So I did and she began to sew. As you can imagine, it hurt like hell, but not so bad as a gutshot does.

"You should really stop messing with Halperin."

And not as bad as a lecture either.

"The man's a crook and a bully. He deserves the trouble I give him."

Jean rubbed her nose against my forehead.

"But do you deserve the trouble he gives you, baby?"

Maybe if it wasn't for the fact that Halperin was Jean's employer I wouldn't be so scornful of him. Then again, it was money I owed him that made me sell my body to Jimmy Plush. It was between how he helped me end up as a teddy bear, how he was party to Jean leading her secret life of waitressing and crime and how he helped her make a fool out of me on account of it. I was no fool, but Halperin helped her think she could make a fool out of me and that was enough to make me hate him all over again for who he was. I might have actually started to like this girl if I could trust her—and I wanted to like her so much.

"No matter what happens to me, Vic Halperin gets no quarter."

"You shouldn't talk like that, Jimmy. Halperin's a big, dangerous man in this town!"

"And I'm a small, dangerous bear, Jean! I'm not gonna be scared of anybody, you hear me?"

Sure I meant it, sure the bravado was real, but it was still a bit much. Being three feet tall and having no penis makes a man want to overcompensate. Dripping cotton from a gaping chest wound makes a man angry. In the future I would have to remind myself that my tough guy private dick outburst count was getting to be a bit high.

"I've got to go."

I mustered the best sad teddy face I could. I was a pretty sad teddy.

"You sure?"

I was hoping this might go where it usually went when I was getting patched up. I lack equipment, but Jean rubs me against all the right places and it feels nice. I could use a rub against all those places, because believe me, they could be oh so right and my day had gone oh so wrong.

"I've got things to do."

I knew what she meant. Waiting tables to help Halperin run numbers, unloading crates of fake name brand cereal, plucking balls of opium so that the poor sods at the den hidden behind J.L Wong's were shortchanged. Things to do. Bad things to do. I was gonna find out what and break my word to Halperin as I always did, possibly getting the ever-loving shit beaten out of me like I usually did. Didn't matter. I was tired of this.

"All right. Dinner Friday?"

"Maybe. I might be busy."

"Suit yourself. No fuzz off my balls. Thanks for the patch job."

"Any time."

"Yeah sure, any time."

I sulked my way out to the car and sat down.

"Chang…"

"Conceal the car, wait for Jean and follow her?"

"Yes, Chang. Do we do this that often?"

Chang didn't answer. He knew he was already on pretty thin ice thanks to the incident with Tusky and Bernstein. We waited and a car picked her up. It drove around in circles for a while to avoid a tail, not knowing Chang's Chinese Shadow Driving skills would be more than enough to evade them. Shadow Driving was a recent addition to the Chinese Fighting Arts, but not an altogether unwelcome one. The car stopped and let her out. I didn't like what I saw.

Jean immediately began a brutal slap fight with a fat girl dressed like a squirrel for the use of her lamppost. In this city, a girl doesn't use a lamppost for reading light.

"So there you go, Chang," I boasted. "Definitive proof."

"That your girlfriend is a prostitute?"

"I'm trying to objectively appraise the situation, Chang. Thinking about that too much will inhibit me. Jean works for Halperin, though. The Furries are on the street, one furry works for Halperin, therefore the Furries are Halperin's."

"I am still not convinced."

"Is there anybody else who might know something then, Chang?"

His voice got more solemn than usual.

"Yes, most honored Mr. Plush, but he hates you."

"Doesn't everybody?" I didn't like the notion, but its veracity could hardly be disputed.

"Okay, Mr. Plush. Just don't expect him to cooperate much. Also, I must warn you, Mittens O' Hara is… unusual."

"Nothing's going to surprise me in this town."

Except that is for an office dominated by a large typewriter. And a fat tiger cat whose porkpie hat rested uncomfortably atop its fat head. There was a slip of paper that read "press" on it. The cat sat down on various keys to type out something in enormous letters. It was a surprise, I've gotta say. I had thought Halperin was the last animal left in this town. As soon as it spotted me, it hissed.

"Beat it, Plush," said the cat in a high, nasal New York huckster voice. "You know you isn't welcome here, not after what you did!"

"I'm afraid I don't know that I *isn't* welcome, Mittens. Otherwise, I wouldn't be here."

"Well now you know, Paddington, so scram!"

I decided to ease up on the tough guy detective stuff for a second. This guy was every bit as abrasive as I was and there'd be no sense starting anything. My temper hadn't done me a whole hell of a lot of good lately.

"Listen, Mittens, I've got a big problem and I need your help. If you can't help me out this city's gonna get filthier and stay filthier. There's a rumor going around that somebody's helping Vic Halperin from the shadows. Somebody with Furry connections. You don't want to mess with angry Furries and how long do you think it will be before you start poking around and get caught by a better class of thug than Johnny Hideous and Skinny Valentine? Think about it, kitty cat!"

The cat did think about it, writing several lines of Qs as he sank down into his spot.

"I've gotta say, you have a point Plush. Guy like me gets into trouble all the time. Lots of tight squeezes, danger around every street corner. One day, Mr. Bartender starts slippin' Fells gin with a knockout drop chaser and then, bang, I'm on the trail and they're on my tail. Dangerous work, Plush. So, I tell ya what, I'll give you the lowdown on the Furries in town, even though I don't like ya, and I want it to be known again, I don't like ya. You're a walking cold sore, Jimmy Plush and you make people regret ever knowin' ya. If I hadn't lost my body in a game of checkers with a cat, I'd have shot you by now, but I'm glad I didn't, because more Furries ain't good for anybody, more Furries always mean more trouble, don't they, Plush? So I'll tell ya, I'll…"

Bang!

The cat went silent and fell from his spot on the typewriter. Reacting quickly, I reached for my gun, realizing somebody had come in while the cat was ranting, took aim and shot him and that somebody now had to be on the run. I could see the culprit running for the door, a guy in a penguin suit. Hopefully, all that padding wouldn't protect the back of his knees.

It didn't. He fell down right away, and it would be hard for him to get up. Particularly if I stood on his spine and pistol-whipped him in the back of his furry penguin head three or four times. Which I did. And he didn't get up. I ordered Chang inside and the two of us retrieved Mittens and the penguin thug. The thug went in the trunk and Mittens got the back seat next to him. Only difference was Mittens was going to the hospital and the penguin thug was definitely not.

"When you drop off Mittens, take me to Jean's, Chang."

"Certainly, most honored Jimmy Plush, but I don't think she'll be home."

"That's the point. She's got sewing needles and a bag of cotton."

Chang trembled a bit. "You're starting to sound like the real Jimmy Plush."

"What was that?" the groggy, wounded Mittens mumbled, revealing that he might just pull through.

"I'll explain another day."

"Savin' my life almost makes up for what you did to me," said the cat, "almost."

So we brought the cat to the hospital. I couldn't stick around to find out if he'd pull through because I had some business with the guy who shot him. Some very unpleasant business. We dragged him into Jean's house and tied him to a chair in her kitchen. I climbed onto the counter and grabbed a sharp knife while Chang peeled the penguin suit off the hood. Underneath it, he was even less to look at. I could see why he wanted so much to be cute.

His eyes opened to find me standing on the table, brandishing a kitchen knife. I had also laid out the bag of cotton and Jean's sewing kit.

"I need some information," I said matter-of-factly.

"I don't know nothin'!"

"Aww, I wouldn't say that. You know how to shoot a cat. You also know that an orange beak is better than that ugly, scrunched up pug nose of yours. That's not nothin'. I know lots of people who know less than that."

The penguin thug spat at me.

"I'm not tellin' you nothin'!"

"See? There we go. Now we're communicating better. There's a difference between the two things."

"Yeah? What it is, bear?"

"If you don't know nothin', I could torture you all day and nothing would come out. But, if you just won't tell me anything then I could probably extract something."

The penguin thug coughed out a nervous fake laugh. "Ha! That's rich comin' from the teddy bear. You ain't got the balls!"

I'm not certain if I had ever intended for this to be a bluff, but if I had, that possibility was gone now. As any man would be who lacked genitalia, I was awfully sensitive. I grabbed the knife with both hands and with all my teddy bear strength, I made a long cut in his bare chest.

"You Furries. You make me laugh. Walkin' around, pretending to be what I am. It's insulting. It's hilarious, too. I'm gonna give you what you want. Chang, stuff 'im."

My chauffeur's yellow skin turned pale.

"Mr. Plush—"

"Take the cotton and stick it in the hole, Chang. Then sew it."

The penguin thug's eyes widened. They must have looked enormous to Chang.

"Please, mister, you can't—"

Chang gave his customary bow. "As you wish, most honored Mr. Plush."

So, Chang stuffed the wound with cotton and sewed it shut. The penguin thug made several noises I never expected to hear out of a man or a penguin. I glared at him with my round, black plastic eyes. I knew he couldn't see any expression behind them, but from the look on his tear-stained face, I could tell that he knew I was glaring and he knew I wasn't above cutting him again.

"I do know somethin' and I'll tell ya."

"You don't say? I'm glad, because Chang could easily undo all those stitches one by one…"

"Halperin's working with a man from outta town who just started coming around. He knew this place was ripe for plucking. Halperin could be scared, could be shaken down. He's a coward underneath the whole Mandarin act."

"Tell me something I don't know. And I mean that literally. Stop stalling. I am not a patient little bear."

"His name's Kewpie Doll Steve."

"Better. If he were in the phonebook, that is. Chang, undo the stitches."

Chang once more gave his customary bow. He elongated it, seeing that this time I actually was bluffing.

"Wait…you don't gotta do that. The Monogram Marshmallow factory's a front for his hideout."

Great. Kewpie Doll Steve was hanging out at the Monogram Marshmallow factory. The worst part of having lost my memory is having to rediscover what a stupid town I lived in one day at a time. There were towns where it was hard to solve a mystery, where it took a smart man and not a guy willing to torture idiot henchmen for answers. There were towns where furry prostitution wasn't a criminal calling. There were towns outside the protectorate of crotchety teddy bears. Somehow, I still felt attached to this one and it bugged the hell out of me.

I juggled my failures in my head like so many oranges: I had failed as a writer and failed as a gambler, so I failed as a person and traded bodies with Jimmy Plush. I had failed as a man for not convincing my girl to get out of Halperin's press-on nailed grasp. I had failed as a detective when I got knocked out and left Lillian Benzedrine to Halperin's very limited mercies. She was probably somewhere dressed up as a French poodle to amuse out-of-town businessmen as her husband dangled in a chair over a vat of acid. My conscience was in the same position and there were scissors at the rope. Snip. Splash. Stab. I plunged the knife deep, penetrating his heart as all the disappointments had mine.

I waited for Chang's reaction. I wanted him to shake his head in disappointment. I wanted him to cry or tell me I'd gone too far and he should've been spared since he gave me the information he needed. But Chang had worked for the real Jimmy Plush, who had done things Chang refused to tell me about, who had done things that made Chang grateful for me, as bitter as I could get and as sick as could I be of his small outbursts of impertinence in the midst of fawning loyalty. Chang wasn't surprised.

"Your orders, Mr. Plush?"

I sighed. "Finish the job, Chang. We need to send a message; we need Halperin to know that Jimmy Plush is no fool, no weakling and isn't going to be pushed around."

So Chang and I got to it. It took hours, stank like nothin' else I've ever smelled and we had to buy a lot more cotton and give Jean's kitchen quite the scrubbing, but it was worth it. Halperin would get the message now, and I wouldn't have to do this again. Hopefully. I can't say I was that crazy about the whole experience.

We dropped off the corpse outside J.L Wong's and drove like the wind for the Monogram Marshmallow factory, where Kewpie Doll Steve or somebody who knew where he was should have been.

I wasn't at all shocked to find Halperin's gunsels Tusky and Bernstein guarding the back door. Might be a big city, but it was a pretty damn small world. Much as I wanted a piece of that walrus, stuffing that penguin had slightly eased my thirst for revenge, and I was thinking clearer.

"Chang, you take down the walrus. I'll take the squid."

Chang seemed concerned. "You realize there is no counter to squid-style martial arts."

"I do, Chang."

"And you are angry at the walrus…"

"Don't worry about me, Chang. I'm sure it will all work out."

I sprang from the car and put a bullet right between Bernstein's eyes. There was no counter to squid-style martial arts, but as of yet the Chinese really hadn't come up with a way to get around being shot in the head. Having untied the Gordian Knot with my gun, Chang readied himself for the walrus' charge. Tusky could have countered the Chinese fighting arts as well, but was, as I suspected, blinded with grief and anger at the death of his lover.

Poor Tusky charged directly into a move whose name Chang says translates roughly into "Gilded Battle Axe Fist." The walrus vomited out a big fishy mess and then imploded. Made me wonder why Chang had never chosen to do that before. It would have made things much easier.

Of course, it wasn't *that* easy. The ruckus of the exploding walrus and the vanquished squid attracted plenty of attention. The door burst open and there were all manner of Furries on the other side of it, from neon yellow opossums, to perpetually smiling wolves, from angry rats to loveable mandrills to cartoonish chipmunks to placid, Zen tortoises. There were some fifty of them pouring out of there, but we were ready to make some fur fly.

High on our victory, we took them three, four at a time; me letting bullets fly, tripping up a pink cow with a low kick as I shot a badger in the eye. With the Gilded Battle Axe Fist and the Decapitation Kick, Chang went through a pair of cuddly coyotes without blinking an eye and then brought the fear of God into a young tortoise that fled surprisingly fast. I took a few punches, dodged a few bullets, but I gave better than I got, because I'm Jimmy Plush and there ain't no walking stuffed animal in this town, real or fake that can stand up to me when I'm angry and I've just put a bullet in the head of somebody who I thought was unbeatable. Plush heads and the real heads underneath them littered the alley outside the Monogram Marshmallow Factory. There's nothing like the scent of fake fur, hot lead and spilled guts in the night to prove you're a real man.

"Chang, you've redeemed yourself," I said to the chauffeur, "but I need you to stay in the car."

"Mr. Plush, who knows what kind of ambush—"

"I think the ambush is over. I'm going in to investigate and hopefully find Kewpie Doll Steve."

"As you wish, most honored Mr. Plush."

Like I said, in some towns mysteries are tough to solve and it takes a real smart man to unravel it all but this ain't one of the towns. Criminals, God bless 'em, were usually found exactly where you expected to find them, completely unafraid of being undermined by the likes of myself or the frequently-absent police department. Emerging from the shadows, walking past two large inflatable sculptures of Murray, the Monogram Unicorn was a figure about my size.

Kewpie Doll Steve stepped into the light. It was eerie, how much he looked like a she. Like my own empty plastic eyes, his showed no feeling, but looked a bit flirty on account of the long, curled eyelashes and nonexistent eyebrows. His huge, infant lips had been painted red, which was the color of the short, checkered dress he wore. The ensemble was completed by a pair of little white party shoes. The illusion broke when he laughed a heavy cigar-burned laugh.

"This is him? The guy who brought down my men? Who gives Vic Halperin trouble? You're a riot, Jimmy Plush. You're just as much of a joke as me!"

I squeezed off a shot at the doll, but now of all times, the gun clicked "sorry, out of ammo".

"Don't worry, Plush. I don't have a gun. Don't need one either, teddy bear!"

The talking doll was quick and caught me off guard, he leapt like a jaguar, pinning me to the ground and punching me hard in the face. A guy like this was strong for the same reason I had to be strong: cause he looked nothing like a man. Cause he looked soft. As the punches rained down like brokers when the market goes south, I understood more than ever why I was so angry. I rolled him off me and took his position on top.

His head squeaked with each of my blows, which left me wondering just what could be done to a guy like this. Could his brain be damaged? Could he be unstuffed? Not by a guy with no hands who doesn't have anything to cut him with. I was out of bullets, too. I'd have to do something the criminals in this town usually didn't require me to do and that was think. I got off him and danced around like a boxer, putting up my knuckleless dukes.

Kewpie Doll Steve kicked surprisingly hard, sending me flying backwards into the side of a marshmallow vat. It was hot. I moved away from it quickly, knowing my own flammability a bit too well thanks to a run-in with Skinny Valentine and a cigarette lighter. I scurried lightly up the ladder leading to the vat, hoping Kewpie Doll Steve might be dumb enough to follow. Naturally, he took the bait.

I scrambled up the ladder one step at a time, defending my position with punch after punch and from punch after punch. Every couple of hits, I would be nearly as oblivious as he was or lose my footing on the ladder, but then the plan would come back to me, along with the knowledge that there would be no other way to bring this guy down. Pathetic that I had to rely on a vat of hot marshmallows.

We reached the top and I shuffled along the rim, balance aided by my relative lack of mass, his balance aided by the same. I risked my position to rush him and nearly fell in myself. Like Holmes and Moriarty, we were caught up in a moment of mortal struggle and almost plunged to the death together. Almost. My hands found the rim as he fell screaming into the white, hot gooey abyss. Awful way to go. I shuffled along the rim again until I reached the ladder and worked my way down to enjoy my moment of triumph.

I should have known I was never that lucky. When I hit the ground, a bullet caught me in the back, bringing me down. I felt my consciousness start to puff out of my body like a wisp of smoke. I wish I wasn't a guy who fainted so easily. The trenchcoated assassin left his hiding place and climbed gracefully up the ladder, reaching in, grabbing the marshmallow covered Kewpie Doll Steve from the pit of ooze and climbing down just as quickly as he climbed up. Before blacking out completely I caught a glimpse of the guy's face. Just when I thought my day had gotten better, it went back to being a regular god-awful day in the life of Jimmy Plush, teddy bear detective. The face had been my own only a month back, the face of one Charles Hatbox, but behind the eyes there was the bear with whom I'd traded bodies, that bastard, the real Jimmy Plush.

HAT

ROY KESEY

He came in through the door, and they gave him a paperclip and told him to make an airplane. When the airplane is finished, they said, you may go, or you may stay. As you wish.

He took off his hat.

- Am I permitted the use of tools?

- Yes, they said. Tools are allowed. Of course, a master would never need them, but the journey is long and you are just beginning. For now, tools are allowed.

- And may I use additional materials?

Of course not. Use what you are given.

With a soldering iron, a file, and two small pairs of needle-nose pliers, in five days he'd made an airplane of the paperclip, and he led them to see it.

No, they said. It is not an airplane.

- But look! The wings, the tail, even the landing gear . . .

It is not an airplane, they repeated. It is a toy. You must make an airplane.

- What does an airplane have that my toy doesn't?

Your toy has almost nothing that an airplane has, they said. Where is the engine? The propeller? The flaps and rudder, the fuel gauge, the gyro horizon? Your toy is no airplane, sir. Please do not call us again until your airplane is ready.

- Then I will need more tools, and additional materials.

All the tools you like, they said, though a master would never need them. But no additional materials. Use what you are given.

For eight months he labored, epoxy and tweezers, loupe and engraver. Finally the paperclip was an airplane with everything that an airplane must have, and again he led them to see it.

- I have finished, he said. May I go?

No, they said. It is still not an airplane.

- Of course it is. Just look—the oil gauge and altimeter, the removable cowling, the engine with its pistons and valves . . .

Very well, they said. If it's an airplane, start the engine. Start the engine, fly the plane, and then you may go.

- I have to make it fly?

Of course. Airplanes fly. If yours does not fly, it is not an airplane.

- But—he began. Then he bowed his hatless head, and they walked away.

For nine years he labored, centrifuge and compound microscope, laser and interferometer, micro-tomes and -pipettes and -needles. By the time he finished he was blind in one eye, but the airplane was ready, a point of silver-gleaming, wingspan of a millimeter and a millimeter from nose to tail. Then he called for them, and they came. One by one they perused his work. Finally they asked, And does it fly?

- Of course.

With a thread of spider-web he spun the propeller, and the plane slipped along the desktop, lifted and dipped and transcribed Giotto's circle before landing once again on the desktop.

It is a fine plane, they said. You are well on your way.

- May I go?

If you insist. But you are not yet a master. Stay with us, and learn to build without tools.

- One can learn on one's own.

Slowly, said one. Poorly, said another. Those who learn fastest and best are those who learn from those who learned first. Stay, learn from us, become a master.

- No. You have said I may go, and I shall.

So saying, he put on his hat and left.

Forty-one years later he returned.

- So at last you have decided to learn more? they asked. You wish to become a master?

No, he said. I have learned what I wished to learn.

- Is that so? We would accept your word if we accepted the word of anyone. As things stand, we must see proof.

Very well, he said. Bring me a thumbtack, and I will make you a submarine.

- How interesting. And which tools will you be needing?

No tools, he said. Just the thumbtack.

The thumbtack was brought, silver-gleaming and sharp. He set it in his hat, and they watched for three days and nights as he taught it to love. On the fourth day he rose, took the thumbtack in his left hand, placed his hat on his head, and led them to the sea. There, he set the thumbtack in the water and taught it to float.

- But it is still just a thumbtack, they said.

Yes, he answered. And no.

So saying, he stepped aboard, took the helm, and submerged.

THE SHARP-DRESSED MAN
AT THE END OF THE LINE

JEREMY ROBERT JOHNSON

He was collecting roaches. They moved faster than he'd expected. They'd be within centimeters of Dean's fingers and suddenly speed left or right with quarterback maneuverability. Crafty fuckers. Even more survival driven than he gave them credit for.

Survival, Dean's modus operandi. He understood the cockroaches on that level. Both of them had a clearly established Goal One:

Do Not Die.

He left out muffins. They swarmed the muffins. Dean harvested the unsuspecting bugs by the handful.

He replaced his regular bulbs with UV black lights, so he could see, but the roaches didn't scatter like they would under normal apartment light.

In between roach round-ups, he watched television. He grimaced. He cringed. Every image on the screen was a fat, flashing sign that read WWIII.

The news showed Conflict with a capital C, international and senseless.

It caused Dean to sweat stress and stink up his flop pad, the worst in all of D.C. Check the rotting floorboards, the dripping faucets. Noise-aholic neighbor bass and baby screams as the soundscape. Swinging bare-bulb ambience. Mildew and asbestos fighting for airspace. Punctured pipes leaking slow into linoleum cracks. Plastered pellets of roach shit as the common denominator.

Living cheap. Barely living.

He watched television. The President poked angry bears with sharp sticks.

We will not relent to this Axis of Assholes!

Take that Iraqi-Bear!

They're hoarding weapons and plannin' rape missions!

Yield before us Korea-Bear!

Commie baby-killers, pure and simple!

Oh, China-Bear, you'll rue the day!

The President was up in the polls. The populace—petrified and war weary, but strangely supportive, Dean included. He'd back a bully as long as El Presidente could guarantee a win. It was that possibility of a loss that spooked Dean to screeching simian defense levels. A loss, at this heavily armed and nuclear point in world history, meant Apocalypse.

Dean's answer—Cockroach Suit. Thousands of cockroaches hand-stitched through the thorax, tightly sewn to a Penney's business suit bought on the cheap.

Dean's days and nights were occupied with the spreading of wings and the careful puncturing of his pathogenic pals with needle and thread. He positioned them all feet-out, so their mouths could still feed.

Dead roaches were of no use to Dean. The live ones carried the instinct.

The instinct had kept them alive for four hundred million years. Their bodies were natural radiation shock absorbers. They could live for ten days after being decapitated. Dean knew that in the event of Apocalypse, he'd be rolling with the right crew.

He knew they were training him for war, and for suffering. He'd already borne the brunt of their bacterial ballast. He'd coped with clostridium. He'd dealt with dysentery.

He was becoming impervious to disease, like them.

He kept and catalogued the roaches, separated into clusters of speedy Smoky-browns, ravenous Germans, and over-eating Americans.

Jars upon jars of the bugs were stored in his deep freezer. They slowed down in the chill. The cold goofed them like opium, kept them still.

It kept them from eating each other.

That insatiable appetite had been the primary problem with the first cock-roach suit. Dean had left it out in the muggy tenement warmth at night, stored along with some chocolate cereal in a microwave-sized cardboard box. When he opened the box in the morning the cockroaches had not only eaten all the cereal, but had ravaged each other. His carefully crafted suit had gone cannibalistic.

He bought another suit. Dean didn't sweat his cash flow. Daddy Dean Sr.'s estate was still kicking out cash in steady intervals. The primary source of cash—royalties from the sale of Daddy Dean's Ivy League approved books on entomology.

Daddy Dean Sr. had been a big time bug man and serious scholar until his car accident. A deer had run into the road. Daddy Dean Sr. swerved hard with his right hand on the wheel. His left hand gripped a cherry Slurpee with a thick red straw. Daddy Dean Sr.'s car hit an elm tree straight on. The dependable airbag exploded and jammed the fortified Slurpee straw straight into Daddy Dean Sr.'s left nostril and right on through to his frontal lobe.

Dean had shown up at the scene in time to see the cops detach the straw and blood-filled cup.

Dean had heard one cop on the accident scene call it a "straw-botomy."

Dean didn't think it was funny.

Dean didn't think a single fucking thing was funny for quite a while, and resolved to find happiness however he could.

For a long while that meant spending Daddy's textbook royalties on hallucinogens. The "straw-botomy" had taught him that the world made no sense anyway, so he traveled the world hunting head-trips. He tongued toads. He feasted on fungus. He inhaled ayahuasca. A bad encounter with a sodomizing shaman and some industrial strength desert peyote finally scared Dean straight.

Then he moved back to the states and began his survival training.

He knew the world wanted to erase him. He'd seen it in visions. He'd seen it in the eyes of the priapic shaman. He saw flash frames of his own father felled by a plastic straw.

Dean moved to the slums of D.C. He wanted to move to a place that resisted and destroyed life. He knew there were survival secrets in the daily struggle.

He holed up and watched television. He watched El Presidente taunting nuclear armed countries anxious to see if they could one-up Hiroshima.

Y'all ain't got the bomb, or maybe y'all just ain't got the balls to use it!

C'mon Korea-Bear, show us you got a pair!

Dean read books about roaches. He studied sewing and stitch types. He bought spools of thread and heat sterilized needles.

Dean developed his cockroach suit and watched it fail.

He cried and sucked up the sick, musty attar of roaches when his first suit dined on itself.

He cursed himself when the second suit crawled through a hole in the crumbling apartment drywall. Fifty seconds to piss. That's all he'd taken. That was all they'd needed. He heard his roach-riddled jacket and pants skittering around in the crawlspace above his kitchen.

Every time he failed, he felt as if Apocalypse was seconds away. He got weak, the blood flow to his head lagged. He thought he could hear the roar of approaching bombs overhead. He worked harder, his hands shaking with fear.

He ignored the doubt that crept into his skull and took up permanent residence.

Dean, don't you know the bomb is coming for you? You think some bugs and some cheap threads can stop a holocaust?

He ignored the fists that pounded on his door, the angry screams, the vulgar notes slipped through the crack of his mail slot.

The note last Tuesday read: Mister room 308, you are the cockroach man and ever since you came all up in here they've gone crazy. My little sister has to wear cotton balls in her ears to keep them roaches from digging into her head and laying eggs, like they did with Brian. You ain't right at all Mister room 308, and you ought to leave and take your roaches with you. I see them coming out from under your front door right now. My dad says if Brian has eggs in his brain, then you die. Go away. Love, Maysie.

The neighbors thought Dean was bad mojo. They threatened litigation. They threatened worse. Dean knew it was part of the world's plan to erase him. He kept working.

Dean actually saw the first bomb hit. He knew it was coming.

He knew from the silence. El Presidente had gone silent for three days. No more TV broadcasts promising patriotic retribution. No more shots on CNN of El Presidente grabbing his balls and shouting, "Eat this, Iran!"

El Presidente was quiet because he was hiding, somewhere, from the grief he saw coming America's way. El Presidente was crafty, even more survival driven than Dean had given him credit for.

In the calm before the atomic shit-storm, Dean finished his third cockroach suit.

It was perfect. A living tapestry of twitching legs and chittering mandibles. Add to the threads a pair of Kroeg blast goggles, a crash helmet, a refillable oxygen tank, and a thick pair of foil-lined tan work boots, and Dean was suited for survival.

When the first newscaster started crying on air, Dean geared up and walked from his apartment to the street. He didn't want to be inside that roach trap when the Earth started shaking.

Dean walked by apartments, heard the crying of the tenants. They could sense the bomb was coming. Their cries were weird and strangely complacent, the mewling of doomed animals with no options. Baby seals, waiting for the spiked bat to spread their skulls wide.

It made Dean sad. He cried and fogged up his goggles. He felt the suit writhing around his body, taking in his warmth, seething. He stayed in motion.

Dean made it into the street and turned to his left, not sure quite where to go, hoping the cockroaches' instinct would take over soon. Then he would just lay down on his belly or his back and let them carry him to survival, like a God.

The D.C. streets were packed with people looking up at the sky, waiting. Dean expected chaos and conflict. No one even gave him a second glance. They were waiting for the Big Delivery from above.

They got it, twenty seconds later.

The flash blinded Dean, even with the goggles and helmet on.

He crouched behind a cement stoop and heard the most cohesive and unified scream any dying species had ever let loose.

Then there was silence, and heat, terrible heat.

And, of course, darkness.

The cockroaches carried Dean, like a God. He woke to dark clouds and electrical storms and drifting gray ash. His retinas were blast burnt, but functional.

He was alive.

That was the part he could not comprehend.

He was fucking alive.

The roaches were too, and they were moving quickly towards a perceived food source. Dean felt them moving, swift and single-minded, driven by constant hunger.

His hands were cold. Nuclear winter was just beginning and the air already approached frosty. He'd forgotten to buy gloves. He hunched his shoulders, pulled his hands inside the living suit. He relaxed and enjoyed the eerie quiet, and reveled in being alive. Being a survivor.

He moved without effort through the ash of nuclear winter. His suit surged beneath him as it crawled up onto a sidewalk. The legion of tiny legs pushed onward as Dean zoned out on the gray snowfall floating down from the sky.

He watched the sky darken. He saw thick red and green clouds of nuclear dust float above him. He saw an obelisk in the distance, stark and tarred jet black by the bomb blast.

It was the Washington Monument, just like he'd seen on T.V. There was something walking back and forth at the base of the monument. It moved like a human, but glowed bright yellow.

Dean let the suit carry him closer, and then stood up when he was within ten feet of the yellow shifting mass.

Dean lifted the visor of his helmet and de-fogged his goggles. He could see clearly after that, aside from the bright imprint of the blast that wouldn't leave his sight.

The peripatetic figure was a man. A man in a Twinkie suit. The thousands of Twinkies were half charred and oozing cream filling.

The man turned to face Dean.

The man's face was slack, and the eyes were empty of thought or feeling. Despite this lack of emotion, El Presidente was still the most recognizable man on Earth.

He looked at Dean and started to weep.

Dean opened his arms, offering a hug.

El Presidente stepped forward, and then hesitated. It was too late. The cockroach suit was upon him, a thousand mouths demanding to be fed.

Dean looked into El Presidente's eyes, caught dilated pupils, animal-level fear.

The eyes no longer promised Dean's destruction, as they had from the static screen of his television. The world's plan to erase Dean had failed; it was vaporized to dust, silt in sick Strontium-19 winds.

The scarred sky above Dean grew darker, the air around him even colder. Dean shivered; El Presidente screamed.

Dean reached up and warmed his hands around El Presidente's throat. He felt the pulse under his hands drop to zero.

The weeping had ended, and the feasting had begun.

HOTEL ROT

AIMEE BENDER

They came to town in long cars, and gathered up all the birds they could find. With tall nets on stems and cleverly seeded traps. Then they stuffed them into one huge room at the biggest hotel for miles. Birds up to the ceiling, birds struggling in the middle, birds layering the floor in featherbeds. Clucking and quacking and trying to build a nest in the tile which was impossible. Trying to make nests of each other which was a bad idea. There was nowhere to fly, the air was so clogged with feathers and beaks, and so each bird flapped in place, or chirped at the floor, or wedged itself into the ceiling. With so much wing pollen in the air, it was very hard to breathe.

Then they charged tickets to go in. Room of Birds, they called it, and they figured people might like to go and look. Twelve dollars for a day-long pass. But it really made you want to explode, when you put your eyes in there, all that flight stuffed inside a corporate auditorium. A few locals jumped at the chance but it was so tightly balanced in there that new bodies upset the equilibrium, and all the birds began shifting. Seagulls dropped out of the ceiling and bluejays panicked and banged against the wall and several robins flew into the window and the emu crumpled into a beige heap. Hysterical chickens ran back and forth on the floor.

Next door. Get away from that infernal squawking. You can hear it from a mile away.

Next door, they took all the flowers they could round up in a day, vans and wagons and twelve-wheeler trucks-full, every floral shop for miles wiped clean, and they crammed them all into the hotel's second ballroom. Room of Flowers. There wasn't space here for terra cotta pots or watering cans or cellophane, so all the tulips, gardenias, wisteria and morning glories were spread on the floor in a huge petal salad. All the roses made triangles with their stems. You paid your six dollars and went inside, and the rainbow spectrum softened the eyes. The whole room smelled so warm, like grandmother's wrist, or July Italy, or a fresh towel on the morning you wake up with new hope. The smell was so intense it actually put color in the air. A couple of folks had asthma attacks and had to leave after a few vivid seconds.

It was very beautiful, briefly.

Most corporate hotels have at least three auditoriums, for cross-over conventions, and the third one here did not get passed over. First Fauna. Then Flora. Finally Bones. Here was an utterly static room and the only one that after several days wasn't a rotting theatre of wings or petals. Bone Room stayed put. In it were the frames of everything you could imagine: femur, skull, bird wing, snake back, spine of woman, feet of antelope, shoulder of gorilla, tiny fish head. All packed in the room, all shades of white and brown, all ready to decay eventually but on a much slower time scale. From inside The Bone Room, you could actually catch a whiff of the flowers biodegrading next door, and hear those birds yelling and weeping in heaps next-next door. The Bone Room itself was silent, and smelled mildly of dirt. The people who paid their three dollars and went inside stayed for awhile and sat with the bones. Calming, it was. Humbling. Not unlike looking up at the wash of stars on a clear night. After a meditative trip to The Bone Room, you might walk in the bare gardens beneath the silent skies and think of the shifts in your life so far.

The Bone Room managed to stay in business.

Four days after Room of Flowers opened, it had to close. The inevitable wilt had turned that corporate auditorium into one huge compost heap. It smelled awful now, withery, and big sympathy for those janitors that had to scoop those piles upon piles of petals into their arms and dump them into the garbage. By the end of their day, all they could stand to sniff was something spicy and nonfloral, like salt or cayenne pepper. One janitor came home to his wife who had dabbed perfume on her throat to entice him into her arms and unfortunately for both of them, as soon as he caught a whiff of her, he had to run in the other direction as fast as he could and throw up, sighing, into the dirt. They had a long talk after she'd showered. He never picked a flower again. Very few were left growing anyway.

I looked back into the Room of Birds on day five, and all the toucans and eagles and doves and pigeons and parrots and seagulls and hawks were dead. All the parakeets and robins and pelicans and bluejays and condors and terns and the two emus and the one ostrich. All seventy of the hummingbirds had slowed to a stop and were strewn like old rosebuds on the floor. All fourteen herons, in leggy piles. All five woodpeckers and both magnificent frigates. All dead. The room was now just a mass of multi-colored stilled feathers.

This was the worst moment of all. Please write a letter to the world, and tell them to stop it.

THE MOBY CLITORIS
OF HIS BELOVED

IAN WATSON & ROBERTO QUAGLIA

Yukio was only a salaryman, not a company boss, but for years he'd yearned to taste whale clitoris sashimi. Regular whalemeat sashimi was quite expensive, but Yukio would need to work for a hundred years to afford whale clitoris sashimi, the most expensive status symbol in Japan.

Much of Yukio's knowledge of the world came from manga comic books or from anime movies which he watched on his phone while commuting for three hours every day. He treasured the image of a beautiful young ama diving woman standing on the bow of a whaling boat clad in a semi-transparent white costume and holding sparklingly aloft the special clitoridectomy knife. An icon far more wonderful than that of Kate Winslet at the front of the *Titanic!* Americans might have their *Moby Dick*, but Yukio's countrymen (or at least the richest of them) had their Moby Clitoris Sashimi.

The beautiful young ama woman would take a deep breath, dive, swim underneath a woman-whale, grasp her 8-centimeter clitoris, then with one razor-sharp slash cut off the clitoris and swim away very fast. On the deck of the whaler the crew would wait for the ama to climb back aboard, her costume now see-through due to wetness.

And then the whalers would harpoon and kill the whale, because it would be too cruel to leave a female whale alive after amputation of her clitoris. In this respect the Japanese differed very much from certain Islamic and African

223

countries which cut off the clitorises of human girls, so that men should not feel inadequate about their own capacity for orgasms.

Whenever the Japanese were criticised for hunting whales, it was the harvesting of clitorises which empowered them to continue. And of course Japan observed a strict clitoris quota, so that enough female whales would continue to copulate pleasurably and repopulate. Thus, while it was true that whale clitoridectomy directly pleasured only the richest individuals, every Japanese citizen who enjoyed eating whales also benefitted.

This Yukio knew. Yet he still yearned to taste whale clitoris sashimi for himself! Most men have licked a woman's clitoris, although probably they haven't eaten one; but the organ of ecstasy of a female whale sliced thinly was said to possess a taste beyond words.

When Yukio's vacation came—the usual very hot and humid fortnight in August—he didn't surrender his holiday back to the Nippon Real-Doll Corporation, as he had done in previous years, in the hope of more rapid promotion through the copyright department. Instead, he took a train from Tokyo (and then a bus) the hundred kilometers to Shirahama City where ama diving women lived. He would seduce an ama to love him. They would marry. She would get a job on a whaling boat. For him she would smuggle clitoris sashimi...

To his consternation Yukio soon discovered that the ama women of Shirahama, who dive for red seaweed, sea snails and abalone, looked nothing like the icon in his mind. For one thing, they weren't slim but were muscular from exercise—and chubby, to cope with cold water. For another, their faces were darkly tanned, not a lovely creamy-white. For a third, their voices were loud and raucous, perhaps due to damage from water pressure; and their speech was quite vulgar. For a fourth, they didn't wear semi-transparent white garments, but orange sweatshirts, thermal tights, and neoprene diving hoods. And for a fifth, their average age seemed to be over sixty. Even if one of those fat vulgar grannies wanted a lover and husband, how could Yukio excite himself enough to woo her?

Disconsolate, he went to get drunk. Presently he found himself outside **The Authentic Ama-Geisha Inn**. The name seemed promising.

Inside, he was amazed to find waiting several beautiful slim young hostesses dressed in the correct long white semi-transparent costumes, and also wearing white high heels. Perched jauntily on their foreheads were diving masks. One hostess wore her very long hair in an oily black rope which would excite a bondage fetishist or a flagellant considerably.

Soon this hostess, whose name was Keiko, was leading Yukio into a private room—which contained a low table, plastic cushions, and a small blue-tiled pool set in the floor of tatami matting, which was plastic too; plastic would dry more quickly than straw matting.

He knelt. Keiko knelt and poured some Johnnie Walker Black Label.

She giggled and said sweetly, "You may splash me whenever you wish!"

Thus revealing more of her breast or thigh or belly...

"But you're the ama of my visions!" Yukio exclaimed. "Why aren't you diving in the sea? You would look so beautiful."

Already he was a bit in love with Keiko, even though the plan had been for an ama to fall in love with him.

"I'm an ama-geisha," Keiko explained. "Only *you* can wet me, not the sea."

"I've seen amas just like you with the whaling fleet! Only," and he recollected his apparently foolish plan, "not with such wonderful hair as yours. They dive for whale clitorises," he added.

Keiko giggled again. "A real ama does that."

"A fat old granny?"

Keiko's job was to please him, and Yukio seemed to prefer intellectual stimulation rather than getting drunk and splashing her, so the astonishing truth emerged—a truth known to most inhabitants of Shirahama, but which the media patriotically chose not to publicise.

Each whaling ship carried a real ama and also a false ama (or rather an authentic iconic ama). The real ama, old and fat, foul-mouthed and lurid, would harvest the clitoris while the false ama—who looked more real—would wait in the water beside the ship. The false authentic ama would then take the clitoris from the real inauthentic ama and would climb a steep gangplank back on board deck, her garment delightfully see-through. Meanwhile the old fat ama would sneak on to the ship from the rear, using the ramp up which dead whales were winched.

This substitution made whale-hunting seem graceful and elegant and sexually exciting in the eyes of the world—slightly akin to marine bull-fighting—and justified the high price to gourmets of clitoris sashimi.

Yukio stared at Keiko. "Wouldn't you rather be on a whaling ship, than here? With your wonderful rope of hair you'd set a new style for cartoon books and films. I can license your image for you." Yukio's work did indeed consist in copyright matters concerning Real Dolls modelled upon porn stars. "I'm a specialist. You'd earn a big fee." And Yukio would be the lovely Keiko's agent and manager, and because of this, he would become her Beloved! And at last he would eat whale clitoris sashimi.

Keiko was wide-eyed.

"Agreed?"

Before Keiko could change her mind, Yukio picked up his glass of Johnnie Walker Black Label and threw the contents over her, wetting and revealing a delightful breast.

"Kampai!" he exclaimed, to toast her—but in his mind he was shouting 'Banzai!' for victory.

The whaling industry normally recruited deep-sea ama from communities such as Shirahama, but Yukio needed Keiko with him in Tokyo to register her image. Keiko could stay in his little apartment in a highrise in the suburbs.

So Keiko exchanged her authentic ama costume and high heels for jeans and a blouse, and piled her rope of hair upon her head, hiding it with a scarf, because nobody must steal her image on a phone en route! Already Yukio felt paranoid and jealous.

On the train Yukio looked at the news on his own phone, and a headline caught his eye: THROW THE WHALE AWAY!

A meeting in South Korea of the International Whaling Commission had ended in confusion. As usual the dispute was about whether to save whales or eat them. The Japanese delegate had suddenly declared that whale clitoris sashimi was a cultural treasure unique to Japan. If foreigners forced the Japanese to stop eating whalemeat, the Japanese would continue to harvest whale clitorises —but to please world public opinion they would throw the rest of the whale away. They would accomplish this grand gesture by compassionately exploding all clitoridectomised whales using torpedos packed with plastic explosive, since nuclear torpedos were unacceptable.

"That will make clitorises even more valuable and prestigious," Yukio said to Keiko.

"I have a clitoris too," she replied.

"But not a whale clitoris." Or at least not yet, he thought.

Maybe the Japanese delegate's statement was intended to bewilder the World Wildlife Fund, which had been picketing the meeting. Under the United Nations' Declaration of Cultural Rights, it was forbidden to attack or slander any country's unique cultural icons, such as the Golden Arches of McDonald's or the Eiffel Tower. Now that Japan had registered whale clitoris sashimi as a cultural treasure, that gourmet experience was protected from criticism—and if there were no clitorises to be sliced, obviously the experience would become extinct. To preserve the cultural experience, the Japanese must continue to hunt whales.

Yukio's apartment was a four-mat one, which was better than living and sleeping in a room only the size of three tatami mats; but still it was rather crowded by two people, unless those two people were intimate. So Yukio found himself examining Keiko's clitoris, causing her to sigh with pleasure. Then he went to sleep and dreamed that every century a magical woman-whale would appear offshore, to provide sashimi from her clitoris for the Empress of the time. On the brow of this whale: a white mark exactly like a chrysanthemum flower. During the subsequent hundred years, the whale's clitoris would regenerate.

Yukio awoke in the morning, thinking immediately about the possibilities of *cloning* clitoris. Keiko had already risen and was now kneeling, dressed in her authentic iconic ama costume which real ama no longer wore. Truly she had the graces of a geisha.

Obviously a woman's clitoris couldn't possibly taste as wonderful as a whale's, yet what if cloned human clitoris could be marketed profitably enough so that the genius who thought of this became rich enough to afford to eat whale clitoris?

Since Yukio had no idea how to clone anything, an alternative occurred to him. These days, because pigs and people are very alike, pigs provided transplant organs for human beings. Maybe a million people had inside them pig hearts or lungs or livers or kidneys. When the pigs were sacrificed to provide transplants, the rest of the pig, including the clitoris in the case of female pigs, would probably go into pet food.

What if Yukio were to buy the sex organs of pigs, to provide a source of clitorises? These could be packaged in tiny jars as human clitorises, and sold over the internet! Upon the label, a photo of a genuine human clitoris, with a certificate of authenticity which would be correct since the picture at least was genuine. *Delicious clitorises, cloned from this very clitoris you see!* Realistically, Keiko might *not* obtain a job on a whaling ship—yet she could still help Yukio to achieve his goal.

Truly, his trip to the seaside had inspired him, probably because the clean air contained more oxygen in it than in the city.

Yukio took his phone, and soon he was photographing Keiko's clitoris while she assisted him. He wasn't quite sure if her clitoris was the usual size but it was certainly very noticeable. Using Photoshop, he could get rid of the surrounding flaps of flesh familiar to users of porn magazines, leaving only the clitoris itself in the picture. His computer could print many labels. In a truly iconic sense he would indeed be cloning Keiko's clitoris, or at least its image. In his excitement he almost forgot to go to work.

On the commuter train, he used his phone to search for Pig Organ Farms and for Food Bottlers. Genius is to perceive connections where none were seen before.

When he returned home that night, Keiko was already lying asleep on the futon, still dressed as an ama and wearing her diving mask for even greater authenticity. Her long rope of hair seemed like an oxygen tube. The TV set was showing young men eating as many worms as they could as quickly as possible. It was the popular weekly show *Brown Spaghetti Race*, sponsored by the Dai-Nippon Cheese Company. The more Parmesan the contestants poured on the wiggling worms, the less difficult it was to pick them up using smoothly lacquered chopsticks.

Would consumers be more excited by "genuine canned cloned human clitoris sashimi" or "genuine ama clitoris sashimi (cloned)"? Maybe the label should show Keiko smiling as she held her photoshopped clitoris to her own lips with *chopsticks*? Would the suggestion of auto-cannibalism excite buyers? Was his ideal market gourmets who couldn't afford whale clitoris, or sexual fetishists? Or both?

Yukio sat on the edge of the futon beside Keiko and regarded her tenderly. He lifted her rope of hair, closed his lips upon the end of it, and blew into the hair as though to supply her with more oxygen, such as she had been accustomed to at the seaside. Maybe, subconsciously at least, that was the reason why she had put on the diving mask.

"Keiko-san," he told her politely, although she was asleep, "there is a change of plan."

It took Yukio some hard work and organisation and most of his savings to set up the Genuine Cloned Ama Clitoris Sashimi Company, or GCACSC for short.

The sexual organs of organ-donor pigs must be rushed by courier, refrigerated and ultra-fresh, to the Greater Tokyo Bottling Company, where a dedicated employee dissected out the clitorises for bottling. Irrelevant vaginas and labia and also penises and balls were cooked and minced and canned to become Luxury Pig-Protein sent as food aid to starving Communist North Korea, with the full co-operation of the government's Japan-Aid programme, which subsidised the project and praised Yukio's initiative and sense of social responsibility, while respecting his wish to remain anonymous. The donor farm believed that the complete sexual organs were being processed, which in the case of male pigs was true; and Yukio had no wish to enlighten them.

He enlightened the gourmet public about the availability of cloned ama clitoris sashimi by means of a clever spam program, which he bought in the Akihabara electronics district. A spam program was appropriate since the word spam originally meant 'spiced American meat.'

Every night after Yukio came home from the Nippon Real-Doll Corporation, he printed labels for the jars and boxes and address labels and dealt with an increasing number of internet orders and payments. He had rented a garage for delivery of the little unlabelled jars of clitorises, which were received there during the day by Keiko, dressed ordinarily. She would then change into her ama costume, stick the labels on to the jars, skillfully fold the beautiful little cardboard boxes which Yukio produced on his printer, fit a jar into each, and stick on an address label.

Keiko was very busy; and so was Yukio. What with Yukio's regular work at the Real-Doll Corporation and his after-hours work at home, he became a bit like a Zen monk who had trained himself in No-Sleep, or not much—now he slept standing up in the commuter train instead of looking at manga and anime on his phone; consequently he never watched the News in either manga or anime format. All he knew was that orders were pouring into his home PC. The spam had done its job sufficiently well that consumers were spontaneously spreading the word of the new and affordable (although not cheap) gourmet delight. Keiko told him that by now magazines were writing stories about, and TV channels were talking—she had done some phone interviews. Apparently Yukio was being hailed as the new Mr Mikimoto, but Yukio had no spare time to pay much attention.

Mikimoto-san was the man who invented cultured pearls by putting irritating grains of sand inside oysters, at Pearl Island. To suggest that his cultured pearls were as good as naturally occuring pearls, he had employed amas to dive into the sea around Pearl Island for tourists to admire, and in fact, according to Keiko, Mikimoto-san had invented or revised the see-through costumes of the amas. The ama water-ballet actresses would bring up real oysters, which might or might not contain real pearls, for the tourists to eat authentically in the Pearl Island Restaurant.

One evening an astonishing thing happened. Yukio had woken up automatically as usual in time to get off the commuter train, and was walking away from the station homeward when he saw Keiko coming towards him along the street dressed in schoolgirl uniform!

"Why have you become a schoolgirl?" he cried out, but Keiko walked past, ignoring him.

Then along the street came another schoolgirl Keiko, then another, then a couple together.

They were real schoolgirls wearing false faces—latex masks of the real Keiko!

"Excuse me," Yukio said to a false Keiko, "but where did you get that mask?"

The schoolgirl paused, but remained silent.

Of course, she couldn't speak while wearing that mask because Yukio wasn't speaking to her but to the mask. Should he reach out and peel the mask from her true face? That might constitute assault, or even a new perversion, of unmasking schoolgirls.

"Please tell me," he begged.

She bowed slightly, then beckoned—gestured him back towards the station.

Like a tourist guide for the deaf she led him inside the station to a vending machine. It was one of those that sold the used panties of virgins, which old men would buy and sniff. But now it also sold something else in little bags: those masks of Keiko.

Quickly Yukio bought one. The packaging showed the upper body and face of Keiko, just as on the labels of the jars of clitorises. Keiko held to her lips with chopsticks a clitoris, although now she was using her left hand rather than her right—evidently she had been photoshopped. A speech bubble above her head read: *Eat my virgin clitoris.*

That was the cheeky message conveyed by the mask. Identities concealed, schoolgirls could tease men naughtily without a blush, without even saying a word or making a gesture. What innocent, or wicked, erotic power they would feel! Clitoris power. Maybe the packaging of other masks had different speech in the bubbles. Or maybe not. Or maybe yes.

Quickly Yukio googled non-manga non-anime News on his phone.

He saw a picture, taken through a window, of a classroom in which all the girls were wearing identical Keiko masks to the consternation of the teacher. He saw a picture of a playground where a dozen Keikos of different heights were strolling. A craze had hit the whole of Japan, probably spreading among schoolgirls everywhere by txt!

Because of trousers, he noticed some boys too, who were also wearing Keiko masks. Ah, the boys were doing that so as to save face!

He asked the Keiko who still lingered by the machine, "Keiko, did you *do* this without consulting me? To prove that you're clever too?" What a perfect ecological loop, that the same machines which sold the used virgin underwear of schoolgirls should provide the same schoolgirls with these masks...

But of course she wasn't the real Keiko, and besides she had no intention of speaking.

How could Keiko have organised the rapid manufacture of all the masks and their supply to vending machines? Yukio ripped open the packaging and unfolded the latex mask. On the back of the chin, to his horror he saw: *â„¢ Nippon Real-Doll Corp.*

Had he fallen asleep at work without realizing and talked in his sleep? Had he been too clever for himself? Had part of him exploited himself schizophrenically out of company loyalty? Or had the company security-psychologist decided that Yukio was behaving oddly, and investigated his computer?

Oh foolish Yukio, to have copyrighted the label with Keiko's image in his own name at work, borrowing the company's copyright software—that was how they had found out!

But then the company perceived a unique business opportunity: the Real-Doll Corporation could turn real schoolgirls everywhere into clitoris-power dolls of his Keiko! A million texting schoolgirls could spread a craze within a few days, or maybe a few hours. And Yukio couldn't complain or sue, nor could Keiko. For one thing, Yukio had committed industrial theft. But, even more worryingly, the Real-Doll Corporation's psychologist-detective may have also found out the true source of Genuine Cloned Ama Clitoris Sashimi.

Yukio bowed to the false Keiko, then hurried home.

"Who are you?" he said to Keiko in the four-mat room. Quickly he explained what he had discovered—Keiko had been too busy labeling in the rented garage that day to watch any news. And he added: "You must wear a mask from now on, or else I won't know you!"

"Do you mean wear my diving mask?"

"More like a mask of Kate Winslet, I think... No, wait!"

The big oval of latex cut from the Keiko mask fitted the diving mask perfectly. Superglue secured it. Her false eyes, false nose, and false mouth squeezed flatly against the inside of the glass, as if she had dived to a depth of such pressure that her features had become two-dimensional. Her photoshopped clitoris forever would touch her flat lips.

Since the false genuine face which she wore a few centimeters in front of her real face was in fact her true face, this negated that falsity and bestowed a mysterious and mystical authenticity upon her actual face, even though that was now invisible, as mystical things often are.

A Zen-like state came over Yukio. He knelt before Keiko, like Pinocchio praying to the Blue Fairy to make him real. By not-seeing what he was seeing, Yukio began to worship her countenance.

Unseeing too, a blind goddess, Keiko heard his mantra of worship.

"My Beloved, My Beloved, My Beloved..."

Whale clitoris sashimi was only an illusion, from which Yukio was now freed by enlightenment. Probably its sublime taste was also an illusion caused by exorbitant price. He would eat Keiko's clitoris instead.

SCRATCH

JEREMY C. SHIPP

Margaret, one of my least favorite wives, blocks the television as if anything she says is as interesting or witty as scripted dialogue crafted by professional writers; as if her smile with the chipped tooth is as enchanting as a celebrity's; as if I haven't seen this one a thousand times already. "I have something special planned for you later," Margaret says. "It involves strawberries, handcuffs and a very lucky umbrella."

I laugh, because she expects me to.

"Be honest," she says. "Is that too kinky? Not kinky enough?"

"You know what, honey?" I say. "I'm not really feeling it tonight. I'm sorry."

"Not feeling it?"

"I don't think I can do this so ... often anymore."

"Oh."

"I'd like to. It's just that my body isn't responding the way that it used to."

"I see."

She should walk away. Run, really.

But instead, she steps closer. She can't help herself. Not because of gravity or magnetism or even attraction. It's because every night after she falls asleep, I sit beside her, and read to her from my notebook with the kitten on the cover. You probably don't know this, but that kitten was run over and killed and run over a few more times three days after that photograph was taken. And if you look close enough, with a magnifying glass would be best, you can see fear in the kitten's eyes. Part of him knows what's coming. Part of him isn't so innocent.

"Don't look so sad," I say. "Our relationship has evolved beyond the physical.

I get so much more pleasure from talking to you now than touching you."

"You don't like touching me?" she says, closer.

"I do. Of course I do. But our bodies aren't what they used to be. We're not built for sex at this age. You can't have children anymore, so we've lost our physical appeal."

"I can get surgery," she says, on my lap now. "I can change."

"Yes, but you can't change into a younger woman. You can never get back what you lost."

She holds me tight. "I don't want to lose you."

"You won't," I say, and smile. "No matter what fades from our relationship, I'll always appreciate what we have. Always."

She squeezes me. She cries on me.

Then she folds into me like a hide-a-bed, and poof. She's gone.

"That's how you do it," I say.

Sonny pops his head out of the enormous vase where he was hiding and says, "I'm not sure exactly what you did, Mr. Grelding."

"Of course you're not sure," I say. "You're a student."

Look at him jumping out of that vase like some green-screened ninja. He thinks he's so great. Just because he's young and good looking and smarter than the average bear. I bet he's never traveled back and forth through time or fought in an intergalactic space war or saved the world from the apocalypse.

I bet he's even a virgin.

After setting down in the forest clearing, I unfasten my rocket pack and let it smash a couple of mushrooms or mice or whatever they were.

"Now I'm going to teach you how to have a baby," I say.

Sonny doesn't unfasten his rocket pack. It's heavy, and he's trying to prove his manliness to me because when he sees me, he sees his father, which is always a nice money maker.

"I didn't think you could have a child without a woman," he says.

"Without a woman?" I say. "Let me ask you something, Sonny. Are you retarded?"

"I take offense to that, Mr. Grelding. My cousin has autism."

"Autism is the same as retarded?"

"I wouldn't call anyone retarded. It's insensitive."

"I am insensitive, retard. The point is, of course you need a woman to have a baby. I have twelve inside me right now."

"Babies?"

"Women. Now pay attention."

I gather the best bits and pieces from each woman inside. Linda's math skills. Margaret's libido. Cindy's looks. Fran's obsessive perfectionism. On and on. I gather them and sculpt them into a little boy. As for the leftovers. Linda's ugliness. Margaret's weak stomach. Cindy's stupidity. Fran's compassion. On and on. I dump the scraps into a little girl.

Soon I'm bent over, heaving, vomiting hard on a wounded mouse that managed to drag itself from under my rocket pack.

I upchuck the boy first. The girl comes second. They're dripping with bile and I pull out my permanent marker and draw an X on the girl's forehead. I carry them both to the cage and lower them inside. I'm careful.

"With everything I put inside him, he'll be the next Einstein," I say. "Or at least the next Bill Gates."

"What will she be?" Sonny says.

"She'll be a meal for the beasts. You might not know this, but in beast society, human children, especially babies, are considered quite the delicacy. I give them a few surplus children and they raise my real children in exchange."

"But what's the point of having children if you're not going to raise them?"

"I take them back after they're older and less annoying. It's easier to assimilate them into human society than you might think. It just takes some tough love, and that's something I have a lot of."

His eyes twinkle, because he's hoping that part of me loves him.

And I keep his hope alive by smiling at him. He's pathetic.

I close the cage.

The troublesome part of having a windup house is that you need to employ a fulltime winder and the turnover rate is 100%, what with the severe hand crippling. Other than the pesky paperwork and interviews, however, it's a blast.

Most people, I suppose, like to detach themselves from the suffering required to keep their opulent lifestyles up and running. Me, I like to watch, sitting in my comfiest chair, gobbling down popcorn.

"Nice work, Hans," I say, between chomps.

"Thank you, Mr. Grelding," Hans says. He's winding up the fireplace, which of course doesn't require any winding. Hans is probably smart enough to know this, but he turns the fake winding key anyway.

Sonny comes in and pulls a Rubik's cube out of a shopping bag. He holds it out to me.

"What?" I say. "I don't want it."

"You asked me to buy it for you," Sonny says. "You said you'd pay me back."

"I wouldn't ask for this. I hate games."

"I must have misheard you." Sonny puts the cube back in the bag.

Hans continues to turn the key. His hands continue to wither and die.

"Sonny," I say. "We need to have a little talk. Sit down." He does.

"First of all," I say. "I want you to know that I believe in you. Really, I do."

"Thank you, Mr. Grelding."

"You have the will to succeed in my program, but your body and mind are going to need a little extra help. I'm afraid I have to increase the cost of your tuition to cover the additional training time."

Sonny scoots closer to me. "I'm already too financially strained as it is, Mr. Grelding. I'll work harder, I promise."

"It's not as simple as that, Sonny."

He moves closer.

"You can't make your flaws disappear by working hard," I say. "They're a deep-seated part of you, and these limitations don't make you a bad person. They make you special. I'm prepared to give you more of my time and energy to compensate for your special needs, but I need to be compensated in return. I don't think that's too much to ask."

Sonny should laugh in my face.

But instead, he sits closer. He can't help himself. Not because of respect or admiration or even fear. It's because every night after he falls asleep, I sneak into the guest room, and read to him from my notebook with the kitten on the cover. You might not know this, but I own a cat. He's small and stupid. Without me, he'd die for sure.

"I'll pay," Sonny says. He starts to hug me, but I stand and head for the kitchen.

"The microwave, Hans," I say.

"Right away, Mr. Grelding," Hans says.

I can tell he's in pain, and that's my pain in his hands. It's my childhood, my traumas. My house runs on suffering, and the whole situation makes me burst with laughter sometimes while I'm in the shower or stuck in traffic. Anywhere, really.

"Damn, I burned it," I say. "The microwave again please, Hans."

"Right away, Mr. Grelding."

The scratch is worse today. I can't say I'm surprised.

It all started a few days or weeks or was it months ago when my small and stupid cat approached me in my living room and clawed my leg for no apparent reason. When he headed for the door, I didn't chase him. I didn't kick him. In fact, I didn't dignify this trivial scraping with any response whatsoever.

I forgot the incident ever happened, and any time I remembered, I forced myself to forget again.

When I first noticed the thick yellow pus on the cut, I laughed.

Days or weeks or was it months passed, and the wound spread, snaking up my leg, around my genitals thank god, and up my stomach. The swollen stretch of skin burns and itches. It's infested with rancid boils spewing green ooze.

Obviously on some level, I should go to a doctor. But I can't. I can't let the cat win.

So I'm trying out another home remedy. Sooner or later I'll invent something that works. Today I drench the injured tissue with gasoline and industrial strength wasp spray. I scream for a while, which probably means it's working.

Before I'm done reapplying the bandages, a young woman enters my room. She points a spear at me and says, "You." She says this as if she's somebody, but she's not glamorous or delicate or skinny or passive in the least. She's nothing.

She slashes the blade across my chest, and I'm not very invulnerable when I'm not wearing my bionic exoskeleton.

I dip my finger in my blood. "Who are you?" I say.

"I'm your daughter," she says.

"I don't have any daughters."

"You left me to die, but a beast named Elina saved me from the others and raised me as her own. She told me who you were. I finally found you." She smiles.

I pick up the phone and try to call the police, but the phone isn't wound up.

"Hans!" I say. "Phone!"

Then I remember he quit earlier today. He even managed to give me the finger, despite his handicap. That was before he stole all the keys.

"Sonny!" I say. Then I remember he left to buy me a new chess set.

The girl swings and slices my arm.

And I do the only thing I can think of doing. I scramble over to my nightstand and read to her from my notebook with the kitten on the cover.

"You're unworthy," I say. "You're ugly. You're stupid. You're a failure. You're unlovable."

She growls at me, from the depth of what must be her soul or something just as frightening, and knocks the notebook from my hands. I know I shouldn't be scared of this nothing of a woman. I know she's small and stupid like my cat.

But I can't stop shaking.

"What do you want?" I say.

"I don't know yet," she says, and cuts my other arm.

"I can give you money."

"We don't use currency in beast society."

"I can try to be a real father to you."

"It's a little too late for that."

She moves fast and carves up my forehead. She draws an X. I should walk away. Run, really.

But instead, I step closer. I can't help myself. Not because of duty or empathy or even love. It's because every night before I fall asleep, I think the things from my notebook with the kitten on the cover. You might not know this, but I'm not very happy.

I hold my daughter and say, "I can change."

She pushes me away. She lifts her spear and brings it down on me. She cuts off my bandages.

I look down at my body, and in my mangled rotting flesh, I see faces. Linda. Margaret. Cindy. Fran. On and on. They're squirming up my stomach, up my chest. They're smiling. They're chewing. I'm itching and scratching, and they're gnawing my finger with sharp chipped teeth.

Finally, the faces reach my head, my childhood, my traumas, and poof.

I'm gone.

THE SEX BEAST
OF SCURVY ISLAND

ANDERSEN PRUNTY

At the sound of the doorbell, Brock Rockhard stopped in mid-thrust. The girl below him, the one they currently called Project 26, opened her eyes wide and stifled a moan.

"It's okay," Carrie Godown called from the next room. "It's just Sheriff Dent."

Brock continued thrusting.

Project 26's moans continued.

The camera ran.

Carrie opened the front door. "Sheriff Dent."

The plump officer stared over her shoulder, trying to find the source of the ecstatic moaning.

"You caught us in the middle of filming."

"I could come back."

"You're welcome to watch." Carrie knew Dent was only into gay animal porn but felt like she should offer anyway.

"I think I'll pass this time."

"What brings you by?"

"I have a favor to ask."

"Come on in."

Carrie retreated across the living room of the old farmhouse to the doorway of the back bedroom, pausing momentarily to look at the rippling muscles of Brock's deeply tanned back and the scabby knees of Project 26. Zeke Loner stood in the corner of the room, recording everything.

"Make sure you get the angles right," she told him. "Most guys don't want to stare at Brock's ass for ten minutes."

He flipped her off. She slammed the door.

She turned back around to see Dent staring at Frump, the dog with perfectly formed male human genitalia, lying on his back and sleeping. Dent's eyes glazed over. He absently rubbed himself through his uniform pants.

"Sheriff?"

He blinked and shook his head. "I think I zoned out. Where was I?"

"You had a favor to ask."

Carrie sat down on the couch in the middle of the room, shoving the napping Emma Inside over. Emma opened her eyes and stretched. Carrie told her to go make some coffee.

Carrie gaped at Dent's blooming erection. "Sit?"

"Maybe I should."

Sadly, she knew the cause of Dent's erection was the poor sleeping dog and not her perfect figure, black hair, and multitudinous piercings.

Dent sat down and stared dreamily into space.

"Your favor?"

"Oh, right." He took his hat off and placed it over his crotch. "I've got this old friend who's the Sheriff down at a place called Scurvy Island."

"I've heard of it."

"You have?"

"Yes. I hear they have some wonderful… local sights."

"And that's the problem, I'm afraid."

"The local sights?"

"All those delicious girls and boys. It seems like most of the young women are pregnant and the young men are getting killed in ridiculous ways."

"Ridiculous how?"

"They had to dig one of them out of a cow's stomach."

"Oh. Did the cow swallow him?"

"They believe he was inserted into the cow's rectum. The Sheriff—his name's Denny Rogers—is pretty baffled. As you know, that's a tourist area and most of the tourists come for the services of the young men and women. A lot of people have stopped coming. Sure, they've had their share of fetishists, and the women and remaining men are still willing to work, but soon Scurvy Island as we know it is just going to dry up."

Frump roused himself from the floor and trotted toward the sound of Dent's voice.

"And you want us to…"

Dent held out his hand and rubbed Frump's head.

"Find out who's doing all the raping and killing and put a stop to it." He scratched vigorously below Frump's chin. "Yeah, that's a good boy."

Carrie looked on in disgust. "Why doesn't the Sheriff do that?"

"To be honest, he's not very smart. And he might be a little corrupt. I think the Grassville Gang can do better. We'll make it up to you financially, of course. And you'll have free room and board while you're down there."

Frump latched onto Dent's leg and began thrusting against it.

"If it's okay with the others, then we'll do it."

Carrie stood up. She could tell she had already lost Dent. His eyes were rolled back in his head as Frump continued to thrust and pant against his leg.

"I'll leave you two alone." She stood up and walked toward the kitchen to check on Emma. As she reached the door, she heard Dent cry out in ecstasy.

"That's twenty dollars," she called over her shoulder.

"On the table," he called back before shutting the door on his way out.

Carrie leaned against the counter. "What a dirty pig."

Emma poured her a cup of coffee. "Dent?"

"Yeah."

"He's all right. Just different."

"So what do you think about going to Scurvy Island?"

Emma let out a resigned sigh. She'd just come off a three day Guzzle bender and felt deflated.

"Not to film. To work."

Emma looked down at the floor, her blonde hair falling over her shoulders.

"I do like to solve crime," she said. "Almost as much as I like to fuck."

"I'll go tell the boys."

"Are we bringing…?"

"Project 26?"

"We're going to have to give her a name eventually."

"When it's time. Maybe we'll just leave her here to keep an eye on Frump."

"You think that's a good idea?"

"It's either here or back to the truck stop glory hole."

Before traveling, the Grassville Gang liked to drink copious amounts of Guzzle Blue to keep them alert.

Together, they charged out of the house shouting, "Grassville Gang to the rescue! Grassville Gang forever!"

Brock Rockhard with his red bandana, sunglasses, cut-off denim shorts, and nothing else save his flip-flops and grossly unhealthy tan.

Carrie Godown with her black dreadlocks and piercings, black tank top, black gypsy skirt, black-framed glasses, and black combat boots.

Zeke Loner with his messy hair, dark brown sweater, khaki corduroys, and whatever his book of the day was.

And Emma Inside, the once-reluctant virgin, now sex-starved and ready for action with her long straight blonde hair, form-hugging white t-shirt, and skintight jeans worn low around the waist.

Together, they charged for the deep purple van. The driver's side of the van featured an airbrushed depiction of two kids in wheelchairs playing badminton.

The girls slid open the side door and hopped in.

The boys jumped in front.

Brock turned the key in the ignition.

Loud music blared.

Brock turned to shout at everyone in his dumb guy party voice: "It's a good thing this baby can flyyyy!"

And he hit the accelerator, taxiing onto the runway cut through the middle of a cornfield and, as the van went faster and faster, as they were almost out of runway, Brock flashed a thumbs up to Zeke, who opened the glove compartment and pulled the super special lever. The van lifted and took to the skies.

Excited, as they always were before a job, and hopped up on Guzzle, the girls disrobed and began going at each other.

Emma feverishly and continuously moaned, "Ow, my pussy's sore."

Brock watched them in the rearview mirror, pulling his cock out and massaging himself. Carrie was covered in tattoos of the ugliest people she had ever seen. She added new ones all the time. Brock found their hideous faces, made even more hideous through Carrie's contortions, quite erotic.

Zeke opened up Camus' *The Stranger* and began to read.

They reached Scurvy Island in no time at all.

Zeke wasn't sure why Brock always flew the van. Maybe he'd been a pilot at one point, but whatever shred of intelligence he'd once possessed had long since been obliterated by copious amounts of Guzzle products.

They circled the island until they found what could have been a runway.

"Landing!" Brock took his hand off his penis to guide the wheel.

They came down rough, in an explosion of vaginal juices, lubricant, sweat, come, and curses.

The girls threw open the sliding door and exited the van, pulling on clothes and adjusting them, buttoning buttons.

Zeke got out and calmly slid his old paperback into his pocket.

Brock got out, slammed the door violently, and sniffed the air for blood or vagina.

The front driver's side wheel was bent under the frame.

"You trashed it," Carrie said.

"I'll fix it!" Brock shouted. He slammed his head into the quarter panel above the tire and rocked the van over on two wheels. Grabbing the tire, he gave it a yank. It came off in his hands. Brock was extreme. In fact, two years ago, he'd changed his name to Brock X-treme. Zeke wasn't sure what kind of Guzzle he'd been on at the time, but it didn't last long and ended with Brock going to jail, followed by rehab.

"Now you really trashed it," Carrie said.

Brock hurled the tire. It landed a few feet away and rolled a while before coming to rest in the sand. Then he collapsed next to the van, pulled his knees into his chest and started breathing heavily.

"It's okay," Emma said. "Just calm down. I'm sure somebody here can fix it."

"I think that's the Sheriff." Zeke pointed across the hood of the van.

A deeply tanned man with shoulder-length gray hair and a well-clipped beard approached them. He looked a lot like Kenny Rogers before the botched plastic surgery. He wore long khaki cargo shorts, ratty white Converse, and a stained white wife beater with SHERIFF written across his ample stomach in black marker.

"Denny Rogers?" Carrie stuck out her hand. She hoped the Sheriff wouldn't notice that it smelled like vagina.

"The one and only."

"We hear you have a problem," Carrie said.

"That I do. You here to help me out?"

"Well, we're always up for a good mystery. We like solving crime. Almost as much as we like to fuck."

Rogers looked momentarily perplexed. "I think there's been too much fucking 'round here, if you ask me."

"Tell us all about it."

"Tell you. Hell, I can show you."

They hopped into the Sheriff's car, a rusted out hulk that would fit about a hundred people, and drove to a barn toward the middle of the island. They didn't pass a single car. Didn't see a single person out walking. The entire island felt abandoned.

Standing in front of the barn doors, Rogers said, "I wasn't really sure what to do with them so I just put 'em in here."

He swung open the doors and entered the barn. The Grassville Gang followed him in.

There must have been a hundred or more stalls. A pregnant woman was in each one. They were all naked, holding their huge stomachs and looking sadly at the Gang, as though they had come to free them.

"I'm running out of room," Rogers said. "And the tourists are running out of entertainment. Therefore, I'm running out of tourists and running out of money."

"Why are they in stalls?" Carrie asked. "It doesn't seem right to just lock them up like that."

"I have to go," Zeke said. He had his book out, holding it in front of his crotch. Carrie wondered if he was appalled by the conditions or really needed to read. He couldn't have been aroused.

"I think we've all seen enough," Carrie said.

Brock moved up to one of the stalls and began massaging a woman's breasts.

"Mmm," the woman moaned. "I'm lactating too… You want summa that? Huh? You want summa momma's milk?"

Brock stepped back as the woman squirted two streams of milk into the air.

"Sick!" Brock shouted. He ran out of the barn in fear. Everyone else followed.

They hopped back into Rogers' cruiser and drove through the quaint island town until they reached a pizza shop. Once inside the pizza shop, they were the only ones there besides the young island boy behind the counter.

They slid into a booth and Brock barked, "Five large pies!"

"Sir," the island boy said quietly. "You're going to have to put on a shirt."

"It's okay," Rogers said. "He's with me."

"But the health code…"

"I have one hundred and twenty-six pregnant women locked in a barn. Fuck the goddamn health code."

"Whatever…" The boy retreated back behind the counter.

"Can we get some beer?" Rogers asked.

"A keg!" Brock shouted.

The boy wheeled out a keg and sat five plastic mugs on the table before struggling to hoist the keg up. The boy filled the glasses. Beer was technically now Guzzle Gold, but most people still just called it beer. The boy disappeared again.

Rogers took a long sip of his beer and shook his head. "I know you guys probably think it's inhumane to keep all them girls locked up like that, but I have reason to believe that… when they deliver the babies, they might be dangerous."

"How do you figure?" Emma asked.

"I personally examined each one of them."

"You mean like their pussies?" Brock said. He held his left hand into a circle and punched his right index finger in and out of the hole.

"Yes." Rogers looked embarrassed. "That's exactly what I mean."

Brock nodded his head up and down knowingly and made a raunchy face.

"Now hold up. I didn't fuck any of them. I just examined them. Anyway, they each demonstrated similar signs."

"Similar signs?" Carrie asked.

"The person who impregnated them had a very large penis."

Carrie wondered if it was larger than Zeke's.

"Have you come to any conclusions?"

"I think the same person impregnated all of them over a three day period. Of course, that's been months ago. I wasn't even aware of the problem until recently and I'm afraid it might be too late."

"It's not too late," Carrie said. "We'll find him. Whatever it takes."

The island boy returned with their pizzas. Everyone was ravenous and busied themselves eating. By the time they were finished, Rogers and Brock were both too drunk to carry on a conversation. Carrie, Emma, and Zeke helped them out to the car and Zeke drove to the Labrador Hotel. They left Rogers in the car and went into the hotel to confer.

The Grassville Gang did their best thinking while shooting porn.

Once inside their hideously dilapidated room, they flopped Brock onto the bed. Emma turned on the docked iPod and tuned it to some mood music. The mood music was one long repetitive piece Zeke's friend recorded using his keyboard under the moniker Your Mom's Face. Carrie opened up the cooler and passed around bottles of Guzzle Pink. Zeke stood behind the camera.

Carrie unbuttoned Brock's denim shorts and pulled them down his legs. Everyone in the Grassville Gang was natural except for Brock, who was a mess of chemical tanning, electrolysis, implants, steroids, and numerous penis modifications. No one was sure where the penile parts came from, but it was so racially diverse it was the genital equivalent of a college brochure.

Carrie began sucking his scarred, multi-colored member and Emma forced some Guzzle into his mouth.

"Wait," Zeke said. "What do we call this one? We can't just start shooting without a title."

"Hmm?" Carrie mumbled around Brock's penis.

"A title?"

"Oh." Carrie came up and held Brock in her hand. "Why don't we just call it *Out of Their Heads (And Clothes) Part 12?*"

"Sounds good."

"Thanks." Carrie went back to sucking Brock.

Emma stood up, downed her Guzzle, and slowly took off her clothes while making eye contact with the camera. She finished off the Guzzle and tossed the bottle into the corner where it shattered.

"Mmm, I'm so wasted," she said into the camera. "And my pussy's sore."

She climbed onto the bed and straddled Brock's face. He was out of it but still knew enough to perform his duties. His tongue began lapping at Emma's pink vagina.

"Ow, my pussy's so sore."

Carrie stopped fellating Brock and began removing her clothes. The more flesh she revealed, the more disgusting tattoos Zeke had to focus on. Her latest addition, just above her left breast, looked like a man who had a horn growing out of his cheek. She left her glasses on.

"You like this one?" She stroked the new ugly man. "I want that horn up my wet cunt."

She slipped off her white underwear and flicked her clitoral ring. She downed the rest of her Guzzle in one gulp. She staggered and took a step backward. Zeke zoomed in on her unfocused eyes.

"Fuck," she said. "I wanna fuck till I puke. Yeah? Does that sound good? You wanna make me puke?"

Then she was on the bed, straddling Brock's wildly erect cock. "Oh, yeah," she said. "Bury that shit in me. Oh fuck. I'm gonna rip off my nipples."

She tugged vigorously at her nipples.

Zeke set the camera up on the tripod and checked to make sure it was focused on the bed.

"Ow, my pussy's sore," Emma cried.

Zeke took his clothes off behind the camera. He was thin, pale, and hairy. His penis hung down to his knees.

"You gonna gag me with that thing?" Carrie said. "Huh? You gonna slide that monkey arm down my throat till I puke? Puke and come?"

"Yes," Zeke spoke in an enunciated monotone. "Whatever. Life is meaningless. Might as well fuck until we die."

He approached the bed. While riding Brock hard, Carrie grabbed Zeke's cock and slowly took it all into her mouth, down her throat.

"Ow, my pussy's sore."

The bass from the stereo had kicked in and the Grassville Gang was lost in the haze of Guzzle and sex.

Carrie gagged and pulled away from Zeke's monster cock. "Aw, fuck, baby. You gonna shoot your jibbles on my teeth?"

"No." Zeke sounded bored. "I just want to (sigh) stick this big cock in your tight hole."

"Get your jibbles off? Aw, fuck! I wish you could fuck my spine. Oh, baby, yeah. I'm gonna roll on the floor."

Carrie pulled herself off Brock and began rolling on the floor. She rolled until she hit the wall and then rolled back until she hit the bed. Zeke went to the head of the bed and bent Emma over Brock. She eagerly started sucking Brock, proffering her ass to Zeke. "Careful," she said. "My pussy's sore."

"The pain will make you feel more alive."

Zeke slapped her ass hard and mechanically.

"Hurdle!" Carrie stood up from the floor and took a running leap over the flesh heap on the bed. She flew into a table and broke it. Bleeding and splinter-pricked, she stumbled over to the bed and started smacking Emma in the face as Emma sucked Brock, Zeke pounding her from behind.

"Stick your fingers in that asshole!" Carrie shouted savagely.

Zeke obeyed, plugging Emma's ass with his middle finger.

Things became even hazier after that. The foursome ran through every combination possible until they reached their grand finale.

"Matter spatter!" Carrie shouted.

"God. Pussy's so fucking sore..." Emma hissed through gritted teeth.

Carrie lay down on her back. Zeke and Emma rolled Brock on top of her. Emma fed his cock into Carrie's vagina. Carrie shouted, "Shitstorm fiasco!" Emma sandwiched her hips between Brock and Carrie's heads so Carrie was lapping at her cunt and Brock was tonguing her asshole.

Zeke lubed up his penis and worked it into Brock's filthy rectum. This was a special scene. They could only do this when Brock was really, really wasted. Zeke worked away for a few minutes and Carrie shouted, "Matter spatter!" again.

Zeke pulled out, kneeled beside Brock and began slapping his back with his feces-covered cock.

Emma crawled up to the head of the bed, splayed her legs, and put a bag of ice on her vagina before sticking her thumb in her mouth, looking into the camera, and crying.

"Get your jibbles out!" Carrie yelled. "Get 'em all in that shit!"

"Yes. I'm getting ready to come in this shit. This shit I got from fucking another man in the ass."

"Oh God. Oh fuck! I'm gonna fucking puke. Puke and bleed and pass out!"

Just as Zeke was ready to come, the power went out.

"What?" he said.

He heard things moving around. Brock wasn't under him anymore.

Carrie kept shouting, "What the fuck is going on!"

"Ow, my pussy's sore? Even though I have ice on it?" Emma called. Zeke wasn't sure where she was.

Then he heard a shrill voice coming from somewhere near the window.

"Ha ha! You may be almost as good at solving crime as you are at fucking, Grassville Gang, but you'll never catch The Impregnator!"

And then the window shattered and all the power came back on.

"Zeke?" Carrie called from the bathroom. "You'd better come here."

Zeke walked into the bathroom, his bare feet crunching across the debris.

"I'm going to be sick," Carrie said.

The bathroom was covered in shit, blood, and entrails. Brock lay in a pool of gore in the bathtub. Carrie vomited into the toilet.

Emma came into the bathroom and said, "I think that guy raped me. My pussy's sore, like, for real this time."

"Okay," Zeke said. "We need to call Sheriff Rogers."

"I gotta get out of this bathroom." Emma turned back into the main room.

"And we should probably all put some clothes on," Zeke said.

He grabbed his clothes from the floor and put them on. He grabbed his cell phone from his pants pocket and called Rogers. It rang and rang.

"He's not answering."

"Did you call 911?" Carrie was now examining herself in the mirror and pulling splinters out of her skin.

"Do you think that even works here?"

"Sure. Why not? It works everywhere."

Zeke shrugged and dialed 911. It rang and rang.

"I'll go down to the lobby," Emma said. "See if they can help us."

"Don't tell them about Brock," Carrie warned.

"Who?"

"The lobby people. We don't want to incite panic or anything."

"Whatever."

Emma left the room and walked down the tiled hallway until she reached the front desk. A rotund islander sat sleeping in his chair, head lolling back, drool slicking his chin.

"Sir?"

She noticed something off to her right, outside.

"Yeah… just a minute." The clerk wiped the drool from his chin and picked some crust from the corners of his eyes.

"Never mind."

"Thanks for waking me up then."

"Fuck you."

"Fuck you."

"Good comeback."

"Fuck your face."

Emma rolled her eyes.

Through the glass doors of the lobby, Emma had spotted Rogers' car, exactly where they had left it. She walked out into the humid night. Rogers was asleep in the front seat. Emma could hear his phone ringing. The windows were open. She wondered how the residents and tourists felt safe. She reached through the window and grabbed the phone.

"Hello," she said.

"I'd like to report an emergency."

"Zeke?"

"Yeah. Emma? Where are you?"

"Right out front. Our beloved and faithful Sheriff is passed out in his car."

"Well get him up here."

Rogers surveyed the crime scene from the doorway. He said he didn't want to get any closer. He already felt queasy.

"Looks like he's the victim of a rapid enema machine."

"A what?" Zeke asked.

"A rapid enema machine. It's a machine that gives enemas in rapid succession. If it's turned up too high, it'll suck the bowels right out."

"I've never heard of one of those. Why would someone need one of those?"

"Well, it's theoretical, but that's what it looks like."

"So you just made that up?"

"I theorized it. We need to get that body out of here."

"We?"

"Yeah. Well, you guys. I'll hurl if I come anywhere near it."

"Aren't you going to call an ambulance? An EMT? A coroner?"

"Dead. Dead. And dead."

"Shit."

"I told you I have a fuckin' crisis on my hands."

"Fine. What do we need to do?"

"We need to get it down to the car and then we'll throw it in the ocean. That's the island way."

"Sounds like that's the lazy way. Don't you need it for evidence or something?"

"If we see a person with a rapid enema machine, I'll assume we have our man."

They rolled Brock's body onto a tarp and loaded it into the trunk of the car. Zeke wondered why working with the Sheriff felt an awful lot like working with a serial killer.

Once at the beach, they rolled Brock's body into the water, but the tide kept bringing it back. Zeke was suddenly emotional.

"Let's go back to the car and hit some Guzzle Green," the Sheriff proposed.

The others followed, Zeke wiping away tears.

Once at the car, Rogers uncapped a bottle of Guzzle and took a swig before passing it to Emma, who did the same.

"Now," Rogers said, "you said this thing raped you?"

Emma nodded her head. "I'm pretty sure. My pussy feels sore. Almost raw."

"But you didn't get a look at him?"

"It was so dark."

"I think it's obvious what we need to do."

The bottle had made its way back to Rogers and he took another healthy swig. The others stared at him, awaiting his answer.

"We need to gather up all the remaining men on the island and you need to have sex with them."

"That's… retarded," Zeke said.

"We'll make them all sign releases. You can film it."

"Now it's starting to sound profitable. Emma? Are you up for that?"

"My pussy's really sore but… if it'll help crack the case of The Impregnator,

I'm up for anything."

"Great." Rogers clapped his hands together. "We'll want to get started right away. Naturally, you'll have to fuck me."

"Can you get this?" Zeke pulled the camera from the backseat of the car and handed it to Carrie.

"Why? What are you doing?"

"Looking for clues."

Zeke hopped into the car and pulled away, watching Rogers stroke his comically small penis in the rearview mirror.

Zeke was terrible with directions and spent two hours driving around the island before he finally found the barn. An erection strained against his corduroys as he pulled to a stop. He walked to the barn doors and realized they were padlocked. If he were Brock, he would have just ripped the wooden doors off the barn. Thinking about Brock made him sad. He went back to the car and pulled the keys from the ignition. There were several keys on the ring. Hopefully, one of them would open the barn.

Zeke paused and made sure he really wanted to go through with this. Maybe this was the only way he could go through with it—in the name of research. Clue hunting.

He had never been with a pregnant woman before. It was something he had always fantasized about. When he was young, his mother was pregnant all the time. She had to have children so she could sell them for food. Zeke's mom and dad thought it was much easier to stay home and fuck and then sell their children than going out to get a real job. Zeke had always thought the pregnant form of a woman was how they were supposed to look.

Now was his chance. A pregnant woman. An absence of cameras. The acquisition of knowledge. It didn't get a lot more exciting for Zeke.

He unlocked the lock and pulled the door open.

The smell that greeted him was not pleasant.

He was sort of hoping they could do it in front of the other pregnant women, but Zeke didn't think he'd be able to put up with that stench.

Over the years, he'd learned that women enjoy sex as much as men. And if you have 126 women in a room, the chances were good that at least one of them wouldn't care who it was she fucked.

He unbuttoned his pants and pulled his colossal cock out. It was fully erect and stood out at a right angle from his body.

"Who wants it?"

Luckily, there was a woman close by so he didn't have to wander back into the stench of the barn. He let her out of the stall and took her back to the car. What followed was brutal, satisfying, and highly informative.

Fucking in the high noon sun had exhausted Emma. Nineteen guys later, she chugged a bottle of Guzzle Clear and threw herself into the ocean to get the sweat and come off her body. Her vagina was beyond sore. While she didn't mind all the sex, she wished they had found a suspect.

She had her suspicions about Rogers, but it had absolutely nothing to do with the length or girth of his penis.

On the beach, Carrie stripped off her clothes and waded out to Emma.

"Any luck?" Carrie asked.

"None." Emma stuck out her bottom lip.

"Who would do something like this?"

"I don't know. There doesn't seem to be a lot of people here."

"Why would someone do something like this? I guess that should be the first question."

Emma splashed at the warm, clear water. "Money?"

"But if their money's in tourism and you impregnate or kill the whores who bring the tourists... That just doesn't seem logical."

"Maybe someone wants to turn the island into a baby factory."

"That practice is still frowned upon by the mainstream."

"Maybe we should just match the DNA from the fetuses."

"You think this place has a lab or anybody who'd know how to do it?"

"Maybe it's a spite crime."

"Like revenge?"

"Could be."

"Look." Carrie pointed further up on the beach. Rogers appeared to be arguing with a bald man in a black suit. "Who's that?"

"That was guy number six."

"Oh, right. I didn't recognize him with the suit."

The men continued to argue, pointing back toward the town and the middle of the island. Things became more animated and the large man in the suit punched Rogers in the stomach, doubling him over.

Emma headed for the shore on rubbery legs. "We need to help."

Carrie reluctantly followed her.

By the time they made it up to the beach, the man had already left. Rogers was collapsed on the sand, dramatically holding his head and kicking his legs.

Carrie noticed a strange deformity on his right arm and couldn't help asking him about it. "What's wrong with your arm?" It looked like he was missing an elbow.

"Jesus, think you could help me up?"

Emma helped him up while Carrie continued to study the odd depression on his arm.

"So you gonna tell me or not?"

"That." He pointed to it, spitting sand from his mouth. "I was born without an elbow, that's all."

"That's stupid. I've never heard of that."

Emma placed a consoling hand on Rogers' shoulder. "Who was that man?"

"That guy… Oh, just an old friend."

"You know," Carrie said, "if we're looking for suspects, you shouldn't keep things secret from us."

"It was Dean Mahoney. He's not a suspect. Is he, Emma?"

"Definitely not." She held her index and forefinger two inches apart.

"So who is he?"

"He's just a guy I owe money too, all right?"

"Maybe he's working with The Impregnator."

"The only person Mahoney works for is Mahoney."

Carrie started to say something else when Zeke pulled up in the car, cutting her off.

"I think I have a clue!" Zeke called from the car. He opened the door and stepped out, holding something up in the air.

"What the hell is that?" Emma cried.

"It's a fetus!" Zeke smiled for the first time Emma could remember.

"Ew, what does a fetus have to do with anything?" Emma asked.

Zeke must have been hitting some sort of Guzzle on the way back. Or maybe he was just excited. He hopped back and forth, holding the fetus around one ankle and waggling it in front of Rogers and the girls.

"Is it still alive?" Carrie asked. "Maybe you shouldn't be handling it like that."

"No. It's okay. I had to snap its neck."

"Zeke!" Emma cried.

"No, it's okay, Em. It isn't human."

"Looks human."

"No. It's not. It's a demon baby. I had to kill it because it kept trying to eat my heart. See? See?" He held the fetus's head in his left hand and pulled back its upper lip. Perfectly formed teeth grew from the gums. Most of them were pointed. Then he poked its navel. "See? See here? No umbilical cord or anything. It just fucking crawled out!"

"Out of the pussy?" Emma asked.

"I think it's called a womb," Carrie said.

"But it still has to come through the pussy."

"It's actually a vagina."

"Whatever. You're a fucking prude. I still don't think Zeke should have killed it."

Rogers stood behind the girls, chewing on his thumb. He looked nervous or maybe nauseated.

"But if it had been a full grown demon trying to eat your heart out, it would have been okay, right?" Zeke goaded.

"Well..."

"So I was just being proactive."

"And this is your big clue?" Carrie asked. "You were in the barn with all the pregnant women, weren't you?"

"I actually took one woman into the car. The barn smelled foul. I don't think they have any bathrooms in there. And they might have lactation wars when they get bored. Anyway, I've always heard that one of the best ways to induce labor was through sex."

"There are other ways," Carrie said.

"Look, we all have needs, okay? Anyway, I almost lost my penis as a result." Zeke dropped the fetus to the ground. "Look at it." He pulled his pants down and brandished his huge cock.

"My god!" Emma cried.

It was raw and gnawed-looking.

"I hope it heals," Carrie said. "I hope it was worth it."

"Regardless, I think we need to have a conference."

Emma said, "It just won't be the same without Brock."

"I could stand in," Rogers said.

"I think we need to be alone," Carrie said.

Rogers looked dejected.

"We could use the girl," Zeke said, pointing to the lifeless-looking woman in the back seat. "They're all kind of hypnotized or drugged. Maybe we can shock her into remembering something."

"Maybe," Carrie said. "Sheriff? Can we get a ride back to the hotel?"

They piled into the car and headed back toward town. Emma gathered up the fetus and held it on her lap like a real baby. Zeke made out with the new girl.

"She's gamey," Carrie said. "She's going to have to shower before the conference."

"You're just jealous," Zeke said.

"Yes. I wish I had a demon fetus growing in me."

Emma looked at the demon, horrified. "Do you think I have one of these in me now?"

"It's possible," Zeke said. "Once we get back, you'll have to go to the doctor. You don't want to carry something like that to term."

"Fuck!" Emma rolled down the window and started to throw the demon out, but Carrie stopped her.

"We might need to examine it."

"Carrie's right," Zeke said before continuing to make out with the girl. She looked mostly comatose. Maybe that's what Zeke liked about her.

Carrie spotted Dean Mahoney walking on the sidewalk on the opposite side of the street, his back to them.

"Isn't that…" But before she could even get his name out, Rogers swerved the car and clipped Mahoney. The bumper hit his right knee, kicking his leg out from under him and sending him rolling off into the parking lot of an abandoned convenient store.

"Shit!" Emma said. "You just hit that guy, what's-his-face."

"Accidents will happen," Rogers said. "I wouldn't worry too much about it."

"But he could be hurt really bad."

"Next stop, Labrador Hotel!" Rogers was clearly changing the subject and refusing to talk about it.

Once at the hotel, they grabbed the demon and the woman and headed for the lobby doors. They were locked. A hand-lettered sign was taped to the door on the left. It read: CLOSED PERMANENTLY.

"That's no good," Emma said.

"Maybe we can confer in the car," Carrie said.

"I don't see any other choice," Zeke said.

Carrie said, "You're gonna have to leave Stinky out here."

"What about shock therapy? What about information? I think she needs to be part of the conference."

"Fine," Carrie said. "But there's no room for Rogers. Besides, he might be a suspect and we might have to talk about him."

They walked back to the car. Zeke asked Rogers if they could use his car to film *Doped Teen 3*. He said he didn't mind, got out of the car, and leaned against the hood. Zeke guessed they would just have to whisper if they needed to talk about him.

The conference was long and vigorous. Emma was sexed out and Zeke's penis was like raw hamburger so it took them forever to come. The other girl was unresponsive and kept dozing off or passing out. Her vagina was loose and bloody from delivering the demon. The demon lay on the dash the entire time. Rogers stood outside the car and played with himself through the pocket of his shorts while looking back over his shoulder and then pretending he hadn't been looking.

They were going to question the girl as soon as they finished, but she drifted off and they were unable to wake her up.

Zeke checked her pulse.

"Dead," he said.

"Dead?" Emma asked.

"Dead," Zeke repeated.

"Who's dead?" Rogers asked.

"The girl. You're not supposed to be listening."

"We should call 911 again," Carrie said.

Zeke found his cell phone in the pile of clothes on the floorboard and punched in the digits.

Rogers' phone rang and he answered, "Scurvy Island Emergency."

"Sheriff?"

"Yep."

"There's a dead girl in the car."

"I'm sorry to hear that."

"Shouldn't we call an ambulance?"

"Are you an idiot? Didn't I tell you everyone was dead?"

"What about you? Don't you know CPR or something? Surely law enforcement must learn some of that stuff. Even security guards learn that."

"I'll see what I can do."

Rogers came around to the rear passenger side of the car, opened the door, and dragged the girl out. He laid her on the ground and began fondling her.

The Grassville Gang, still naked, stood around him and looked down with disapproval.

"Are you even trying?" Zeke asked.

"Why don't you go take a walk or something," Rogers said. He continued looking down at the dead girl. He might have been crying. "I know you just want to talk about me anyway. You think maybe I'm this sex monster, this Impregnator... But you're wrong."

Carrie said, "I guess we should put our clothes back on."

Zeke said, "Don't have sex with the corpse, okay?"

Rogers shook his head. "I can't promise anything. Remember to take your dead baby with you."

The remaining members of the Grassville Gang put on their clothes, grabbed their dead demon baby, and headed for the beach. Once at the beach, they walked along in the fading daylight, passing around a bottle of Guzzle Green. Carrie produced a dossier and flipped through it. She always had one of these. No one was really sure where they came from.

"Maybe we should sit down," she said.

They found a bench. Carrie and Zeke sat on the bench and Emma sat in the sand, facing them.

"So," Carrie began. "Nearly every male on the island is dead and nearly every female pregnant. We know the perpetrator is someone calling himself The Impregnator."

"And," Zeke raised a finger of proclamation, "he may not necessarily be human."

Carrie continued to flip through the dossier. "I would say with all the women getting pregnant within a few days of each other, he's not human at all."

"Or he's superhuman." Emma giggled. "Maybe we should hire him to be part of the Gang."

"This is serious, Em." Carrie kicked sand at her.

"One man was filled with helium. One man was beaten to death with a shoe. One man was sodomized to death with a chair. Grisly. One man drowned in his toilet. One man choked to death on an ice cream cone. One man..."

Zeke waved a hand. "We get the point."

"So why would someone do this?"

"It sounds like someone wants the island to himself."

"But who?"

"Sheriff Rogers comes to mind."

"But Emma had sex with both Rogers and The Impregnator and said they were nothing alike."

"I've been thinking," Emma said. "About my test. I don't know how accurate it is."

Carrie looked up from her dossier. "What do you mean? I thought your vag was a hundred percent accurate."

"It usually is. But it was dark when The Impregnator raped me. What if he was wearing some kind of prosthetic? Do you want to hear my theory?"

Zeke and Carrie both nodded their heads.

"I think this Impregnator character does have a prosthetic penis. And I think he's outfitted it with some kind of demon semen."

"Demon semen?" Carrie asked.

"Yes. Some chemically altered substance he's been shooting into the girls. How else could he get so many of them pregnant in such a short period of time?"

"And they would have to be ovulating within a few days of each other..." Carrie said.

"And none of them could be on birth control or anything..." Zeke said.

"Unless," Emma said, "the demon seed just needs a warm body and not necessarily a womb."

"That's a good point," Zeke said. "But then why wouldn't he have just used the men, too?"

"Who knows," Emma said.

"Maybe he did use the men. Did anyone check to see if they were pregnant?"

Zeke leapt to his feet. "Let's go to the cemetery and dig up a body!"

Carrie pulled him back down to the bench. "They don't use cemeteries, remember? They just throw them in the ocean. That's the island way."

"Again," Zeke said. "Who could it be?"

Carrie stood up from the bench. "I think we need to find Rogers and ask him a few more questions."

The sun was now almost completely gone from the sky, sinking into the ocean and turning it a dazzling orange.

He noticed the tide creeping in at an alarming rate.

On closer inspection, it wasn't the tide at all.

"Demon babies!" Zeke shouted.

Carrie squinted her eyes.

Emma turned around.

"Oh, fuck!" Carrie shouted.

"Quick," Zeke said. "We need to get to the car and get out to the barn. These things were probably incubating in the corpses tossed out to sea."

"And we need to get into the van. Get the weapons out," Carrie said.

"You girls go get the car. I'll get the shit out of the van."

They stood in a circle, even though they didn't really have time, and put all their hands on top of one another. "Grassville Gang to the rescue. Grassville Gang forever!" And they brought their hands up into the air, the horde of demon babies only a few feet away.

Carrie and Emma ran toward town.

Zeke ran for the van, which was only a little way down the beach.

The demon babies were not hard to outrun, even though they were able to chug along on their legs rather than crawl. Zeke made it to the van, panting and tired, with a few minutes to spare. Beside the driver's side of the van was an odd shape on the ground. Only, it wasn't really odd. Just out of place. For a brief moment, Zeke thought it was Brock. Drawing closer, he saw that it *was* Brock.

Was he somehow still alive?

Had he crawled back here to the van to try and fix it in his final moments of life? Even after his closest friends had thrown him into the ocean, watched him wash back up onto shore, and then left him for dead?

But now he was definitely dead.

Lying out in the sun all day had not done great things for him.

Zeke tried not to become emotional as he crouched down beside him and ran his fingertips along Brock's red bandana.

"We'll miss you, buddy."

Zeke looked at the wheel of the van, hoping the tire would be there, hoping the van would be fixed.

But it wasn't.

He opened the doors at the back of the van. He crawled inside and collected their weapons. He preferred a battle axe. There was something very traditional about it. Brock had used a flame thrower. Emma used a small chainsaw and Carrie used a garrote.

It was a lot to carry.

Turning to step out of the van, Zeke was confronted with three demon babies, hissing as their little hands clutched the shiny chrome bumper.

Zeke primed the flame thrower and strapped it onto his back. He pulled the trigger and flames burst from the barrel.

"This is for you, Brock!" Zeke thought that was something Brock would have said. He pulled the trigger again.

Then he leapt from the van, through the stench of fuel and burning baby demon flesh, and ran into the early dark.

As soon as they'd taken off running, Emma had tossed the dead demon baby over her shoulder, hoping it would ward off more of the demons. They had run as hard as they could.

Now, halfway into town, Emma stopped.

She leaned against a palm tree and stuck her hand down her pants.

Carrie stopped and walked toward her. "Come on, Em. Now's not the time to rub one out."

"Ow, my pussy's sore. And it itches." She giggled. "And kind of tickles."

She pulled her hand out of her pants.

Carrie knew that Emma couldn't have crab lice because she didn't have any pubic hair. She moved closer to see what Emma held between her thumb and forefinger.

"What is it?" Emma had her eyes closed, holding her hand as far as she could away from her body.

"It looks like a very tiny demon baby." Carrie took it from her. It was almost microscopic, but it was definitely a demon baby.

She threw it to the sidewalk and stomped it with her boot.

Looking back, she saw the demon horde approaching.

"We need to go. Quickly."

They took off in the direction of the town.

Zeke was not used to long distance running. Apparently, it used completely different muscles than lengthy and borderline supernatural sex.

Or maybe it was the extra weaponry he carried.

His vision blurred.

He knew the demon babies were behind him.

Sweat rolled down his forehead and stung his eyes. His vision blurred.

Was that a dune buggy in front of him?

It looked like it was in the middle of the street. An odd sight since they had hardly seen any cars on the road since arriving.

The dune buggy's lights flipped on. Bright. Blinding.

Zeke drew to a stop, his breathing ragged.

He heard the high whine of the dune buggy in front of him, the engine revving, the tires gripping the road and squealing toward him.

Behind him, the angry and hungry sounds of the demon horde.

Just as the dune buggy closed in on him, he dived to his right, rolling on the ground and pulling himself up quickly, readying his battle axe.

The dune buggy plowed through the demon horde.

Was someone here to help him?

Maybe the driver just didn't know the demons were there, even though they'd already taken out four or five.

And then the demons swarmed the buggy.

Zeke was still unable to make out the driver. He wanted to run, but he was exhausted from all the running. Plus, if the driver of the dune buggy had tried to help him, he didn't want to abandon him or her to the demon horde.

He approached the dune buggy, battle axe poised.

The little demons were crawling all over the driver.

Maybe it was too late.

Then the driver stood up in the dune buggy.

He was huge. Heavily muscled. Red. Winged.

Zeke noticed the wings as the driver spread his arms, the baby demons lining them like birds come to roost.

Then Zeke noticed the huge appendage dangling between his legs.

This thing, Zeke thought. *This thing is definitely not human.*

Now that he didn't care about torching them all, Zeke fastened the battle axe to his belt and primed the flame thrower.

"Halt!" The Impregnator shouted at him. "The Grassville Gang stands no chance against The Impregnator and his minions. If you kill me... everyone dies."

Zeke wasn't sure what he was talking about. Wasn't everyone already dead? Maybe the women were still alive. But they were dazed, traumatized, possibly lobotomized.

Zeke shot a spray of flame toward the dune buggy and took off running. He scrambled off the road, zigzagging around palm trees, stands filled with employment guides and free newspapers, benches, and parking meters.

The Impregnator followed him for a couple of blocks and then abruptly slammed on his brakes and headed in the opposite direction.

Zeke craned his head to make sure no demon babies were following him —and promptly smashed into a palm tree. He sat there for a few moments, surrounded by the weaponry he'd dropped. The air was still. The humidity was intense.

In the distance, he heard the drone of the dune buggy and the high-pitched cackle of The Impregnator.

He needed to find the girls.

They needed to get to the barn.

He couldn't help but think something very bad was going to happen.

"Shit!"

"Fuck!"

"Where the fuck is he?" Carrie said.

Approaching the Hotel Labrador, there was no sign of Rogers' car.

"The shit skipped out," Carrie said.

"And left the girl behind," Emma said. The girl lay facedown on the sidewalk.

"He didn't even have the decency to put her clothes back on." Carrie shook her head in disgust.

"What a fucking goat's ass."

"What do we do now?"

"Zeke said something about meeting at the barn."

"No way." Carrie shook her head again. "There's no way I'm going there without my weapon."

"It's just a bunch of pregnant ladies."

"Are you crazy? They're pregnant with demons! Demons, Emma! Are you so fucking oblivious you don't realize some really bad shit is going on here? Because if you don't, you seem to be the last one." Carrie swept her hands around her, motioning to the dark and hushed town.

Emma slapped Carrie hard, in the face.

Carrie punched Emma in the stomach.

It wasn't long before they were pulling at each other's hair and ripping clothes that would miraculously mend only moments later. Then they were on the sidewalk, tongues and fingers everywhere. Dildoes appeared out of nowhere. Five minutes later, the island shook with the crescendo of their simultaneous orgasms.

They rolled off one another, sticky from their engagement, and stared dazedly into the night…

…and into a net dropping down over them. The net closed and they were lifted up and slung over the back of The Impregnator, thrown into the back of his dune buggy, and speeding away from the hotel.

Zeke arrived at the Hotel Labrador, only to find the place abandoned.

No girls.

No Rogers.

Just the girls' clothes.

He was exhausted. But he was also horny.

He picked up the girls' clothes, buried his face in their underwear.

He pulled his pants down and masturbated.

Then he went in search of a bike shop.

Soon they were cruising through the dark night in the back of The Impregnator's gasoline-reeking dune buggy. There was another smell coming from The Impregnator. An awful smell. It smelled like death and spoiled milk.

"You better let us out of here." Carrie struggled against the cargo netting.

"I'm afraid I can't do that," The Impregnator said. His voice was sinister. Was it electronically altered? It didn't sound like any type of voice either of the girls had heard before, save the abbreviated conference they'd had their first night here.

"I'll rip your cock off? And shove it down your throat?" Emma threatened, but it came out in her porno voice.

"I'm afraid not. All I need to do is get you back to the barn and lure that other boy there. I have an especially ridiculous death planned for him. And as soon as he's gone, the island will be mine. ALL MINE!" The Impregnator laughed giddily.

"And what about us?" Carrie moved as close as possible to him, trying to hiss in his ear. It wasn't hard. The dune buggy wasn't very large. "You'll never impregnate us…"

The Impregnator laughed again. "But I already have." And he looked smarmily over his shoulder.

"We aborted Emma's," Carrie said.

"I gave you both another one. While I was carrying you to the buggy."

"My pussy is kind of sore," Emma said. "Again."

"I told you," The Impregnator half-sang.

"You're forgetting one thing about the Grassville Gang," Carrie said.

"And what's that, darling?"

"We like to solve crime almost as much as we like to fuck."

"Liking and doing are two separate things." The Impregnator laughed and stomped the accelerator, throwing the girls back against the roll bars.

Zeke found something even better than a bike. He found a pedal car. It had two big bicycle tires on the back and a smaller tire up front. It had an orange flag on a stick attached to the back of it. The flag made Zeke think of golf. He hated golf. He tore the flag and the skinny pole off and threw them into the street. He stowed the weapons in the wire basket between the two back tires. He positioned himself in the pedal car. He was almost lying down. It took him a minute to get situated. Then, his eyes clouded with hate, he pedaled furiously, hoping he was traveling in the right direction.

The Impregnator and the girls reached the barn, the dune buggy skidding to a vicious halt.

The Impregnator lifted the net and suspended it from a nearby tree.

The demon baby horde surrounded the barn.

They parted for The Impregnator.

"Even if you get Zeke, Sheriff Rogers will stop you!" Emma shouted in a moment of desperation.

The Impregnator turned and approached the net. He batted savagely at it. "Don't you ever mention that name to me. That man is an unlanced anal wart. That man is a truckload of AIDS. That man is worthless... And you can rest assured that he's long gone."

"But he's the one who called us for help."

"After letting this go on for how long? He's too stupid to exist."

"He'll..."

"Shhh..." The Impregnator held a taloned finger up to his lips. "There are other things to do at the moment."

"But—"

The Impregnator struck the net again. "Please be quiet. Please? Can you do that? Or do you want me to feed your cunt to your friend?"

Emma was silent.

"Very good."

The Impregnator strolled back to the barn, flourishing his cape and switching his tail.

What had they gotten themselves into?

Zeke carried the girls' clothes in his lap. He knew they wouldn't have just gone off and left them. That meant The Impregnator probably had them. Zeke couldn't just go storming the barn. He would have to sneak.

Somewhere ahead of him, he heard the most awful sound.

Like a knight or an asshole, he followed.

"Witness the birthing!" The Impregnator cried out.

He threw open the barn doors and all the women came dazedly wandering out.

They were all nearly barking with screams.

The first one dropped to the ground and spread her legs. Emma wondered how she could have let her vagina get so hairy, how anyone could just let themselves go like that. She guessed if you were pregnant it just didn't matter.

The woman screamed and breathed rapidly.

Another woman dropped down next to her and began doing the same.

"The labor of multitudes!" The Impregnator shouted.

Carrie and Emma watched open-mouthed as the first woman's vagina ripped open in a shower of blood. A demon baby clawed his way out and crawled into the dirt.

"In only moments, my demon army will be complete."

"Not so fast, Impregnator!"

The girls heard the voice off to their right. As best they could, they turned in the net.

"Zeke!" they shouted in unison.

Zeke turned toward them and hurled his battle axe and their clothes. The axe sliced through the net and the girls landed on their feet, miraculously clothed, only a second later.

"Demons attack!" The Impregnator shouted. "I will not let you ruin my moment of triumph, Grassville Gang!"

One group of demons moved toward Zeke and another group moved toward the girls.

Zeke threw them their weapons.

They threw him his battle axe.

More women dropped to the ground. The Impregnator began seizing them, reaching up into their vaginas, and forcefully pulling the demon babies out, tossing them onto the dirt where they landed and scampered toward their prey.

Zeke struggled to prime the flame thrower. One of the demons clambered up his leg and bit at his neck. Frantic and desperate, Zeke gnashed his teeth and tore into the flesh of the baby demon, and then swallowed by accident.

He brought the battle axe down on another demon, splitting it in half.

He looked over at the girls. They were surrounded. The Impregnator was now forcing the pregnant women to the ground as they exited the barn, ripping the demons from between their legs. The night was alive with the screams of laboring women and the scent of their blood. Zeke didn't see any way out of this.

He started to feel weird.

Dizzy.

He dropped to his knees.

He kind of felt like vomiting but he fought to keep his gorge down.

It felt like he was spinning, but he also felt… stronger.

A demon baby crouched at his ankle, sprang toward him, and latched on.

Zeke didn't feel a thing.

He picked the demon baby up and ripped it in half, saving a chunk to shove down his throat.

He turned to the girls.

"Emma! Carrie!" Even his voice was more powerful.

Emma finished sawing two of the demons' heads off at once. Carrie finished dragging the garrote through a neck. Then the girls turned toward him.

"You have to eat the babies! It'll make you stronger!"

Carrie garroted another one and drank from the geyser of blood spurting from its neck. Emma took off a tiny hand and popped it into her mouth.

In only a few seconds, they felt indestructible.

Now the Grassville Gang had the distinct feeling that the tide had turned. They fought their way toward where The Impregnator crouched. They also ripped fetuses from wombs and gobbled them down like Guzzler Fried Chicken.

And just when they closed in on The Impregnator…

…he was nowhere to be seen.

In the distance, they heard his laughter. Around them, the demons' mothers were screaming and dying. The demon babies were all dismembered and either twitched in puddles of their own blood or attempted to make a wounded retreat.

"What do we do?" Emma asked.

"We have to get The Impregnator," Carrie said.

Zeke nodded his affirmation.

The Grassville Gang loaded up in the dune buggy and shot back toward town. Toward the Sheriff's office.

They reached the Sheriff's office to find Rogers' car haphazardly parked across the sidewalk. The front door was broken from its hinges. The window was shattered.

From inside the office, The Impregnator shouted, "You'll never stop me! You can never come between me and my life's work!"

Zeke approached the door and cautioned the girls. "Careful. It's slippery."

Once in the office, he flipped on the lights to reveal The Impregnator ensnared in a finely constructed prison of bondage cord, novelty handcuffs, dildoes, and fake vaginas.

Zeke approached with caution.

"Who did this?" Carrie asked.

"You see," Zeke began, "when I found your clothes lying on the sidewalk, I naturally assumed The Impregnator had taken you prisoner. I quickly acted on our suspicions and assumed it had to be Sheriff Rogers. I knew he would have to come back to his office sooner or later, so I broke into the Hotel Labrador and used whatever supplies I could find to construct this trap. He walks in the door, slides on the lubricant, and falls victim to the tensile strength of bondage rope and various latex products."

Zeke sauntered over to The Impregnator, placed his hand on the top of the villain's head, clutched his mask and, yanking it away, proclaimed, "Girls, I give you Sheriff Rogers."

The face of Rogers was before all of them.

"I'm afraid you're not correct, Zeke," Emma said.

"What do you mean? That's Rogers."

"Yes. It is *a* Rogers. But this is the Sheriff's evil Siamese twin."

Zeke shook his head. "You must be joking."

"I'm afraid not." She approached The Impregnator and ripped away the sleeve of his left arm. "While The Impregnator was raping me, I noticed this unique deformity."

She pointed midway down his arm.

"A missing elbow!" they all shouted.

"That's right," Emma said. "Just like Sheriff Rogers. Only his was on the other arm."

"Where they were separated at birth!" Carrie said.

"Exactly. Sheriff Rogers had no reason to do these things, but he did have a reason to wait so long to report them. He didn't want to imprison his only brother. Unfortunately, his brother was almost able to turn the complete island into his secret demon training ground and prepare for world domination!"

"And I would have gotten away with it too if it wasn't for you filthy pornographers."

"So Sheriff Rogers is innocent..."

"Well, not entirely," a voice said from the back of the office. Sheriff Rogers emerged. "This island's ruin is as much my fault as Lenny's... my brother's. I'd invested in everything until I practically owned the entire island. But I'm not good with money. I'm addicted to Guzzle and prostitutes and this is the wrong place for that. Eventually, I just couldn't make payments on my holdings. Everything fell into disrepair. The fewer tourists were a blessing at first. Things weren't so embarrassing..."

The Sheriff brought a hand up to his eyes and wiped the tears away.

"But you didn't do anything wrong," Carrie said. "You're just stupid."

The Sheriff nodded.

"So what now?" Emma said.

"Well," Zeke said. "I think we leave The Impregnator right here, get the hell off this island, and let the Feds sort it out."

"Only one thing left to do," Carrie said. She approached The Impregnator and pulled a blade from the waistband of her skirt. While Zeke braced The Impregnator's head, she carved a "G.G." into his forehead.

Reaching behind The Impregnator, she pulled a canister from his back.

"Nooo!" The Impregnator howled. "Not my secret alchemical formula!"

"That must be the demon semen," Emma said.

There was a tube running down to the prosthetic penis outfitted in his costume. Carrie pulled the tube free and spurted the semen on The Impregnator while he wept tears of humiliation.

It was dawn by the time they finished. Stepping outside, the air had cooled considerably.

"Say," Sheriff Rogers said, "there really isn't too much here for me. Seeing as how you guys lost one, does that mean you have room for one more? I kind of like to solve crime. And I really like to fuck."

Carrie said, "Your penis isn't very large but, I guess if it's okay with everyone else, we could give you a trial run."

"You ever take it up the ass before?" Zeke asked.

The Sheriff didn't answer.

When they reached the van, they remembered it was damaged.

Zeke went around front to reinspect the axle.

"Hey!" he called to the others. "Look at this!"

The wheel was back on the van.

"How did this happen?" Zeke asked.

"I wasn't just hiding out from trouble," Rogers said.

"Welcome aboard," Carrie said. She and Emma slid the side doors open and crawled in.

Zeke was excited about finally being able to fly the van, but when he opened the door, Brock was sitting in the driver's seat.

"Hope you're into necrophilia, buddy!" Brock said with a shit-eating grin.

Zeke, realizing he was into anything, climbed into the passenger side of the van.

Rogers climbed on top of him and began giving him a seductively hideous lap dance.

Brock powered the van down the street and bellowed, "It's a good thing this baby can flyyy!" in his dumb guy zombie voice.

And Zeke, he showed the Sheriff the super special lever.

INHERITANCE

JEDEDIAH BERRY

At first they didn't talk about it, the beast Greg brought with him to the Saturday night poker game. He tugged it leashed down the basement steps and it sat cross-legged in a corner, muzzled but more sad than mean. Greg said, "It'll stay right there, don't worry about it." And they tried not to, but it was a worrisome beast, its snout long and searching, head furry with woolly clumps around the ears, cloven hooves at the ends of its lean legs. Even harder to ignore were the almost human parts—the navel visible through wiry hair, the hairless brown nipples, eyes with something like a soul behind them. The beast perked its ears while Abe shuffled and dealt the cards.

It was Phil who finally said, "You think it wants a drink?"

"Hell, it might," Greg said, so off came the muzzle, off the cap from another beer, and Phil thrust the bottle into the beast's big-knuckled hand. It held the bottle up to the light, squinting at the brown glass. Phil showed it what to do—"Here, lift and swallow, partner, lift and swallow"—and it tried with teeth and tongue to get at the liquid inside, to hold the bottle's mouth with its bullish lips. Most of the beer spilled foaming onto its chest.

Abe, from the card table, said, "Christ, get the thing a mug and ante up."

So they sat down and played the next hand. But the beast, encouraged by all the attention, maybe, stood and started to explore the basement, its hooves clacking against the slab. It had a dank smell about it, like moldering leaves, strong enough to overpower the smoke from Phil's cigarettes, Abe's cigars. It was taller than any of the men by a foot or more, and there were signs in its ragged fur they did not care to read: bare spots, and rings around wrists and

271

ankles worn bald and red.

It found Abe's model ships. These were arrayed on shelves sponge-painted blue to simulate ocean waters. The ships were delicate constructions of thin polished wood, with thread for rigging and real cloth sails. Each had taken Abe a month to build, and there were nine of them, one for each month since Corey left him. The beast picked one up and blew on its sails. It was the *Bonne Homme Richard*.

Abe set down his cards and prepared to say something, but the beast got bored and carefully set the ship back on its custom-made stand. Then it ambled over to the table, as though for a closer look at the game.

It grabbed Greg's beer bottle and poured the contents straight down its throat without spilling a drop, set it down empty.

"Learns quick," Phil said.

The beast snorted and shook its head like it was in on the joke, and Greg thought, okay, maybe this *will* work.

Lilith was still up when he got home that night—Greg could see her through the front window. A black and white movie was on television, and in that light the living room looked black and white, too, with Lilith the black and white wife, her nightgown made of bluish light, her pinned-up nighttime hair an illusion of elegance.

She would want to know how things had gone. It had been her idea to bring the beast to the poker game, "to socialize him," she had said. And that was when Greg noticed she called "him" the thing Greg called "it." He had felt responsible for the beast the moment he saw it. But it was Lilith who took it into the backyard that first day and washed it, not with the hose, but with shampoo and warm water from a bucket. Lilith who had made a bed of old blankets in the garage, who peeked in on the beast while it slept. Greg had agreed to take it to Abe's not because he thought getting the beast out of the house would be good for it, but because he thought it would be good for her.

They went in and the beast waited beside him while he took off his jacket. It watched each of his movements, making Greg more aware of them, too: down off the shoulders, left arm out, right arm out.

Lilith came from the living room and said, "Oh God, he's bleeding."

She took the beast by the arm and led it toward the bathroom. Greg followed. When she switched on the light he saw the dark patch below the beast's right ear, remembered how it had bumped its head getting into the car. The blood had matted the fur down to its shoulder and was dripping onto the linoleum in red coins.

Lilith whispered consolingly as she searched for the wound with her fingers, but the beast didn't seem to know it was hurt. She opened the cabinet beneath the sink and found peroxide, cotton balls, scissors.

"Head wounds just bleed a lot," Greg said, "even small ones."

She didn't say anything, and there wasn't space for all three of them in the bathroom, so he went to the kitchen for paper towels to clean out the car. He couldn't find any. He filled a bowl with water, took the sponge from the sink, and went outside.

On the back seat only a little blood was smeared, but Greg took his time cleaning it up. A light was on in the house across the street. He saw Mrs. Heck peering at him, her curled silver hair hovering at the edge of the lace curtains. Her husband Bill Heck, dead fifteen years now, had been a friend of his father's, had fought with him in the war, and Greg remembered her at their house some Sundays, seated in a corner with a pair of scissors, carefully cutting coupons from the newspaper—*their* newspaper—and stuffing them into her purse. Greg had almost expected to see her at his father's wake last week, sitting in the back row, cutting coupons. But she hadn't come to the wake.

Greg closed the car door so that the interior light went out—now he was invisible. He whispered, "Your move, Heck." The woman emerged from behind the curtains, realized she'd been caught, and quickly withdrew. A moment later her light went out. Greg got out of the car and poured the water onto the lawn.

Back inside, he could hear Lilith's voice coming from the garage. She wasn't singing, but the words had a lullaby quality about them.

He sat down and watched the movie while he waited. A pair of cops had just stepped out of their car in front of a big house on a hill. The house looked like his father's, not because of the hill but because of the old slate roof, the big porch, the broad woods behind it. The cops looked business-as-usual as they climbed the porch steps and rang the doorbell, but the music suggested trouble.

Lilith came in and Greg said, "It went well tonight."

"I don't want a divorce," she said.

Five years together and neither of them had mentioned the possibility, so Greg said, "That's good."

Now they were both in that black and white world he'd glimpsed through the window. Her hair was down, messier without the pins. He had no idea what she was thinking. Then she came across the room and straddled him where he sat, blocking his view of the television. She kissed him very seriously. The music on the television reached a crescendo and one of the cops said, "Oh, for the love of God," and the other said, "Get ahold of yourself, son," and when Greg kissed his wife he smelled in her hair that faint rotting-leaves scent beneath the sweetness of her shampoo.

Phil's son Gordon raised his hand in Greg's third period history class and asked, without waiting to be called upon, if the monster was coming to school for Halloween.

Gordon's question came out of nowhere; they were talking about the bombing of Hiroshima. But Greg had expected the question, not just because Phil would have told his family what happened on poker night, but because all day Sunday the neighborhood kids rode their bikes back and forth in front of the house, hoping for a glimpse of the new lodger. And Lilith, not wanting to disappoint, dressed the beast in a pair of faded blue overalls and took it outside, even let some of them touch its fur.

Gordon went on, "I was just thinking, it's like it's already got a costume."

Greg rolled the chalk slowly between his fingers. "We'll have to see," he said.

On Thursday, skeletons, witches, and mummies poked their heads into Greg's classroom. Gordon was dressed as the beast itself, with pointed ears on top of his head and false hooves over his shoes. But Greg, himself costumeless, said, "Sorry, kids. It got a bad cold and couldn't make it."

Greg looked sick, too. He hadn't been sleeping well, he needed a haircut. He took his break in the teacher's lounge and Meredith, the assistant principal, pulled him aside. "Greg," she said, "you never took any time off while your father was ill."

It was true he hadn't missed any classes, but he'd thought that was a good thing. There had been only those long nights beside the hospital bed while the morphine doses were rising, Lyle muttering commandments regarding the upkeep of his lawn, hedges, and roof gutters. His father's face had been whiskered for the first time Greg could remember, and when he saw him again in the casket, he wondered who had shaved him, whether they had used warm water or cold.

Meredith said, "You could take some time now if you need it, Greg. It's just that some of the parents are concerned. I heard that you spent a week and a half on the Holocaust. The World War Two unit's only supposed to be a week long."

"A week didn't seem like enough time," Greg said.

"It isn't, but you know they get this stuff again in high school."

He was thumbing the school's copy of the newspaper. Meredith looked at it and said, "Have you seen the letter to the editor yet?"

Greg turned the page and read aloud, his voice making the statement into a question: "Devious elements springing up around this town like mushrooms overnight?"

The author was anonymous.

"It's just one person," Meredith said. But as she left, Greg noticed a few of his colleagues, silent in their seats, exchanging glances.

Lilith was in the kitchen when he got home, the beast seated on the chair before her, waiting patiently while she trimmed off clumps of fur with electric clippers. "Sorry," she said to Greg. "You're going to have to sharpen these by the time I'm done."

He went to the office and graded papers until the buzzing stopped. When he came out again, Lilith was sweeping mounds of hair into the trash. The beast was gone.

"So it was nothing but fur after all."

She nodded toward the bedroom. "He went that way."

Greg loosened his tie and went down the hall. The beast was curled at the center of the bed, brown hairs shedding onto the white comforter. Pale flesh was visible under the coat now. Greg grabbed its arm. "Come on," he said, "off the bed."

It rolled glassy brown eyes at him and sank deeper into the mattress, wiped snot from its nostrils with its free arm.

"Up!" Greg shouted, and slowly the beast relented, rising from the bed and following him out of the room.

Lilith said, "You could let him rest, hon. He isn't feeling well."

Greg pushed the beast into the garage and locked the door. "*It* stays out *there*," he said.

She turned her back to him and stood at the sink, gripping its edge with both hands. The fancy pillows were on the living room couch, the camera mounted on the tripod. She'd been getting it ready for a family portrait.

Phil and Elise came for dinner and brought Gordon with them. Elise handed Lilith a bottle of wine, but was already peering past her into the house. Phil nodded toward the open kitchen door and said, "There's the fellow." The beast was crouched near the wet churning warmth of the dishwasher, watching them.

"I heard he was sick," Elise said, searching for signs of contagion.

"He's better now," Lilith assured her. "You should have seen all the get well cards."

Gordon ran past them and into the kitchen, halting just in front of the beast, his arms raised. The beast inched away from the boy, blinking. "Now it knows who's boss," Gordon said.

"Leave it alone," Elise said to him, and Gordon went into the living room to watch television.

Greg and Phil stood with hands in pockets while their wives squatted beside the beast. Phil said, "Those wrists are looking better."

It quickly lost interest in the newcomers and resumed its game of rolling oranges across the floor. When dinner was ready, Lilith shooed the beast into the garage. It sat and gazed up at her as she closed the door.

"It's hard to keep up with him these days," she said, picking the oranges off the floor.

"Asserting his personality," said Elise.

Greg didn't talk much during dinner. He drank a lot of water, always going into the kitchen to refill his glass. Afterward, he and Phil retreated to the office, and Greg took out a stack of photographs of his father. In the pictures, all from the war, Lyle appeared as a taller, handsomer version of Greg, dancing with women in flared skirts, smoking a cigarette in front of the Egyptian pyramids, on a runway in England with arms around his buddies, always grinning, sometimes pointing straight at the camera as if to say, "Hey, you there!"

"You going to sell the house?" Phil asked.

"As soon as I can," Greg said. "Got it pretty much cleaned out now. I found these in his dresser. He never showed them to me."

"And what about the big guy? Where'd you find him, anyway?"

Greg held the last photo—Lyle behind the controls of his bomber plane— and flipped it rapidly against his knee. "In the basement," he said. "There's a little room down there where they used to store coal, for the old furnace. It was just chained up back there. Dirty and half-starved."

Phil whistled and shook his head. "And he never mentioned it. Wonder where he picked the thing up."

Greg said, "For the last thirty years the man and I were strangers. Now he's dead and I feel like he's around me all the time."

From the next room came the sound of Elise's laughter. Lilith had commenced the nightly lesson. "A," she said, and then again, insistent, "A."

"Ahgg," came the beast's rasp.

"B," Lilith said.

"Ahgg," it said.

Phil said, "Elise told me you've got the kids studying the atomic bomb. Gordon's really into it. He was telling me about how people's shadows were left on the walls, you know, afterwards. Pretty creepy stuff. Anyway, Elise is wondering how long you're planning to spend on that?"

Greg put the photos away. "Not sure," he said.

Elise drank most of the bottle of wine she brought that night. She and Phil were standing at the door with their jackets on when she remembered Gordon. "Where is that boy?" she said. The television was still on but the couch was empty.

Greg went across the house to the garage. The beast was curled up on its bed of blankets and Gordon was crouched over it. When the boy pulled his hand away Greg saw the bruise on the beast's nipple.

"It isn't so tough," Gordon said.

"Your parents are leaving now," Greg said. He waited in the doorway until Gordon walked past him. The beast watched the boy go, then settled its head down with a sigh.

Greg and Lilith were coming home from the supermarket when a police cruiser came up behind them and flashed its high beams. Greg pulled over and watched in the rearview as the cop stepped out of his car. It was Abe. He waved as he approached, and Greg rolled down his window.

Abe leaned over and said, "Just got a call from Mrs. Connor over on Myrtle. Says there's a bear chewing on her barbecue grill. You want to come check it out with me?"

"Oh Jesus," said Lilith.

Greg said to her, "You go home and check."

"No, I'm coming with you."

Abe got back into his car and Greg followed him around the block. The Connor place was dark when they arrived. The three met on the walk and Abe explained, "Said she didn't want to attract its attention."

They walked around the side of the house, keeping close to the wall. Dogs were barking from the neighboring yards, and Abe had his hand on the butt of his pistol.

At first they could see nothing but Mrs. Connor's rows of tulips. Then from the shadow of a tree came another shadow, bent and shaggy. The beast's eyes were bright in the moonlight.

"Nice and easy now," Abe said, like a television cop. He handed Greg his cuffs. "You want to do this?"

But Lilith walked past them, one hand raised. The beast seemed to catch her scent.

"Come here," she called, but the beast ignored her.

"Doesn't look good," said Abe.

"Come here to mommy," Lilith said.

Abe shot a glance at Greg that he was careful not to return.

When the beast still didn't budge, Lilith said, "Come here *right this instant.*"

It put its snout in the air and produced a gurgling sound, almost a howl.

"Yes," Lilith said. "A."

"Bahgg," the beast said.

"A, B," said Lilith.

It rolled its shoulders and came slowly over the lawn, stood before her with head hung. She took its wrist and said, "Okay, let's go."

They put the beast in the back seat and Lilith got in beside it, moving groceries out of the way.

"I'll call Mrs. Connor in the morning," Greg said to Abe.

"Gave her quite a scare. You folks going to be all right?"

"Just fine, Abe. Thanks for grabbing us when you did."

Abe tipped his hat. "Poker tomorrow," he said, and headed up the sidewalk to the house.

Greg got behind the wheel and met Lilith's eyes in the mirror. She held the beast's right arm and squeezed it gently. Greg couldn't see its face, but he smelled the earthy breath, felt it hot on the back of his neck.

They could have played on the dining room table, since Abe had the place to himself now, but it was tradition to take the cooler into the basement, check the progress of the model ship of the month, pull out the folding chairs and pass around the plastic poker chips. Abe had remodeled the basement the year before Corey went back to Minneapolis. Using any other room would have been an insult to the man's craftsmanship, and too much like acknowledging his wife's absence.

That night, though, even in the sanctum beneath the house, nothing was right. The cooler leaked water over the floor, the pretzels were stale, and Phil, usually the risk-taker, folded quickly almost every hand. Finally Abe said, "Have to close up now, boys. Early day tomorrow."

The men shuffled back up the stairs. As Greg took his jacket from the wall rack, Abe put a hand on his arm and asked him to stay a moment. When the others were gone, Abe's face went tight and he said, "Your father was a good man, Greg. He was a friend of mine."

Abe was older than Greg but younger than his father. Lyle never joined them for their poker games, but Greg knew that he and Abe shared a few beers sometimes down at Cooley's.

Greg said, "He always spoke well of you, Abe."

"That's why I feel a little responsible, like I should look out for you. I think your dad would want that. Not that I knew him too well, mind you. But this much about him I had figured. Either he took care of business or he kept his business his own. You follow me?"

"You bet," he said.

"Good. Now this guest of yours, Greg, a beast like that shouldn't be taught to speak. Nobody wants to know what it would have to say. You just call me if you need help with this thing, okay? I'm always here."

That room was tidy, pristine, just the way Corey had left it. And there were Abe's white socks, sunk in the thick blue carpet.

Greg put his jacket on. "Thanks, Abe."

At the door they wished each other goodnight. The porch light went off as Greg got into his car.

Greg got up early, made coffee, eggs, toast. He took the beast through the sliding glass door into the backyard, where birds twittered angrily from the trees. Greg tossed an orange into the grass, said, "Go for it, boy. Let's see your stuff."

It hesitated, then bounded after the orange, rolling it along with its snout while Greg sipped from his mug. "That's it," he said. "Keep it moving, keep it moving."

The beast snatched the orange in its teeth and flung it across the lawn. Greg put his mug down and went after it, tossed it back into the air. The beast caught the orange in its mouth. "Yeah," Greg said. "Now rip that thing apart. Just tear into it."

The beast shook its head and bit down, juice spilling over its chin. It dropped the remains into the grass. "All right," Greg said, and took the beast back inside.

He arrived at school early, claiming the best spot in the parking lot. His lesson plan was the best he'd ever written. He filled the board with notes for first period, using four colors of chalk, then sat in the first row to admire his work.

Meredith appeared at the door, in shorts and a t-shirt. "Morning, Greg. What are you doing?"

"Just getting ready for another day of junior high school," he said brightly.

"But Greg, it's Sunday."

Even the sixth-grader seat felt too big for him. "Sunday?" he said. "Then what are you doing here?"

She held up a basketball. "JV practice." Her shorts were orange and blue, the school colors.

"Right," he said. "I guess I'll just keep these notes up for tomorrow."

"Let the janitor know," Meredith said, "or he'll wash it clean." She jogged down the hall toward the gym.

It was well after midnight, and under the harsh streetlights the block looked a little like a museum exhibit. Greg was watching out the window when Abe's cruiser came to a halt in front of the house. It was Mrs. Heck who'd called—he'd seen her light go on, seen her standing at the window with the telephone to her ear.

Greg opened the door to let Abe in, and Lilith asked if he wanted coffee.

"No, thank you."

Phil and Elise were on the couch with Gordon sandwiched between them. The boy's face was red and puffy, one eye already blackening. Greg had been awakened by the sound of the boy's screaming. In the garage, he'd found Gordon crumpled in the corner and the beast settling back onto its blankets, the old scab on its head opened up again.

"You see what that thing did to my son?" Elise said. "He could be dead right now."

Lilith said to Abe, "He stole the spare key to our house. He's probably the one who let him out into Mrs. Connor's yard last week." To Elise she added, "And what the hell was he doing in our garage, anyway?"

Gordon sank into the cushions and whimpered, "I just wanted to pet it."

Lilith stopped herself from saying something and went into the kitchen.

Abe said, "You want to get dressed, Greg?"

Greg had been standing in silence in the middle of the room. He went down the hall and put on the clothes he'd worn to school that morning. When he got back, Phil was saying, "Look, Abe, we don't have to make a big fuss out of this." Elise glared at him, but Phil went on, "Let's just work this out in the morning. We shouldn't have bothered you at this hour."

"You take your son home," said Abe. "School night tonight. Gordon, you gave the key back?"

Gordon nodded.

"We're all set here, then."

"What about this eye?" Elise said.

"Ice for the swelling," said Abe.

Phil ushered them outside and into their station wagon. A minute later it crawled away down the street.

Lilith exploded from the kitchen. "That little twerp had it coming."

"Lilith," Greg said.

"She's probably right," said Abe. "Greg, you better bring your guest."

The beast sauntered sleepily from the garage and allowed itself to be led outside. Its hooves clacked against the sidewalk. Greg saw Mrs. Heck's curtain swish closed.

From the door Lilith said, "I got him to say my name, Greg. Damn it, he knows my name."

They took Abe's car; the beast rode in the back. Abe kept the chatter of the police radio low while he drove to the edge of town, out to Lyle's place. Greg used to drive past the house at night, if he had to go to the store for something. And sometimes the kitchen light would be on, and he'd wonder what his father was doing in there—taking in a cowboy movie, probably, or a gin and tonic. But Greg never stopped and went in. Now the place was dark and a realtor's sign was up in the front yard. But the hedges needed trimming, and the gutters would have to be cleaned before winter.

When the beast stepped out of the car, it snuffled the air and blinked.

"Knows its own home," said Abe.

Greg took the beast's arm. They walked up to the house, then past it toward the woods beyond. When they reached the backyard Abe said, "This is where I stay." He handed Greg his pistol.

Greg felt like he was sleepwalking as he went into those woods, the beast beside him, he dressed for school. Dead pine needles crackled underfoot. He found a clearing that looked familiar and sat down in the damp weeds. He'd built a fort in this spot when he was nine or ten, and his father had helped, bringing him twine to bind the wood, a piece of burlap for the roof. Greg slept in the teepee a few times that summer but water leaked in when it rained. His father told him that next time he would have to use a deer skin like the Indians did, and when Greg asked where to get one, his father said, "Off a deer." Greg took the teepee down and never built another.

The beast had been wandering, nose to the ground. It came back to Greg now and looked up at him—it had pushed a pinecone across the clearing with its snout. It opened its mouth as though to speak, but Greg got up before it could.

He didn't know how to fire a gun, but he fired it. Then he walked back to the yard and Abe took the gun and strapped it into its holster.

They drove past the school on the way back into town. The lights were on over the tennis courts, over the soccer field, too, and inside the school Greg knew his notes were still on the board. On the radio the police dispatcher spouted a series of codes, then said something about a stalled car abandoned on an overpass, and a woman with pains in her chest, and a couple who had woken the neighbors with their arguing, and a man who'd cut his hand trying to chip ice out of his freezer.

Abe silenced the radio. "Could use some quiet now," he said.

EVERYBODY IS WAITING FOR SOMETHING

ANDREA KNEELAND

When fish started falling from the sky, Karen just shut herself up in the house with her family, hunched on the couch, waiting for some sign of reception from the television. Her husband, always the extremist, killed himself within the first twenty-four hours. Three days later, her eldest daughter, Rosalie, ran off to the Baptist church down the road, although Karen had expressly forbidden her to do anything of the sort.

Rosalie came home an hour later. The church was packed so tight with sweaty flesh that dozens of people had already lost their lives in the throes of ecclesiastical ecstasy. The causes of death were numerous: suffocation, trampling, dehydration, hyperventilation. Still, the masses inside the church were unfazed, convulsing on top of the fallen bodies in desperate prayer, speaking in tongues. The line of new converts wrapped up the church steps and around the block, hundreds of people wallowing through the thick slush of iridescent scales and reddish guts, shielding themselves from the sky with trash can lids. Rosalie told her mother this between bites of a ham sandwich, famished from her rebellion.

Within a year, life had returned to normal, as much as could be expected. Churches emptied out. Suicide rates dropped. People became embarrassed of their overreactions. Karen, for example, pretended that her husband had disappeared during a particularly intense fish storm; refused to admit his folly.

Karen's life had become microscopic, settled into a radius of three miles, the farthest she could walk without becoming sick from the smell of fish. Cars, airplanes, trains—any standard method of escape had become useless beneath the onslaught. She learned to predict what would be for supper that night. Thunder always indicated shellfish. Tiny clouds of gauzy cumulus suggested a smattering of shrimp. Dark autocumulus, lumpy as new black wool, foreshadowed mackerel. Everyone she knew quit their jobs (if there was any job left to quit) and settled into their respective routines: waiting for some miracle of technology to bring their television reception back, waiting for the water to finally run out beneath the absence of rainfall, waiting for the rats to get tired of rotting fish and come after the infants instead.

This, you see, was the new life. *The new life*, Karen thought, *is a tiny little thing*. She never discussed this sentiment with her daughter or her neighbors, but she knew that they agreed: the core of her bones told her so. She set a bucket out on her back porch and retired to a lawn chair beneath the eaves of the house, waiting for her dinner to fall from the sky.

It was Jim Rourke who surprised everyone. Inventing a way to extract water from fish; to separate that liquid as precious as gold from the salty guts and flesh. The news was spread the old fashioned way, through gossip; through leaflets stapled to obsolete telephone poles; through a murmur of electricity, of agitation, that permeated the air.

Karen believed she remembered the name "Jim Rourke." The letters, the vowels, the composite of the alphabet spelled just that way, sparked a distant memory in her; she would have called it "nostalgia" if she hadn't already worn out the meaning of that word. She wandered about in a daze for weeks, waiting for her body to spark into excitement, the words "Jim Rourke" escaping her lips haphazardly, an accidental mantra. Finally, she pulled her yearbook from the attic and found his picture, two rows down and to the left of her own. His face, as blank and as indistinguishable as the rest of them.

The next day, she found an announcement flour-pasted to one of the telephone poles. The black lines above hung like old rubber snakes, broken and useless. She eased into her lawn chair, watching the dinner bucket, and thought about Jim's yearbook portrait, about what had to become of the world before a person like him could ever be a hero.

Karen sat in at the town hall demonstration, swaddled fast between rows upon rows of collapsible metal chairs and sweaty flesh, her tennis shoes rubbing nervously against the high school's sticky gymnasium floor. Everybody was waiting for something to happen. She craned her head behind her shoulder, eyed the plain white clock that hung just above the closed double doors. Her head realigned itself with the front of her body and her eyes swam to the man in the front of the room. He moved toward the machine.

She watched the fish disappear inside a small box of metal, watched Jim turn the outer dial; the sputtering spigot, the tiny drops of pure, clear water running out into the little glass bowl. This water: this unbearable possibility of life.

When Karen heard the gunshot, she felt her insides shudder with queer relief; with a vague empathy for the assassin. Jim slumped across the stage, his arms flapping like the fins of a fish, blood leaking out from his heart like a faucet. The second bullet sliced clean through Jim's contraption. Glistening shards of metal and trout swam above the stage in a violent rainbow.

Karen squeezed her eyes shut. In the distance, just beyond the screams and clattering of chairs and the deafening tick of the clock, she could hear trout slapping against the roof of the building.

EAR CAT

CARLTON MELLICK III

Irene's fingers are wiggly today. They curl in and out of her hand like she is trying to snap all of her fingers at the same time.

"Quit it with the fingers already," Martin says over the videophone.

Irene paces the living room, straightening pictures of her dead parents on the coffee table, wiggling her fingers, and avoiding the pile of cats in the corner.

"Please," Martin says. "I need you."

Irene stops in front of the videophone, but she avoids looking into the screen to Martin's house. The room he's in might be dimly lit, decorated with calming earth tones, but it is still too unsettling for her. She faces his video image, but her eyes are locked on a red clay lamp directly above the monitor.

"What if it got lost in the mail?" Irene says.

"I'm sure it will come," he says. "Be patient."

Irene has been a member of the Kitty of the Month Club for over six years, and never once has a kitten been delivered this late. Her monthly kitty is the only thing that ever truly calms her down, and it has been several days since the last one expired.

"I can't be patient without it," she says.

"You're making me nervous," he says. "Calm down."

Irene realizes her fingers are wiggling, so she clenches them into fists until her knuckles go white. Then she decides to reorganize her antique lamp collection.

"Not the lamps again," Martin groans. "You just rearranged them this morning."

Irene's lamp collection covers every free inch of wall in her living room.

287

Shelves of antique lamps start at the floor and go all the way up to the top of the seventeen-foot-high ceiling, only leaving free space for windows, a couple of couches, the front door, and the fireplace.

Each lamp is a unique work of art. There is a purple mushroom-shaped lamp, a blue porcelain lamp with sparrows painted on the side, a marble lamp shaped like a fat little German boy, a wooden withered tree-shaped lamp, a frog lamp, a shoe lamp, a fishbowl lamp. There are so many varieties of lamps clashing chaotically on her shelves that they are dizzying to the eye; the fact that she absolutely must keep every single lamp turned on at all hours of every day only amplifies this effect.

Martin sneers at Irene's lamp collection. "Why do you even bother organizing them? They look ugly no matter what order you put them in."

Irene pulls lamps off the shelves and places them on the floor. A seahorse lamp, a rainbow lamp, a child's teddy bear lamp. She keeps them all plugged in as she moves them. She can't handle seeing any of them turned off, even for a minute.

"Last time they were organized by their monetary value, from most expensive to least expensive," Irene says. "Now I want to organize them by their size from biggest to smallest."

"But they're all the same size," Martin says.

Irene holds a zebra-striped lamp up to a white slinky-shaped lamp. "This one is at least an inch and a half taller than this one."

Martin groans and turns off the visual on his videophone.

"What did you do that for?" she asks the blank screen where the image of Martin used to be.

His voice comes out of the speakers on the side of the monitor. "Sorry, I can't take it anymore. Everything's so *busy* at your house."

"But you're supposed to be helping me," she says.

"And you're supposed to be helping *me*," he says. "But all you do is make me nervous."

She wiggles her fingers at the black screen. "But we had only twenty minutes left to go. Now Dr. Ash is going to make us do it all over again tomorrow."

"I'm sorry," he says. "I hate redoing these phone sessions as much as you do, but you drove me to it."

"Fine," she says.

Irene shifts her weight back and forth in front of the screen for a few minutes. Martin remains quiet.

"Well, we might as well just cancel our conversation for the day," she says. "If we have to redo it again tomorrow, there's no point in talking anymore today."

"Sounds good," Martin says.

He disconnects before she has a chance to say goodbye.

Irene pinches the chunk of skin above the bridge of her nose. A lot of tension builds up in this area of her face, so pinching it often relieves a bit of stress. She calls this area of her face her *tickle*, because it often tickles if she goes without pinching it for too long.

She holds her tickle, her facial muscles slowly relaxing, as she sways toward her collection of previous Kitties of the Month piled sloppily on the brown-checkered carpeting.

Although the cats were once living, they are now more like stuffed animals. Gen-cats always revert to stuffed animals immediately upon expiration; their innards expel themselves out of various orifices and they can be filled with cotton fluff. That's the way they were designed.

Irene picks up an ex-cat with red and tan swirls, and snuggles it against her chin. It was last January's kitty, which they called a *cinnamon cat*. Remembering back to that time, the cinnamon cat was a frisky playful kitten that freshened her house with a nice cinnamon smell all month long.

Each kitten in the Kitty of the Month Club is bio-engineered by scientists that are referred to as Kitty Artists. Their job is to invent new varieties of cats. So far, Irene has received an orange basketball kitty that bounced when it hit the ground, a unicorn kitty that had a long horn growing from its white forehead, a plushy kitty that was like an animated cat-shaped plush toy, a raspberry blue kitty, an avocado kitty, a circus clown kitty, a helicopter kitty.

They seem to have an endless variety of bio-engineered cats. So far, Irene has loved every single one of them. And once dead, they have all made great additions to her stuffed animal collection.

Normally, Irene keeps her stuffed kitties displayed on shelves in her bedroom, but whenever she is feeling lonely she likes to take them all downstairs and pile them in the living room. That way, they can be at-hand just in case she needs comfort from them.

The Kitty of the Month Club has a motto:
Comforting, High-Quality Companions, Guaranteed.

Dr. Ash refuses to call Irene on the videophone during their therapy sessions. He always insists on seeing her in person. Irene never lets him inside, so he speaks to her through a crack in the doorway. When they speak, she holds a limp goldilocks cat in her arms, with her back to the door. She doesn't want to catch even the smallest glimpse of the miserable world outside, which looks more like a long-abandoned construction site than a neighborhood street.

"You have been avoiding again," Dr. Ash says with a miniature smile. "The more you avoid, the harder it will be to confront."

Irene sticks her finger in her nose. She hates Dr. Ash. She hates that he is only twenty-two and thinks he knows everything just because he's part of the 3.5 percent of the population that isn't agoraphobic.

"I want a different therapy partner," Irene says.

Dr. Ash rubs out the wrinkles in his electric blue suit.

"What's wrong with Martin?" he says.

"He's impossible," she says.

"You said that about your last eleven therapy partners," he says.

"I'm sick of seeing him on my phone," she says. "I'm sick of talking about stupid things with stupid people just because you think it will help me."

"It will help you," Dr. Ash says.

His eyebrows tighten to his eyelids to show her how genuinely concerned he is.

"What if I don't want to be helped?" Irene strokes the long golden locks hanging from the stuffed kitten on her lap.

"Don't you?" Dr. Ash says. "Don't you want to be able to go outside again?"

Dr. Ash flips through pages in a notebook. "Don't you want to go to the beach? Go out with friends? Travel to other cities, to other countries?"

She hugs the cat to her chest with all her strength. Then she pinches her tickle.

"No," she says. "I don't need any of that. What's the point in going out anymore? I've got everything I need right here. If I've got to talk to anybody, I've got email. When it's time to go to work, I log online. If I need to buy something, I shop at an online store and have it delivered. If I want to see anything interesting, the internet has millions of pictures of places that a single person could never visit in a lifetime."

"Doesn't that sound like you're just making excuses?" says Dr. Ash. "I've got dozens of other patients who say exactly the same thing."

"Whatever," Irene says, stretching her fingers out as far as she can until they begin to hurt.

"I'm going to keep you with Martin," says Dr. Ash. "I want you to stick with the same therapy partner for at least three months. The more you talk to him the more comfortable you will feel around him. Just stick with it and stop avoiding. It will get easier."

"I don't want to talk to him anymore this week," she says. "At least not until I get this month's cat."

"I want you to talk to him tomorrow afternoon for two hours," he says. "Even without the cat."

"But I can't think straight without one."

"The cat doesn't matter," he says.

"But you're the one who said I should get a pet," she says.

"I said you should get a pet," he says. "There's a big difference between getting a pet and signing up for the Kitty of the Month Club."

"What difference is that?"

"Just stop worrying about the cat," he says. "I'm sure it will come later in the day."

"It better come," she says, wiggling her fingers.

Irene logs onto the Kitty of the Month Club website to see if there is any mention of a delay in shipping this month. The front page of the site has the Kitty of the Month logo in sparkling glitter letters with cartoon kitties hopping and dancing to accordion music.

The site hasn't been updated in over a week. The This Month's Selection page is still an advertisement for last month's kitten, which was a Cheshire Kitty based on the cat from Alice in Wonderland, complete with a wide toothy grin.

After clicking on all the different pages, even checking the message board for recent announcement posts, Irene gives up. There is no mention of a delay. There is no information on what the new cat is going to be like. She begins to wonder if the company has gone out of business.

"What if there aren't any more coming?" she says to her lamp collection. "What if I'll never get another one?"

She tries not to think about it and goes to a different website that sells brass instruments. Irene is a collector of horns. Hanging on the wall in her cellar, she has a fine collection of French horns, Vienna horns, double horns, and other brass instruments that Irene likes to call *curly horns*.

Although Irene has no idea how to play any of the instruments she owns, she likes to try. All that ever comes out when she plays are loud obnoxious noises, but there is something relaxing about feeling her lips vibrate against a mouthpiece. It's not really playing the instruments that appeals to Irene. She just likes the look of her collection on the wall.

Irene loves collecting things. She has her horn collection, her lamp collection, her cat collection; these things are important to her. They are the only friends she needs.

Since she hasn't gotten her Kitty of the Month selection, Irene decides to order a new French horn. She pays to have it shipped overnight. If she doesn't get her Kitty of the Month selection, at least she will get a new horn as a kind of consolation.

The delivery machine arrives at her front door with smoke drizzling out of its faceless spherical head, its body trembling and making a loud clanking sound. Irene spies out her window at the caterpillar-shaped device as it reaches into its hollow body with rubber-coated limbs. Irene's lower lip flickers as she sees the condition of her package. The rickety delivery bot drops it out of its chest, leaving it lopsided on her doorstep. The box is wrinkled and wet, one of its sides is completely smashed inward.

"You piece of junk!" Irene yells through the door.

The machine turns around and sputters toward the next house on the gray, muddy suburban street.

Irene waits for the delivery machine to get out of sight before making her move. As she opens the door, she focuses her eyes on the package. She steps out of the doorway with only one foot, keeping the other safely inside. Her arms stretch out to their limit and seize the edge of the package. In one jerking motion, she pulls the package inside and slams the door.

"Crappy delivery machines," Irene says, staring down at the dilapidated box.

The Kitty of the Month Club logo is scraped down to the cardboard, as if the package had been dragged across asphalt for thirty yards.

"If anything happened to it I'm going to... "

The package moves. Something is alive inside. The kitten was not destroyed during transport.

Irene smiles so wide that her lips crack. She frantically cuts the packaging tape with her front door key. It is the only thing her door key is good for anymore. While cutting, she wonders what kind of cat it will be. She thinks, will it be a rainbow-colored cat? Will it be a flying cat? Will it be a ninja cat that hides in shadows and sneak-attacks your toes when you least expect it?

When she opens the box, her smile fades away. There is something hideous inside. She's not quite sure what it is. All she can see are... ears.

The cat jumps out of the box and stretches against the carpeting, giving Irene a good look at it. The kitten doesn't have any hair. Instead of fur, the kitten has ears. It has a coat of human ears of all different sizes and shapes, sewn together in a sort of ear-kitty Frankenstein way.

Irene backs away from the cat. She isn't sure how such a monstrosity got into her Kitty of the Month Club box. She is sure that the company made a mistake. She is sure the Kitty Artists accidentally sent a failed experimental cat instead of the real one. Her hand reaches for the box. Each monthly cat comes with an introduction card explaining its unique characteristics. She is sure there will be a different cat listed on the card.

As her hand digs through the litter in the box, the thing turns its head and looks at Irene. The cat's face is like a tiny person's face, with a human's mouth, nose, and eyes.

"Meow," says the cat.

The thing doesn't meow like a cat; it says *meow* in the way that a person might say it.

Irene wonders if the thing has the intelligence of a human.

"Meow," says the cat, glaring at her with tiny blue human eyes.

The card says that it is an Ear Cat. It wasn't a mistake. This mutant animal is the right Kitty of the Month selection they sent out to everyone.

"What the hell were they thinking?" Irene says to the ear cat as it licks the lobe of an ear on its hip.

Normally, the card will give a paragraph-long story about the unique personality and physical attributes of the monthly cat, but this time all the card says is:

It has ears.

Irene's fingers are wiggly again, but this time they are wiggling faster, with more frenzied jerks. She is trying to avoid the ear cat, but the thing keeps following her around the house. She paces through the kitchen to the dining room to the entry room to the living room back to the kitchen, with the ear cat walking casually behind her. When she stops, the cat stops with her and sits down.

"Meow," says the ear cat, looking up at her with all ears raised at once as if to listen carefully to what she has to say.

"Stop following me," she says to the ear cat, wiggling her fingers at it.

"Meow," says the ear cat.

"What do you want?" she cries.

It wags its hairless tail, which ends in a tiny baby ear instead of a point. Irene pinches her tickle until her nerves become smooth.

The ear cat makes itself at home. It curls up on the top of the pile of stuffed ex-cats, clawing at their fur until they become squishy and comfortable.

"No!" Irene cries at the ear cat.

The ear cat snuggles in, smearing earwax all over Irene's cat collection.

"You're ruining them!" she says.

"Meow," the ear cat whispers, its face squished against the side of a limp pirate cat.

Irene goes to her computer and visits the Kitty of the Month Club website. She is going to send them the nastiest email she has ever written in her life. On the contact page she realizes there isn't an email address. Just a phone number.

"Just a phone number?" Irene says. "I'm not going to call anyone to make a complaint."

She looks at the videophone. She knows she has been practicing phone conversations with Martin for a while, but she isn't ready to call a complete stranger. She prefers to complain by email.

During the night, Irene keeps herself locked in her bedroom. The ear cat wanders through the house. It sometimes coughs and sneezes. When it coughs, it sounds like a person coughing. It sounds like there is someone else in the house with her.

Irene lies in her bed, unable to sleep. Every time she closes her eyes and drifts halfway to sleep, she dreams there is a strange man pressing his ear against her bedroom door, trying to listen to what she is doing, and saying, "Meow."

The next day, Irene calls Martin on the videophone. Martin answers with audio only. His screen is black.

"This is a first," Martin says with a melancholy voice. "You're the one calling me."

"Turn on the video," Irene says.

"And you want me to turn the video on?" he says, trying to be witty through the quivers in his voice. "What's Dr. Ash done to you?"

Irene decides not to argue. "I'm having another panic attack."

"What is it over this time?" he says. "Did you run out of coffee again? Did one of your lamps' light bulbs burn out?"

"No," she says. "There's this strange thing in my house."

The ear cat rubs earwax against Irene's black velvet sofa.

"What kind of thing?"

"It's this cat made of ears."

"Of course."

"It was this month's kitty. It finally came and turned out to be the most horrible thing I've ever seen. It looks more like a little deformed baby than a cat."

The ear cat scratches at the wrinkles on its forehead.

"So why are you calling me about it?"

"I don't know what to do. It keeps listening to me."

"Call Dr. Ash. Ask him."

"I can't get through to him for some reason."

"Look, Irene," he says. "I'm hanging up."

"You can't hang up. You're my socialization buddy."

"I... " he says. "I don't think I want us to be socialization buddies."

"But Dr. Ash said... "

"I don't care what Dr. Ash said. Ever since I partnered with you I've become more anxious than I've ever been. I'm not going to do it anymore."

"But you can't quit."

Irene's fingers go wiggly.

"I don't care. I'm done."

"But I need your help."

"Who cares about the stupid cat?" he says. "The thing is going to die in a month anyway. Just put up with it until it dies."

"I can't put up with it," she says. "The thing is invading my home."

"Don't call me anymore. I'm disconnecting. Don't bother calling back."

The sound cuts off. Irene tries to redial his number, but he doesn't pick up.

The French horn Irene ordered arrives a day late, even though she paid for overnight shipping. The delivery machine is smoking twice as much as last time. Sparks are raining out of its abdomen. Its head is on crooked as though some kid was trying to break it off with a bat.

The box is slightly blackened on the outside, as if it had been cooking for a while within the delivery machine. At least it is not as smashed as the previous package she received.

Irene pulls out the brass instrument. Once she holds it in her hand, she realizes that it's not doing anything for her. It's not making her instantly happy the way she normally feels when she adds something new to one of her collections. It seems like just another horn. Nothing special.

She takes it into the living room. The ear cat sits down by her feet and says,

"Meow." She inches away from it. It inches toward her, glaring with a frowny little man face.

Irene turns her back to the cat. She can't handle the sight of the thing, but it just leaps up onto one of the lamp shelves so that she is forced to look at it.

"Meow," says the ear cat.

Irene looks down at the French horn. It didn't make her happy to get it in the mail, but if she plays it she'll at least be able to get that vibrating mouth feeling that relaxes her.

Sucking in a large breath of air and then blowing into the mouthpiece, Irene hits one of the loudest, most obnoxious notes she has ever played.

When the ear cat hears the noise, its face cringes up. All of its ears tense up at the same time and its claws dig into the shelf. Then it flees. It charges through Irene's antique lamp collection, knocking them off the shelves. The shelf collapses, knocking down the shelf below. Like dominoes, all her shelves of rare and unusual lamps come crashing down around her.

Irene's eyes bulge open as she sees her precious collection shattering to pieces. In the center of the destruction, the ear cat licks at its wounded ears. Irene tosses her new French horn into the mess. She throws herself back into a chair, exhausted.

"That's it," she says to the ear cat. "All those years of collecting. Gone. It's ruined. I have no reason to buy another lamp, ever again."

The ear cat jumps up onto the coffee table in front of her. It cocks its head and says, "Meow."

She shudders at the little black hairs growing out of some of the ears.

Irene contemplates killing the cat. It has messed up her cat collection, ruined her lamp collection, caused her to lose interest in her horn collection. Without these collections, she has lost all her friends in the universe. The ear cat deserves to die.

She looks down at the freakish kitten. The kitten stares at her with sad raised eyebrows and pouting lips. She realizes she doesn't have the heart to kill even the ugliest of cats.

Irene opens the door a crack, without looking outside. She motions for the ear cat to go out. Although she doesn't want to kill it, she doesn't have a problem with getting rid of it.

"Come on," Irene says, snapping her fingers. "Get out."

The ear cat walks up to the door and sits down at her feet. It looks up at her and says, "Meow."

"Go on," Irene tells the ear cat.

"Meow," the ear cat tells Irene.

Then the ear cat wanders away, toward the kitchen.

Irene pinches her tickle. Before closing the door, she glances outside and contemplates leaving. It would be good to get away from the hideous creature that lives in her home. But then she reminds herself that the ear cat will not be alive for very long. She just has to wait.

A month passes and the ear cat is still alive. It has been a long month of hiding in the bedroom, cleaning earwax off her clothes, and cringing whenever the cat coughed or cleared its throat.

She has never had a Gen-cat last so long. Normally they expire after three weeks. Sometimes two. On a couple occasions they last most of the month, but there has never been a cat that has lasted long enough to see the next month's cat.

Several days late, the smoking delivery machine crawls like a snail up the muddy street and spits out the Kitty of the Month package onto the faded welcome mat.

When Irene opens the box, her eyes tremble at the sight of the new kitten. She pulls the introduction card out of the box.

It says:

Muscle Cat—He's got muscles.

Like the ear cat, the muscle cat has a mostly human face and no fur on its body. However, the muscle cat does have hair on its head, blond hair with a surfer-style haircut. Its four limbs look like small human arms, with human hands instead of paws. These arms are incredibly muscular, as if the cat were a professional bodybuilder. The muscle cat also wears a tiny pair of purple spandex shorts.

"Meee-ow," says the muscle cat to Irene, as it flexes its muscles and flicks its blond bangs out of its blue eyes.

Irene inches away from it.

The ear cat and the muscle cat become fast friends. They play together in Irene's living room while Irene hides in her bedroom, watching them through a crack in the door.

The muscle cat bench-presses a couple of the cracked lamps that had been piled on the floor. The ear cat rocks in a rocking chair, listening to the birds singing in the dead trees outside.

The muscle cat grunts as it works out.

The ear cat coughs and clears its throat.

Irene tries to pinch her tickle to make the stress go away, but it doesn't seem to work anymore.

Irene calls Dr. Ash. He answers his videophone with the video off. She wants to see him. She thinks seeing him would make her feel more comfortable, more safe. It is the first time she has needed the company of another person.

"Irene?" he says as he answers, surprised to hear from her.

She wants to ask him to turn the video on, but can't get herself to ask the question. She hopes he will decide to turn it on himself. She waits for him to.

"Irene, I'm really busy, what do you want?" he asks.

"I need help," she says. "I can't breathe in this house. I'm drowning. I need to get out."

"Need to get out?" he says. "I thought it was the outside that made you feel like you were drowning?"

"Did you get my emails?"

"You said something about a Gen-cat that disturbed you?" he says. "You said it didn't die after a month?"

"No, it didn't," she says. "There's two of them now! The second one makes me even more uncomfortable than the first!"

"Why don't you just throw them away or kick them outside?" he asks. "They're only Gen-cats."

"I'm not touching those things," she says. "You have to come over and take them away."

She hears him exhale severely.

"Irene," he says. "I don't know how to tell you this, but I'm no longer able to be your counselor."

"What do you mean?"

"People are becoming more and more agoraphobic every day," he says. "Fifteen months ago, 94% of the population was considered severely agoraphobic.

Just a few months ago, it jumped by two percent. Last month, it jumped up another two percent. Our civilization can't function with everyone locked up in their homes. We have to get outside and put the world back together."

"Then why are you dumping me as your patient?" she asks. "Especially at a time like this."

"Because I've been told to dump the hopeless cases and focus only on the ones with the best chance for recovery."

"But I'm not a hopeless case," she says.

"I'm sorry," Dr. Ash says. "Unfortunately, I really don't have time to discuss this anymore. I have to go."

"You can't do this to me," she says.

"Good luck, Irene," he says to her.

The phone disconnects.

Her internet stops working. She isn't sure what's wrong with it. She doesn't know what to do. Everything is connected through the internet: her television, her videophone, her job. She has become completely disconnected from the rest of the world. It is just her, the two freakish cat-things, and her wiggly fingers.

"Meee-ow," says the muscle cat, flexing its arms as it does pull-ups from a curtain rod.

She tries to ignore them, but they won't leave her alone. They follow her, meowing at her, as though they are trying to communicate.

Sitting at her computer, her twitching fingers tap on the mouse button. If she can't log online soon she could lose her accounting job. There are so many people who need online jobs and so few jobs available that she could easily be replaced within a day. Her employers have no personal connection to her. They have never met her in person nor have they even heard her voice, so they would feel no guilt in getting rid of her.

Muscle Cat strikes a pose at Irene, flexing for her. She tries not to make eye contact. Muscle Cat takes the keyboard from her lap and bends it in half, then proudly hands it back to her.

Irene glares at the mutant animal. She holds the L-shaped keyboard with three fingers, trying not to get earwax on her hand.

"Meow," says the muscle cat, striking another pose.

Irene looks at the door. If she could go to a neighbor's house, she could see if their internet is working and perhaps order a repairman to come out to help her. She hasn't met or seen any of her neighbors, but she assumes other people live in the surrounding houses.

She crosses the room and puts her hand on the door, but she cannot get herself to open it. She convinces herself that the neighbors have surely lost their internet connection as well, so there's no reason to bother them. She convinces herself that the internet will come back very soon.

Another month goes by and the internet still hasn't come back. Every day, Irene looks at her front door and contemplates leaving, but she always finds a reason to keep it closed.

Both cats are still alive without any sign of expiration. In their final days, Gen-cats usually grow thin and don't move around so much, but her freakish cats are as frisky as ever.

One morning, Irene finds the delivery machine collapsed outside her front door. In one of its rubber hands is another package from the Kitty of the Month Club. Irene doesn't want to open it. She doesn't want any more creepy cats walking around her house.

She takes the box inside. The muscle cat and the ear cat sit in front of it, curious about the contents within.

The box moves.

"Maybe this one will be different," she says.

When she opens it, a tiny man pops out. He is two feet tall and wears a gray business suit, a black bowtie, and a matching derby on his head. Tiny spectacles perch on the end of his nose, as he brushes a dark curly mustache with a tiny mustache comb.

Irene grabs the introduction card and steps away from the box.

It reads:

Gentleman Cat.

That is all. It is not even accompanied by a tiny description.

"But it looks like a man," she says to the card. "It doesn't look anything like a cat."

The gentleman cat walks over to Irene and bows to her. It holds out its little hand. She shakes its hand.

"Meow," says the gentleman cat, in a very sophisticated British accent.

"Meow... " Irene finds herself saying.

The gentleman cat sits on her couch, drinking tea and eating orange cranberry scones. After it takes a bite of scone, it wiggles the crumbs out of its mustache.

Irene stays far away from him. She is positive that this one isn't even a cat. It is a man. A very, very small man. She isn't sure why it is eating. Gen-cats don't need to eat. They live on protein stored in their flesh cells that lasts them long enough to survive their month-long lifespan.

She worries about him eating her food. Now that she can't order groceries, she has to survive on what she has until the internet comes back.

Gentleman Cat notices Irene glaring at the scones on his plate and tips his hat to her.

The internet doesn't come back and the food is running low. Irene tries to conserve her food, but Gentleman Cat does not understand conservation. He likes to make extravagant four-course meals for her, and prepares enough food for a family of seven.

Every morning, Irene awakes to breakfast in bed. Gentleman Cat places a tray on her nightstand and reveals the delicious meal as if revealing his latest masterpiece. Salmon benedicts, sausages, soft-boiled eggs, dried fruits, a variety of toasts, juices, and jams are all artistically arranged on the serving platter.

If Irene does not wake before breakfast is served, Gentleman Cat will stare down on her face and wake her with gentle breaths from his miniature nostrils. As soon as she begins her breakfast, Gentleman Cat will bow at her, and say, "Meow."

She knows the food isn't going to last if he keeps up this way, but she does admit to herself that the food is the best she has tasted in years.

One day, Irene goes into her living room. The muscle cat is doing pushups on the floor. The gentleman cat is playing a miniature violin as the ear cat sways to the romantic melody.

The cabinets are bare. Irene hasn't had anything but tap water in a week, and though her intense hunger has faded she has become tired and light-headed from the fast. She doesn't even know how long she will have tap water to drink. Although a human can live quite a long time without food, they can't go very long without water.

She looks at the front door. She thinks about opening it, but she just can't.

Instead, Irene leans against a wall and slides to the floor. She knows she doesn't have a choice, she has to leave, but the anxiety she feels when she goes outside can be so overwhelming that she almost prefers death.

"Why am I so weak?" Irene yells at the ear cat by her foot. "I wish I was one of the strong ones."

Gentleman Cat continues to play the violin, while Muscle Cat strikes a pose.

"Do you know how great the job market is for people who aren't agoraphobic? I could get three times the amount of pay by doing half the work. But I'm weak. My mother was weak. My father was weak. They were both agoraphobic, too, back when it was still pretty rare. When I was a kid, my mother wouldn't let any of my friends come over. She was uncomfortable with the idea of strangers in her house, even kids. She also wouldn't let me go over to my friends' houses because she was too scared to drive me. I was lucky that the school was within walking distance or she would have had me homeschooled and I never would have had any friends at all."

The ear cat sits there, listening to her through all of its ears.

"Of course, I was homeschooled eventually. When I was in 6th grade, a car hit me on the way home from school. I was rushed to the emergency room with two broken legs and a concussion. My mother never came for me. She was too paranoid to leave the house. My dad came, but only to drive me home once the doctors were done with me. Then my parents never let me leave the house again. They were afraid I would get hurt again somewhere and they wouldn't be able to come help me. They wanted me to stay home, where it was safe."

The ear cat cuddles against her hand. She doesn't even realize the earwax greasing across her fingers when she pets its back.

Irene stands up and stares at the door again.

She's got to go through it. If she doesn't leave the house she's going to starve to death. She might have the worst panic attack of her life, but a panic attack is not going to kill her.

The gentleman cat stops playing his violin as Irene's hand wraps around the doorknob.

"Meow?" the ear cat says, looking up at Irene from the floor.

The door opens.

The withered, muddy neighborhood has been a frightening two-dimensional painting to her for the past ten years. She thought she would never have to enter that painting again.

She takes one step and closes her eyes. Then she takes another. Her fingers start wiggling. At first, they wiggle slowly. After she takes another step, her wiggly fingers become frantic.

The gentleman cat steps outside and stops Irene's fingers from wiggling. He holds her hand in his tiny warm palms. She looks down at him and he bows to her. She takes another step. The gentleman cat stays with her, holding her hand as firmly as he can.

The ear cat and the muscle cat come outside with them. She takes another step. Then another. The painting of the neighborhood becomes three-dimensional. She is inside of it. It is a dizzy swirling of colors. It overwhelms her so much that she can hardly feel her body from the neck down, as if her head is floating.

When she gets to the edge of her driveway, she keeps going. She walks through the withered neighborhood. The street looks as if it hasn't been used in decades. Weeds have broken through the asphalt and overtaken the road, the sidewalks, and the walls around yards.

There aren't any more grocery stores, so she doesn't know where to go for food. Everything is delivered through the mail. All the food is hidden away in warehouses that she'll never be able to find. But she can't think about that now. She has to focus on each step. She can't let her surroundings overcome her.

There is a maple tree collapsed in the road in front of her. She stops moving. She shifts her weight from foot to foot, not sure what to do. She wants to pop her fingers, but the gentleman cat holds her hand too firmly for her to do it.

The tree rises off the ground. Underneath, Irene sees Muscle Cat. He is lifting the tree over his head as high as he can. He tosses it out of the road, into a muddy yard.

Irene nods at Muscle Cat.

The muscle cat says, "Meee-ow."

She continues on. She tries not to think too much about it. She just takes one step at a time.

Ear Cat leads the way, using his powerful sense of hearing to guide them. His body is tense. He can hear something in the distance.

Once they get closer to downtown, Irene realizes what her city has become. The streets look like a tornado swept through ages ago and nobody ever bothered to clean up afterwards. The buildings are overgrown with vines, the roads have been ripped apart by roots and weeds, there are cars rusted into the sides of the street, there are piles of rubble as if bombs had gone off.

"Meow," says the ear cat, gesturing its head to the distance.

"What is it?" Irene says.

Up ahead, people are coming out of buildings. Thousands of people spill out of the surrounding apartments and houses. They climb down fire escapes, they rappel out of windows, they climb up from the sewers. All of them are confused and anxious. They look uncomfortable, fearful to be so close to each other, yet they are still drawn together. And accompanying each of these nervous people, staying close by their sides, are three cats: a gentleman cat, a muscle cat, and an ear cat.

"Meow?" says the ear cat, looking up at Irene with a wide childlike smile.

Irene nods.

She moves toward the crowds of people, taking one baby step at a time. Her head is still dizzy, her fingers are still trying to wiggle, but the three Kitties of the Month stay by her side every inch of the way.

NUB HUT

KURT DINAN

Four of us surround the hole in the ice, each lying with an arm submerged deep in the water. This is nothing like I pictured. In my mind I saw smaller, individual holes and a sense of transformation. Instead, the hole is one large opening maybe ten feet across, and all I feel is the great freeze as we wait under the Alaskan moon, the snow twinkling down like millions of tiny flash bulbs.

Hannah wears only jeans and a Gamecocks sweatshirt. She hasn't moved or said a word since we began, but her frozen breath still occasionally drifts up. Beside her, Nigel Nine Toes is pants-less. His argument that his missing toe should make him an automatic for the Nub Hut ended with the admission that he lost it to a lawnmower when he was sixteen. The Nub Hut, Sheila proclaimed, must have standards.

The smart money is on Gillian. She's built like a lumberjack, even wearing flannel shirts and boots like she's off to chop down sequoias. Gillian's worked the slime line at the cannery for years. She'll be radiating fish stink the rest of her life, however long that is.

Me, I'm in true winter wear—thermals, rubber-soled boots, an arctic jacket —and am resting on a blanket I swiped from the bunkhouse. Using a gutting knife, I cut off a coat sleeve so nothing would come between my bare arm and the water. All four of us are alike in that respect. That and the mandatory rope, of course, one end tied around an ankle and the other spiked through the ice.

We wait in the glow of the Nub Hut. What once housed two Snow Cats and the back-up generator now sits thirty yards away onshore. The windows are covered with thick black plastic, but orange fire light seeps through the slats. A spray painted "Nub Hut" streaks down the door. Muffled music plays inside, evidence someone scavenged a battery.

"Think you can guess how long it's been, Alan?"

Nigel Nine Toes speaks through chattering teeth. He may be thirty, he may be fifty; it's hard to tell. Alaska weathers a man, and that's just what he wants. "To be reduced to my base animal" is how Nigel puts it. He stalks camp spouting about the chaotic beauty of the tundra while making sure we're all aware of his Che Guevara shirt. To most of us though, he's just the guy who complains that his recreations of famous paintings infused with aborted fetuses are kept out of galleries due to an elaborate conspiracy.

"Come on," Nigel says. "Take a guess. How long?"

I can't turn his way because my ear is frozen to the ice. "An hour?"

"Forty minutes. And that's why you won't make it. Your mind is weak. Only the primal can survive. All humanity must be whittled away until all that remains is a god, a creator, an explosion and implosion of raw energy."

So that's Nigel.

This is the first conversation in some time. All of us shouted in solidarity when we first plunged our arms in, but the camaraderie wore off fast. This isn't about friendship; this is about the Nub Hut. Tell four people only two will be chosen and inevitably this is what happens.

"I'm having a hard time breathing," Gillian says. "Can't catch any air."

"Arm feels like it's in a vice," I tell her.

"I can't keep my thoughts straight."

"I'm seeing double."

And on and on.

The first few minutes of submersion were the worst. Nothing but burn. The icy water collapsed around my arm squeezing out the blood. Only through sheer will power was I able to keep it in the hole. But you want will power? Sheila's nothing more than a torso now. There's talk she'll do her ears soon. None of us doubt it.

The door to the Nub Hut opens and music pours into the night. Nigel Nine Toes says it's Neil Young but Gillian says it's America and now they're arguing over who sang "A Horse with No Name."

For a brief moment I see inside—firelight, shadows, maybe a table—then someone steps out and shuts the door before anyone can see. Whatever happens inside the Nub Hut is a mystery, but it must be wonderful.

At the sound of boots crunching snow, I tear my ear off the ice, leaving behind a pulp of skin. Warm blood trickles down my neck, dotting the ice. As the silhouette draws closer, the outline becomes clear and Gillian says, "MilaGino."

Between them, Mila and Gino have been married separately five times. Sheila presided over their sixth attempt last week in the Nub Hut. They spent their wedding night holding hands under water. Afterward, Mila sacrificed her right arm, Gino his left. Now they're sewn together at the shoulder.

They take a knee and I feel stale breath on my face. MilaGino speak as one, both mouths repeating the words a moment apart, creating a strange echo.

"How are you holding up?"

I attempt to respond, but my tongue is a balled-up sock.

"It's okay, Alan," they say putting a hand on my shoulder. "We understand."

But they can't understand. Maybe they could when they wandered camp as lonely hearts before the takeover. Or maybe they could have understood in the days after the revolt when we were all unified, everyone joyous in having a place to call our own, a place where we belonged. But they can't understand anymore. Now they're muscle for Sheila. Now they belong to the Nub Hut.

While the wind chips at my face, MilaGino survey the others. Everyone smiles through frozen lips. Hannah and Nigel push their arms deeper into the water. We're all dogs hoping to go home from the pound.

MilaGino draw out the choice, discussing us privately, their faces inches apart. But it's all show. Everyone knows who makes the final call. They nod simultaneously then say, "Hannah, come join us in the Nub Hut" and my arm burns all over again.

Just one look at Hannah, with her hangdog face and saddle bags making it appear that she's carrying hundreds of pennies in her pockets, and you can understand how it's a thinly disguised pity pick. Every society needs a target. And who's easier than the woman who spends her free time talking of Renaissance festivals and reading her silly backward comics? I might feel sorry for Hannah if I didn't hate her so much right now.

Hannah's sweatshirt clings to the ice as MilaGino help her up. With a jerk, her hoodie tears away, leaving white university letters behind. MilaGino lose their footing for a moment, slipping on the ice and tumbling sideways before regaining balance. As they guide Hannah up the path, her feet barely touch the snowy ground.

"There's gotta be some sort of mistake," Nigel says.

"That it wasn't you?" Gillian says. "Let's see, Nigel. Sweet Hannah without an offensive bone in her body, or you with your pseudo-intellectual bullshit and babies playing poker."

"They're fetuses. It's symbolic."

"What it is, is asinine."

"I have a hundred dollars that says you played softball in college, Gillian."

"Asshole."

"Dyke."

It's like that.

My lips twitch as if electrified and now I've lost all sensation in my feet. My eyes are closed before I realize it.

This is how it happens. No matter what you try, you never take root. It's years of no luck with work, no luck with women, no luck at all. You're on an endless search without a clear destination. You tell yourself it's in the next city or the next town, but everywhere you go you're a cipher. On the outside you look like everyone else, but inside you're ash and isolation. Then on the Discovery Channel you see Alaska's promise of endless possibilities as the last frontier. And if you're twenty-nine and have traveled nothing but dead-end roads, you'll follow whichever star lights the way. It's only when you get here that you realize the entire state is filled with mirror images of yourself waiting for further directions.

Cheers erupting inside the Nub Hut shake me from my haze. We crane our necks for any sign. Hannah must be submitting to the blade. She belongs to them now. As the ovation dies down, we all crumble back onto the ice. No one has to mention the resentment surging through each of us.

Minutes later, Gillian whispers, "Alan?" A thin layer of frost covers her face. Her lips are white in the moonlight, but it's her eyes, wide and bottomless, that frighten me.

"It's so strange," she says, "I'm not even cold anymore."

Gripping the hole's edge with her free arm, Gillian pulls herself into the water. She drifts downward like a snow flake before disappearing altogether. The rope around her feet snakes behind her until going taut. Someone will reel her in later.

I'm too cold to move, too cold to respond. I just stare into the abyss. Maybe in the daylight I could see her, but in the darkness the black water reveals nothing.

Nigel begins laughing and can't stop choking on his words. Finally he roars, "Ophelia of the Arctic," and pounds the ice with his free hand until I think bones might break.

In the beginning, only two others joined Sheila in the Nub Hut. Lorna iced her toes, Trevor his hand. After that, everyone flocked to the hole for a chance at metamorphosis. Now supposedly there's a pile of severed nipples on a table. Gillian said the Asian from Toledo sliced off his lips. Rumor is some are talking castration next. No one can touch Sheila though. She sacrificed both legs the day after removing her arms. Even God's terrified of Sheila at this point.

"Why don't you take a swim too, Alan?" Nigel says. "Join your friend. This is beyond you. Your core self isn't—"

Even with Nigel's yammering and the wind howling across the Chukchi Sea, I hear the party in the Nub Hut. Harriet must've finished the sawing by now. She used to go through three hundred fish an hour, so it makes sense that she commands the knife. Once done, Marco does a fishing line suture, closing the wound in a criss-cross of railroad tracks. Sometimes though the soldering gun is necessary.

There's no burn anymore, no freezing, not even any pressure. I even have to double check to make sure my arm's still in the water. Gillian watches me through the ice. She stares wide-eyed, our faces separated by inches. Free from the confines of her hat, red hair swims around her face. With her eyes, she blinks out Morse code messages I can't decipher.

In the weeks leading up to the revolution there were grumblings throughout camp as if Alaska had reneged on her promise. Then one day Sheila pulled the conveyor belt's emergency shutdown and Milo sledgehammered the control panel announcing, "This belongs to us now." There wasn't much thinking after that, just years of frustration pouring out in busted jaws and smashed machinery while Sheila smiled surveying the chaos. Outnumbered, and with no help for hundreds of miles, management evacuated in the buses. Two days later, Sheila birthed the Nub Hut.

"They won't take you." Nigel's voice creaks like a rusty hinge. "You don't belong here. You never have."

I want to tell him how there isn't anywhere else. How he'll never get up because his bare legs are welded to the ice. But what comes out instead is, "Sherrshingfel" before my tongue freezes and my vision fails.

I'm not sure how long I'm out. I'm dreaming of roads clogged with hitchhikers heading north to the Nub Hut when plastic sliding across the ice snaps me back. With my free hand I paw at my face, chipping away the frost sealing my eyes. The noise grows louder until it is right in front of me. Nigel bays with excitement. When I can finally see again, I am staring at four rubber-soled boots. MilaGino.

Trailing behind, pulled in her red disc sled, sits a triumphant Sheila ready to announce her final selection. She is propped on a pillow, little more than a face peeking out from the blanket bundled around her. MilaGino scoops her from the sled, holding her high like a newborn.

Sheila's teeth, now filed to sharp points, gleam in the moonlight. No one mentions the scar anymore, zigzagging across her face, that in the old world kept her working alone in backrooms away from the public. Now Sheila is beautiful. Now Sheila is someone. Now Sheila rules the Nub Hut.

"After tonight, we will be complete," she says. "There is only room for one more. The Nub Hut is not for everyone."

It's Nigel. Sheila doesn't have to say anymore for me to know. I can instinctively recognize defeat. The decision radiates from Sheila's eyes, from her aura, even from the air.

Nigel Nine Toes must sense it too because he kicks spastically, contorting his body in anticipation. For the briefest of moments, his arm leaves the water. The withered limb is nothing but a shriveled birch twig. He thrusts it back in, his eyes wide. When he speaks, each word is a tiny earthquake.

"I'm sorry, Sheila," he says. "Please."

She surveys Nigel Nine Toes like a saddened parent, then gives a private shake of her head. She whispers to MilaGino who reverently place her back on the disc before turning to Nigel.

Despite the thrashing and screaming, it only takes a moment for MilaGino to cut the rope around Nigel's ankle. At first I think he will refuse to move, but Nigel gets to his feet wailing endlessly. His bare legs are nothing but charcoal down the front. The crying doesn't stop even as he stumbles away from the hole, away from the camp, away from the Nub Hut. He disappears across the ice into the darkness until he is nothing but a beast howling in the distance.

MilaGino reaches under my armpits and lifts me, careful not to touch the dead limb. My entire left side hangs slack. Dynamite detonates throughout my body.

"Welcome," Sheila says finally. She smiles from atop her cushioned throne. Sheila the sacrificer. Sheila the leader. Sheila of the Nub Hut.

But the smile can't disguise her disappointment. This wasn't the plan. She wanted Nigel. To her, I'm the also-ran, now substituted as a last-minute replacement for the Nub Hut.

"We need to set you down for a minute, Alan, so we can get Sheila back," MilaGino says, lowering me. "After we get her inside, we'll—"

They slip like before, teetering on the hole's edge, but this time there's no quick recovery. Their arms flail, and there's a moment where I know I can reach with my good hand to steady them. Instead, I let MilaGino tumble into the hole. The splash is a muted explosion. They scream in harmony before the water immobilizes their bodies and drags them under.

Moments pass before Sheila finally says, "Take me back inside, Alex." She wants to sound commanding, but her voice waivers. She can't keep my eye. Sheila can't even get my name right.

But I couldn't care less. Because now I am engulfed in the transformation of the Nub Hut. The change is nothing physical; it's more a clarity of purpose. Is this what Sheila felt when she first conceived the Nub Hut? Is this what surges through her when she selects new citizens? Maybe. It doesn't matter anymore.

I watch the water until its surface is a glass-topped table. Sheila begs for help, but whether it's the wind or the music drowning out her cries, no one appears. When she finally quiets, her change is also complete. No longer is she Sheila of the Nub Hut—she's simply Sheila with the scar-carved face.

I pull her towards me, then use my head to bump the sled the remainder of the way to the hole. Then I begin the long crawl home. Up ahead the Nub Hut awaits.

PUNKUPINE MOSHERS
OF THE APOCALYPSE

DAVID AGRANOFF

Year 35

Dressica Killmaiden held a stick over the fire and watched the bottom of her marshmallow blacken slowly. The fire snapped, and she felt its warmth on the clean-shaven sides of her head. An old man looked across the fire and smiled at her. His features were as weathered as his leather jacket; there was no one older back in town. More than just the wise old farmer on the hill, he was her Uncle Max. The other children had fallen asleep more than an hour ago in tents set up on the edge of a corn patch, but Dressica wanted to talk to her uncle.

"You need to sleep," he said.

Dressica shook her head. "Not tired."

Most of the other children were afraid of the old man, but the school made them visit him to learn the basics of farming. Max was a mystery. He rarely came out to shows, still wore the skin of animals and seemed to want no part of life in the city.

Max popped a handful of nuts in his mouth and chewed. "Kids never admit to being tired. Why is that? You want to be a grown-up right? Grown-ups like to sleep."

His dreadlocked mohawk was gray at the roots. His walking sick was almost six feet tall, wrapped in vinyl stickers for bands his niece knew only as legends:

Circle Jerks, Black Flag and Bad Religion. He didn't give a shit what anyone thought. He was *Max-imum Damage*, punk vocalist and mosh pit gladiator who had survived more shows than anyone had a right to. But he had left it all to grow salad greens and ginger root, only coming into the city to sell his crop at the market.

Dressica turned her eyes away from the fire. The lights of Crassville shone across the high desert. This was the farthest she had ever been from the city in her six years. She knew there were farms and smaller villages throughout the land of Dischargia but had never seen them.

Uncle Max's farm was as far as she had dared to go.

"Uncle Max," she asked, "can I be honest with you?"

The wind turned the fire and lifted her uncle's hair. "About what, love?"

Dressica didn't trust her mother, didn't know who her father was. Teachers seemed more interested in engineering, farming, guitars—anything but history. "I think you adults are lousy liars," she said, finally.

"Is that so?" Max snorted and took a drink from his canteen. "The Punks got old, just like everyone else. Adults sometimes feel they must lie to kids to protect them."

"I can take care of myself."

Max stoked the fire with a stick. When the flame lowered, the old man had a sour look on his face.

"Your mother told me you have been asking about the nether-lands beyond Dischargia," he said. "No such lands exist. They're nothing more than myth."

Max had been Dressica's only hope. She wanted the truth from him, yet he sat across the fire and lied through his broken teeth.

Dressica kicked the fire pit. "Bullshit!"

Max sighed and patted the ground. His niece walked around the fire and sat next to him.

"I didn't lie, but there are things you must understand. If I tell you, it must remain our secret," Max said at just above a whisper.

"I swear I won't tell anyone."

"What year is it, Dressica?"

"Thirty-five."

"Here in Dischargia, yeah. Beyond the red line, however, it is the year twenty-twenty-two."

Dressica's mind boggled just thinking about so many years.

"In the year nineteen-eighty-seven, there were many tribes with massive cities, and they waged a great and destructive war. So, you see, I didn't lie. The great lands of old are gone."

She felt dejected. She had always hoped there would be life beyond Dischargia.

"They can't all be gone."

"They are, and it's a good goddamn thing, too. The world of old was driven by greed and hatred."

Dressica shivered in the cold and moved closer to the fire. She watched the flames. "Sounds scary," she said.

Max smiled at her. "You like the music in the city?"

She thought of the bands at school. Raging punk rock. The children of Dischargia received their first guitar and drum lessons at five.

"You like your clothes? Your piercings?" he continued.

Dressica looked at her holey jeans and played with her nose and lip rings. She didn't understand why Max was asking her this.

"If you like the way of life we have here in Dischargia, then you'll never cross that red line on the map. Because if anyone is still alive out there..."

Dressica waited for him to finish.

Max looked up at the night sky and back down at her. "Go to bed."

"But Uncle Max—"

He stood up and turned away. Never did he bring up the subject again.

CHAPTER ONE

Year 45

Dressica tightened her grip on the microphone and took a deep breath.

"One, two, three, four!"

The band launched into a blast of high-speed punk, and the circle pit swirled in front of the stage like the outer edge of a hurricane. Dressica leaned over the crowd, spitting her lyrics. Blood splattered across her face and, for a moment, she dropped the mic to wipe away the blood. Bodies rammed into one another and fists were thrown. Legs stomped to the beat.

Reality Asylum was a huge venue that had the meanest pits in all of Dischargia. When Combat Vehicle hit the stage, the chaos was at an all-time high. Looking out into the crowd, Dressica saw a figure skanking his way across the floor. The pit cleared like the Dead Sea. He was Razorback—Raz to his friends. Three long blades protruded from his back. Two smaller blades were attached to his arms. He swung those arms as the beat of the music slowed down to a groove.

A drunk mosher pumped his fist at the front of the stage. He didn't see Raz circle the pit behind him. The blades slid across his back, and the man shrieked.

His blood drenched the stage monitors.

Dressica finished the song. She looked at her band mates. John, her guitar player, hit a few notes and started tuning. The crowd waited impatiently for the next song to begin, milling around on the blood-slick floor.

"How you doing tonight? We're Combat Vehicle!"

"No shit! Really?" Raz called out and laughed.

Dressica moved nearer to him and stared. Raz smiled wickedly at her. His hair was done up in liberty spikes so tall he needed to duck into every doorway he entered. The crowd was thick with spiked mohawks. It was the genetically engineered razors protruding from his back and arms that made Raz punk as hell.

"So, Raz," Dressica said from the stage. "Why didn't the engineers give you a dick when they gave you those razors, huh?"

The crowd oohed as Raz held up a middle finger. John hit a note that told the rest of the band he was ready. Raz pumped his fist.

The band started playing their next song as Raz got the chant going.

"Stage dive! Stage dive! Stage dive!"

Everyone in the crowd ran at each other. A riot of bodies, the sound of bones breaking was almost louder than the band.

Dressica had had enough. "Fuck you, Raz!" she shouted.

But people were happy. They came to see Combat Vehicle to experience uncontrolled chaos. Dressica jumped off the stage. The crowd cleared as she landed in the middle of the pit. Putting her right thumb and pinky together, Dressica felt a burst of energy travel up her spine. Almost instantly, long and sharp metal quills burst through the skin on the nape of her neck. She extended her arms, and the quills snapped through the back of her shirt and down the length of her legs.

The music shook her quills. Dressica spun through the crowd like a windmill, her fists and legs pumping to the beat. She was queen of the pit. If any moshers were to run into her, their bodies would be utterly destroyed.

The show was over. Dressica touched her thumb to her index finger. The quills receded, and she allowed herself time to relax on the couch set up off-stage. She examined the tattered remains of her shirt.

John pushed a large amp past her and winked.

"Great show!"

She waved at him. Her hands were covered in blood and shaking. She wiped the blood on her shredded pant legs.

At that moment, another voice called out to her.

"Hey, Dressica!"

It was Dez—a great engineer. He had rebuilt the city's solar panels. In his spare time, however, he worked for her, engineering Dressica's modifications because he had a crush on her.

She looked him over. His dyed green hair and spike belts looked fresh. Apparently, he had gotten dressed up for a night on the town.

"You should see your face," he said.

"It's not my blood, dude. The quills worked perfectly, but they could have been a bit longer."

He stood over Dressica and shook his head. Pulling out an electric clipboard, he used his thumb to scroll through his notes. "If I make them longer it will cause internal scarring, or worse."

Dressica knew her quills had achieved maximum-length. Still, she felt she needed something extra to remain competitive.

"Who's engineering for Raz?"

Dez looked up from his pad. He seemed concerned. "I doubt they're from Crassville. Maybe Blitz," he said. "Whoever it is, they're good. You keep getting in the pit with him, you're going to die."

Dressica had heard this warning before, but she lived for the pit, spent every quiet moment thinking about the rush she got when she danced her way through the madness.

"Come on, Dez," she said. "You can walk me home while you lecture me."

They stepped out into the cool night. Two shows broke up in different venues along Rimbaud Avenue, where street vendors sold bootleg cassettes and food. Dozens of people were lined up for grilled soy products at the tofu dog stands. Street barbers were dying hair and cutting fresh mohawks—so many barbers that they sounded like garden crews mowing lawns. They had used up all their solar power and had assistants who worked pedals to generate energy.

It was a typical Friday night in Crassville.

Dressica led Dez to a food stand without a line. A woman sat behind the stand. Her dreads were tied back and her feet up on a chair as she read from Crassville's peace punk newspaper.

"What does a pit gladiator need to do to get some food around here?"

The woman glanced up from her paper, looking past Dressica's eyes to the cuts on her forehead. "I have potatoes," she said. "Home fries with rosemary ketchup."

Dez made a sound of approval.

"Dez," said Dressica, "I'd like you to meet my cousin, Isa."

Dez couldn't help but stare at Isa's right arm. It was mechanical, hidden by a sleeve. The engineer in him was impressed. Her flesh and blood arm had been lost in one of the most famous pit maulings in all of Dischargia. It happened during a Combat Vehicle show down in Blitz. The legend was that, by the time the song was over, Isa was screaming on the floor and Dressica had used her cousin's severed arm to chase Raz out of the club.

Isa worked the serving tools awkwardly. She was still new to the cybernetic arm.

"I wondered why you weren't at shows…" Dressica pointed at the peace punk paper lying on her chair. Isa ignored her and scraped the taters from the pan. The tension was so thick Dez took a step back.

Dressica narrowed her eyes. "So, you're some kinda of peace punk now?"

Isa's mechanical arm creaked and wheezed unnaturally as she held the paper container of potatoes out for her cousin.

"Just take them and go."

Dressica put her mutual aid credits on top of the newspaper. The credits acknowledged to the Dischargian council that Isa had traded community aid. When they sat at a table and opened the container, Dez still had one eye on Dressica's cousin.

"Didn't Raz do that to her?"

"Eat your potatoes," Dressica said as she unfolded the fork on her multi-tool.

CHAPTER TWO

Max walked across his field. On his belt, a small radio played "Wild in the Streets" by the Circle Jerks. He didn't like the stuff kids today called *punk rock*. Even in the field at night, he could hear faintly the shows down in Crassville.

He had fond memories of shows before the Great War, when punk was rebellion, not culture. They happened in rented warehouses, abandoned buildings and all sorts of funky places. Often, cops would step in and break them up. Max thought about cops and laughed.

Once, he had understood why the council had decided to make shows so violent, fatal even. There were, after all, only limited resources in Dischargia. But years of pit fighting had worn him down. Now, it all seemed senseless to him.

He simply had to make a break from a culture he no longer recognized.

His soy crop bent with the wind. He would have to harvest it in the next week. He would also have to trade food for some workers. That meant going into the city. Max sighed in frustration as he walked up to his wooden irrigation control. He expected he'd have to brush away mosquitoes, but the air was clear of them.

Max grabbed the wooden handle and lifted the latch, but the water didn't pour out as it always did. Only a tiny drop of water, more like a tear, rolled out and hit the ground. Max climbed up the structure. There was no water coming down from the river that headed into town.

Using his walking stick to balance himself, Max swung to the ground. When he stepped onto the riverbank, he saw the extent of the problem. The river was usually the width of a basement venue's stage. Now, only a small stream trickled between the large rocks in the empty riverbed. The water had flowed normally when he'd been here just hours before.

He looked upriver to the mountain in the north. The mountain was more than a hundred miles away, beyond what the council had determined to be the red line. As far as the younger generation was concerned, it was the edge of the world. Thirty years had passed since anyone had crossed that line.

Max squeezed his walking stick and walked toward the city. He knew what was required: a town meeting.

CHAPTER THREE

"If you want to speak, enter an agenda item on your clipboards, or raise your hand and the moderator will put your name on the stack."

Dressica heard the voice call out from the speaker system outside the great hall as she and Dez approached it. The great hall had been built to seat over a thousand people, but it wasn't mandatory that the public attend its meetings. The proceedings were broadcast live across the city.

Looking inside, Dressica saw Uncle Max sit down in the third row of seats. She stepped into the chamber.

Dez followed her like a puppy. "Are you sure you want to sit through this?" he asked.

She did not reply.

Eve-al, the second longest-serving member of the council, was moderator. Like all council members, she had multi-colored hair and wore spiked and studded clothing held together with safety pins. She tapped her gavel as members of the community continued to pile into the hall.

Keith Tesco, a councilor from the north side of town, rose from his seat. "I donate my position on the stack to Max—former vocalist of Max-imum Damage and a farmer from my district with excellent mutual aid standing."

Dressica found a seat in the fifth row as her uncle addressed the council.

"A dark time has fallen upon our land. The river no longer flows from the north."

Murmurs spread through the crowd. A young man sitting beside Dressica spoke out of turn. "But the water is supposed to come from the edge of the world," he said.

Uncle Max pointed across the room. "The elders here must face the truth. If we continue to lie, then this community will be torn apart."

"Does the floor accept a followup question?" Eve-al asked. Max nodded, and she continued. "I understand your concerns, but what point are you trying to make?"

"I contacted farmers to the north. The flow stopped this evening, somewhere just below the red line."

One of the young council members signaled a followup question. Max motioned for him to speak.

"The red line is the last space before the world ends."

Uncle Max shook his head gravely.

Dez whispered to Dressica. "I knew the world was bigger than Dischargia." She agreed, but shushed him anyway.

Uncle Max spoke to a video camera. "Children, we taught you a story, one you had no reason to doubt. But we can no longer force your heads into the sand. Life comes from the river, and its flow starts beyond our world."

People stood, pointed fingers and broke into shouts. Eve-al beat her spiked hammer on the table, bringing the crowd to order.

"Most of us grew up hearing tales of lands beyond the red line," she said. "And most, I admit, never believed them, but it seems that something on the outside is killing our river."

"It's a monster!" someone called out.

"Fuck you all!" someone else yelled.

Eve-al rapped her hammer. The council conferred and, moments later, a resolution was typed and transmitted to electric clipboards across the city. Provided the citizens of Crassville reached a consensus, a team would be dispatched to cross the red line. Dressica picked up the pad in front of her seat and entered her mutual aid number. She watched the votes tally. A few citizens voted in favor of the resolution, but hundreds of others countered with negative votes.

Dressica watched Uncle Max sit down and dip his head in sorrow. She typed her name into the stack, as no one else seemed willing to speak. Standing up, she said, "I'll go!"

Everyone in the hall turned to look at her.

"You're afraid that you will be called to cross the red line on behalf of punk-kind. But I know there is more to this world, and I'm not afraid."

Uncle Max smiled at his niece then looked at his clipboard. Suddenly, two hundred votes shifted to the affirmative. "That settles it," he said, using his walking stick to push himself up from his seat. "I'll join you."

More votes switched over. Now, only thirty citizens blocked the resolution. Dressica sighed. The peace punks were afraid that the others would start fights beyond the red line. She knew it.

At that moment, the door opened. Everyone turned to see Isa—former pit gladiator—enter the hall. A peace symbol was embroidered on the butt flap that hung over her gray pants.

"I'll do it," she said. "Someone has to provide a voice for peace."

Dressica watched her clipboard. Twenty-nine more votes shifted. She looked at Dez. He hid his clipboard, but she didn't need to see it to know how he had voted.

"We're gonna need an engineer," she whispered to him.

"One warrior, a cripple and an old man?" Dez shook his head as a wave of frustration washed across the room.

"Change your vote, asshole!"

"We'll die without water!"

"Eat dog shit, you fucknut!"

Dez stood and shouted, "I won't change my vote!"

Dressica glared. She could have punched him.

"I'm in!" The voice came from the back of the hall, causing Dressica to drop her clipboard.

Raz strode into the room, and there was silence except for the sound of the spurs on his combat boots. Both Dressica and Isa shook their heads. Dressica was about to say 'hell no' when she heard the signal.

Consensus reached.

CHAPTER FOUR

A crowd of citizens had gathered around the team as they stood by the 'Welcome to Crassville' sign. Uncle Max's hair tied back; two shotguns crossed on his back in slings. Isa had throwing knifes strapped to her legs. The same ones she had used for years in the pit.

Dressica slung a rifle over her shoulder. She felt confident. If Mama Killmaiden were here, she would surely try to talk her daughter out of this mission, or even block the vote. But she wasn't, and Dressica was an adult capable of making this journey.

She heard the sound of spurs as Raz arrived late to join them. He didn't look at Dressica, and she didn't look at him.

Eve-al and Keith Tesco of the council stepped away from the crowd. "The hopes of our great society rest in your capable hands," Eve-al said.

Suddenly, a dust cloud was kicked up. Something massive rounded the corner. Dressica unslung her rifle, ready to fire at whatever monster might be upon them. The rest of the team pulled out their weapons as Dressica loaded a round into the rifle's chamber.

"Back! Back!" she shouted to the crowd.

Slowly, the dust cleared. The thing was, in fact, a Ford Mustang with its roof cut off. Its body, painted like a shark's open mouth, was haloed by barbed wire, its wheels covered in sharp spikes. Dez stood up in the front seat.

"Need a ride to the red line?"

"I almost shot you."

Isa sniffed the air. "I smell something cooking."

Uncle Max walked the length of the car. "How did you get one of these old things moving again?"

Dez jumped out of the car. "Been working on it for months. It runs on recycled cooking oil and a system of pedals. I call it a hybrid."

Dressica examined it, too. There was no floor in the vehicle, just six sets of bike pedals. She slung her rifle and jumped into the muscle car. Sitting behind the driver's seat, she positioned her feet on the pedals. Raz jumped in next, the car bouncing with his weight. Once all were inside, they locked their feet into the pedals.

Eve-al approached the car. She smiled at Dressica but went past her, stopping at Uncle Max. She leaned over the barbed wire to whisper into his ear.

"Tell them why."

Dressica's ears were damaged, but she could still hear her. Eve-al then patted Uncle Max's shoulder and stepped back to join the crowd.

"Rock on!" she yelled.

Dez showed Dressica how to put the car in drive. "Pedal!" he then shouted.

All five of them did so, and the car revved slowly to life. The stereo blared "Rise Above" by Black Flag. Raz pumped his fist once the drumbeat kicked in.

"Fuck yeah!"

Uncle Max nodded, smiling as the team rolled away.

"Get us some fucking water!" Keith Tesco screamed and shoved his fellow councilor. Eve-al pushed him back. Everyone in the crowd began to mosh.

"Rise above! We're gonna rise above!" the crowd chanted as the Mustang rolled out of Crassville on its journey with destiny.

CHAPTER FIVE

Dressica had worked up a pretty good sweat. There were times the car could coast, but, after a few minutes, the tape deck would slow and the sound of sluggish music would cue everyone that it was time to pedal again.

They took a road that led up a hill and away from Crassville. They saw a few farms along the side of the road but mostly empty desert. Isa stood up every couple miles and looked through binoculars at the river.

The flow had not increased. The mountain that had always been a snow-capped dot grew larger as they pedaled closer to it. Raz bored easily, so he spent most of his time releasing and sharpening his razors. He didn't seem to notice that it made everyone else nervous.

Dez studied Raz's bladed shoulders. Raz glanced at him and said, "Think you could do better?"

Dez laughed. "I *have* done better. You can't get close to Dressica once she's in the pit."

Raz retracted his blades with a snap. He flexed, the steel casing becoming visible beneath his skin. He turned to Isa and grinned.

"Sorry about the arm."

Isa started pedaling. They were coasting down the road, so she didn't need to pedal. Still, it kept her from ripping out Raz's throat.

Uncle Max tapped Raz on the shoulder. "You know, when I was your age, the pit was a celebration of unity."

Isa smiled at him, and the old man continued, "We danced together as an outlet for aggression but when someone fell, we picked them back up again."

Raz glared at the old man. "Fucking hippie."

"Have you ever seen a hippie?" Dressica asked.

"No, but I've read about them."

"Bullshit," she said. "Hippies are a myth."

Uncle Max took his niece's hand into his own and shook his head. "Is the way you do things really so fun?" he asked.

Dressica smiled just thinking of the excitement of the pit. "Fuck yeah! The pit is awesome! The energy, the emotion…"

Isa shook her head. "It's all bullshit. The council uses it as population control."

Dressica saw that they were nearing the border. Otherwise, she would have told Isa that she was being crazy.

The pavement ended abruptly. The car slowed to a stop before it reached the drop-off. A small sign stood just in front of a long red line of paint. It read: 'Enter the Phantom Zone at your own risk.'

Dressica jumped out of the car and walked to the line. Dez followed her. Just the idea of crossing it went against everything they had been taught since they were children. From the backseat, Isa scanned the area with binoculars, but could see very little. A fog bank hung around the base of the mountain.

Raz pounded on the dashboard. "Let's fuckin' do it!"

Dressica returned to the car. "Tell us why," she said to her uncle.

Uncle Max played dumb. "Why what?"

"That's what Eve-al told you. I think she meant the red line. Or maybe something even bigger."

He shook his head. "It's not the right time."

"We're crossing into the Phantom Zone. It's fucking time."

Raz bounced in his seat like an excited chimp. "Those sound like fuckin' lyrics, man!" He started pedaling, and the stereo came on. Raz ejected the tape in the deck and put in a mix he had made. "Sick Boy" by G.B.H. blared through the speakers. "Let's go!"

Uncle Max smiled, letting the classic punk song provide him with an excuse to remain silent.

Dressica put the vehicle into drive. Dez still stood at the line, shaking his head. "No, there's nothing across the red line."

"That's fucking elder talk, dude!" Raz shouted over the music. "Don't be a wuss!"

"Get in or walk back," Dressica added. "Your choice."

Dez jumped into the back seat. "I shouldn't have taught you how to put this thing in drive," he said.

Dressica floored it. As they blew past the line, Isa let out the breath that she had held.

The car disappeared into the fog at the base of the mountain.

CHAPTER SIX

They could see nothing as the car cut through the fog. Dressica turned the volume down as the mix tape rolled on to an Angry Samoans song. She felt the power weaken when Dez took his feet off the pedal and looked down. He shook Dressica's seat.

"Fuck! Turn around!"

Dressica looked down, too. She couldn't see the ground beneath them, just fog.

"It's all true!" Dez cried. "We're going to die!"

"Keep going!" Uncle Max yelled.

But Dressica stopped the car. Isa groaned. Dez looked around nervously. Dressica slammed her fists against the steering wheel and shifted in her seat to face her uncle.

"When I was a kid, you told me something about the world. Was it true?"

Uncle Max took a deep breath. "Just keep going forward," he said. "You'll find a road."

"Fucking knew it!" Raz laughed and turned up the music.

Dressica punched the eject button. "Come on, just tell us! Eve-al wanted you to do it!'"

Uncle Max nodded. "Okay, I'll tell you everything." He sighed. "It was Reagan's fault. He isn't just a myth. Back in the day, he was—"

PSSSSPAT!

An arrow penetrated Max's chest. He clutched the arrow to his chest and screamed. Dressica squinted through the fog in the direction the arrow had come from. A beast, taller than the car, could be seen in the fog a short distance away. It stood on four legs and was taller than the car. A man sat on its back, holding a bow and arrow.

"Drive!" Max shouted, coughing up blood. He pulled one of his shotguns free and fired it.

The beast rider's head exploded in a shower of skull shards and brain matter.

Uncle Max said nothing, just pulled one of his shotguns free and fired it. The man flew off the back of the beast, his head coming apart in a shower of brain matter.

"Pedal!" Dressica shouted. Everyone pedaled hard as she hit the gas. The car lurched as its wheels found the start of a road.

The lifted as they ascended, but more of the giant beasts appeared, galloping beside them on both sides. They heard a sound like a lawnmower as a bike with a motor pulled up on the right. The man on the bike loaded a shotgun. Raz jumped up and swung his arm-blade at the biker's throat. Blood sprayed; the bike fell away.

"Pedal harder!"

The car sped past the beasts. It seemed the riders were holding them back.

Isa looked at the riverbed through binoculars. "I can't tell if it's flowing or not. We need to get closer."

Dressica pulled the car off the road and stopped the car. Isa jumped out. Dressica turned to Uncle Max. He had pulled out the arrow. His shirt and pants were soaked through with blood. His eyelids fluttered; he barely breathed. Dez searched his pack for the first aid kit, but Dressica knew it was too late.

"I never lied to you," said Uncle Max with his last breath.

Dressica closed his eyes just as Dez pulled out the first aid kit.

"Put it away."

He returned it to his bag.

Isa returned from the riverbed. "The water is here, but the flow is very weak. We just need to keep following it."

Dressica looked up at the sky. The sun was setting.

"We'll bury Uncle Max. Then, in the morning, we'll find the bastards who are taking our water."

That night, Raz fell asleep slumped against a tree. Isa slept close to the fire, and Dez, who never spent time outside of Crassville, slept on the back seat of the Mustang.

CHAPTER SEVEN

The sun poked over the ridge and shined on Raz. He awoke, startled, blades out. Once he realized there was no threat, he retracted his blades.

Dressica laughed at him and turned to watch the sun rise over the mountain. On the far side of it, she could see the lights of a village. It was smaller than Crassville, but well lit even at dawn. Dressica peered through the binoculars. To the east of city, large fields rolled with crops.

"See anything?" Raz asked.

Dressica pointed north. "A city." She broke a small branch in frustration. "The people there must be diverting our river."

Raz kicked Isa awake. She smacked his foot with her mechanical hand.

"Wake up, sleeping beauty."

"Fuck you," she said, smacking his foot with her mechanical hand.

"Really," he continued. "It's time to kick some ass."

Isa sat up. Dressica handed the binoculars to her.

"We have to talk to them," Isa said. "They probably don't realize that we need the river, too."

"Are you daft?" Raz snorted. "They were riding on monsters and killed Max! You can't talk to them!"

"I'm sure it was just a misunderstanding," said Isa.

"Maybe, maybe not. But we're going to help them, offer some mutual aid. It's what we do."

Dez stumbled sleepily from the Mustang. "What if they want to kill us?"

"Then the pit fighting starts…"

Raz grinned, exposing food stuck between his teeth.

CHAPTER EIGHT

The Mustang slowed as the team reached a large painted sign.

WELCOME TO GOLDWATER!

Spread out before them were homes laid out in row after row of straight lines. A small patch of short green stuff surrounded each home, looking like prairie grass, though green rather than yellow. None of the homes had band posters on the outside; none had stages built out front.

Dressica had never seen such odd buildings. They didn't even look lived in.

"Are those houses?" asked Dez.

"I don't know."

Suddenly, one of the strange beasts came running toward them down the main road.

"Quick! Turn!" Dez screamed behind Dressica. She aimed the car toward the first side street she saw. *William F. Buckley Drive.* The car sped past countless identical homes with well-manicured lawns.

"What the fuck is this place?" Raz yelled.

"Look!" Isa shouted. "People!"

The car slowed as they came upon a man who stood in front of a house, holding a hose. His white shirt featured no band logo. The things on his feet were not boots. His skin was pale white, free of tattoos. He had very little hair on his head, just a small patch like pubic hair.

The car rolled up beside the man. He looked at them in shock as Raz stood on his seat and ejected the razors on his arm.

"That's our fucking water, bro!"

The man dropped the hose and ran toward his house. The door opened, and a woman in a white skirt and blue blouse stepped outside. She had a full head of un-dyed hair the color of desert straw.

"What the hell are they?" the woman yelled, but the man just pushed her back into the house and slammed the door.

"What the fuck are *you*?" Raz retorted as he jumped out of the car and picked up the end of the hose. He drank from it. "Here's our fucking water!"

A group of men rounded the corner onto the street, riding on the backs of beasts. Raz rubbed his hands together. Dressica hopped out of the car, and Isa followed her. Dez remained in the car, too afraid to leave it.

"Keep it cool, Raz."

The men stopped their animals and people emerged from the houses to form a crowd. None of them had mohawks, dyed hair or wore normal-looking boots. They sported plaid shorts and plain white shirts. Dressica counted at least five who held shotguns.

She put up her hands. Isa and Dez looked over at her. Quickly, they raised their own hands.

"Raz, do it!" Dressica said, just loud enough for him to hear.

Raz raised his hands. A man with a gold star pinned to his chest stepped forward. Dressica guessed that the star must've been some symbol of authority.

The man spoke. "I'm the sheriff of these here parts. Who are you and where did you come from?"

Dressica breathed a sigh of relief. He spoke Dischargian.

"Some kind alien weirdos!" yelled a woman in the crowd.

"Us, weird? Look at *you*, you fuckers!" Raz shouted.

"We came from a land beyond the red line," Dressica said.

The crowd gasped.

"Nothing lives below the red line," the sheriff said.

"That's not true. Our land is called Dischargia."

The sheriff shared a long glance with one of the men holding a shotgun.

"Lady," he said, finally, "the red bastards dropped a few nukes on us, but this is still the US of A."

Dressica looked wide-eyed at Isa. No one their age back in Dischargia believed the United States had ever existed. That country which promoted violence, war and greed. That encouraged conformity and brutal repression of the self. It was just an ugly monster that punk parents sang about in songs to scare children into behaving like good punks.

"We crossed into America?" Isa whispered.

"Fucking myth," said Raz.

The sheriff watched them carefully. Dressica stepped forward; guns were raised. She kept her hands up.

"Look," she said, "we need to talk about the river."

The sheriff shook his head. "No, I think we need take to *you* to Chancellor Reagan."

Dressica took a step back. Her stomach twisted in knots. "Did you say Reagan?"

Reagan was the ultimate boogeyman. His name was spit in anger in more songs of the elder bands than any other. The bastard Reagan, the man whose name Uncle Max had uttered just before his death. The man responsible for all evil in the world.

Reagan.

Raz had heard all the songs, too. He reacted out of sheer panic, swinging his bladed arm and spinning in a classic pit move. He closed his eyes, imagined his favorite TSOL song and slammed through the crowd to the beat in his head. Many standing in the front row fell to their knees, bleeding.

Dressica touched her thumb to her pinky. She spun like a top and her quills came free in time for her to roll her body against the crowd. Screams rang through the town of Goldwater. The people didn't have it in them to riot. They just ran. The sheriff pulled out his pistol and fired at Dressica. She moved too quickly, and his aim was off. Isa threw a knife at the sheriff that hit him in the leg. Dez jumped into the front seat of the car, but couldn't start it without lifting his head. He was too afraid to do that.

The sheriff came up behind Isa, kicked the back of her knees. She fell to the ground, and he placed his gun against her temple.

"Stop, or I'll kill her."

Dressica stopped and, in a single motion, retracted her quills. Raz stopped too, but didn't retract his quills.

"Fine," Dressica huffed. "Take me to your leader."

CHAPTER NINE

Crowds of freakishly plain-looking people stared at the team as the sheriff pushed them through the main street of Goldwater. A guard held onto Dressica by her mohawk. Raz looked ready to explode, but the sheriff walked at the front with his gun still pressed against Isa's temple. People yelled at the punks, and many laughed. The older citizens just shook their heads in disbelief.

Then Dressica heard something she had longed to hear: the river. After another minute of walking they came upon it—clear, blue water flowing toward a large dam near the mountain. The guard twisted Dressica's mohawk when she raised her head to gaze up at it. She almost released her quills out of pure anger.

"Keep moving!"

Dressica obeyed, but attempted to speak with the guard.

"Where does the river go after the dam?"

He kept pushing her, silently.

"Does it go to your farms?"

He remained silent as they reached a building, the tallest Dressica had ever seen. It had at least twenty floors and looked like it was made of glass. The sheriff pushed Isa through a revolving door.

Inside, the building felt like a refrigerator; cold air blew out of slots in the walls. Even Raz got gooseflesh and shivered. The guards herded the team into a small room with silver walls.

The sheriff and the guards made disgusted faces.

"What's wrong?" Raz asked. "You have to take a dump?"

The sheriff shook his head. "No, but it smells like you people did."

Raz laughed. "At least I don't look fuckin' weird."

The sheriff approached Raz and pressed a finger into the punk's chest. "Have you looked in mirror, freak?"

At that moment, a bell sounded and a robotic voice spoke:

"Welcome to Chancellor Reagan's penthouse."

The door opened to reveal a spacious glass-walled room. The guard released Dressica's mohawk, but the sheriff and four guards kept their guns pointed at them. Cautiously, Dressica approached the far glass wall.

The mighty river surged below. A water plant that serviced the town had been diverting it. Beyond that, she saw forests being torn down by work crews and fields of animals lined up to be led, single-file, into a building. Dressica knew these barbarians planned to eat those animals. North of the city, more trees were being destroyed. Houses were going up in their wake.

"Well, what do you think of my empire?"

Dressica turned at the sound of the raspy voice. There were two large desks at the end of the room. A man sat behind the desk on the left. He was old and shriveled with black, greasy hair. Dressica couldn't see his eyes. Just empty sockets. A woman sat behind the desk on the right. Her eyes were gone too. Her skin wrinkled and her graying blonde hair was done up in a bouf.

The man's right arm lifted, but his hand remained frozen. Dressica heard a voice, though his mouth didn't move.

"Those damn reds thought they could destroy us, didn't they, Maggie?"

The woman's arms trembled. Dressica observed this was because they were attached to sticks. Someone covered by a black curtain sat behind the office chair and directed these "people." Dressica stepped toward the desks. The guards and the sheriff all readied their guns. Dressica raised her hands.

"Who are you?" she asked.

The Reagan puppet flopped behind its desk. "I am Chancellor Reagan, savior of the American dream. And this is my partner, Prime Minister Thatcher."

The Thatcher puppet clapped and spoke with a ridiculous accent that Dressica had only heard between songs on The Damned and Sex Pistols bootlegs.

"Oh thank you for saving the world, my sweet Chancellor," it said.

The two puppets took a moment to blow kisses to each other. Raz squeezed his fists in frustration.

The Reagan puppet's head shifted as if scanning the group. "And just who the hell are you freaks?" it said.

"My name is Dressica Killmaiden. I come from a land downriver called Dischargia." She pointed out the window. "Is this your empire?"

"I thought Gorby was weak." The Reagan voice giggled, the puppet dancing falsely in its chair. "That was before he blew the piss out of our silos in Turkey. Crazy, red-splotched motherfucker. I'll have you know, little lady, that we leveled Moscow like a truck stop pancake."

"I don't care about the old world."

"It's coming back, darling," the Thatcher puppet said.

"It took a few years, but I made a promise that the American Dream would be reborn. Hamburgers, banks, no trees causing pollution and, goddamn it, the lowest tax rate imaginable."

"For the wealthy, right?" Dressica scowled. "My mom played me songs about Reagan."

"Songs about me?"

"It's how my people pass down history, and those songs told of a boogeyman bent on exploitation. I think you believe those myths. But I would ask that you think for yourself. That is ultimate law in my land."

The Reagan puppet stared blankly at her.

Dressica stepped closer to the window. "Your river flows downstream and provides the water for my people. Surely, we can work together and share it."

The puppet knocked pictures of Nancy Reagan and her children off the desk.

"My America! My river!"

Feminine laughter burst out from the curtain behind the desks. A woman rolled forward on a scooter, her gray hair pulled back in a tight ponytail. Her voice was shaky. "I warned you about these vulgar punk rockers!"

Another old woman walked robotically on mechanical legs to the Reagan puppet. Wrinkled, stretched skin hung off her head, which was her body's only remaining biological part. Brown dyed hair, curled in a perm, shook as she walked. Blood flowed through tubes coiled around her artificial body back to her head.

"Tipper's right, Ronnie," she said. "They want to undermine our new America."

"What should be done about them, Nancy?"

A smile: "Public execution."

The Reagan and Thatcher puppets clapped. The guards stepped forward. Dressica looked at Isa. Both knew the score. They had tried to talk, but now they had to act. Dressica jumped onto the Reagan puppet's desk and released her Punkupine quills. She swung the quills at the puppet, but it dropped to the ground. Isa shoved the sheriff to the floor. Dressica grabbed the pistol out of his hand. The Nancy-bot leapt onto the desk and swung at her with inhuman strength. The mechanical arm bashed into her quills. Dressica shrieked as the quills bent beneath her skin.

"You fucking fucker!" the Nancy-bot screamed. She hit Dressica again. Dressica fell against Thatcher's desk, and the puppet of the prime minister came at her, but she batted it away.

Raz swung with his blades, cutting open the belly of a guard. The guard's guts raced to the floor even as he fired off a final shot. The shot went wide of Raz, striking the Tipper lady's face. Her head exploded in skull fragments and brain chunks. She never had time to scream.

"Guards!" the Nancy-bot called out. "Seal the building!"

Two of the guards disappeared into the elevator. Raz punched the door after it closed. Dez ran over and pushed the *down* button repeatedly.

The Nancy-bot shook her head. "It won't work. You're trapped."

Dressica shook out her quills. "Sorry, lady, but we're going down."

The Nancy-bot laughed. "That's where you're wrong. In less than a minute, my minions will surround this building, ready to kill at my command."

Dressica ran the length of the table and slammed the Nancy-bot against the window, shattering the glass. Dressica closed her eyes as she flew out the window with the Nancy-bot.

The last thing she heard was Raz yelling, "Fuckin' A!"

They fell faster than Dressica thought possible. Clinging to the Nancy-bot, she opened her eyes to see the river coming at her. She hoped it would be deep. She closed her eyes and held her breath just as they hit water.

CHAPTER TEN

Dressica flailed her arms and legs in the wild flow of the river. Her head popped to the surface just long enough for her to hear Dez screaming and the plops as the rest of her team landed in the river. Dressica held her breath as she slid back beneath the surface.

After a few seconds of struggling, she again found air, but Raz and Dez still fought to get their heads above water. In front of them, Isa gripped the floating body of the now headless Nancy-bot.

"Grab on!" Dressica shouted. "We'll all float down to the dam!"

Raz had to pull Dez toward the Nancy-bot. The whole team held onto it. Crowds had gathered on the shoreline.

Raz shook their flotation device. "Where's the fucking head?"

Dressica shrugged. "Paddle to the right!"

They started shifting their weight, directing themselves toward the main control center. Over on the far bank, the sheriff ran, barking commands while trying to catch up with them. Shots were fired, but they were moving fast enough downriver to avoid being hit. The team passed an armory and a truck depot before reaching the dam.

"Are they going to have someone meet us there?" Dez asked.

Raz nodded as they rolled up on the beach.

Water collected behind the dam. Traps and ducts had been built to divert the water around Goldwater.

Suddenly, a blast knocked up sand at Dressica's feet. Even sopping wet, she was too fast for the Goldwater cop. Dressica unleashed her quills seconds before Raz opened his razors. Dressica spun, stabbed the cop with her quills and took the shotgun from him in one swift motion. The three other cops protecting the dam nearly shit themselves. They lowered their guns in fear.

With his arm blades, Raz opened up one cop and spun to take out another with his razorback. He grabbed a machine gun and threw it to Isa, who caught it with her mechanical hand and fired bullets into the remaining cops' path. The cops scattered for cover.

Finally, they reached the control center. The room was filled with blinking lights, keypads and monitors. Raz entered the room soon after and tapped the screen on one monitor.

"The whole city is coming down on us, Dressy. What's the plan?"

She stared at all the blinking lights. She had no idea.

Dez approached one of the computers and pushed a number of buttons. "This is perfect, really."

"What's perfect, Dez?"

He turned to Dressica. "I just closed everything off."

Raz punched his shoulder. "You fucking wank, we need water! Open it back up!"

"The dam is brand new. It's not strong enough to hold all that water back."

Dressica hugged Dez. He squeezed her tighter than was appropriate, but right now she didn't care. Breaking the embrace, she traded guns with Isa and broke open the firing chamber. She shook out her quills before firing multiple rounds into the control equipment. Red lights flashed; sirens blared.

"Follow me to the truck depot!"

Raz flipped off the room and followed everyone else down the hall and to the exit.

Outside, a crowd had gathered. Dressica spun through it. Some people fell away screaming; others ran. Dressica saw frustrated cops across the river in boats. They were almost to the shore and in firing range when a tremendous cracking diverted everyone's attention.

Those in boats fell overboard as the river surged. Dressica ignored the screams of panic. She waved her team into the truck depot.

"Find the mechanics shop!"

Isa pointed to a garage where four big trucks were opened up as though in mid-surgery. There, Dressica saw what she needed.

"Get those empty tire tubes!"

Raz grabbed his with a laugh. "Hell yeah! We're tubin'!"

Dressica found a pump station, and everyone began to inflate the tubes. It was too long. The earth was shaking and the dam would soon burst.

Dressica wasn't sure how Raz and Dez had done it, but their tubes were already full, and they were heading toward the river. Both Isa and Dressica continued to struggle with inflating their tubes.

Finally, Dressica's tube felt firm. She capped it seconds before Isa capped her own.

The dam had almost completely broken apart. Dressica and Isa ran to the riverbed and dropped their tubes in the water.

Isa floated away but then a voice rang out: "Stop her!"

The Reagan puppet was set up in a convertible with America flag decals on the hood. Dressica could see the puppeteer lying in the back seat. She lifted her middle finger.

"Fuck you, Reagan!"

The power of the unleashed river picked her tube up and, in a matter of seconds, Dressica had disappeared down the river.

CHAPTER ELEVEN

Sheriff Newt took a deep breath as he entered Chancellor Reagan's penthouse, carrying the Nancy-bot's decapitated head by her permed hair. It was amazing how the perm had held after being submerged in the river, stuck beneath a floating log. But that stump kept the head from flowing downstream.

"Oh, thank God! You found my dear Nancy!" Chancellor Reagan's arm went up, and a headless, robotic body clunked forward from behind the curtain.

The sheriff held the head aloft. Metallic arms reached and took the head. It made a few squishy noises before clicking into place. Then the robot stabbed the head with two tubes. After a third tube went into the head, its eyes shot open and Nancy's mouth vomited week-old river water and a dead frog onto the chancellor's desk.

"Nancy?" Chancellor Reagan said, speaking without the assistance of a puppeteer.

"Goddamn it, Ronnie! What happened?"

"Uh, well..."

The Nancy-bot moved away from the chancellor's desk and looked out the window. No one had even begun repairs on the broken dam. The river still flowed naturally down toward the red line and beyond. She saw lawns dying in the suburbs of Goldwater. She saw empty fields where they had released the cows they no longer had the water to support.

Turning away from the hellish sights, the Nancy-bot slammed her mechanical fist against the desk.

"I swear, Ronnie, one day I'm gonna destroy that Dressica Killmaiden!"

"Well, Nancy, what can I say? They just beat us. Those goddamn punk rockers beat us."

THE OCTOPUS

BEN LOORY

The octopus is spooning sugar into his tea when there is a knock on the door.

Come in, says the octopus over his shoulder, and the door opens.

It is Mrs. Jorgenson.

Got your mail, Mr. Octopus, she says, moving daintily into the apartment.

Thank you, Mrs. Jorgenson, says the octopus. Would you like some tea?

Why yes, I'd love some, comes the response. Do you mind if I sit down?

Not at all, says the octopus, getting down another cup. Not at all.

He brings the tea to the table.

Oh, my aching feet, says Mrs. Jorgenson. I've been up and down those stairs so many times today already.

I do appreciate your bringing up my mail, says the octopus, laying a spoon beside the sugar bowl for Mrs. Jorgenson.

Oh, for you I don't mind at all, she says. It's just some of these other tenants. Everyone's got a problem, you know. And I nearly tripped and fell on the third floor; there was some kind of puddle.

Puddle? says the octopus.

Puddle! says Mrs. Jorgenson. Just sitting there in the middle of the staircase.

The octopus looks confused. Then he sees the mail.

Do you mind if I . . . ? he says to Mrs. Jorgenson.

Heavens, no, she replies. You go right ahead. Mmm, this is good tea.

Darjeeling, says the octopus, leafing through the mail.

There's really nothing good, just the usual stuff. Bills, catalogs, junk mail, more bills . . . and then the octopus gets to the last piece of mail. He sits there,

337

holding it gently in one tentacle.

What is it? says Mrs. Jorgenson.

It's from the ocean, says the octopus, staring at the postmark.

I didn't know you still had folks there, says Mrs. Jorgenson.

Oh yes, says the octopus. Oh yes, I do. My brother, my brother's children.

How nice, says Mrs. Jorgenson. Perhaps it's from them?

Perhaps it is, says the octopus, and he slits the envelope open.

He reads for some time.

Hmm, he says, when he gets to the end.

He looks up to see Mrs. Jorgenson staring at him.

It's from my little nephews, he says. Would you like me to read it?

I wouldn't dream of it, says Mrs. Jorgenson. I mean, unless you wanted to.

The octopus smiles and holds up the letter again. He begins to read.

Dear Uncle Harley, he reads—interjecting, *My name is Harley*—Hello from the ocean! We hope everything on land is going well. The other day Aunt Hattie got into a fight with a cuttlefish. It was funny! We think we might like to come visit you, just the two of us. We've heard so much about you, we'd like to meet you in person. Would that be okay? Please let us know. Your nephews, Gerald and Lewis.

He finishes reading and lowers the letter.

Gerald and Lewis, says Mrs. Jorgenson. They sound like nice young boys.

Oh, they are, says the octopus. Or at least, so it seems. I never really met them in person. I mean, they were only just hatched when I left, so they hadn't quite developed personalities.

Ah, says Mrs. Jorgenson. Are you going to let them come?

Well, says the octopus, looking around, I don't really have a lot of room. Just the couch, really. Where would the other one sleep?

I have a cot I could bring up, says Mrs. Jorgenson.

Do you? says the octopus. Well, that would work. It would be nice to see some of the old gang again.

How long have you been here? asks Mrs. Jorgenson.

About fifteen years, says the octopus.

That's a long time, says Mrs. Jorgenson.

Yes, but I love it, says the octopus, looking around at his apartment. Yes, but I do love it so.

Well, says Mrs. Jorgenson, I guess you should be writing back. If you dash something off, I'll put it in the mailbox when I get down to the lobby.

Would you? says the octopus.

Yes, of course, says Mrs. Jorgenson.

And so it is done.

A few days later there is a knock on the door.

Come in, hollers the octopus, who is cleaning his spoons.

But the door does not open. The octopus grumbles a bit, then gets down from his chair and glides across the room. He opens the door a crack.

Gerald and Lewis! he says, in surprise.

Uncle Harley! they say, and they all embrace.

Come in, come in, says the octopus.

Gerald and Lewis move inside the apartment.

So this is what an apartment looks like, says Gerald, his eyes roving over everything.

It's a little dirty right now, says the octopus.

Dirty? says Gerald. It's amazing—so many treasures!

He is looking at the octopus's collection of spoons, laid out on the table for polishing.

Those are my spoons, says the octopus. I collect them.

What are they for? says Lewis. His voice is rather squeaky.

They're for moving small volumes of liquid around, says the octopus. Or solids, like sugar. I use them all the time.

All three octopi stand there and stare at the spoons.

We don't have anything like that in the ocean, says Gerald.

No, says the octopus, you don't.

Well, he says suddenly, turning. Gerald, you will have the couch. And Lewis, you will have the cot. Unless you want to trade off from night to night.

No, that will be fine, says Lewis. I don't mind. I've never slept on a cot before.

He goes and sits on the cot. He bounces up and down.

So where will we go first? he asks.

Go? says the octopus, looking at him.

Go, says Lewis. What will we go to see first?

The octopus doesn't know what to say.

You mean in the, in the city? he asks.

Of course, says Lewis. We just came from the ocean.

Oh, well, I don't know, says the octopus. I don't really go out there.

You don't go into the city? says Lewis.

No, says the octopus. Not really.

Ever? says Lewis.

No, says the octopus. I like it here.

Gerald and Lewis look at each other.

We thought you were going to take us around to see the city, Gerald says. That's why we came.

I thought you came to see me, says the octopus.

Well, that too, of course, says Gerald. It was both, it was both.

They said we could only come if you'd show us around and take care of us, says Lewis.

Who? says the octopus. Who said that?

Daddy and Aunt Hattie, says Lewis.

Ah, says the octopus. I see.

And now we're here, says Lewis.

Indeed, you are, says the octopus.

The three stupid octopi regard one another in silence.

Well I guess I'll be your tour guide, the octopus says, finally.

Gerald and Lewis smile broadly.

They spend the next day walking the streets of the city. Gerald has a map, and Lewis is in charge of sunscreen. The octopus himself merely walks, staring up at the huge, awe-inspiring buildings and trying not to be terrified of the passing buses and cars.

You're more scared than we are, Uncle Harvey, says Gerald.

And Lewis and the octopus both laugh.

They go to the museums and libraries. They listen to a concert in a park. They have lunch and dinner, and go to an opera.

At the end of the day, they find themselves sitting at an outdoor cafe. Gerald and Lewis are drinking root beer; the octopus has tea.

So? says the octopus. What do you think?

It certainly is large, says Gerald.

It certainly is huge, says Lewis.

The octopus nods.

Yes it is, he says. Yes, it is.

Is it true that you'll live forever? says Gerald out of the blue. I mean, if you stay here?

The octopus looks at him thoughtfully.

It is, says the octopus. It is true. Supposedly, of course. I guess the only way to tell for sure is to stay here and find out.

But why does it work that way? says Lewis. Why can't we live forever in the ocean?

I don't know, says the octopus. That's just the way it is. When an octopus comes to land, he lives forever. It's just the way it is, like the way some people have brown hair and some people are blond.

Gerald and Lewis sit and stare at their sodas.

Has Dad ever been here? Gerald asks.

No, says the octopus. Your dad was never much interested in land.

Why's that? says Lewis.

I don't know, says the octopus. He just wasn't. He met your mom and they were very happy, and then they had you. So there was never really time for coming to visit the land, or for thinking about living here.

But why don't we all live here? says Gerald.

The octopus looks at him and smiles.

It just doesn't work that way, he says. It just doesn't work that way.

That night the octopus tucks Gerald and Lewis into bed.

Sleep tight, he says. Tomorrow you go back to the ocean.

What? Already? say Gerald and Lewis.

I'm sorry, says the octopus, but yes. I have a lot of things to do and I can't do them with you boys hanging around all the time. I love you, though. You boys know that?

The boys grumble a little, but say yes.

Good, says the octopus. Then good night.

He pats the boys on their heads and then goes into the kitchen. He makes himself a cup of tea and stirs sugar into it with a spoon. He listens to the clanking noise the spoon makes against the cup, and watches the liquid as it swirls around: a circle, a circle, a circle.

When he returns to the living room, the boys are fast asleep. He stands there in the darkness, watching them. Then he returns to the kitchen and opens a cabinet. Inside, the silver polish; in the drawer, the spoons.

The next morning they are all off to the beach.

Shall I carry your suitcase? the octopus says to Lewis.

Oh no, says Lewis, I got it.

They move down the staircase. In the lobby, they pass Mrs. Jorgenson.

Why Mr. Octopus, says Mrs. Jorgenson, you're out and about!

Just taking the boys back to the sea, says the octopus, and the boys wave hello and good-bye.

They take the subway to the beach. The subway is very crowded.

Where are all these people going? says Gerald. There are so many of them.

I don't know, says the octopus, looking around. I always wondered that myself.

When they get to the beach, Gerald and Lewis trudge down to the waterline.

Are you sure we can't stay with you another day? asks Gerald.

I'm positive, says the octopus. I'm sorry.

But why can't we stay? says Lewis.

There's no reason, says the octopus. I just can't let you. Please, boys, just do as you're told.

The boys grumble some more, but they're not really angry. They give the octopus great big hugs.

Good-bye, Uncle Harley, Gerald says.

Good-bye, Uncle, says Lewis.

Good-bye, boys, says the octopus. Now off with you.

And he stands there and watches as the boys slap down into the surf and wade out beneath the waves.

Thank God that's over, thinks the octopus. Now I can go back to my life.

But, strangely, the octopus does not turn. Instead, he stands there and stares—off into the gently rolling surf, down into the water, after Gerald and Lewis. In his mind the octopus pictures his brother—their father—and poor Aunt Hattie, and all those other octopi he used to know in the days before he lived on land. He remembers the day he turned away from them—the day he swam away—the day he walked up onto the beach, and headed into the city and found the apartment. He remembers the day he began drinking tea, and the day he started collecting spoons. He remembers the day he stopped getting his mail and let Mrs. Jorgenson bring it up to him. He remembers in turn all of these things, all of them and more. He remembers the tea as it swirled around and around in a circle in his cup.

The octopus suddenly finds himself walking down the beach to the water. He feels the sand under his tentacles, and then the water washing over them.

My God, the water feels good, he thinks. I had almost forgotten.

He stands in the shallows, gazing out, and then, in one motion, he dives in.

The octopus swims toward the depths—his tentacles waving free—and something inside him opens up. Suddenly, he can breathe.

I'm coming, brother, he calls out, in his mind and in the sea. I'm coming, nephews. I'm coming, friends. I'm coming home. It's me!

YOU SAW ME STANDING ALONE

KRIS SAKNUSSEMM

Ben was cruising across a stretch of farmland, through endless acres of rice fields, gleaming acres of canola, big irrigation spindles and combine harvesters. He couldn't switch the country station—it was driving him crazy. He came to a crossroads. There was a boarded-up, shotgunned remnant of a Polar Freeze and a Cherokee gas station. He looked down at his gas gauge. The dashboard was blank. No numbers, no mileage. He glanced over at the front seat. It was littered with Denny's coffee cups and naked lady playing cards. He pulled in to get some gas. He didn't know how much he had.

A bell rang when he drove into the forecourt. The gas pumps were old but brilliant white and shining in the heat. A slightly stooped, salt-and-pepper haired man in a mechanic's suit waved to him out of the shadows of the garage, the silver of the hydraulic lift catching a flash of light, like a pillar of mirror. The man made no motion to come out of the garage so Ben began pumping the gas himself. The nozzle was immense and ancient, and the numbers behind the glass clicked over slowly and mechanically like years on a calendar. It seemed to take forever to fill the tank. His hand got sore. The sun sank. Suddenly he felt a splosh of gasoline splurge up. It smelled like liquor and perfume. Thank Christ, he thought. Tank full at last. Then he saw that the numbers had all turned around to 00. It was dark by then, a full moon rising over a peeling billboard, crickets everywhere like gravel. He crushed them with his feet that he found were bare. No other cars had pulled in and the man in the garage had never come out. Ben walked over to the window looking for where he should pay. The older man in the garage worked by the light of a caged bulb suspended from a steel beam. He was busy with a socket wrench, tinkering with what appeared to be an old-fashioned race car. The sleeves of his dark green coveralls were rolled up and Ben could see that both his arms were artificial. The prosthetic flesh looked real but the fingers weren't that dexterous—the man kept dropping his socket wrench. Ben realized he'd been hearing that sound the whole time he'd been pumping the gas.

"Built it myself," the man said, dropping the wrench again and patting the fireball orange metal with one of his plastic hands. "You go on inna office—Lucy Tee will fix you up."

Ben went outside and finally found the office. The window was full of fan belts and women's underwear. An old Coke machine was stocked with a drink called Orange Pep, which had the face of a laughing giraffe on it. Inside the office, he found a counter with a girl of about sixteen behind it. She had on a soft white cotton bowling shirt and she was wearing a blindfold. Behind her, on a set of display shelves where cigarettes or candy bars might've been, were boxes of condoms and those yellow plastic corn cobs with forks in them for holding corn on the cob so you don't burn your fingers.

"How come you're wearing a blindfold?" Ben asked.

"In case anybody tries to cheat me," the girl answered.

"What do you mean—wouldn't it be easier for 'em to cheat you—if you can't see?"

"Sometimes," the girl answered. "But most times they give themselves away."

"How much do I owe you?" Ben asked.

"Whatever's right," the girl answered. "Ain't no standard rates. Everything's on an in-di-vid-shool basis."

"Then how can you be cheated?" He noticed the cash register was open and the drawer was empty.

"Don't you think I'm pretty?" the girl asked and closed the drawer.

"S-ure," Ben said, fidgeting, wondering where his wallet had gone.

"Then why don't you ask me what my favorite song is!"

"What—what's your favorite song?"

"'Blue Moon.'"

"Oh, yeah?" Ben said, examining the girl more closely. "Which version?"

"The one on the jukebox," the girl answered.

"Which jukebox?"

"The one out by the door."

He wanted to see what she looked like without that bowling shirt on. He didn't know how much gas he'd bought.

"Why don't you play it for me?"

Ben felt in his pocket for any change and found he had only beer caps.

"It don't take no money," the girl said.

He went outside to the Coke machine. He eyed the row of laughing giraffe faces advertising Orange Pep and bashed one with his fist. The machine teetered and made a mechanical complaint inside, and then to his surprise the girl began singing *"Blue Moon...you saw me standing alone..."* with a beautiful professional voice—only it sounded amplified as if a radio or a CD were playing and the girl only moving her lips. Ben clapped when the song was over. "I gotta be goin'," he said.

"You can't," the girl said. "Daddy's not finished building the race car. Then we're gonna git married and you're gonna run the station—and build a car of yer own."

Ben sniffed with disdain. "Honey," he said, pulling his cock out of his shorts. "How tight is that blindfold?"

"I know what you're doin'," the girl answered.

"And I knew you could see through that blindfold."

The girl whisked off the white cloth and Ben saw that where her eye sockets should be, her face was blank. Smooth, undifferentiated skin. The breath died in his throat. His cock was now too large to grasp with one hand. The girl smiled. Ben had never exposed himself before and the thrill of it made his knees creak. With both hands he began to stroke the organ, rolling the foreskin back and forth. It was like pulling a baby's head in and out of a sweater. His arms grew weary but he was too excited to stop. The girl didn't move, but she seemed to be listening with her entire body. The pressure was building up inside him. Then the bell rang outside at the pumps.

"Uh-oh," the girl said.

"What?" Ben gasped—just on the edge.

"Lucy's back."

"I—I thought you were Lucy..." he sputtered...so close to climax...

The girl snorted at this and then began laughing uncontrollably.

Her hysterics had a deflating effect on Ben—and then he heard a sound that outright unnerved him. He heard it the way a mother might jump at the cry of her child from another room. It was the horn of his car—a very distinctive honk. Loud and long—and then the sound of his car peeling out.

"My car!" Ben shouted, still flopping out of his shorts as he watched his taillights recede down the lonely strip of old two-lane highway.

The girl behind the counter remained doubled over with hiccupping laughter—but even over her wheezings he heard the telltale plink of metal on concrete behind him. The old mechanic with the prosthetic hands had slipped up behind him and dropped his socket wrench.

"C'mon son," the older man smiled as he stooped to retrieve the wrench.

"What have you done with my car?" Ben demanded, tucking himself back in.

"Ah, Lucy Tee's just gone back to get the malted milks. She forgot 'em. You got a full tank," the man smiled and dropped the socket wrench again.

Ben picked it up and held it menacingly. "Get me my car back."

The wrinkled mechanic's face beamed.

"We got us a race car to finish! Don't wanna disappoint Lucy. You know what she's like when she gets upset."

As he said this he held up his artificial hands as if he had never seen them before. Then he turned and headed back to the garage whistling "Blue Moon," leaving Ben gripping the wrench as the girl behind the counter, who had at last managed to stop laughing, reinstated her blindfold.

MR. BEAR

JOE R. LANSDALE

For Michelle Lansdale

Jim watched as the plane filled up. It was a pretty tightly stacked flight, but last time, coming into Houston, he had watched as every seat filled except for the one on his left and the one on his right. He had hit the jackpot that time, no row mates. That made it comfortable, having all that knee and elbow room.

He had the middle seat again, an empty seat to his left, and one to his right. He sat there hoping there would be the amazing repeat of the time before.

A couple of big guys, sweating and puffing, were moving down the aisle, and he thought, yep, they'll be the ones. Probably one of them on either side. Shit, he'd settle for just having one seat filled, the one by the window, so he could get out on the aisle side. Easy to go to the bathroom that way, stretch your legs.

The big guys passed him by. He saw a lovely young woman carrying a straw hat making her way down the center. He thought, someone has got to sit by me, maybe it'll be her. He could perhaps strike up a conversation. He might even find she's going where he's going, doesn't have a boyfriend. Wishful thinking, but it was a better thing to think about than big guys on either side of him, hemming him in like the center of a sandwich.

But no, she passed him by as well. He looked up at her, hoping she'd look his way. Maybe he could get a smile at least. That would be nice.

Course, he was a married man, so that was no way to think.

But he was thinking it.

She didn't look and she didn't smile.

Jim sighed, waited. The line was moving past him. There was only one customer left. A shirtless bear in dungarees and work boots, carrying a hat. The bear looked peeved, or tired, or both.

Oh, shit, thought Jim. Bears, they've got to stink. All that damn fur. He passes me by, I'm going to have a seat free to myself on either side. He doesn't, well, I've got to ride next to him for several hours.

But, the bear stopped in his row, pointed at the window seat. "That's my seat."

"Sure," Jim said, and moved out of the middle seat, and out into the aisle, let the bear in. The bear settled in by the window and fastened his seat belt and rested his hat on his knee. Jim slid back into the middle seat. He could feel the heat off the bear's big hairy arm. And there was a smell. Nothing nasty or ripe. Just a kind of musty odor, like an old fur coat hung too long in a closet, dried blood left in a carpet, a whiff of cigarette smoke and charred wood.

Jim watched the aisle again. No one else. He could hear them closing the door. He unfastened his seat belt and moved to the seat closest to the aisle. The bear turned and looked at him. "You care I put my hat in the middle seat?"

"Not at all," Jim said.

"I get tired of keeping up with it. Thinking of taking it out of the wardrobe equation."

Suddenly it snapped. Jim knew the bear. Had seen him on TV. He was a famous environmentalist. Well, that was something. Had to sit by a musty bear, helped if he was famous. Maybe there would be something to talk about.

"Hey," the bear said, "I ask you something, and I don't want it to sound rude, but...can I?"

"Sure."

"I got a feeling, just from a look you gave me, you recognized me."

"I did."

"Well, I don't want to be too rude, sort of leave a fart hanging in the air, though, I might...Deer carcass. Never agrees. But, I really don't want to talk about me or what I do or who I am...And let me just be completely honest. I was so good at what I do...Well, I am good. Let me rephrase that. I was really as successful as people think, you believe I'd be riding coach? After all my years of service to the forest, it's like asking your best girl to ride bitch like she was the local poke. So, I don't want to talk about it."

"I never intended to ask," Jim said. That was a lie, but it seemed like the right thing to say.

"Good. That's good," said the bear, and leaned back in his seat and put the hat on his head and pulled it down over his eyes.

For a moment Jim thought the bear had gone to sleep, but no, the bear spoke again. "Now that we've got that out of the way, you want to talk, we can talk. Don't want to, don't have to, but we can talk, just don't want to talk about the job and me and the television ads, all that shit. You know what I'd like to talk about?"

"What's that?"

"Poontang. All the guys talk about pussy, but me, I'm a bear, so it makes guys uncomfortable, don't want to bring it up. Let me tell you something man, I get plenty, and I don't just mean bear stuff. Guy like me, that celebrity thing going and all, I can line them up outside the old motel room, knock 'em off like shooting ducks from a blind. Blondes, redheads, brunettes, bald, you name it, I can bang it."

This made Jim uncomfortable. He couldn't remember the last time he'd had sex with his wife, and here was a smelly bear with a goofy hat knocking it off like there was no tomorrow. He said, "Aren't we talking about your celebrity after all? I mean, in a way?"

"Shit. You're right. Okay. Something else. Maybe nothing. Maybe we just sit. Tell you what, I'm going to read a magazine, but you think of something you want to talk about, you go ahead. I'm listening."

Jim got a magazine out of the pouch in front of him and read a little, even came across an ad with the bear's picture in it, but he didn't want to bring that up. He put the magazine back and thought about the book he had in the overhead, in his bag, but he hated to bother. Besides, the book was the usual thriller, and he didn't feel like bothering.

After a while the flight attendant came by. She was a nice looking woman who looked even nicer because of her suit, way she carried herself, the air of authority. She asked if they'd like drinks.

Jim ordered a diet soda, which was free, but the bear pulled out a bill and bought a mixed drink, a Bloody Mary. They both got peanuts. When the flight attendant handed the bear his drink, the bear said, "Honey, we land, you're not doing anything, I could maybe show you my wild side, find yours."

The bear grinned, and showed some very ugly teeth.

The flight attendant leaned over Jim, close to the bear, said, "I'd rather rub dirt in my ass than do anything with you."

This statement hung in the air like backed up methane for a moment, then the flight attendant smiled, moved back and stood in the aisle, looked right at Jim and said, "If you need anything else, let me know," and she was gone.

The bear had let down his dining tray and he had the drink in its plastic cup in his hand. The Bloody Mary looked very bloody. The bear drank it in one big gulp. He said, "Flight drinks. You could have taken a used Tampax and dipped it in rubbing alcohol and it would taste the same."

Jim didn't say anything. The bear said, "She must be a lesbian. Got to be. Don't you think?"

The way the bear turned and looked at him, Jim thought it was wise to agree. "Could be."

The bear crushed the plastic cup. "No could be. Is. Tell me you agree. Say, IS."

"Is," Jim said, and his legs trembled slightly.

"That's right, boy. Now whistle up that lesbian bitch, get her back over here. I want another drink."

When they landed in Denver the bear was pretty liquored up. He walked down the ramp crooked and his hat was cocked at an odd angle that suggested it would fall at any moment. But it didn't.

The plane had arrived late, and this meant Jim had missed his connecting flight due to a raging snow storm. The next flight was in the morning and it was packed. He'd have to wait until tomorrow, mid-afternoon, just to see if a flight was available. He called his wife on his cell phone, told her, and then rang off feeling depressed and tired and wishing he could stay home and never fly again.

Jim went to the bar, thinking he might have a nightcap, catch a taxi to the hotel, and there was the bear, sitting on a stool next to a blonde with breasts so big they were resting on the bar in front of her. The bear, his hat still angled oddly on his head, was chatting her up.

Jim went behind them on his way to a table. He heard the bear say, "Shid, darlin', you dun't know whad yer missin'. 'ere's wimen all o'er 'is world would lige to do it wid a bear."

"I'm not that drunk, yet," the blonde said, "and I don't think they have enough liquor here to make me that drunk." She got up and walked off.

Jim sat down at a table with his back to the bar. He didn't want the bear to recognize him, but he wanted a drink. And then he could smell the bear. The big beast was right behind him. He turned slightly. The bear was standing there, dripping saliva onto his furry chest thick as sea foam.

"Eh, buddy, 'ow you doin'." The bear's words were so slurred, it took Jim a moment to understand.

"Oh," he said. "Not so good. Flight to Seattle is delayed until tomorrow."

"Me too," the bear said, and plopped down in a chair at the table so hard the chair wobbled and Jim heard a cracking sound that made him half-expect to see the chair explode and the bear go tumbling to the floor. "See me wid dat gal? Wus dryin' to roun me ub sum, ya know."

"No luck?"

"Les'bin. The're eberyware."

Jim decided he needed to get out of this pretty quick. "Well, you know, I don't think I'm going to wait on that drink. Got to get a hotel room, get ready for tomorrow."

"Naw, dunt do 'at. Er, led me buy ya a drank. Miz. You in dem tidht panss."

So the waitress came over and the bear ordered some drinks for them both. Jim kept trying to leave, but, no go. Before he knew it, he was almost as hammered as the bear.

Finally, the bear, just two breaths short of a complete slur, said, "Eber thang 'ere is den times duh prize. Leds go ta a real bar." He paused. "Daby Crogett killed a bar." And then the bear broke into insane laughter.

"Wen e wus ony tree...three. Always subone gad ta shood sub bar subware. Cum on, eds go. I know dis town ligh duh bag ob muh 'and."

They closed down a mid-town bar. Jim remembered that pretty well. And then Jim remembered something about the bear saying they ought to have some companionship, and then things got muddled. He awoke in a little motel room, discovered the air was full of the smell of moldy bear fur, alcohol farts, a coppery aroma, and sweaty perfume.

Sitting up in bed, Jim was astonished to find a very plump girl with short blonde hair next to him in bed. She was lying facedown, one long, bladder like tit sticking out from under her chest, the nipple pierced with a ring that looked like a washer.

Jim rolled out of bed and stood up beside it. He was nude and sticky. "Shit," he said. He observed the hump under the sheet some more, the washer in the tit. And then, as his eyes adjusted, he looked across the room and saw another bed, and he could see on the bedpost the bear's hat, and then the bear, lying on the bed without his pants. There was another lump under the blanket. One delicate foot stuck out from under the blanket near the end of the bed, a gold chain around the ankle. The bear was snoring softly. There were clothes all over the floor, a pair of panties large enough to be used as a sling for the wounded leg of a hippopotamus was dangling from the light fixture. That would belong to his date.

Except for his shoes and socks, Jim found his clothes and put them on and sat in a chair at a rickety table and put his head in his hands. He repeated softly over and over, "Shit, shit, shit."

With his hands on his face, he discovered they had a foul smell about them, somewhere between working man sweat and a tuna net. He was hit with a sudden revelation that made him feel ill. He slipped into the bathroom and showered and re-dressed, this time he put on his socks and shoes. When he came out the light was on over the table and the bear was sitting there, wearing his clothes, even his hat.

"Damn, man," the bear said, his drunk gone, "that was some time we had. I think. But, I got to tell you man, you got the ugly one."

Jim sat down at the table, feeling as if he had just been hit by a car. "I don't remember anything."

"Hope you remembered she stunk. That's how I tracked them down, on a corner. I could smell her a block away. I kind of like that, myself. You know, the smell. Bears, you know how it is. But, I seen her, and I thought, goddamn, she'd have to sneak up on a glass of water, so I took the other one. You said you didn't care."

"Oh, god," Jim said.

"The fun is in the doing, not the remembering. Trust me, some things aren't worth remembering."

"My wife will kill me."

"Not if you don't tell her."

"I've never done anything like this before."

"Now you've started. The fat one, I bet she drank twelve beers before she pissed herself."

"Oh, Jesus."

"Come on, let's get out of here. I gave the whores the last of my money. And I gave them yours."

"What?"

"I asked you. You said you didn't mind."

"I said I don't remember a thing. I need that money."

"I know that. So do I."

The bear got up and went over to his bed and picked up the whore's purse and rummaged through it, took out the money. He then found the other whore's purse on the floor, opened it up and took out money.

Jim staggered to his feet. He didn't like this, not even a little bit. But, he needed his money back. Was it theft if you paid for services you didn't remember?

Probably. But...

As Jim stood, in the table light, he saw that on the bear's bed was a lot of red paint, and then he saw it wasn't paint, saw too that the whore's head was missing. Jim let out a gasp and staggered a little.

The bear looked at him. The expression on his face was oddly sheepish.

"Thought we might get out of here without you seeing that. Sometimes, especially if I've been drinking, and I'm hungry, I revert to my basic nature. If it's any consolation, I don't remember doing that."

"No. No. It's no consolation at all."

At this moment, the fat whore rolled over in bed and sat up and the covers dropped down from her, and the bear, moving very quickly, got over there and with a big swipe of his paw sent a spray of blood and a rattle of teeth flying across the room, against the wall. The whore fell back, half her face clawed away.

"Oh, Jesus. Oh, my god."

"This killing I remember," the bear said. "Now come on, we got to wipe everything down before we leave, and we don't have all night."

They walked the streets in blowing snow, and even though it was cold, Jim felt as if he were in some kind of fever dream. The bear trudged along beside him, said, "I had one of the whores pay for the room in cash. They never even saw us at the desk. Wiped down the prints in the room, anything we might have touched. I'm an expert at it. We're cool. Did that 'cause I know how these things can turn out. I've had it go bad before. Employers have got me out of a few scrapes, you know. I give them that. You okay, you look a little peaked."

"I...I..."

The bear ignored him, rattled on. "You now, I'm sure you can tell by now, I'm not really all that good with the ladies. On the plane, I was laying the bullshit on...Damn, I got all this fur, but that don't mean I'm not cold. I ought to have like a winter uniform, you know, a jacket, with a big collar that I can turn up. Oh, by the way. I borrowed your cell phone to call out for pizza last night, but before I could, dropped it and stepped on the motherfucker. Can you believe that? Squashed like a clam shell. I got it in my pocket. Have to throw it away. Okay. Let me be truthful. I had it in my back pocket and I sat my fat ass on it. That's the thing...You a little hungry? Shit. I'm hungry. I'm cold."

That was the only comment for a few blocks, then the bear said, "Fuck this," and veered toward a car parked with several others at the curb. The bear reached in his pocket and took out a little packet, opened it. The street lights revealed a series of shiny lock pick tools. He went to work on the car door with a tool that he unfolded and slid down the side of the car window until he could pull the lock. He opened the door, said, "Get inside." The bear flipped a switch that unlocked the doors, and Jim, as if he were obeying the commands of a hypnotist, walked around to the other side and got in.

The bear was bent under the dash with his tools, and in a moment, the car roared to life. The bear sat in the seat and closed the door, said, "Seat belts. Ain't nobody rides in my car, they don't wear seatbelts."

Jim thought: It's not your car. But he didn't say anything. He couldn't. His heart was in his mouth. He put on his seat belt.

They tooled along the snowy Denver streets and out of town and the bear said, "We're leaving this place, going to my stomping grounds. Yellowstone Park. Know some back trails. Got a pass. We'll be safe there. We can hang. I got a cabin. It'll be all right."

"I...I..." Jim said, but he couldn't find the rest of the sentence.

"Look in the glove box, see there's anything there. Maybe some prescription medicine of some kind. I could use a jolt."

"I..." Jim said, and then his voice died and he opened the glove box. There was a gun inside. Lazily, Jim reached for it.

The bear leaned over and took it from him. "You don't act like a guy been around guns much. Better let me have that." The bear, while driving, managed with one hand to pop out the clip and slide it back in. "A full load. Wonder he's got a gun permit. You know, I do. Course, not for this gun. But, beggers can't be choosers, now can they?"

"No. No. Guess not," Jim said, having thought for a moment that he would have the gun, that he could turn the tables, at least make the bear turn back toward Denver, let him out downtown.

"See any gum in there," the bear said. "Maybe he's got some gum. After that whore's head, I feel like my mouth has a pair of shitty shorts in it. Anything in there?"

Jim shook his head. "Nothing."

"Well, shit," the bear said.

The car roared on through the snowy night, the windshield wipers beating time, throwing snow wads left and right like drunk children tossing cotton balls.

The heater was on. It was warm. Jim felt a second wave of the alcohol blues; it wrapped around him like a warm blanket, and without really meaning to, he slept.

"I should be hibernating," the bear said, as if Jim were listening. "That's why I'm so goddamn grumpy. The work. No hibernation. Paid poon and cheap liquor. That's no way to live."

The bear was a good driver in treacherous weather. He drove on through the night and made good time.

When Jim awoke it was just light and the light was red and it came through the window and filled the car like blood-stained streams of heavenly piss.

Jim turned his head. The bear had his hat cocked back on his head and he looked tired. He turned his head slightly toward Jim, showed some teeth at the corner of his mouth, then glared back at the snowy road.

"We got a ways to go yet, but we're almost to Yellowstone. You been asleep two days."

"Two days."

"Yeah. I stopped for gas once, and you woke up once and you took a piss."

"I did."

"Yeah. But you went right back to sleep."

"Good grief. I've never been that drunk in my life."

"Probably the pills you popped."

"What?"

"Pills. You took them with the alcohol, when we were with the whores."

"Oh, hell."

"It's all right. Every now and again you got to cut the tiger loose, you know. Don't worry. I got a cabin. That's where we're going. Don't worry. I'll take care of you. I mean, hell, what are friends for?"

The bear didn't actually have a cabin, he had a fire tower, and it rose up high into the sky overlooking very tall trees. They had to climb a ladder up there, and the bear, sticking the automatic in his belt, sent Jim up first, said, "Got to watch those rungs. They get wet, iced over, your hand can slip. Forest Ranger I knew slipped right near the top. We had to dig what was left of him out of the ground. One of his legs went missing. I found it about a month later. It was cold when he fell so it kept pretty good. Wasn't bad, had it with some beans. Waste not, want not. Go on, man. Climb."

Inside the fire tower it was very nice, though cold. The bear turned on the electric heater and it wasn't long before the place was toasty.

The bear said, "There's food in the fridge. Shitter is over there. I'll sleep in my bed, and you sleep on the couch. This'll be great. We can hang. I got all kinds of movies, and as you can see, that TV is big enough for a drive-in theater. We ain't got no bitches, but hell, they're just trouble anyway. We'll just pull each other's wieners."

Jim said, "What now?"

"I don't stutter, boy. It ain't so bad. You just grease a fellow up and go to work."

"I don't know."

"Nah, you'll like it."

As night neared, the light that came through the tower's wraparound windows darkened and died, and Jim could already imagine grease on his hands.

But by then, the bear had whetted his whistle pretty good, drinking straight from a big bottle of Jack Daniel's. He wasn't as wiped out as before, not stumbling drunk, and his tongue still worked, but fortunately the greased weenie pull had slipped from the bear's mind. He sat on the couch with his bottle and Jim sat on the other end, and the bear said:

"Once upon a goddamn time the bears roamed these forests and we were the biggest, baddest, meanest, motherfuckers in the woods. That's no shit. You know that?"

Jim nodded.

"But, along come civilization. We had fires before that, I'm sure. You know, natural stuff. Lightning. Too dry. Natural combustion. But when man arrived, it was doo-doo time for the bears and everything else. I mean, don't take me wrong. I like a good meal and a beer," he held up the bottle, "and some Jack, and hanging out in this warm tower, but something has been sapped out of me. Some sort of savage beast that was in me has been tapped and run off into the ground...I was an orphan. Did you know that?"

"I've heard the stories," Jim said.

"Yeah, well, who hasn't? It was a big fire. I was young. Some arsonists. Damn fire raged through the forest and I got separated from my mom. Dad, he'd run off. But, you know, no biggie. That's how bears do. Well, anyway, I climbed a tree like a numb nuts cause my feet got burned, and I just clung and clung to that tree. And then I seen her, my mother. She was on fire. She ran this way and that, back and forth, and I'm yelling, 'Mama,' but she's not paying attention, had her own concerns. And pretty soon she goes down and the fire licks her all over and her fur is gone and there ain't nothing but a blackened hunk of smoking bear crap left. You know what it is to see a thing like that, me being a cub?"

"I can't imagine."

"No you can't. You can't. No one can. I had a big fall too. I don't really remember it, but it left a knot on the back of my head, just over the right ear... Come here. Feel that."

Jim dutifully complied.

The bear said, "Not too hard now. That knot, that's like my Achilles heel. I'm weak there. Got to make sure I don't bump my head too good. That's no thing to live with and that's why I'm not too fond of arsonists. There are several of them, what's left of them, buried not far from here. I roam these forests and I'll tell you, I don't just report them. Now and again, I'm not doing that. Just take care of business myself. Let me tell you, slick, there's a bunch of them that'll never squat over a commode again. They're out there, their gnawed bones buried deep. You know what it's like to be on duty all the time, not to be able to hibernate, just nap. It makes a bear testy. Want a cigar?"

"Beg your pardon?"

"A cigar. I know it's funny coming from me, and after what I just told you, but, we'll be careful here in my little nest."

Jim didn't answer. The bear got up and came back with two fat, black cigars. He had boxed matches with him. He gave Jim a cigar and Jim put it in his mouth, and the bear said, "Puff gently."

Jim did and the bear lit the end with a wooden match. The bear lit his own cigar. He tossed the box of matches to Jim. "If it goes out, you can light up again. Thing about a cigar is you take your time, just enjoy it, don't get into it like a whore sucking a dick. It's done casual. Pucker your mouth like you're kissing a baby."

Jim puffed on the cigar but didn't inhale. The action of it made him feel high, and not too good, a little sick even. They sat and smoked. After a long while, the bear got up and opened one of the windows, said, "Come here."

Jim went. The woods were alive with sounds, crickets, night birds, howling.

"That's as it should be. Born in the forest, living there, taking game there, dying there, becoming one with the soil. But look at me. What the fuck have I become? I'm like a goddamn circus bear."

"You do a lot of good."

"For who though? The best good I've done was catching those arsonists that are buried out there. That was some good. I'll be straight with you, Jim. I'm happy you're going to be living here. I need a buddy, and, well, tag, you're it."

"Buddy."

"You heard me. Oh, the door, it's locked, and you can't work the lock from inside, cause it's keyed, and I got the key. So don't think about going anywhere."

"That's not very buddy like," Jim said.

The bear studied Jim for a long moment, and Jim felt himself going weak. It was as if he could see the bear's psychosis move from one eye to another, like it was changing rooms. "But, you're still my buddy, aren't you, Jim?"

Jim nodded.

"Well, I'm sort of bushed, so I think I'll turn in early. Tomorrow night we'll catch up on that weenie pull."

When the bear went to the bedroom and lay down, Jim lay on the couch with the blanket and pillow the bear had left for him, and listened. The bear had left the bedroom door open, and after awhile he could hear the bear snoring like a lumberjack working a saw on a log.

Jim got up and eased around the tower and found that he could open windows, but there was nowhere to go from there except straight down, and that was one booger of a drop. Jim thought of how easily the bear had killed the whore and how he admitted to killing others, and then he thought about tomorrow night's weenie pull, and he became even more nervous.

After an hour of walking about and looking, he realized there was no way out. He thought about the key, but had no idea where the bear kept it. He feared if he went in the bear's room to look, he could startle the bear and that might result in getting his head chewed off. He decided to let it go. For now. Ultimately, pulling a greased bear weenie couldn't be as bad as being headless.

Jim went back to the couch, pulled the blanket over him and almost slept.

Next morning, Jim, who thought he would never sleep, had finally drifted off, and what awoke him was not a noise, but the smell of food cooking. Waffles.

Jim got up slowly. A faint pink light was coming through the window. The kitchenette area of the tower was open to view, part of the bigger room, and the bear was in there wearing an apron and a big chef hat. The bear turned, saw him. The apron had a slogan on it: If Mama Ain't Happy, Ain't Nobody Happy.

The bear spotted him, gave Jim a big-fanged, wet smile. "Hey, brother, how are you? Come on in here and sit your big ass down and have one of Mr. Bear's waffles. It's so good you'll want to slap your mama."

Jim went into the kitchenette, sat at the table where the bear instructed. The bear seemed in a light and cheery mood. Coffee was on the table, a plate stacked with waffles, big strips of bacon, pats of butter and a bottle of syrup in a plastic bear modeled after Mr. Bear himself.

"Now you wrap your lips around some of this stuff, see what you think."

While Jim ate the bear regaled him with all manner of stories about his life, and most were in fact interesting, but all Jim could think about was the bear biting the head off of that hooker, and then slashing the other with a strike of his mighty paw. As Jim ate, the tasty waffles with thick syrup became wads of blood and flesh in his mouth, and he felt as if he were eating of Mr. Bear's wine and wafer, his symbolic blood and flesh, and it made Jim's skin crawl.

All it would take to end up like the whores was to make a misstep. Say something wrong. Perhaps a misinterpreted look. A hesitation at tonight's weenie pull...Oh, damn, Jim thought. The weenie pull.

"What I thought we'd do, is we'd go for a drive, dump the car. There's a ravine I know where we can run it off, and no one will see it again. Won't even know it's missing. Excuse me while I go to the shitter. I think I just got word there's been a waffle delivery called."

The bear laughed at his own joke and left the room. Jim ate a bit more of the waffle and all the bacon. He didn't want the bear to think he wasn't grateful. The beast was psychotic. Anything could set him off.

Jim got up and washed his hands at the sink, and just as he was passing into the living room, he saw the gun they had found in the car lying on a big fluffy chair. Part of it, the barrel, had slipped into the crack in the cushions. Maybe the bear had forgotten all about it, or at least didn't have it at the forefront of his mind. That was it. He'd been drunker than a Shriner's convention. He probably didn't even remember having the gun.

Jim eased over and picked up the weapon and put it under his shirt, in the small of his back. He hoped he would know how to use it. He had seen them used before. If he could get up close enough—

"Now, that was some delivery. That motherfucker probably came with a fortune cookie and six pack of Coke. I feel ten pounds lighter. You ready, Jimbo?"

In the early morning the forests were dark and beautiful and there was a slight mist and with the window of the car rolled down, it was cool and damp and the world seemed newborn. But all Jim could think about was performing a greased weenie pull and then getting his head chewed off.

Jim said, "You get rid of the car, how do we get back?"

The bear laughed. "Just like a citizen. We walk, of course."

"We've gone quite a distance."

"It'll do you good. Blow out the soot. You'll like it. Great scenery. I'm gonna show you the graves where I buried what was left of them fellows, the arsonists."

"That's all right," Jim said. "I don't need to see that."

"I want you to. It's not like I can show everyone, but my bestest bud, that's a different matter, now ain't it?"

"Well, I don't..." Jim said.

"We're going to see it."

"Sure. Okay."

Jim had a sudden revelation. Maybe there never was going to be a weenie pull, and as joyful as that perception was, the alternative was worse. The bear was going to get rid of him. Didn't want to do it in his tower. You don't shit where you eat...Well, the bear might. But the idea was you kept your place clean of problems. This wasn't just a trip to dump the car, this was a death ride. The bear was going to kill him and leave him where the arsonists were. Jim felt his butthole clench on the car seat.

They drove up higher and the woods grew thicker and the road turned off and onto a trail. The car bumped along for some miles until the trees overwhelmed everything but the trail, and the tree limbs were so thickly connected they acted as a kind of canopy overhead. They drove in deep shadow and there were spots where the shadows were broken by light and the light played across the trail in speckles and spots and birds shot across their view like feathered bullets, and twice there were deer in sight, bounding into the forest and disappearing like wraiths as the car passed.

They came to a curve and then a sharp rise and the bear drove up the rise. The trail played out, and still he drove. He came to a spot, near the peak of the hill, where the sun broke through, stopped the car and got out. Jim got out. They walked to the highest rise of the hill, and where they stood was a clean wide swath in the trees. Weeds and grass grew there. The grass was tall and mostly yellow but brown in places.

"Spring comes," the bear said. "There will be flowers, all along that path, on up to this hill, bursting all over it. This is my forest, Jim. All the dry world used to be a forest, or nearly was, but man has cut most of it down and that's done things to all of us and I don't think in the long run much of it is good. Before man, things had a balance, know what I mean? But man....Oh, boy. He sucks. Like that fire that burned me. Arson. Just for the fun of it. Burned down my goddamn home, Jim. I was just a cub. Little. My mother dying like that...I always feel two to three berries short of a pie."

"I'm sorry."

"Aren't they all? Sorry. Boy, that sure makes it better, don't it. Shit." The bear paused and looked over the swath of meadow. He said, "Even with there having been snow, it's dry, and when it's dry, someone starts a fire, it'll burn. The snow don't mean a thing after it melts and the thirsty ground sucks it up, considering it's mostly been dry all year. That one little snow, it ain't nothing more than whipped cream on dry cake." The bear pointed down the hill. "That swath there, it would burn like gasoline on a shag carpet. I keep an eye out for those things. I try to keep this forest safe. It's a thankless and continuous job...

Sometimes, I have to leave, get a bit of recreation...like the motel room...time with a friend."

"I see."

"Do you? The graves I told you about. They're just down the hill. You see, they were bad people, but sometimes, even good people end up down there, if they know things they shouldn't, and there have been a few."

"Oh," Jim said, as if he had no idea what the bear was talking about.

"I don't make friends easily, and I may seem a little insincere. Species problems, all that. Sometimes, even people I like, well...It doesn't turn out so well for them. Know what I'm saying?"

"I...I don't think so."

"I think you do. That motel room back there, those whores. I been at this for years. I'm not a serial killer or anything. Ones I kill deserve it. The people I work for. They know how I am. They protect me. How's it gonna be an icon goes to jail? That's what I am. A fuckin' icon. So, I kinda get a free ride, someone goes missing, you know. Guys in black, ones got the helicopters and the black cars. They clean up after me. They're my homies, know what I'm saying?"

"Not exactly."

"Let me nutshell it for you: I'm pretty much immune to prosecution. But you, well...kind of a loose end. There's a patch down there with your name on it, Jimbo. I put a shovel in the car early this morning while you were sleeping. It isn't personal, Jim. I like you. I do. I know that's cold comfort, but that's how it is."

The bear paused, took off his hat and removed a small cigar from the inside hat band and struck a match and took a puff, said, "Thing is though, I can't get to liking someone too good, 'cause—"

The snapping sound made the bear straighten up. He was still holding his hat in his paw, and he dropped it. He almost made a turn to look at Jim, who was now standing right by him holding the automatic to the bump on the bear's noggin'. The bear's legs went out. He stumbled and fell forward and went sliding down the hill on his face and chest, a bullet snuggling in his brain.

Jim took a deep breath. He went down the hill and turned the bear's head using both hands, took a good look at him. He thought the bear didn't really look like any of the cartoon versions of him, and when he was on TV he didn't look so old. Of course, he had never looked dead before. The eyes had already gone flat and he could see his dim reflection in one of them. The bear's cigar was flattened against his mouth, like a coiled worm. Jim found the bear's box of matches and was careful to use a handkerchief from the bear's paw to handle it. He struck the match and set the dry grass on fire, then stuck the match between the bear's claws on his left paw. The fire gnawed patiently at the grass, whipping up enthusiasm as the wind rose. Jim wiped down the automatic with his shirt tail and put it in the bear's right paw using the handkerchief, and pushed the bear's claw through the trigger guard, and closed the bear's paw around the weapon so it looked like he had shot himself.

Jim went back up the hill. The fire licked at the grass and caught some more wind and grew wilder, and then the bear got caught up in it as well, chewing his fur and cackling over his flesh like a crazed hag. The fire licked its way down the hill, and then the wind changed and Jim saw the fire climbing up toward him.

He got in the car and started and found a place where he could back it around. It took some work, and by the time he managed it onto the narrow trail, he could see the fire in the mirror, waving its red head in his direction.

Jim drove down the hill, trying to remember the route. Behind him, the fire rose up into the trees as if it were a giant red bird spreading its wings.

"Dumb bear," he said aloud, "ain't gonna be no weenie pull now, is there?" and he drove on until the fire was just a small bright spot in the rearview mirror, and then it was gone and there was just the tall, dark forest that the fire had yet to find.

ZOMBIE SHARKS WITH METAL TEETH

STEPHEN GRAHAM JONES

It's supposed to be like killing a mouse, killing this mouse, that's what Ronald said, but it isn't.

'Ronald,' I say, trying to make my voice loop over my shoulder to him.

He's in his chair by the specimen refrigerator.

'Just do it,' he says.

'He's looking at me, though.'

Ronald's chair scrapes, air hisses through his teeth, and then he's there, with me.

'You're supposed to be a research *assistant*,' he says, taking the mouse from me, the syringe riding from its back like a tranquilizer dart, 'not a *trainee*.'

The mouse. I was thinking about naming him Mr. Cheese. Or Danger Bob, from his trick with the wheel.

Ronald slams the plunger down and it doesn't even have to be sodium pentathol. There's enough of it that it could be water, or even more blood: it floods Danger Bob's internal organs, stretches his skin taut so that it's pink under his white hair, like an old man going bald.

Sodium pentathol isn't really standard for mice, but neither's what Ronald had been doing to it for the last week.

He holds it up to his face, watches it die, and I think maybe Danger Bob is going to whisper something to him finally, some secret of biology, of rodent psychology, but then, instead, all we get is a drop of sodium pentathol seeping out Danger Bob's right nostril, spidering down to the end of a whisker.

Ronald drops the mouse cadaver— his term, like with everything— into the red biohazard bag and looks around the lab for the next great experiment, his eyes narrowing on each station, each cage, each device.

I hate my job.

In the supply room after work I mouth a silent prayer for Danger Bob, and nod again like I'm watching his trick on the wheel.

The next morning Ronald gets to the lab before me, leaves the door chocked open. I walk in slow, trying to see everything all at once, and Ronald's in his chair by the fridge, watching me.

"Good morning," he says.

I nod, shrug, tell him to tell me, please.

He's already smiling.

It's Danger Bob, back from the afterlife.

I take a long step back.

"He was sleeping by the door to his cage," Ronald says.

"This isn't Bob," I say.

"Ask him."

I watch his eyes after this, not sure I heard right.

"Ask Bob?"

Ronald nods.

"You could have just painted that on his back," I say.

Ronald agrees.

"Ask him," he says again.

I don't want to but I do.

"Louder," Ronald says, like it should be obvious.

"Are you Danger Bob?" I say, again, and it's only because I've been here for four months now that I notice Ronald's right hand is behind his back. His trigger finger. The vein in his neck rises with the tendons in his bicep when the mouse who isn't Danger Bob shakes his head no, and Ronald can't help laughing now.

There's a little white-furred, radio-controlled servo collar around Imposter Bob's neck, its copper leads wired into the neck musculature. So he can shake his head no.

"Quit fucking around," Ronald says, still smiling. "I've got something new for us today."

Some days I'm not sure who's the lab mouse.

The project Ronald was working on when he hired me involved applied telekinesis. What we would do is anesthetize gophers and moles and whatever else we could buy, sever their spinal cords up near their brain stems, then try to condition them to use their own bodies as puppets, lurch across the stainless steel exam table.

The servo collars were what Ronald had to finally use when the financial backers sent their people to check on their investments. It was then that Ronald told me the secret of funding: never do enough to make money, just do enough to get people to give you more.

He thinks when I empty the red biohazard bag, I empty it into the small green medical waste dumpster in the parking lot. But I don't. Instead I fill my pockets with dead rodents then go up onto the roof during break, lay the limp bodies in the white gravel. The hawks scream with delight, fall all around me, and take the moles and gophers and rabbits away. For the mice, because they're white, I have to push all the white gravel away, frame them against the tar. I tried standing them up with toothpicks at first, for dignity, but finally had to just lay them on their sides, their forelegs curled up against their chests.

We're going to hell, of course, me and Ronald. Not just for the animals we kill with truth serum and electricity and surgery, but for the birds that fall sick from the sky into the lives of ordinary people, far, far away, wherever they are.

What Ronald has for us today that's new is beyond telekinesis, beyond Danger Bob's faux-prehensile tail.

I watch him and listen and feel my face making expressions of doubt, then curiosity, then think of a green butterfly for a while, because now he's practicing his pitch on me. Everything bullet points, something Edison would have thought of if he'd had access to the formative experiences of Ronald's childhood.

Or if he'd hated mice.

The green butterfly is an angel, of course. She has the face of a girl I knew in high school.

I nod for Ronald, and for her.

What we're doing today is removing a late-stage mouse fetus from its mother then immersing it in the oxygen rich solution left over from the experiment with the two squirrels. Immersing it in there so it can breathe.

367

"Nutrients?" Ronald asks, as if I'd said it.

I nod, as if I'd just been about to say it, yes.

"They're in there," he says, dismissing my lack of education, staring at me to be sure I get the point.

"Sorry," I say. "Go on."

He smiles, does.

After the mouse— I'm already calling him Zipper Boy— after the mouse is successfully transferred to his glass womb, the fish tank the squirrels had died in, too stubborn to evolve gills, after the mouse is in there, that's when the real science begins: his arms in the long rubber gloves, Ronald will remove Zipper Boy's cartilage skull, exposing the still-developing brain.

He touches the side of his own head to be sure I'm following, not picturing myself on the roof, holding Zipper Boy up in my palm, eyes cast down, a great, moist shadow darkening around me, the underside of her wings iridescent.

I touch my own head back, right in the temple, and Ronald stares at me, looks away.

"The *folds*," he says, "it's the basic mammalian *characteristic*, right? Why are they there, though?"

"So the brain can fit," I say back.

He nods, smiles, says it again: "So the brain can fit. Because, if it didn't fold, then the mother's pelvis would break and there would be no rearing of the young, and it wouldn't matter *how* smart we were, *how* many tools we could *eventually* make."

I tell him okay.

He shrugs, like I'm challenging him. "So what do you think we could accomplish without that limitation?" he says, low, still paranoid that the bats that were delivered by accident are actually industrial spies.

I'm supposed to be catching them, but keep not doing it.

"Anything?" I say.

He nods.

"Anything," he says back, and then for the rest of the morning I have to hold the suction tube to Zipper Boy's head while Ronald performs minor surgery. I'm supposed to catch the blood, keep the water clear, cycle in more.

"Scuba Mouse," Ronald says, through his mask.

I shake my head no.

Two weeks later, Zipper Boy's brain blooms open in the tank like the enhanced pictures you see of distant, exploding galaxies.

I find myself holding my breath each morning in my car, before I walk in. It's not enough.

By the forty-second day, the investors want to see what they're paying for. I lay on the roof looking over the edge. Their cars pull up just before lunch. The only thing different for them about Ronald is how he's bald now, shaved. The eye solution he uses to hide the red around the rims is his own compound. He offers it to me on a regular basis, and on a regular basis I decline.

I walk down the metal stairs in time to hear his latest pitch for time travel, how of *course* you can't send living tissue through any kind of disintegrating field then expect it to be reassembled properly on the other end. But *inert* matter, yes. Ronald's solution is typically elegant: the time traveler should simply offer to be killed moments before passing through the field, moments *after* his team has pushed through all the medical equipment and information brochures the people on the other end will need to revive this dead man from the future, or the past.

I see one of the investors holding his chin, nodding, thinking of the tactical uses this could provide, but when he sees the way I'm looking at him he stops, rubs his cheek.

"Don't worry about him," Ronald says about me.

They don't.

Eight minutes later— the same amount of time it takes sunlight to get here— Ronald is demonstrating what they all saw last time: the modified television set he's learned to tune the future in with. One *hour* in the future, anyway. For the area right around the specimen table. He's not showing them the modified set so much, though, as what's on it's screen: the investors, all signing checks. It's really a tape of them from last time.

"Show us why, though," one of them says.

Why they'll sign. Ronald smiles, nods, is already standing amid all the bent silverware before Zipper Boy's tank, waiting for them to see it.

"Like he's a *god?*" one of the investors says, looking around for support. Like Zipper Boy's a god is what he's saying. One we bring offerings to.

Ronald shushes him, his teeth together.

"I don't think so . . . " another investor says, staring hard at Ronald, as if reading his eyes. "You didn't leave this for him did you, son?"

Ronald shakes his head no, his dimples sucking into a smile he's trying hard to swallow.

"No *way,*" the third and final investor says.

Ronald shrugs, is a carnival barker now, holding his hand out for the third investor's stainless steel, monogrammed pen.

Zipper Boy bends it into a nearly perfect circle with his unfolded mind, then, bored with it, allows it to clatter to the ground.

The milky surface of his water bubbles.

He could live forever in there.

The girlfriend I choose, because I want this all to be over but for it not to be my fault, she's ASPCA. Militant, probably a vegetarian even. I wear leather to get her to introduce herself, then lure her to my car, to lunch, a series of dinners and movies and phone calls, until one day, not on accident, I leave an expired rodent in my right hand pocket, plan to pull it out to open my car door with, only notice it's a mouse when its nose won't fit into the keyhole.

The movie we see that night is about a submarine family chosen, for obvious reasons, to be astronauts. Which is all good and fine until the mother has her third child, her first in space. The amniotic fluid floats through the space station and into the ventilation system, then, with the help of alien spores or cosmic rays— a movie device— transforms the whole station into a womb in which the family gestates, emerging nine months later to look down on earth's blue sphere, and cry, the vacuum of space wicking their tears away. Finally, the firstborn son flares the new membrane around his neck out and it catches the solar wind and the family holds hands, retreats into the outer reaches of the solar system, still together.

My girlfriend— Mandy, I think, if I heard right— cries with the aliens, holds my hand, and I hold onto the armrest.

Afterwards, by the water fountains, I try to tell her about Ronald but fail, just lead her out to the parking lot for my charade, which fails too when I open my pocket and, instead of a dead mouse, pale green butterflies flutter up around us.

Mandy starts to catch one but I stop her, and my hand firm around her wrist is the beginning of the end for us: that I would deny her that.

The next morning Ronald asks me how my experiment went?

I'm tapping vitamins into Zipper Boy's tank when he asks it, and I'm not sure if his lips move, or if they move with the words he's saying.

On the surface of the water, dead, is a pale green butterfly.

Love is a spoon, Zipper Boy says to me in my head.

Across the room, Ronald waits for me to answer, to agree.

Zipper Boy's brain is seventeen times the size of his body now.

We're not sure what he can do if he really wants to.

The thing I notice about the silverware on the ground that afternoon is that it's real silver. Which should be less of a challenge, really. An insult. Another thing is that it's straight, all of it. I bend down to it, know instantly without wanting to that this is Ronald's mother's mother's silverware. And that the only reason it would be straight, now, on the ground, is that Ronald brought it to Zipper Boy bent.

Across the lab, Ronald is hunched over the circuit board of the echolocation device he's retroengineering from the dolphin head he had delivered in a cooler of ice. It cost four thousand dollars, is supposed to locate the bats for us somehow. When I opened the cooler, the dolphin was smiling. But maybe that's all they know how to do.

I don't care about the bats, really.

But the silverware. The swimming goggles Ronald's wearing now, each lens sloshing with his compound.

Love is love, Zipper Boy says in my head, like he's finishing an argument.

Without looking at his tank I think back that he was never even *born*.

The surface of his water undulates with thought, and either he speaks back to me through Ronald or Ronald speaks back himself: "A mother's love for her unborn young is the purest love there is," he says. "Because it hasn't yet fallen victim to the large eyes of infancy."

I sweep up the bat guano until noon then climb the stairs to the roof.

Danger Bob is waiting for me. I cry into my hands, think maybe the whole world can see me up there.

"It's okay," Danger Bob says from behind his three-inch exhaust pipe, and to show, he scurries furiously across the white gravel, invisible until the last moment when his small body is about to silhouette itself against the low, brick-red retaining wall.

I see whiskers, the shadow of an ear, then look away.

In my pocket now is all of Ronald's mother's mother's silverware. I don't know what to do with it.

Two days later I find the first draft of the article Ronald's writing for the neuromags. In it, Zipper Boy is Scuba Mouse, and I've been betrayed.

Beside me, too, I can feel Zipper Boy watching me.

It's something Ronald's tracked in his article— how his Scuba Mouse is now discovering his body, learning to use it, look through it. In a footnote, Ronald sketches out the helmet he's going to build his Scuba Mouse. It's filled with water, a failed diving bell. There will be no leash, either, no air hose, no tether. Just a mouse, teetering out into the world, wholly unaware what love is, even.

Already all the other caged rodents in the lab are dead, overflowing from the red biohazard container.

Ronald says Zipper Boy tells him it's not murder, because they were never really *alive*.

He's the one talking to a mouse now. I don't tell that to him, just shrug, look away, at a bat crawling nose first down the wall, stalking a cricket.

Ronald throws the dolphin head at it, misses.

My hand is shaking from something— from *this*.

When Ronald collects his precious dolphin head he finds the cricket lodged in the basal ganglia and stares at it for an unhealthy period of time. Embarrassed, I look away. Zipper Boy's water is 92 degrees Fahrenheit. The phone rings fourteen times, and fourteen times, we don't answer it.

When the human race ends, this is the way it will happen, I know.

That night I kidnap Mandy a little bit then sit with her— bound hand and foot in the trunk of my car— and watch the city bats coalesce above the three-inch exhaust pipe of the lab. Insects are swirling up out of it, clockwise, and I smile, rename the insects *manna bug*, *moses beetle*, and realize I can't take Mandy into this place. That I either love her too much or I could love her too much, which, really, is the same thing.

I inject her with a non-lethal dose of sodium pentathol and lead her into her building, careful not to ask her any questions, even in a disguised voice. Her doorman takes her without question, nods to me once, and I fade back into the night.

The green butterfly from the girl in high school was the one I found on her windshield one day at lunch, when I'd finally got my nerve up to wait for her, say something.

From across town Zipper Boy says into my head, in her voice, *Hungry there?* and I sulk away, my hands in my pockets.

Love isn't a spoon, I say back to him from the parking lot, the next morning, and this time when I walk in Ronald has the dolphin head on a long, metal stick.

"Scarecrow," he says, about it, then explains in his most offhand voice how bats are really just mice with wings, meaning the mouse part of their brains must still remember the long winters spent under the snow, walking lightly, because the coyotes were up there somewhere, listening, listening, finally slinking off to the water's edge, for clam, then fish, then they keep going out deeper and deeper, testing their lungs, until they're dolphins. "Look at the teeth," he says, running his finger along the dolphin's jaw line.

I close my eyes to think.

"They— they weren't coyotes then, though," I say, pinching the bridge of my nose between the thumb and forefinger of my right hand.

"Doesn't matter," Ronald says. "They didn't know they were mice then either, right?"

He stares at me until I nod, hook my chin to the tank.

"You fed him already?"

He shrugs— maybe, maybe not. This is kindergarten. The new title of his article on Zipper Boy is "Tidings from the Tidal Pool." Even I know it won't translate well— that, being a scientific article, it *needs* to— but before I can tell him, something pops above our heads.

Ronald doesn't look up from his paper. I have to.

"Security," he says.

It's a row of cameras, motion activated. *Bat*-activated.

"What?" I ask.

Ronald shrugs. "Scuby here says their REM patterns are— unusual for rodents. Like how when a dog dreams about chasing a car, its leg will kick?"

"Maybe it's having a karate dream."

"Whatever. It's a luxury bats don't have, right? One kick, they're falling . . ." He shrugs again, already bored with this. " . . . think it has something to do with circulation to their brain. Probably need to get an opossum in here to see, though— upside down, all that. It's a marsupial, though, I don't know . . ."

"I'm not doing it," I tell him.

"What?"

"Sleeping upside down."

"I'm not asking."

"Okay."

"Well."

"Yeah."

I work at my table counting salmon eggs into vials, careful to keep my back to the leering dolphin.

Love isn't a spoon, I know. It's got to be something, though

That night while I'm gone, Ronald somehow manages to spray the dolphin head with liquid nitrogen, to keep it from rotting.

Over lunch, from his office, I call Mandy's work number to report a crime but she doesn't answer. I hang up, hold the phone there for what I know is too long.

Through the plate glass of Ronald's open-air cubicle, Zipper Boy watches me, manages to rewind my memory to the movie about the submarine family then play it again, without the zero-g amniotic fluid. This time, the birth is achieved through a primitive but functional teleportation device: one moment, the baby isn't there, and the next it is, the mother's stomach already deflating, the father guiding it back down like deflating a raft.

I shake my head no, don't want to see anymore, but Zipper Boy forces it on me, in me, and I have to watch this infant grow into an adolescent who appears normal until we follow him into his cabin. There, he reads books on what appropriate emotional reactions are to certain social stimuli, then, as a young man, standing over the father he's just slain, we understand that the reason he is the way he is is that he was denied the essential violence of birth. That his whole life he's been searching for that.

It's Zipper Boy's story. He's never been born either.

I'm sorry, I think to him, but it's too late, he's dreaming with the bats again, flitting with them through their night made of sound, his small, atrophied feet perfectly still.

I envy him, a little. But the rest of me knows what's happening.

The mechanism I'm reduced to is ridiculously simple, as most are: I simply take Ronald's mother's mother's silverware down to the pawn shop, get a ticket for it, then leave it on the bulletin board.

Ronald sees it first thing after lunch, stares at it, and walks away, then comes back again and again, until he looks across the room to me.

"You do this?" he says.

"We needed supplies," I tell him.

Zipper Boy's water gurgles. Ronald looks from it to me.

"*Supplies?*" he says.

"Guess the lab fairy skipped us this month," I say back.

Ronald smiles; it's what he told me my first week here, when I forgot to pick up everything he'd ordered—that the *lab fairy* wasn't going to bring it, was she?

I have no idea what Zipper Boy is telling him.

Ronald shrugs, stands, looking in the direction of the pawn shop already.

"It wasn't really as great as you thought it was," he says, in parting. "Number four's trick."

Danger Bob, on his wheel.

My right hand wraps itself into a fist and I have to look away, swallow hard. Science isn't cold. Not even close.

Ronald laughs on his way out, trailing his fingers over his shoulder.

"Stay off the roof, too," he calls back. "I think it's shaking the cameras."

I stare at him until he's gone then track up to the cameras. Because there's no way in a world of brick and stone that my footsteps could come through the ceiling. But Ronald was just saying that, I see now; what he wanted me to see was that each camera is on one of the old, radio-controlled servos. That he still has the trigger out in the parking lot. That the guidewires their board is hanging from are the perfect antenna. That he's going to be documenting whatever I wanted him out of the lab for.

Zipper Boy smiles, with his real mouth. His teeth dull from disuse. From never-use.

But his mind.

I take a step towards his tank and the room fills with pale green butterflies, the dust on their wings graphite-fine, and I have to breathe it, can hear the cameras snapping me in sequence, one after another, down the board, and the butterflies start to fill me. Light-headed.

But no.

Like the girl from high school said, *meant*, I take the first one I can catch, take it between my teeth, and swallow, and then the next, and the next, until they're all gone, and I say it to Zipper Boy. That every experiment needs a control. Someone to exercise it. That I understand that now.

He's just staring at me now.

Love, he says in my head.

You understand, I say back. *That's why I'm doing this. Please.*

In his water, for me, Zipper Boy tries to do Danger Bob's trick with the wheel, to save himself, but he's not a mouse anymore, and there's no wheel anyway, and it's too late in the game for gymnastics to save us from what we're doing here.

The tears he cries for himself are bubbles of carbon dioxide— spent breath, his infant lungs still new, uncoordinated. The bubbles seep from the corner of his eye, collect on the surface of his water, and he nods, looks away to make this easy on me, but it's not.

Through the cameras, in what will be time-capture, Ronald is watching me, a future Ronald, an hour-from-now Ronald, and I'm sitting by him, trying to explain, to keep my job.

Listen, Zipper Boy says. It's a kindness and I do, and the-me-from-then knows, has it right: what I have to do now is what I can feel myself already doing—move my arms from the wrist, my legs from the foot, my head from the chin, so that, on film, when I take the salt shaker, empty it into the tank, it will look like suicide. Like Zipper Boy had made me his puppet. Chose me instead of Ronald because I was weaker.

It's a thing Ronald could buy. That he would buy.

But then, without meaning too— scientific curiosity, the reason I responded to Ronald's ad in the first place, maybe—I look too long, another hour into the future, past him accepting my explanation for homicide, to the way he stands up from his chair smiling, holding one of the early bat-dream negatives up to the light, so that the colors are reversed. This is one of the images from the camera on the end of the board, which was aimed wrong. Instead of the bats, it had been snapping pictures of the dolphin head, only—looking along his arm I can see it in the modified television set— the dolphin's teeth in the reverse-color image are silver, silver nitrate, *metal*, and from the angle the camera was at the dolphin isn't even a dolphin anymore, but a predator that can never die, not if Ronald builds it right, this time. Not if it keeps moving.

THE PLANTING

BENTLEY LITTLE

I planted her panties by moonlight.
  I watered them with piss.

The desire came over me suddenly, although where it came from or how I got the knowledge, I could not say. One day she was my neighbor, the nice mom next door, and the next I was climbing over our shared fence into her backyard while she went to pick up her youngest from preschool. The family's laundry was hanging from the line, children's clothes mostly, but her underwear was pinned behind a row of small jeans, and I carefully inspected each of them before picking a pair of pink bikini briefs. I folded them carefully, crotch-up, then put them in my pocket and climbed back over the fence.

I was in my front yard setting up the sprinkler when she came home, and I waved to her and the little boy as they walked into their house for lunch.

That night, I went into the woods, dug a hole at the foot of an old oak and planted the panties.

It was a drought year, and the bears were coming down. Mike Heffernon saw one over on Alta Vista, and the police had to take one out who sat in the center of Arbor Circle and refused to budge. People in town were warned to stay away from uninhabited areas, and the Forest Service not only put fire restrictions on the campgrounds but closed them entirely, along with the hiking trails.

But I still went into the woods on each night that the moon was out and pissed on the spot where I'd buried her panties, waiting to see what would grow.

Her name was Anna. Anna Howell. And despite the fact that she was in her late-thirties/early-forties, at least ten years older than me, and a mother of three, she was still the most beautiful woman I had ever seen. Mine was an objective appreciation, however. I didn't covet her, had no plans to try and seduce her, no fantasies about having an affair with her, neither her face nor body entered my thoughts when I masturbated alone at night.

But I was still compelled to steal her panties and plant them, and the impulse to water them when the moon was out was always with me, a vague urge that was almost—but not quite—sexual.

Sometimes I thought of her panties when I masturbated, lying crumpled in a ball in the wet dank ground, deteriorating.

And it made me come much faster.

There was a circle of old cabins out past Dripping Springs in one of those pockets of private land in the middle of the national forest. I'd heard that it had once been a resort—or that the onetime owner had tried to make it into a resort—but it had failed and been abandoned long before my time, and now was the type of place that local kids said was haunted. I didn't know if it really was haunted, but it was certainly a spot that bums might make their own or that drug dealers might find desirable: remote, isolated, far from civilization and the prying eyes of others.

Because it was technically on private land, when a late-summer lightning fire started and word came down that the cabins were burning, they called out the volunteer fire department rather than have the Forest Service put it out—which would have been the most logical thing to do. But, as usual, jurisdictional concerns trumped common sense, and shortly after midnight the ten of us were speeding down the control road through mile after mile of oak and juniper and ponderosa pine, between rugged bluffs and rolling hills, in and out of hidden gorges and seasonal stream-carved canyons, until we reached the flat land on the other side of Dripping Springs.

The cabins were gone when we got there, little more than charred piles of ash hemmed in by black and still-burning sections of frame. Luckily, a dirt road circling the perimeter of the old resort had acted as a break and contained the fire somewhat, keeping it from setting the entire forest ablaze. A lone finger stretch of brush on the north end was burning brightly and had created the only real problem we had to face, but we had ten men, two trucks and full pumpers—and even if we ran out of water, we had snake hoses long enough to tap any nearby creek, spring or pond we could find.

We set to work.

It was nearly morning before we finished, the sky in the east brightening enough to turn the trees into silhouettes by the time the last of the flames were extinguished. Blue-white smoke rose from the ashes around us, dimming the sun as the day dawned and we finished repacking the trucks. Through the haze, I saw a building behind the burned brush, a cabin of rough hewn wood that looked more ancient than the old growth trees surrounding it, although I did not understand how that could be possible. Either the cabin had not been there before or else the fire had cleared out the brush that hid it from view because none of us had seen it previously. I stepped closer to get a better look, then immediately stepped back. The façade of the windowless structure bespoke great age, and there was about it an air of dread and unsettled malevolence that shook me more than I was willing to admit.

"God lives there," Andre said, sidling next to me.

I looked at him askance. "What the hell are you talking about?"

"That's always been the rumor. That God lives out here. That's why there's no graffiti, no beer bottles or syringes or cigarette butts or McDonald's bags. Everyone's always been afraid to come out this way because God is here. And watching."

"You knew about this cabin?"

"Not this cabin exactly. But I knew God's home was in these woods, somewhere near the resort, and when I saw this place, I knew this was it."

"Yeah," Rossi said. "And the Easter Bunny's vacation house is right behind it."

The rest of us laughed, but Andre remained resolute in his conviction, and I had to admit that his somber certitude freaked me out a little. If it had only been the two of us, I would have acceded to his wishes, left the cabin alone and we would have returned to town. But there were others here, and they were curious, so I had to be curious, and I joined the group as we made our way over the still smoldering ashes across the charred dirt to the ancient shack.

It was small, I saw as we approached. Not small as in limited square footage —although it was that, too—but small as in short, as though it had been made for people not as tall as we were. The top of the front door was just about eye level. I reached up and was able to place my hand on the roof.

The door was stuck but unlocked, and after several shoulder shoves, it opened, scraping the dirty wooden floor. I'd been expecting a one-room cabin based on the exterior of the structure, but instead we found ourselves in a narrow hallway that ran the width of the structure. We filed in one by one, Mick and Garcia and Big Bill and Ed Barr flipping on their flashlights, all of us ducking, and it occurred to me that this would be a perfect place for an ambush, that some psycho could be lying in wait just around the corner and take us out one-by-one as we stepped into the next room. There were no cries of shock or pain, however, only the ordinary speech of continued conversation as my stooping fellow firefighters rounded the end of the hallway.

I followed, and once again, I was surprised. The cabin went back far deeper than its exterior façade would indicate, and the long room in which we found ourselves sloped steeply downward from the door, with the ceiling at the entrance barely above five feet and that at the opposite end twelve to fifteen feet high. The room had obviously been dug into the ground at an angle, but there were no windows, the floor was wood as were the walls, and that gave the room the appearance of space that grew as it moved away from us, like the optical illusion of an amusement park haunted shack.

"It's like a fuckin' fun house," Big Bill said, shining his light around.

Andre remained silent.

We clomped down the sloping floor in our heavy boots. There was furniture only on the sides of the room: two twin tables with collections of nearly identical gray rocks arranged on their dusty tops. Though it stretched back far, the room was half the width of the hallway, so there had to be another chamber behind the wall to our left, although no way to enter it from this room. In front of us, however, a closed door was built into the back wall, a construct of solid wood hewn from a single section of tree that had been bolted to the surrounding planks. It had no handle or knob, no visible means by which it might be opened, and there was something both secretive and intriguing about the tightly sealed entrance. It was Ed Barr who said what all of us were thinking: "Let's see what's back there."

"No!" Andre said, and there was fear in his voice.

"This building's obviously abandoned, the area around it's burned to a crisp, let's break down the door and see what's behind it."

"You can't!" Andre shouted.

"Out of the way." Rossi pushed him aside and hefted his ax.

Andre actually started crying, and that, more than anything else, creeped me out. Standing half-underground in an ancient windowless cabin in front of a knobless door watching a grown man the size of a football player sob was just plain unnerving, and at that moment I wanted to get the hell out of there.

The door was tough and it took several swings, but Rossi finally managed to smash a hole through the wood large enough to put his hand and arm through. There was an inside latch, and he used it to open the door. Four flashlights shone into the darkness, and there was sudden silence as we saw what lay in the small dank room beyond.

It was a mummified creature of some sort, a wrinkled shriveled figure that looked like a dried black monkey. The skin of its face had been pulled back from its skull, and it appeared to be grinning, its sharp rotted teeth exposed in a way that made it seem insanely gleeful. It was seated on the floor of the small room, next to a small pile of those gray rocks. Behind it, a rounded section of the wall had been bleached white, as though exposed to harsh sunlight or radiation.

Andre fell to his knees in front of the monkey thing like some primitive tribesman worshipping a stone idol. Rossi dropped his ax and followed suit. I would have laughed, but I could see similar expressions of awe on the faces of the others, and I have to admit that I felt something myself. I thought of Anna Howell's buried panties, and at that moment I wished that I had not stolen them, had not planted them, had not peed on them. I was filled with an emptiness, a sadness, a sense that I had gone off track somewhere, that I had lost something that should have been very important to me. The feeling radiating from the dead creature was one of great sorrow, and its mood affected my own, made me want to get the hell out of there as quickly as possible.

And then . . .

Something changed.

I don't know what it was, if it came from that mummified creature in the middle of the floor, if it came from my fellow firemen or if it was simply a figment of my imagination, but the sadness I felt was suddenly replaced by fear, a cold bone-deep terror that left me rooted in place, filled with the certainty that all of us were doomed, that we would never leave this place but would spent eternity in this tiny room with that hideous black monkey.

To my left, Ed Barr let out a strangled stifled cry. Andre was sobbing, though from religious fervor or despair it was impossible to tell. Garcia's flashlight dimmed, went out. Big Bill's and the others followed suit and moments later we were in darkness, an inky jet so deep and penetrating that I could not tell whether my eyes were open or closed. I stood there, stock still, waiting for the end. Someone cried out. Someone else giggled. There were more noises, more cries, and I felt soft fingers gently stroking my hand and then teeth sink painfully into my right calf.

I have no idea how much time we spent in that place, but by the time we emerged, the sun was high in the sky. Everyone was disheveled. Big Bill was naked.

We left the mummy there, sealing up the room as best we could with additional branches and mud from a small slough to the side of the shack. That was Andre's idea, and the rest of the brigade went along with it, some more willingly than others. I wanted to burn the fucking place down—whatever that dried black creature was, it did not deserve to exist—but I knew I was a minority of one and kept my feelings to myself. It would be enough just to get away from here and make sure that I never came anywhere near that cabin and its horrid occupant again.

I quit the volunteer fire department a few days after.

So did Rossi.

So did Ed Barr.

And though we saw each other on almost a daily basis, we didn't talk about it, didn't ask each other why, didn't discuss what we'd seen, what had happened in that shack.

A week later, Andre killed himself. Ate his shotgun in the woods.

And we didn't talk about that either.

After that, the panties sprouted. I was standing in front of the oak tree when the moon finally reemerged after a week of cloudy nights, and I saw a pale shoot poking upward through the mulchy dirt, a blue-white almost gelatinous tendril that was clearly growing, aspiring to some greater form.

What would it be, I wondered, when it reached maturity?

I pulled out my pecker and pissed on it.

I saw Anna Howell the next day, waved to her over the fence while she hung her laundry out to dry, tried not to look at the underwear she was pinning on the clothesline. She smiled at me, waved back, said it was a nice day, and if she suspected that I had stolen a pair of her panties she did an amazing job of hiding it.

I slunk back inside and realized that I had some soul searching to do. What exactly did I want from that thing I was growing in the forest? As much as I admired and recognized Anna Howell's beauty, I still did not desire her, and I did not think that I was growing the woman for a sex partner, as a substitute for the real McCoy.

The woman.

I said it to myself for the first time, admitting what I had known subconsciously all along—that I was growing a person from Anna Howell's panties.

A woman.

But why?

That was still not clear to me, though I felt the impulse to continue even more strongly than I had before. My every waking moment seemed consumed with the thought of my secret in the woods, and I got through each boring day only with the knowledge that at night, if there was a moon, I would be able to visit my spot at the foot of the oak where I had buried my neighbor's freshly laundered underwear in the soft and fertile soil.

The next time I saw the sprout, it had a face. Under the moonlight, it had grown to nearly two feet high and now had the vague contours of a woman. Although they were closed, there were eyes, and while there was no nose to speak of, the thing had Kewpie doll lips pursed in an unappealing fashion that needed only color to grant them authenticity. Small nubs halfway down the form looked as though they would eventually differentiate themselves into hands and arms.

It seemed wrong to water the figure at this stage of its growth, so I turned my back and relieved my bladder on a bush, then zipped up and crouched down before the oak tree to look at what I'd wrought. The sight was horrible, a travesty of humanity so fundamentally unnatural that my first impulse should have been to destroy it. But instead I sat on my haunches and examined its emerging form. The figure was small but perfectly in proportion rather than dwarflike, and despite the garish elements of its evolving face, I could tell that it would grow into a beautiful woman. Looking closely, I could see a slight indentation that would become the vaginal cleft, two small bumps that would expand into breasts. It was composed of that same translucent bluish-white material, a slimy looking substance that shone in the moonlight and appeared sticky to the touch. I wanted to reach out and press my finger against the shiny skin to see if it felt the way it looked, but I did not want to jeopardize the form's growth by tainting it with my touch, so I refrained.

The night air was moist and dewy, the ground itself damp, but I wondered if that would be enough to keep the budding woman watered and facilitate her growth. I looked at the nascent crotch, thought about what Anna Howell's own vagina must look like under her panties and found myself thinking that I should masturbate on the figure to provide it with moisture and nutrients.

I stood, pulled down my pants, took my penis in hand and started stroking, my head filled with dark thoughts, my fantasy scenario one of depraved perversity, but at the last minute I pulled away, spurting all over a lushly growing fern rather than onto that blue-white flesh, grunting with animal abandon as I emptied my loins on the hapless plant.

The pursed colorless lips seemed to me to be almost smiling.

I arrived home long after midnight, too wound and wired to sleep, my head filled with ideas I did not want to acknowledge, my body wracked with impulses I dared not act upon. Under a lone lamp in the living room, I read the local paper which had been delivered with the mail that afternoon. On the front page was a photo of Giff McCarty, head ranger for the region. He was wearing a woman's wig and thick mascara, his dark lipstick obvious even through the black-and-white newsprint. FOREST SERVICE OFFICIAL ACCUSED OF MOLESTATION, the banner headline read, and I suddenly understood why we had been called to put out the fire at the old resort. I remembered what had happened inside that shack

God lives there

and saw the madness in the old ranger's eyes, the whorishly roughed cheeks bookending his carefully drawn lips, and I crumpled up the paper and made my way to bed.

In my dream, I was standing at the dirty urinal of an old gas station—Enco, Richfield, Gulf, one of those chains that no longer existed—and next to me, at the adjacent urinal, was a wino, a filthy man with wild gray hair and an unkempt beard, wearing a greasy topcoat and smelling of spilled beer and sewer stink. He was nearly a head shorter than me, and when I glanced over at him, he winked. I saw that he was peeing not in the urinal but on the tiled floor between his shoes. From the growing puddle on the chipped stained tile slithered reptilian creatures of every hue and color, horrid creatures with too many legs, small sickening monsters with multiple eyes but no legs at all, formless pulsating slime that inched wormlike toward me.

"The piss of life," the old man said, cackling. "It's the piss of life."

And in the instant before I woke up, I realized that he was God.

I made myself stay away after that.

There was nothing I wanted more than to go out into the woods and continue to care for the budding being I had created, to monitor its growth by moonlight and experience the joy of watching it blossom. But I knew those drives were not mine, I knew they had been imposed on me, and as desperately as I desired to sneak into the forest in the dead of night, I forced myself to remain indoors, trying in vain to fall asleep, fighting the urge to check on the status of the woman I had grown.

Finally, however, I could no longer resist, and exactly two weeks after my last visit, I once again found myself slipping between the trees under the cover of night.

The danger warnings had been heightened over the past week. Two bears had come down into the town, one of them killing a collie, and a mountain lion had mangled a cache of stuffed animals that had inadvertently been left out on a back porch at night. But I was not thinking rationally as I made my way into the woods. I was not thinking at all. I'd made no conscious decision to return, I simply found myself walking through the forest to the old oak, the action as involuntary and devoid of thought as taking a breath.

It was gone.

There was a hole at the foot of the tree, a ragged cavity roughly the size of a woman that was lined with old leaves and a twisted net of roots and smelled of raw sewage. I searched around for footprints or a trail of slime or something that would indicate to me in which direction she had headed, but I was not a woodsman or a tracker, and the forest looked the same to me as it always had.

Staring into the white netted roots that formed the womanly contours of the hole, I was reminded of something I'd seen before, a specific sight or image that nagged at the corner of my mind begging to be identified. The roots were clearly of the same substance that had formed the woman, but their bleached quality, as though they'd been exposed to a blast of radiation or a blinding burst of sunlight, reminded me of another scene entirely.

I stepped closer, peered into the bottom of the space and saw a rotted piece of panty held down by several small gray rocks.

It was the rocks that jiggled my memory.

I suddenly knew where I had to go.

I ran through the trees back to my neighborhood, back to my house, then hopped in my old Jeep and sped down the control road through hills and canyons and forest, braking to a dusty stop on the flat land past Dripping Springs where the resort had been.

I got out of the Jeep. The door of the shack was open, and though the moon was temporarily behind a cloud, leaving the woods in darkness, a soft yellowish light spilled from the small rectangular entryway, granting the surrounding brush a disturbing malevolence.

The last time I had been here, it had been with the fire brigade. That had been scary enough. But now I was all alone, and though part of me wanted to turn tail and run, the part of me that had quit the fire department and vowed never to return to this spot, another more instinctual portion of my brain was urging me forward.

I'm out of here, I could imagine Rossi saying. But Rossi was not here. No one else was here. And though I didn't really want to, I walked up to the shack, ducked into the doorway.

There were candles lighting the hallway that ran the width of the structure, even more candles in the long narrow room that sloped down to the chamber containing the mummified monkey thing.

God lives there

Like the doorway to the shack, the entrance to the back chamber was open, as though waiting for me, and I accepted the invitation and stepped inside.

There were no candles here, but the entire room was suffused with a rosy glow that reminded me of those Victorian prostitute's lamps with scarves and stockings thrown over them, although there was no lamp in sight and indeed the illumination did not have an identifiable source.

I stopped just inside the doorway. A naked woman was seated next to the desiccated mummy on a wooden bench that looked older than the earth itself, and there was something about the way she reclined next to the diminutive figure, something about the way her arm was wrapped about its small skeletal shoulder that bespoke intimacy. They're married, I thought, and the second the idea occurred to me, I knew it was true. She was the wife of that thing. She had always been its intended.

The woman's skin was no longer a slimy bluish white. Instead it was the soft peach of a newborn infant, its fresh color emphasized by the mysterious rose lighting of the chamber. She had blonde hair like Anna Howell, and her pubic hair was blond, too. Which made the dried blackened features of the creature next to her seem that much more grotesque. The face of that monkey and its hideously gleeful rictus had haunted my nightmares, and I looked now upon that dead parchment skin pulled back from those sharp rotted teeth and felt the same fear I had before. The fear was not tempered by the presence of the foolishly grinning woman next to it. If anything, the juxtaposition of the two was even more frightening.

The woman nodded at me, wiggling the fingers of her free hand.

She wasn't a real person, I had to remind myself. She had sprouted from the panties. I had grown her.

As I watched, she spread her legs wide, and from the shadowed cleft between her thighs came flowers, an endless bouquet that flowed out like water from a spring, a floral fountain that cascaded over the edge of the chair onto the floor in an almost liquid wave, covering the dirt and the small gray rocks so completely that the floor of the chamber was buried beneath a rainbow of color. I smelled the perfume of my mother, my grandmother, my aunts and cousins, my teachers, every girlfriend I had ever had. The scents of all women were tied up in that olfactory cornucopia, each of the wonderful flowery fragrances triggering memories of the females in my life, and I was momentarily overwhelmed by nostalgia that was at once happily welcome and profoundly sad.

The blackened figure had not changed its expression—it couldn't change its expression—but emotion still emanated from its unmoving form, and the feeling I got from it now was one of gratitude. I had given it a wife, and it was thankful.

God was no longer alone.

That was crazythinking. I knew this wasn't God. It wasn't even a god. Yet there was no doubt in my mind that the emotion washing over me was real, and though no words were spoken, no thoughts or images transmitted to me, I suddenly understood that the mummified creature wanted to show its gratitude.

In my mind, I saw Andre falling to his knees in worshipful adoration, and I thought about what had happened in this room after the lights went out. Once again, I was filled with that permeating sense of evil and doom.

I knew I should get out of there as quickly as possible, run out of the shack and back to my Jeep, drive back home and never even look at the woods again. But I found myself staring at the flowers still flowing from between the woman's legs, and my mind was soothed by the emotion spreading outward from her immobile companion.

God is grateful

I thought about my empty existence, my boring job and nonexistent lovelife, all of the pointless routines that made up my usual day.

I considered several possibilities.

Then made a wish.

The feeling imparted to me now from the desiccated monkey was one of approbation, but when I looked at the mismatched faces of the couple on the bench I felt colder than I ever had in my life. The fear was back, stronger than ever, and I knew instantly and with utter certainty that I had just made a huge mistake, the biggest mistake of my life. My first impulse was to try and take it back, to drop to my knees and beg for another chance, a do-over. But I knew that was not possible.

I thought for a moment, then picked up a flower that smelled like my mother, turned away, and walked out of the chamber, out of the shack, into the darkness, tears streaming down my face.

And as I headed toward the spot where I'd parked the Jeep, I wondered what went through Andre's mind at the second he pulled the trigger.

SURF GRIZZLIES

DAVID W. BARBEE

Tua was tending bar when the Surf Grizzlies came.

Some countries didn't let their twelve-year-olds have jobs, much less jobs serving a cornucopia of alcoholic beverages to clueless white people. But the Dongo Isles was a tiny little nation on the Pacific Rim suckling at the teat of international tourism, so the grownups figured that if Tua had a knack for serving mojitos to the rich tourists, then they should let the boy earn a living.

His bar was a square tiki hut up on the beach. Tua served his patrons, who slouched on their stools nursing afternoon buzzes, and they all cheered and complimented his precocious bartender act. The boy only shrugged at their sly compliments.

The beach was full of umbrellas and tents and recreational junk. There were tons of people with sizzling bare skin, lounging about and building sandcastles. Swimmers floated on boogie boards and foam noodles out in the salty waves.

But then it happened.

Cresting over the horizon on a giant tidal wave came the Surf Grizzlies.

Surf Grizzlies rode the waves across every ocean of the world, an army of massive bears on surfboards. Their origin was a mystery, and no one ever knew where or when they would show up. All anyone could be sure of was that the Surf Grizzlies only took to shore when they were hungry.

Tua saw hundreds of them, roaring loudly over the sound of the crashing waves. They stood square on their boards, dark fur spiky with wetness, and roared as they closed in on the beach. Tua hurried across his tiki hut and grabbed a megaphone from under the bar.

"Surf Grizzlies!" he announced, and then ducked down under the bar. Everyone was on their own now.

The bar patrons scattered. Some down on the beach looked out and saw the giant bears riding the wave. There were screams. Panic. Those quick enough to understand what was happening began stampeding up the beach away from the water. Swimmers frantically paddled for shore, the strong ones kicking past the slow. Children were left behind.

As the wave behind them grew bigger, the bears rode their boards down the swell, closing in on the beach. A Grizzly that had to be six hundred pounds ripped ahead of the pack, zigging and zagging toward the swimmers. The beast grabbed a small child in its maw and bit into its skull, sending blood and brains exploding out. The beast whipped the corpse back and forth in its jaws and then dropped it into the rushing water as it surfed towards bigger game.

More of the bears charged in towards the beach, crushing swimmers under their thick boards and slicing bodies in half with swipes of their great claws. The bears roared again in unison and more of them spilled onto the beach as the wave crashed down.

Dozens of bears made landfall and abandoned their boards to chase down any humans straggling behind. They killed dozens of people and the tide surged red from the carnage.

Overall, most of the people escaped into the jungle or for the safety of the resort. The bears roared after them but didn't follow. Tua looked up from his hiding place behind the bar. The bears were standing on their hind legs and sticking their surfboards into the sand. Then they turned and ambled up the beach towards him.

Tua had heard stories of the Surf Grizzlies. They hated walking on land, and wouldn't stay on the island long. Just long enough for a quick drink.

As they came up to the tiki hut, Tua began mixing up mai tais. The bears grunted at him and he served up their drinks in a hurry. The Surf Grizzlies drank and roared and Tua managed to keep all of them happy, even as their entire pack crowded around his bar. He mixed cosmos and kamikazes as fast as he could to prevent being eaten.

The Surf Grizzlies got royally and savagely drunk over the next hour.

Just before Tua ran out of alcohol, the Surf Grizzlies left his bar and took to their boards. They surfed away into the sunset, leaving the Dongo Isles behind. Tua didn't know if he'd ever see a Surf Grizzly attack again. But he hoped that whatever place the bears struck next would be stocked with plenty of booze.

THE MISFIT CHILD GROWS FAT ON DESPAIR

TOM PICCIRILLI

Fate arrives disguised as choice.

As if you could actually say, *Screw this, I'm out of here*, or just get down on your knees like everybody else.

But John's got to shrug and go, "Hmmm." He knows that even here at the end of the line, holding his pitiful check for $188.92—boss took out $40 for the broken dishes even though he was the one who slopped soapy water onto the kitchen floor—watching the teller tremble with the eleven-gauge in her face, standing behind some weight lifter with muscles coming out of his asshole and piss pooling over his shoes, and despite what he knows is going to happen after this, John realizes Mr. Teddy Bear has got to be eaten.

Teddy doesn't like how slow the terrified twenty-year-old teller is moving and continues shrieking at her, "Move it. Hurry, goddamn you, hurry! I saw that! You put a dye pack in there? Did you?"

Of course, she hasn't; she can't even move or speak, hyperventilating like that. She's too much a daughter of television and can't do anything much besides keep her arms straight up over her head and pray to Christ in Spanish. The gray stretch marks on her underarms clearly mark how much weight she's gained and lost after her first couple of kids, but her pouty full lips are especially sexy now, the lower one quivering with the name of Jesus.

Teddy's rubber bear mask doesn't fit him all that well. His beard is so thick that the mask won't rest flush against the steep angles and planes of his contorted face. It lifts an inch or more whenever he speaks, which allows the sweat that's been puddling in the curves and hollows of the rubber to drip out all at once. Spittle works its way out of the thin mouth slit. Ted tries to wipe his eyes clear, the back of his hand mopping the bulging forehead of the growling bear head.

Teddy's partner, Mr. Lucifer, might hold things together for another minute or two—if only his easy, muted voice can settle the situation long enough to soothe Teddy and the frantic teller. He's got to get the other cowering folks in the bank to follow his orders, lay down on their bellies, hit no silent alarms, and just face the walls.

"Ladies and gentleman, hush please." The devil repeats himself twice more, and a respectful amount of Southern flavor seeps out of his hanging cadence, friendly and mannered like he might be talking to a group at a church social. His red mask has curved horns, a wide smile, and pencil-thin mustache. The voice matches it perfectly.

"Gentleman and sweet ladies, if you'll let us get on with this, we'll be gone in no time a'tall. This here is government money we're taking, not yours. We're workingmen, too. Now just lay back and relax, and we'll all be on with our day before you know it."

"It's a dye pack. I saw it!" Teddy shrieks, hitting a high note that rings around the small enclosed room, picking up speed. There! There it is!"

John is the only bank patron still on his feet, but the smash-and-grab thieves haven't noticed him standing there yet, as two old women and the weight lifter sob against the floorboards. John is a prime three hundred eighty-four pounds of graceful obesity and dire energy, almost as wide as he is tall (about five seven), dressed entirely in black: well-ironed jeans, a fine button-up, long-sleeve shirt and tie, standing so near the lacquered bank slip table in the center of the place that he appears to be a part of it. He is as immutable and immobile as obsidian.

His arms hang loosely at his sides, his massive hands open for when he has to hug the dead to him.

Teddy Bear isn't having any of it though, still screaming and finally realizing the teller's already out of her head, her voice rising and begging the Mother of God to save her. Those heaving, swaying breasts are doing things to Teddy, who prods one tit with the barrel of the shotgun. Without benefit of a bra, it jiggles for a while before finally settling.

Mr. Lucifer is about to say something else, but it's already too late, all the choices have been made. There's only one way out now as Teddy pokes the girl's other breast and she lets loose with a screech. The slobber pumps freely from his mouth slit, as he gives a braying laugh and pulls the trigger.

No one ever gets used to the hypnotic sight of flesh and fluid applied to an area where it shouldn't be. Everybody in the bank lifts his head and watches as her lower jaw alters into cherry gel rushing across her chest and the cash drawer in one violent splash. The corpse wheels completely around on its toes, revolving one and a half times in a pirouette, before taking a final awkward step and pitching forward.

Most of her teeth are somehow intact, though, and a handful of them do a slow slide across the floor until they stop just outside the growing circle of the weight lifter's piss. John can't help himself as her ghost floats past him, still praying as her breasts finish bouncing, adrift and being reeled towards an aurora of seething golden light that hovers and opens just over her body's left shoulder.

His enormous hand flashes out and he eats her.

The bank manager has seen this sort of thing before, and he enjoys murder. He's done in one ex-wife already and is getting ready to do in another. He hides his smile well, but not in so dark or carefully guarded a space that John can't see it.

The weight lifter is sort of thrashing around on the ground, his muscles so taut that it looks as if he might snap in seven places before this is all over. A security guard stands there with his gun in its holster and his hands straight out in front of him, wrists twirling, ass angled to one side like he's at a disco doing the bump and having a pretty good time. A few people continue to moan and murmur, so far down on the floor that they're licking it.

The dead teller is already inside John, and he can feel her settling into Gethsemane Hills, her arms still over her head and standing beside Manfred Filkes, the mailman who'd died from an aneurysm walking up John's driveway six years ago. Filkes is digging the look of the frightened teller, who sways on her feet as she touches down in the middle of Juniper Boulevard. Filkes had been a pedophile, his mail cart full of illegal photos and magazines that would have sent him away for twenty-five years if only his brain hadn't burst. His madness is palpable and unshifting, the primeval energy of hate and lust rising from him like heat from a brick oven.

Filkes goes after her, even though she's well out of his preferred age range. He manages to get one of his pale hands on her throat before John can get the thin John, the true John, down among the ghosts to slap the shit out of Filkes all the way across the cypress-lined street. Filkes can't get rid of his mind full of baby rot even now, and cowers and sobs as he goes ass backwards over a plastic flamingo planted on a well-groomed lawn.

The dead teller, whose name is Juanita Perez, is too shocked to cry anymore, staring through her fingers at the true John, muttering passages out of the Bible, but getting a lot of the words wrong. Almost everybody does. He whispers and tries to comfort her, saying, "It will be all right, Juanita. Be calm. I won't let anybody hurt you here."

This place is no different from anywhere else in the world, the John inside himself tries to explain, and he's right. When Juanita can finally move again, holding a palm to her bruised breast and glancing over at Filkes sitting on the curb, who's bleeding heavily from his broken nose, she discovers large signs looming above her in the starlight.

This is the town of Gethsemane Hills, population now 1,604, including thin John, who comes and goes, but is always on hand to keep things from spiraling too far out of control. About six square blocks of suburbia, where people occasionally still say hello to you on the street.

There are no hills, but the name is the only one this hometown could have. There is power in names. It is a perpetual twilight of coiling shadows, violet-drenched dusk, and a blood-soaked sun, always with a gleeful moon glowing. Streetlights take the form of the gaslit globes of nineteenth-century London. There is no smog, but there's a smoggy feel. The yards are flawlessly landscaped, flower beds weeded and fertilized, gardens tilled, rooftops all recently reshingled, the dogs well fed. John takes great pride in the place and does all the work himself.

Indistinct, silent people sit on their stoops and front porches, watching Juanita closely. A few insubstantial shapes rise and begin to make clumsy eager gestures, stopping and starting and abruptly stopping again. These are the ambiguous movements of the uncertain, who see no reason to act but are propelled by memories of action. There is some laughter though, as well as angry men's giggling, and a few whispered entreaties.

A hand flashes out, silhouetted in the always failing sunlight—the fingers are crooked, the hand little more than a claw, damaged by arthritis, tension, or heaving doubt. Juanita whirls, gazing around at the rows of dimly lit duplicate houses, each of the similar staggering shadows weaving a bit, forward and back. They are waving to her, and then they recede. Doors are closed quietly—locks are thrown, televisions squawk, and children are tapping at upstairs windows, begging to be let out.

Mr. Lucifer scans the bank one more time, finally noticing John standing there in the middle of the room. He shakes his head because he can't figure out how the hell he'd missed the fat guy in the first place. The devil points his nickel-plated .38 and says, "Excuse me, sir."

"Be quiet," John tells him, "or I will eat you."

"Pardon me?"

"Shh."

"Hey, now, we'll have none of that. You might have some trouble doing squat thrusts, but even a fella your size ought to be able to get down on the ground when he's told."

Teddy Bear doesn't look up. He's intent on getting the other cashiers to empty the banded stacks of cash into his oversized rucksack. Juanita's corpse propels them on so that everybody is really moving now, shoveling money like crazy. Rolls of change fall and break open, so Ted stomps on rolling coins and picks them up. John sees everything that needs to occur actually happening in about eight seconds. If he had a stopwatch he would click it . . . now. The arching, wavering lines of chance and force of will solidifying into a pattern he can put to use.

He takes a step sideways as thin John, the true John weaves and thinks of ushering the lovely Juanita to bed. His heart is hammering and the flush of ticklish heat is flooding his groin. His breathing begins to speed up and a light sheen of cold sweat forms on his upper lip.

Her house is already picked out at the end of the block: a one-story cottage with a bouquet of freshly plucked forget-me-nots already in a vase on the dining room table. Photos of her kids are framed on the mantel, and their crayon drawings are held in place by magnets and exhibited on the refrigerator door. He's filled a bookshelf with some of the greatest volumes of poetry and classic literature. He'll teach her metaphor and symbolism and the definition of subtle underpinning. A single white rose lies across the pillow of her queen-sized bed. The vanity is laden with lace undergarments, stockings, and garter belts. There are condoms in the nightstand drawer, along with several brands of spermicide and tubes of lubrication. He likes the way her rack bobbles.

Juggling some change, Mr. Teddy Bear steps over Juanita's lower jaw, still expecting to find dye packs everywhere. His eyes are flitting like mad, his eyelashes swiping against the rubber loudly. He spots Lucifer's .38 and follows where it's pointing until he spots John calmly standing before them. Somehow the bear mask manages to contort. "Get on your knees!"

"I don't do that," John tells him.

A large splash of sweat falls out from the mask and threads through Teddy Bear's beard. "You don't . . . ?"

"No. Never. Not for anyone."

"You grotesque fat piece of shit freak!"

John is lissome and quick without ever showing his speed, even while he's in motion. It's funny and impressive to see him bringing it on. He reaches into his gully-deep pocket and draws out his nail clipper, carefully stepping around the weight lifter's yellow zone of urine. Ted has been holding the shotgun crooked in his arm for so long that as he turns, he wavers and spins two or three inches too far the other way, and John is already reaching.

The devil politely says, "Hey, now . . ."

The timing is impeccable, as if John had seen this happen many times before, perhaps in a recurring dream. Ted has to correct himself and bring the shotgun back again, as if to take John in his tremendous stomach.

The bank manager is hoping for more viscera and mayhem; maybe the loan department supervisor he's been banging will get it in the head next. In his mind, he runs scenes of bloody ballets, old women being blown upwards onto their tiptoes, hoisted through the air eight or ten feet, and splattering across his desk. He's getting jittery just thinking about it.

But John has already slid inside Mr. Teddy Bear's space, too close now for Ted to do anything but growl.

The security guard lets out the squeaky yip of a toy poodle because he understands this is the moment of finality. So does everyone else, even those not looking, breathing dirt in the corners beneath the teller windows.

John grabs the barrel and pushes it aside, carefully aiming it toward Mr. Lucifer. His other hand rises, holding the nail clipper, going up and inside for Teddy's throat. If Ted hadn't been so pumped during the robbery, his arteries and major veins wouldn't now be so thick and pulsing. It would've been a lot more difficult for John to lunge in there and clip Teddy's jugular.

The pain does what it's expected to do. In his agony and panic, the arterial spray spritzing the bank counter and showering the Plexiglas, Ted yanks hard on the trigger and blows off the greater percentage of Mr. Lucifer's face.

One long line of blood spurts across John's shirt before he can move Teddy Bear's head far enough to one side so Ted's spraying throat only paints the checking account brochures and tray of free pens with the bank's name on them.

The blackness of his shirt and tie is so complete and wet with sweat that the blood doesn't stand out at all. This is also how it should be. He opens both his immense hands wide hoping to catch Mr. Lucifer's soul, but despite the fact that the devil's got considerably less face than the dead Juanita Perez, Lucifer lives on. Thick colorful fluids bubble up as his esophagus gurgles wildly to clear a path to air.

The bank manager is in such a state of arousal that he nearly passes out from the force of his orgasm. He can't wait to get home and murder his wife.

John hisses in expectation, hands clenching and unclenching, but Lucifer isn't about to let go. There's only one eye left in the sparse wedge of his face, and who knows if it can see anything. But it peers at John, gazing sullenly and all the while still blinking.

Teddy, however, is waning fast. He coughs and tries to lean back away from the counter, but John holds him there against the nice marble tile so that no more of the slackening slurp of blood gets on his clothes. Ted's heart gives three final hesitant beats before giving out.

The aurora of roiling power opens again, dragging at Mr. Teddy Bear's soul, but John's enormous arms snatch the floating Ted out of the air and haul him from the draw of the raging eddy. John can't help but give a smirk. From that golden light ushers the voice of a wounded man who suffered and offered what he could before the eyes of the world, and now rages with all the condemnation he can, claiming, *"You are not the way."*

John laughs as he always does, watching the maelstrom dissipate and diminish, because the voice is his own, but full of contrition and fear.

Mr. Teddy Bear touches down in Gethsemane Hills and doesn't take off his mask. He stares wide-eyed through the tiny slits and groans, "Oh, oh my, oh my sweet Jesus on the cross, take me home." His voice, when not incensed by frustration and cocaine, is soft and almost melodious.

Juanita Perez takes a step toward Ted because her murderer is now the only connection she has left to the lost world of the living. The sign above them is covered in a blur of black motion and soon reads POPULATION 1,605. The house across the street has an open front door.

Thin John, the true John says, "You're home," and shoves Ted toward the house. First he's got to pass some guy on the curb with a broken nose. He looks sort of familiar, like Mr. Filkes, the son-of-a-bitch mailman who sodomized Teddy when he was eight. He's still got teeth-mark scars on his shoulders and thighs.

Inside there's half a key of coke already laid out in lines on the dining room table. His favorite video, Scarface, is in the VCR, and the television has surround sound, two motherfucking-huge speaks attached, and two others on either end of the couch. Teddy doesn't know what to do and tries even harder to hide under his mask, going a little more insane.

John eyes Juanita Perez, licking his lips. The nerve endings in his fingertips are igniting. Some of that K-Y jelly is cherry flavored, and her ass has a very nice slope to it. He smiles and takes her wrist, leading her to the new house.

When Juanita begins to struggle, he wraps his bony fingers in her hair and drags her down the block. Her mind not quite numb enough to let her pass out and fade from this awful endless twilight of corrupted colors. She starts to sob and works up to a scream, even while John's ripping her clothes off, leaving the rags draped across the perfectly trimmed hedges, the blooming azaleas.

Kids are banging on their windows, watching, excited and sick. Juanita's front door shuts and the whole neighborhood can hear laughter and squealing prayers for hours to come, with the revolting odor of cherries on the wind. They turn up their television sets and air conditioners.

John gains a full two-and-a-half pounds and goes up to the counter, slipping his check into the small deposit slot. Mr. Lucifer is still crawling and gagging on the floor, staring at John with his one eye and trying to back away.

John toes Juanita's teeth aside. The horrified cashier stares through the Plexiglas at him as he continues to click the nail clippers.

"Cash this," he tells her.

He is filled to bursting with the juice of despair and wants to buy himself a whore tonight.

ACKNOWLEDGMENTS

This anthology would have never come together without the helping hands of many incredible people. I owe a lifetime of thanks to the following:

Carlton Mellick III, for suggesting the idea in the first place and providing guidance on it over the last year and a half.

Rose O'Keefe, Carlton Mellick III, Jeff Burk, and Kevin Shamel, for taking this crazy trip together.

Kirsten Alene, for her infinite patience and wisdom, passionate heart, and for our countless conversations about this book.

Kevin L. Donihe, Kirsten Alene, and Andrew W. Adams, for throwing down the gauntlet when time was against us.

Alan M. Clark, for his supernatural drive and dedication, keen eye, and ceaseless outpouring of bizarre imagery.

David Daley, Kevin L. Donihe, Ross E. Lockhart, Thomas F. Moneteleone, Kevin Sampsell, Bradley Sands, John Skipp, and all the other editors who offered advice, story suggestions, assistance, and/or provided inspiration in the form of their own excellent anthologies.

The Multnomah County Library and Powell's Books, for the thousands of anthologies and publications I had access to.

The Portland Bizarro Community, for keeping it weird.

My father, for the nights he let me stay up late to watch *Alien* and *Creepshow* and *Tales from the Crypt* and a hundred other things that scared the shit out of me.

My mother, world's greatest teacher, who made a lifetime reader out of me.

All the authors in this anthology, for granting me permission to republish their stories. My heroes, all of you.

And to every reader and every writer of bizarro fiction on the planet. The time to shine is now.

ABOUT THE AUTHORS

DAVID AGRANOFF is the author of *The Vegan Revolution . . . with Zombies* and other books. He lives in Portland, Oregon.

DAVID W. BARBEE was born and raised in central Georgia. He is the author of the novel *A Town Called Suckhole*, which has been praised as "the finest post-apocalyptic southern gothic mudpunk buddy-cop blow-out ever put to print." His fiction has appeared in *Amazing Stories of the Flying Spaghetti Monster* and other publications.

AIMEE BENDER is the author of four books; the most recent, *The Particular Sadness of Lemon Cake*, won a SCIBA award, and has been translated into sixteen languages. Her short fiction has been published in *Granta*, *The Paris Review*, *Tin House*, *McSweeney's*, and more. She lives in Los Angeles and teaches creative writing at USC. "Hotel Rot" originally appeared in an online journal that makes flash animation for stories called locusnovus.com.

JEDEDIAH BERRY'S first novel, *The Manual of Detection*, won the Crawford Fantasy Award and the Dashiell Hammett Prize, and has been translated into over a dozen languages. His short stories have appeared in journals and anthologies including *Conjunctions*, *Unstuck*, *Chicago Review*, *Fairy Tale Review*, *Best New American Voices*, and *Best American Fantasy*. He has served as an editor at Small Beer Press, and currently teaches at the MFA Program for Poets & Writers at the University of Massachusetts Amherst.

RYAN BOUDINOT is the author of two novels, the critically acclaimed *Blueprints of the Afterlife* and *Misconception*, a PEN/USA Literary Award finalist; and a story collection, *The Littlest Hitler*, which was selected as a best book of the year by Amazon.com and *Publishers Weekly*. His work has appeared in the *Best American Non-Required Reading*, *Real Unreal: Best American Fantasy*, *Monkeybicycle*, *Post Road*, *The Lifted Brow*, *Torpedo*, and *McSweeney's*. He lives in Seattle.

BLAKE BUTLER is the author of *Nothing: A Portrait of Insomnia*, *There Is No Year*, *Anatomy Courses* (with Sean Kilpatrick), *Scorch Atlas*, and *Sky Saw*. He edits HTMLGIANT and writes a weekly column for *Vice*.

GARRETT COOK is the author of several books, including *Jimmy Plush, Teddy Bear Detective* and *Archelon Ranch*. He plays guitar and sings in the band Mayonnaise Jenkins and the Future Kings of the Delta Blues.

ROBERT DEVEREAUX made his professional debut in *Pulphouse Magazine* in the late 1980's, attended the 1990 Clarion West Writer's Workshop, and soon placed stories in such major venues as *Crank!*, *Weird Tales*, and Dennis Etchison's anthology *MetaHorror*. Two of his stories have made the final ballot for the Bram Stoker and World Fantasy Awards. His books include *Santa Claus Conquers the Homophobes*, *Baby's First Book of Seriously Fucked-Up Shit*, and *Deadweight*. Robert lives in northern Colorado.

KURT DINAN writes and teaches high school English in Cincinnati where he lives with his wife and three sons.

KEVIN L. DONIHE is the author of *Space Walrus*, *Night of the Assholes*, *The Traveling Dildo Salesman*, *House of Houses*, and other books. He is also the editor of the first ever walrus-themed anthology, *Walrus Tales*. Kevin lives in Tennessee.

CODY GOODFELLOW (STR11; CON15; DEX13; INT16; WIS4; CHA6; HP 42; AC: 2; ALIGN: Chaotic Neutral) is a Level 8 Bizarro Writer and a Level 6 Bookseller. In battle he wields a +3 Whiffle Mace and a Wand of Skullbuggery. Spells known: Cone of Apathy, Wall of Outrage. Quests Completed: Perfect Union, Silent Weapons For Quiet Wars, All-Monster Action.

AMELIA GRAY is the author of *AM/PM* (Featherproof Books) and *Museum of the Weird* (FC2). Her first novel, *THREATS*, was published by Farrar, Straus and Giroux.

In just twenty short years of effort, MYKLE HANSEN has become one of the nation's leading obscure authors. He is the author of two novels, three story collections and a wide variety of innovative cusswords. His work has been called hilarious, brilliant, insane, gravelly, over-the-top, poignant, plyometricizing and moist. He lives and works in Portland Oregon, hibernating in midwinter and foraging all summer for ideas, berries and salmon. If you encounter Mykle Hansen while hiking, do not run away; instead, wave your arms over your head and shout "Bravo!" This will confuse him long enough for you to dial 911.

JEREMY ROBERT JOHNSON is the author of *We Live Inside You*, the cult hit *Angel Dust Apocalypse*, *Siren Promised* (w/Alan M. Clark), and the end-of-the-world freak-out *Extinction Journals*. In 2008 he worked with The Mars Volta to tell the story behind their Grammy-winning album *The Bedlam in Goliath*. In 2010 he spoke about weirdness and metaphor as a survival tool at the Fractal 10 conference in Medellin, Colombia (where fellow speakers included DJ Spooky, an MIT bio-engineer, and a doctor who explained the neurological aspirations of a sponge). He is also the founder of indie publishing house Swallowdown Press and is at work on a host of new books.

STEPHEN GRAHAM JONES is the author of *The Last Final Girl*, *Zombie Bake-Off*, *Demon Theory*, *The Ones that Got Away*, *It Came from Del Rio*, *Growing Up Dead in Texas*, and probably twice that many more. Stephen's been an NEA Fellow, a Stoker Award finalist, and has won the Texas Institute of Letters award for fiction. He lives in Boulder, Colorado, and teaches in the MFA programs at CU Boulder and UCR Palm Desert.

ROY KESEY was born and raised in northern California, and currently lives with his wife and children in Maryland.

He's the author of a novel called *Pacazo* (the January 2011 selection for The Rumpus Book Club), a collection of short stories called *All Over* (a finalist for the *Foreword Magazine* Book of the Year Award, and one of The *L Magazine's* Best Books of the Decade), a novella called *Nothing in the World* (winner of the Bullfight Media Little Book Award), and a historical guide to the city of Nanjing, China.

His work has appeared in several anthologies including *Best American Short Stories*, *New Sudden Fiction*, *The Robert Olen Butler Prize Anthology* and *The Future Dictionary of America*, and in more than eighty magazines including *McSweeney's*, *Subtropics*, *The Georgia Review*, *American Short Fiction*, *The Iowa Review* and *Ninth Letter*.

ANDREA KNEELAND'S first collection of stories, *the Birds & the Beasts*, is forthcoming from The Lit Pub this year. She has been lucky enough to have her work appear in lots of neat journals and she hopes that will keep happening. She's also a web editor for *Hobart*.

Champion Mojo Storyteller JOE R. LANSDALE is the author of over thirty novels and numerous short stories. His work has appeared in national anthologies, magazines, and collections, as well as numerous foreign publications. His work has been collected in eighteen short-story collections, and he has edited or co-edited over a dozen anthologies. He has received the Edgar Award, eight Bram Stoker Awards, the Horror Writers Association Lifetime Achievement Award, the British Fantasy Award, the Grinzani Cavour Prize for Literature, the Herodotus Historical Fiction Award, the Inkpot Award for Contributions to Science Fiction and Fantasy, and many others. His novella *Bubba Hotep* was adapted to film by Don Coscarelli, starring Bruce Campbell and Ossie Davis. His story "Incident On and Off a Mountain Road" was adapted to film for Showtime's "Masters of Horror." He is currently co-producing several films, among them *The Bottoms*, based on his Edgar Award-winning novel, with Bill Paxton and Brad Wyman, and *The Drive-In*, with Greg Nicotero. He is Writer In Residence at Stephen F. Austin State University, and is the founder of the martial arts system Shen Chuan: Martial Science and its affiliate, Shen Chuan Family System. He is a member of both the United States and International Martial Arts Halls of Fame. He lives in Nacogdoches, Texas with his wife, dog, and two cats.

BENTLEY LITTLE was born in Arizona a month after his mother attended the world premiere of Alfred Hitchcock's *Psycho*. He is the author of eleven novels, including *The Haunted, The Revelation, The Mailman, The Summoning, Death Instinct* (published under the name Phillip Emmons), *University, Dominion, The Ignored, The Store, The House* and *The Town*. An acknowledged master of horror, he is currently at work on his next novel.

BEN LOORY lives in Los Angeles, in a house on top of a hill. He was born in Dover, New Jersey, and is a graduate of Harvard College. His short stories have appeared everywhere from *The New Yorker* to *ESPN Magazine*. In 2012, his story "The Duck" was featured on the Valentine's Day episode of NPR's *This American Life* ("What I Did For Love").

His book *Stories for Nighttime and Some for the Day* (Penguin, 2011) is now in its fourth printing. It was chosen as a selection of the Barnes & Noble Discover Great New Writers Program and the Starbucks Coffee Bookish Reading Club, and was named one of the 10 Best Fiction Books of the Year by the Hudson Booksellers retail chain.

As a screenwriter, Ben Loory has worked for Jodie Foster, Alex Proyas (director of *Dark City* and *The Crow*), and Mark Johnson (Academy Award-winning producer of *Rain Man*). He is a member of the Writers Guild of America west, and holds an MFA from the American Film Institute.

CARLTON MELLICK III is one of the leading authors of the bizarro genre. Since 2001, his books have drawn an international cult following, despite the fact that they have been shunned by most libraries and chain bookstores.

His short fiction has appeared in *Vice Magazine*, *The Year's Best Fantasy and Horror #16*, *The Magazine of Bizarro Fiction*, and *Demons: Encounters with the Hungry Dead*, among others. He is also a graduate of Clarion West, where he studied under the likes of Chuck Palhaniuk, Connie Willis, and Cory Doctorow.

He lives in Portland, OR, the bizarro fiction mecca.

ALISSA NUTTING is author of the short story collection *Unclean Jobs for Women and Girls*. The book was selected by judge Ben Marcus as winner of the 6th Starcherone Prize for Innovative Fiction. She received her PhD from the University of Las Vegas, Nevada in 2011.

TOM PICCIRILLI is the author of more than twenty novels including *The Last Kind Words*, *Shadow Season*, *The Cold Spot*, *The Coldest Mile*, and *A Choir of Ill Children*. He's won two International Thriller Awards and four Bram Stoker Awards, as well as having been nominated for the Edgar, the World Fantasy Award, the Macavity, and Le Grand Prix de l'Imaginaire.

ANDERSEN PRUNTY is the author of *Fuckness*, *The Driver's Guide to Hitting Pedestrians*, and other books. He lives in Ohio.

Former bartender, prize-winning photographer, and Surrealist Party City Councillor in his home town of Genoa, Italy, ROBERTO QUAGLIA won the British Science Fiction Award in 2010 for a story in *The Beloved of My Beloved* (NewCon Press, UK) co-written with Ian Watson, perhaps the only full-length genre fiction book by two authors with different mother tongues. Of his masterful parody, *Jonathan Livingshit Pigeon: A Tail of Transcendence* he declared: "Once in your life you have to write a shitty book."

2011 saw publication in English of his mammoth (628 page) and disturbing analysis, *The Myth of September 11: The Satanic Verses of Western Democracy*. Roberto divides his time mainly between Italy and Bucharest in Romania since it came to pass that he started speaking fluent Romanian in addition to German (and Italian, and English).

MATTHEW REVERT is the author of *The Tumours Made Me Interesting*, *How to Avoid Sex*, and *A Million Versions of Right*. He lives in Australia.

KRIS SAKNUSSEMM is the internationally acclaimed author of the novels *Zanesville*, *Private Midnight*, *Enigmatic Pilot*, *Reverend America* and *Eat Jellied*

Eels and Think Distant Thoughts. Lazy Fascist Press brought out a collection of his early stories called *Sinister Miniatures* (from which this story is taken) and is publishing his first play in 20 years entitled *The Humble Assessment.* His latest work is a "Memory Book" called *Sea Monkeys*, published by Soft Skull Press.

VINCENT SAKOWSKI is the author of *Some Things Are Better Left Unplugged*, *Misadventures in a Thumbnail Universe*, and *Not Quite One of the Boys.* He lives in Saskatoon, SK, Canada.

JEREMY C. SHIPP is the author of several books, including *Cursed*, *Vacation*, and *Sheep and Wolves.* His stories have appeared in *Cemetery Dance*, ChiZine, Apex Magazine, and many other publications. He lives in southern California.

ATHENA VILLAVERDE is a bizarro fiction writer from Toronto. She is the author of two books: *Clockwork Girl* and *Starfish Girl.* Her fiction has appeared in *The Bizarro Starter Kit (Purple)* and the Bram Stoker Award-winning anthology, *Demons: Encounters with the Devil and His Minions, Fallen Angels, and the Possessed* (edited by John Skipp).

Extremely former lecturer in literature in Dar es Salaam and in Tokyo, IAN WATSON wrote the Screen Story for Steven Spielberg's *A.I. Artificial Intelligence* after a year's work eyeball to eyeball with Stanley Kubrick. Numerous SF novels and a dozen story collections (most recently *Saving for a Sunny Day* from NewCon Press, UK) followed his prize-winning debut in 1973 with *The Embedding*, including 4 books set in the lurid, psychotic universe of Warhammer 40,000, which seem to be his best-selling titles. After 30 years in a tiny rural English village, he now lives in Gijón in the north of Spain.

D. HARLAN WILSON is an award-winning novelist, editor, literary critic and English prof.

ABOUT THE COVER ARTISTS

Alan M. Clark grew up in Tennessee in a house full of bones and old medical books. He has a Bachelor of Fine Arts from the San Francisco Art Institute. His illustrations have appeared in books of fiction, non-fiction, textbooks, young adult fiction and children's books. Awards for his illustration work include the World Fantasy Award and four Chesley Awards. Two of his novels, *Of Thimble and Threat: The Life of a Ripper Victim* and *A Parliament of Crows*, have been published by Lazy Fascist Press. He and his wife, Melody, live in Oregon.

Kevin Ward is a native of Nashville, Tennessee. He has been drawing and illustrating his whole life. He has worked with Doubleday Publishing Group, Grolier Science Encyclopedia, Funk and Wagnalls, TSR, Inc., and NASA, among others. His work has been featured on the covers of authors such as Anne McCaffrey, Piers Anthony and Norman Spinrad.

ABOUT THE EDITOR

Cameron Pierce is the author of eight books, including *Die You Doughnut Bastards*, *Ass Goblins of Auschwitz*, and the Wonderland Book Award-winning collection *Lost in Cat Brain Land*. He has edited two anthologies, *In Heaven, Everything Is Fine: Fiction Inspired by David Lynch* and *Amazing Stories of the Flying Spaghetti Monster*.

Cameron also serves as the head editor of Lazy Fascist Press, publishing books by such authors as Stephen Graham Jones, Alan M. Clark, Molly Tanzer, Sam Pink, Ross E. Lockhart, Blake Butler, Patrick Wensink, David Ohle, and Scott McClanahan.

He lives in Portland, Oregon with his wife, author Kirsten Alene.

BIZARRO BOOKS

CATALOG   SPRING 2012

**ERASERHEAD
PRESS**

Your major resource for the bizarro fiction genre:

WWW.BIZARROCENTRAL.COM

Introduce yourselves to the bizarro fiction genre and all of its authors with the Bizarro Starter Kit series. Each volume features short novels and short stories by ten of the leading bizarro authors, designed to give you a perfect sampling of the genre for only $10.

BB-0X1
"The Bizarro Starter Kit"
(Orange)
Featuring D. Harlan Wilson, Carlton Mellick III, Jeremy Robert Johnson, Kevin L Donihe, Gina Ranalli, Andre Duza, Vincent W. Sakowski, Steve Beard, John Edward Lawson, and Bruce Taylor. **236 pages $10**

BB-0X2
"The Bizarro Starter Kit"
(Blue)
Featuring Ray Fracalossy, Jeremy C. Shipp, Jordan Krall, Mykle Hansen, Andersen Prunty, Eckhard Gerdes, Bradley Sands, Steve Aylett, Christian TeBordo, and Tony Rauch. **244 pages $10**

BB-0X2
"The Bizarro Starter Kit"
(Purple)
Featuring Russell Edson, Athena Villaverde, David Agranoff, Matthew Revert, Andrew Goldfarb, Jeff Burk, Garrett Cook, Kris Saknussemm, Cody Goodfellow, and Cameron Pierce **264 pages $10**

BB-001 "The Kafka Effekt" D. Harlan Wilson — A collection of forty-four irreal short stories loosely written in the vein of Franz Kafka, with more than a pinch of William S. Burroughs sprinkled on top. **211 pages $14**

BB-002 "Satan Burger" Carlton Mellick III — The cult novel that put Carlton Mellick III on the map ... Six punks get jobs at a fast food restaurant owned by the devil in a city violently overpopulated by surreal alien cultures. **236 pages $14**

BB-003 "Some Things Are Better Left Unplugged" Vincent Sakwoski — Join The Man and his Nemesis, the obese tabby, for a nightmare roller coaster ride into this postmodern fantasy. **152 pages $10**

BB-004 "Shall We Gather At the Garden?" Kevin L Donihe — Donihe's Debut novel. Midgets take over the world, The Church of Lionel Richie vs. The Church of the Byrds, plant porn and more! **244 pages $14**

BB-005 "Razor Wire Pubic Hair" Carlton Mellick III — A genderless humandildo is purchased by a razor dominatrix and brought into her nightmarish world of bizarre sex and mutilation. **176 pages $11**

BB-006 "Stranger on the Loose" D. Harlan Wilson — The fiction of Wilson's 2nd collection is planted in the soil of normalcy, but what grows out of that soil is a dark, witty, otherworldly jungle... **228 pages $14**

BB-007 "The Baby Jesus Butt Plug" Carlton Mellick III — Using clones of the Baby Jesus for anal sex will be the hip sex fetish of the future. **92 pages $10**

BB-008 "Fishyfleshed" Carlton Mellick III — The world of the past is an illogical flatland lacking in dimension and color, a sick-scape of crispy squid people wandering the desert for no apparent reason. **260 pages $14**

BB-009 **"Dead Bitch Army" Andre Duza** — Step into a world filled with racist teenagers, cannibals, 100 warped Uncle Sams, automobiles with razor-sharp teeth, living graffiti, and a pissed-off zombie bitch out for revenge. **344 pages $16**

BB-010 **"The Menstruating Mall" Carlton Mellick III** — "The Breakfast Club meets Chopping Mall as directed by David Lynch." - Brian Keene **212 pages $12**

BB-011 **"Angel Dust Apocalypse" Jeremy Robert Johnson** — Meth-heads, man-made monsters, and murderous Neo-Nazis. "Seriously amazing short stories..." - Chuck Palahniuk, author of Fight Club **184 pages $11**

BB-012 **"Ocean of Lard" Kevin L Donihe / Carlton Mellick III** — A parody of those old Choose Your Own Adventure kid's books about some very odd pirates sailing on a sea made of animal fat. **176 pages $12**

BB-015 **"Foop!" Chris Genoa** — Strange happenings are going on at Dactyl, Inc, the world's first and only time travel tourism company. "A surreal pie in the face!" - Christopher Moore **300 pages $14**

BB-020 **"Punk Land" Carlton Mellick III** — In the punk version of Heaven, the anarchist utopia is threatened by corporate fascism and only Goblin, Mortician's sperm, and a blue-mohawked female assassin named Shark Girl can stop them. **284 pages $15**

BB-027 **"Siren Promised" Jeremy Robert Johnson & Alan M Clark** — Nominated for the Bram Stoker Award. A potent mix of bad drugs, bad dreams, brutal bad guys, and surreal/incredible art by Alan M. Clark. **190 pages $13**

BB-031 **"Sea of the Patchwork Cats" Carlton Mellick III** — A quiet dreamlike tale set in the ashes of the human race. For Mellick enthusiasts who also adore The Twilight Zone. **112 pages $10**

BB-032 "Extinction Journals" Jeremy Robert Johnson — An uncanny voyage across a newly nuclear America where one man must confront the problems associated with loneliness, insane dieties, radiation, love, and an ever-evolving cockroach suit with a mind of its own. **104 pages $10**

BB-037 "The Haunted Vagina" Carlton Mellick III — It's difficult to love a woman whose vagina is a gateway to the world of the dead. **132 pages $10**

BB-043 "War Slut" Carlton Mellick III — Part "1984," part "Waiting for Godot," and part action horror video game adaptation of John Carpenter's "The Thing." **116 pages $10**

BB-047 "Sausagey Santa" Carlton Mellick III — A bizarro Christmas tale featuring Santa as a piratey mutant with a body made of sausages. 124 pages $10

BB-048 "Misadventures in a Thumbnail Universe" Vincent Sakowski — Dive deep into the surreal and satirical realms of neo-classical Blender Fiction, filled with television shoes and flesh-filled skies. **120 pages $10**

BB-053 "Ballad of a Slow Poisoner" Andrew Goldfarb — Millford Mutterwurst sat down on a Tuesday to take his afternoon tea, and made the unpleasant discovery that his elbows were becoming flatter. **128 pages $10**

BB-055 "Help! A Bear is Eating Me" Mykle Hansen — The bizarro, heartwarming, magical tale of poor planning, hubris and severe blood loss... **150 pages $11**

BB-056 "Piecemeal June" Jordan Krall — A man falls in love with a living sex doll, but with love comes danger when her creator comes after her with crab-squid assassins. **90 pages $9**

BB-058 **"The Overwhelming Urge" Andersen Prunty** — A collection of bizarro tales by Andersen Prunty. **150 pages $11**

BB-059 **"Adolf in Wonderland" Carlton Mellick III** — A dreamlike adventure that takes a young descendant of Adolf Hitler's design and sends him down the rabbit hole into a world of imperfection and disorder. **180 pages $11**

BB-061 **"Ultra Fuckers" Carlton Mellick III** — Absurdist suburban horror about a couple who enter an upper middle class gated community but can't find their way out. **108 pages $9**

BB-062 **"House of Houses" Kevin L. Donihe** — An odd man wants to marry his house. Unfortunately, all of the houses in the world collapse at the same time in the Great House Holocaust. Now he must travel to House Heaven to find his departed fiancee. **172 pages $11**

BB-064 **"Squid Pulp Blues" Jordan Krall** — In these three bizarro-noir novellas, the reader is thrown into a world of murderers, drugs made from squid parts, deformed gun-toting veterans, and a mischievous apocalyptic donkey. **204 pages $12**

BB-065 **"Jack and Mr. Grin" Andersen Prunty** — "When Mr. Grin calls you can hear a smile in his voice. Not a warm and friendly smile, but the kind that seizes your spine in fear. You don't need to pay your phone bill to hear it. That smile is in every line of Prunty's prose." - Tom Bradley. **208 pages $12**

BB-066 **"Cybernetrix" Carlton Mellick III** — What would you do if your normal everyday world was slowly mutating into the video game world from Tron? **212 pages $12**

BB-072 **"Zerostrata" Andersen Prunty** — Hansel Nothing lives in a tree house, suffers from memory loss, has a very eccentric family, and falls in love with a woman who runs naked through the woods every night. **144 pages $11**

BB-073 "The Egg Man" Carlton Mellick III — It is a world where humans reproduce like insects. Children are the property of corporations, and having an enormous ten-foot brain implanted into your skull is a grotesque sexual fetish. Mellick's industrial urban dystopia is one of his darkest and grittiest to date. **184 pages $11**

BB-074 "Shark Hunting in Paradise Garden" Cameron Pierce — A group of strange humanoid religious fanatics travel back in time to the Garden of Eden to discover it is invested with hundreds of giant flying maneating sharks. **150 pages $10**

BB-075 "Apeshit" Carlton Mellick III - Friday the 13th meets Visitor Q. Six hipster teens go to a cabin in the woods inhabited by a deformed killer. An incredibly fucked-up parody of B-horror movies with a bizarro slant. **192 pages $12**

BB-076 "Fuckers of Everything on the Crazy Shitting Planet of the Vomit At smosphere" Mykle Hansen - Three bizarro satires. Monster Cocks, Journey to the Center of Agnes Cuddlebottom, and Crazy Shitting Planet. **228 pages $12**

BB-077 "The Kissing Bug" Daniel Scott Buck — In the tradition of Roald Dahl, Tim Burton, and Edward Gorey, comes this bizarro anti-war children's story about a bohemian conenose kissing bug who falls in love with a human woman. **116 pages $10**

BB-078 "MachoPoni" Lotus Rose — It's My Little Pony... *Bizarro* style! A long time ago Poniworld was split in two. On one side of the Jagged Line is the Pastel Kingdom, a magical land of music, parties, and positivity. On the other side of the Jagged Line is Dark Kingdom inhabited by an army of undead ponies. **148 pages $11**

BB-079 "The Faggiest Vampire" Carlton Mellick III — A Roald Dahl-esque children's story about two faggy vampires who partake in a mustache competition to find out which one is truly the faggiest. **104 pages $10**

BB-080 "Sky Tongues" Gina Ranalli — The autobiography of Sky Tongues, the biracial hermaphrodite actress with tongues for fingers. Follow her strange life story as she rises from freak to fame. **204 pages $12**

BB-081 **"Washer Mouth" Kevin L. Donihe** - A washing machine becomes human and pursues his dream of meeting his favorite soap opera star. **244 pages $11**

BB-082 **"Shatnerquake" Jeff Burk** - All of the characters ever played by William Shatner are suddenly sucked into our world. Their mission: hunt down and destroy the real William Shatner. **100 pages $10**

BB-083 **"The Cannibals of Candyland" Carlton Mellick III** - There exists a race of cannibals that are made of candy. They live in an underground world made out of candy. One man has dedicated his life to killing them all. **170 pages $11**

BB-084 **"Slub Glub in the Weird World of the Weeping Willows"** **Andrew Goldfarb** - The charming tale of a blue glob named Slub Glub who helps the weeping willows whose tears are flooding the earth. There are also hyenas, ghosts, and a voodoo priest **100 pages $10**

BB-085 **"Super Fetus" Adam Pepper** - Try to abort this fetus and he'll kick your ass! **104 pages $10**

BB-086 **"Fistful of Feet" Jordan Krall** - A bizarro tribute to spaghetti westerns, featuring Cthulhu-worshipping Indians, a woman with four feet, a crazed gunman who is obsessed with sucking on candy, Syphilis-ridden mutants, sexually transmitted tattoos, and a house devoted to the freakiest fetishes. **228 pages $12**

BB-087 **"Ass Goblins of Auschwitz" Cameron Pierce** - It's Monty Python meets Nazi exploitation in a surreal nightmare as can only be imagined by Bizarro author Cameron Pierce. **104 pages $10**

BB-088 **"Silent Weapons for Quiet Wars" Cody Goodfellow** - "This is high-end psychological surrealist horror meets bottom-feeding low-life crime in a techno-thrilling science fiction world full of Lovecraft and magic..." -John Skipp **212 pages $12**

BB-089 "Warrior Wolf Women of the Wasteland" Carlton Mellick III
— Road Warrior Werewolves versus McDonaldland Mutants...post-apocalyptic fiction has never been quite like this. **316 pages $13**

BB-091 "Super Giant Monster Time" Jeff Burk — A tribute to choose your own adventures and Godzilla movies. Will you escape the giant monsters that are rampaging the fuck out of your city and shit? Or will you join the mob of alien-controlled punk rockers causing chaos in the streets? What happens next depends on you. **188 pages $12**

BB-092 "Perfect Union" Cody Goodfellow — "Cronenberg's THE FLY on a grand scale: human/insect gene-spliced body horror, where the human hive politics are as shocking as the gore." -John Skipp. **272 pages $13**

BB-093 "Sunset with a Beard" Carlton Mellick III — 14 stories of surreal science fiction. **200 pages $12**

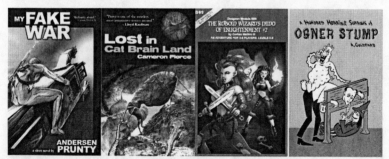

BB-094 "My Fake War" Andersen Prunty — The absurd tale of an unlikely soldier forced to fight a war that, quite possibly, does not exist. It's Rambo meets Waiting for Godot in this subversive satire of American values and the scope of the human imagination. **128 pages $11**

BB-095 "Lost in Cat Brain Land" Cameron Pierce — Sad stories from a surreal world. A fascist mustache, the ghost of Franz Kafka, a desert inside a dead cat. Primordial entities mourn the death of their child. The desperate serve tea to mysterious creatures. A hopeless romantic falls in love with a pterodactyl. And much more. **152 pages $11**

BB-096 "The Kobold Wizard's Dildo of Enlightenment +2" Carlton Mellick III — A Dungeons and Dragons parody about a group of people who learn they are only made up characters in an AD&D campaign and must find a way to resist their nerdy teenaged players and retarded dungeon master in order to survive. **232 pages $12**

BB-098 "A Hundred Horrible Sorrows of Ogner Stump" Andrew Goldfarb — Goldfarb's acclaimed comic series. A magical and weird journey into the horrors of everyday life. **164 pages $11**

BB-099 **"Pickled Apocalypse of Pancake Island" Cameron Pierce**—A demented fairy tale about a pickle, a pancake, and the apocalypse. **102 pages $8**

BB-100 **"Slag Attack" Andersen Prunty**— Slag Attack features four visceral, noir stories about the living, crawling apocalypse.A slag is what survivors are calling the slug-like maggots raining from the sky, burrowing inside people, and hollowing out their flesh and their sanity. **148 pages $11**

BB-101 **"Slaughterhouse High" Robert Devereaux**—A place where schools are built with secret passageways, rebellious teens get zippers installed in their mouths and genitals, and once a year, on that special night, one couple is slaughtered and the bits of their bodies are kept as souvenirs. **304 pages $13**

BB-102 **"The Emerald Burrito of Oz" John Skipp & Marc Levinthal** —OZ IS REAL! Magic is real! The gate is really in Kansas! And America is finally allowing Earth tourists to visit this weird-ass, mysterious land. But when Gene of Los Angeles heads off for summer vacation in the Emerald City, little does he know that a war is brewing...a war that could destroy both worlds. **280 pages $13**

BB-103 **"The Vegan Revolution... with Zombies" David Agranoff** — When there's no more meat in hell, the vegans will walk the earth. **160 pages $11**

BB-104 **"The Flappy Parts" Kevin L Donihe**—Poems about bunnies, LSD, and police abuse. You know, things that matter. **132 pages $11**

BB-105 **"Sorry I Ruined Your Orgy" Bradley Sands**—Bizarro humorist Bradley Sands returns with one of the strangest, most hilarious collections of the year. **130 pages $11**

BB-106 **"Mr. Magic Realism" Bruce Taylor**—Like Golden Age science fiction comics written by Freud, *Mr. Magic Realism* is a strange, insightful adventure that spans the furthest reaches of the galaxy, exploring the hidden caverns in the hearts and minds of men, women, aliens, and biomechanical cats. **152 pages $11**

BB-107 **"Zombies and Shit" Carlton Mellick III**—"Battle Royale" meets "Return of the Living Dead." Mellick's bizarro tribute to the zombie genre. **308 pages $13**

BB-108 **"The Cannibal's Guide to Ethical Living" Mykle Hansen**— Over a five star French meal of fine wine, organic vegetables and human flesh, a lunatic delivers a witty, chilling, disturbingly sane argument in favor of eating the rich.. **184 pages $11**

BB-109 **"Starfish Girl" Athena Villaverde**—In a post-apocalyptic underwater dome society, a girl with a starfish growing from her head and an assassin with sea anenome hair are on the run from a gang of mutant fish men. **160 pages $11**

BB-110 **"Lick Your Neighbor" Chris Genoa**—Mutant ninjas, a talking whale, kung fu masters, maniacal pilgrims, and an alcoholic clown populate Chris Genoa's surreal, darkly comical and unnerving reimagining of the first Thanksgiving. **303 pages $13**

BB-111 **"Night of the Assholes" Kevin L. Donihe**—A plague of assholes is infecting the countryside. Normal everyday people are transforming into jerks, snobs, dicks, and douchebags. And they all have only one purpose: to make your life a living hell.. **192 pages $11**

BB-112 **"Jimmy Plush, Teddy Bear Detective" Garrett Cook**—Hardboiled cases of a private detective trapped within a teddy bear body. **180 pages $11**

BB-113 **"The Deadheart Shelters" Forrest Armstrong**—The hip hop lovechild of William Burroughs and Dali... **144 pages $11**

BB-114 **"Eyeballs Growing All Over Me... Again" Tony Raugh**— Absurd, surreal, playful, dream-like, whimsical, and a lot of fun to read. **144 pages $11**

BB-115 **"Whargoul" Dave Brockie** — From the killing grounds of Stalingrad to the death camps of the holocaust. From torture chambers in Iraq to race riots in the United States, the Whargoul was there, killing and raping. **244 pages $12**

BB-116 **"By the Time We Leave Here, We'll Be Friends" J. David Osborne** — A David Lynchian nightmare set in a Russian gulag, where its prisoners, guards, traitors, soldiers, lovers, and demons fight for survival and their own rapidly deteriorating humanity. **168 pages $11**

BB-117 **"Christmas on Crack" edited by Carlton Mellick III** — Perverted Christmas Tales for the whole family! . . . as long as every member of your family is over the age of 18. **168 pages $11**

BB-118 **"Crab Town" Carlton Mellick III** — Radiation fetishists, balloon people, mutant crabs, sail-bike road warriors, and a love affair between a woman and an H-Bomb. This is one mean asshole of a city. Welcome to Crab Town. **100 pages $8**

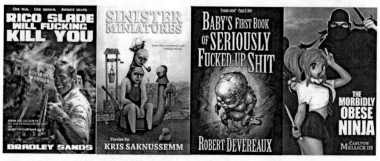

BB-119 **"Rico Slade Will Fucking Kill You" Bradley Sands** — Rico Slade is an action hero. Rico Slade can rip out a throat with his bare hands. Rico Slade's favorite food is the honey-roasted peanut. Rico Slade will fucking kill everyone. A novel. **122 pages $8**

BB-120 **"Sinister Miniatures" Kris Saknussemm** — The definitive collection of short fiction by Kris Saknussemm, confirming that he is one of the best, most daring writers of the weird to emerge in the twenty-first century. **180 pages $11**

BB-121 **"Baby's First Book of Seriously Fucked up Shit" Robert Devereaux** — Ten stories of the strange, the gross, and the just plain fucked up from one of the most original voices in horror. **176 pages $11**

BB-122 **"The Morbidly Obese Ninja" Carlton Mellick III** — These days, if you want to run a successful company . . . you're going to need a lot of ninjas. **92 pages $8**

BB-123 **"Abortion Arcade" Cameron Pierce** — An intoxicating blend of body horror and midnight movie madness, reminiscent of early David Lynch and the splatterpunks at their most sublime. **172 pages $11**

BB-124 **"Black Hole Blues" Patrick Wensink** — A hilarious double helix of country music and physics. **196 pages $11**

BB-125 **"Barbarian Beast Bitches of the Badlands" Carlton Mellick III** — Three prequels and sequels to *Warrior Wolf Women of the Wasteland*. **284 pages $13**

BB-126 **"The Traveling Dildo Salesman" Kevin L. Donihe** — A nightmare comedy about destiny, faith, and sex toys. Also featuring Donihe's most lurid and infamous short stories: *Milky Agitation, Two-Way Santa, The Helen Mower, Living Room Zombies,* and *Revenge of the Living Masturbation Rag.* **108 pages $8**

BB-127 **"Metamorphosis Blues" Bruce Taylor** — Enter a land of love beasts, intergalactic cowboys, and rock 'n roll. A land where Sears Catalogs are doorways to insanity and men keep mysterious black boxes. Welcome to the monstrous mind of Mr. Magic Realism. **136 pages $11**

BB-128 **"The Driver's Guide to Hitting Pedestrians" Andersen Prunty** — A pocket guide to the twenty-three most painful things in life, written by the most well-adjusted man in the universe. **108 pages $8**

BB-129 **"Island of the Super People" Kevin Shamel** — Four students and their anthropology professor journey to a remote island to study its indigenous population. But this is no ordinary native culture. They're super heroes and villains with flesh costumes and out-landish abilities like self-detonation, musical eyelashes, and microwave hands. **194 pages $11**

BB-130 **"Fantastic Orgy" Carlton Mellick III** — Shark Sex, mutant cats, and strange sexually transmitted diseases. Featuring the stories: *Candy-coated, Ear Cat, Fantastic Orgy, City Hobgoblins,* and *Porno in August.* **136 pages $9**

BB-131 "Cripple Wolf" Jeff Burk — Part man. Part wolf. 100% crippled. Also including *Punk Rock Nursing Home, Adrift with Space Badgers, Cook for Your Life, Just Another Day in the Park, Frosty and the Full Monty*, and *House of Cats*. **152 pages $10**

BB-132 "I Knocked Up Satan's Daughter" Carlton Mellick III — An adorable, violent, fantastical love story. A romantic comedy for the bizarro fiction reader. **152 pages $10**

BB-133 "A Town Called Suckhole" David W. Barbee — Far into the future, in the nuclear bowels of post-apocalyptic Dixie, there is a town. A town of derelict mobile homes, ancient junk, and mutant wildlife. A town of slack jawed rednecks who bask in the splendors of moonshine and mud boggin'. A town dedicated to the bloody and demented legacy of the Old South. A town called Suckhole. **144 pages $10**

BB-134 "Cthulhu Comes to the Vampire Kingdom" Cameron Pierce — What you'd get if H. P. Lovecraft wrote a Tim Burton animated film. **148 pages $11**

BB-135 "I am Genghis Cum" Violet LeVoit — From the savage Arctic tundra to post-partum mutations to your missing daughter's unmarked grave, join visionary madwoman Violet LeVoit in this non-stop eight-story onslaught of full-tilt Bizarro punk lit thrills. **124 pages $9**

BB-136 "Haunt" Laura Lee Bahr — A tripping-balls Los Angeles noir, where a mysterious dame drags you through a time-warping Bizarro hall of mirrors. **316 pages $13**

BB-137 "Amazing Stories of the Flying Spaghetti Monster" edited by Cameron Pierce — Like an all-spaghetti evening of Adult Swim, the Flying Spaghetti Monster will show you the many realms of His Noodly Appendage. Learn of those who worship him and the lives he touches in distant, mysterious ways. **228 pages $12**

BB-138 "Wave of Mutilation" Douglas Lain — A dream-pop exploration of modern architecture and the American identity, *Wave of Mutilation* is a Zen finger trap for the 21st century. **100 pages $8**

BB-139 **"Hooray for Death!" Mykle Hansen** — Famous Author Mykle Hansen draws unconventional humor from deaths tiny and large, and invites you to laugh while you can. **128 pages $10**

BB-140 **"Hypno-hog's Moonshine Monster Jamboree" Andrew Goldfarb** — Hicks, Hogs, Horror! Goldfarb is back with another strange illustrated tale of backwoods weirdness. **120 pages $9**

BB-141 **"Broken Piano For President" Patrick Wensink** — A comic masterpiece about the fast food industry, booze, and the necessity to choose happiness over work and security. **372 pages $15**

BB-142 **"Please Do Not Shoot Me in the Face" Bradley Sands** — A novel in three parts, *Please Do Not Shoot Me in the Face: A Novel*, is the story of one boy detective, the worst ninja in the world, and the great American fast food wars. It is a novel of loss, destruction, and--incredibly--genuine hope. **224 pages $12**

BB-143 **"Santa Steps Out" Robert Devereaux** — Sex, Death, and Santa Claus ... The ultimate erotic Christmas story is back. **294 pages $13**

BB-144 **"Santa Conquers the Homophobes" Robert Devereaux** — "I wish I could hope to ever attain one-thousandth the perversity of Robert Devereaux's toenail clippings." - Poppy Z. Brite **316 pages $13**

BB-145 **"We Live Inside You" Jeremy Robert Johnson** — "Jeremy Robert Johnson is dancing to a way different drummer. He loves language, he loves the edge, and he loves us people. These stories have range and style and wit. This is entertainment... and literature."- Jack Ketchum **188 pages $11**

BB-146 **"Clockwork Girl" Athena Villaverde** — Urban fairy tales for the weird girl in all of us. Like a combination of Francesca Lia Block, Charles de Lint, Kathe Koja, Tim Burton, and Hayao Miyazaki, her stories are cute, kinky, edgy, magical, provocative, and strange, full of poetic imagery and vicious sexuality. **160 pages $10**

BB-147 "Armadillo Fists" Carlton Mellick III — A weird-as-hell gangster story set in a world where people drive giant mechanical dinosaurs instead of cars. **168 pages $11**

BB-148 "Gargoyle Girls of Spider Island" Cameron Pierce — Four college seniors venture out into open waters for the tropical party weekend of a lifetime. Instead of a teenage sex fantasy, they find themselves in a nightmare of pirates, sharks, and sex-crazed monsters. **100 pages $8**

BB-149 "The Handsome Squirm" by Carlton Mellick III — Like Franz Kafka's *The Trial* meets an erotic body horror version of *The Blob*. **158 pages $11**

BB-150 "Tentacle Death Trip" Jordan Krall — It's *Death Race 2000* meets H. P. Lovecraft in bizarro author Jordan Krall's best and most suspenseful work to date. **224 pages $12**

BB-151 "The Obese" Nick Antosca — Like Alfred Hitchcock's *The Birds*... but with obese people. **108 pages $10**

BB-152 "All-Monster Action!" Cody Goodfellow — The world gave him a blank check and a demand: Create giant monsters to fight our wars. But Dr. Otaku was not satisfied with mere chaos and mass destruction.... **216 pages $12**

BB-153 "Ugly Heaven" Carlton Mellick III — Heaven is no longer a paradise. It was once a blissful utopia full of wonders far beyond human comprehension. But the afterlife is now in ruins. It has become an ugly, lonely wasteland populated by strange monstrous beasts, masturbating angels, and sad man-like beings wallowing in the remains of the once-great Kingdom of God. **106 pages $8**

BB-154 "Space Walrus" Kevin L. Donihe — Walter is supposed to go where no walrus has ever gone before, but all this astronaut walrus really wants is to take it easy on the intense training, escape the chimpanzee bullies, and win the love of his human trainer Dr. Stephanie. **160 pages $11**

CPSIA information can be obtained at www.ICGtesting.com
Printed in the USA
LVOW081327140313

324305LV00001B/30/P